MW01245611

THE BLACK PELICAN

Vadim Babenko

Ergo Sum Publishing
www.ergosumpublishing.com

Published by Ergo Sum Publishing, 2013

Translated from Russian by Henry Whittlesey and Vadim Babenko
Russian text copyright © Vadim Babenko 2005, 2013
English text copyright © Vadim Babenko 2013

E-book ISBN 978-99957-42-10-2
Paperback ISBN 978-99957-42-11-9
Hardback ISBN 978-99957-42-12-6

This novel is a work of fiction. Names and characters are the
product of the author's imagination and any resemblance to
actual persons, living or dead, is entirely coincidental.

Cover design: damonza.com
Editor: Robin Smith

www.ergosumpublishing.com
www.blackpelicanbook.com

PART I

CHAPTER 1

To this day I remember the long road to the City of M. It dragged on and on while the thoughts plaguing me mingled with the scenes along the way. It seemed as if everything around me was already at one with the place, even though I still had a few hours to go. I passed indistinct farms in empty fields, small villages and lonely estates surrounded by cultivated greenery and forest hills. Manmade ponds and natural lakes skirted the road and reeked of wetlands, which later, right before M., turned into peat bogs and marshes. The countryside was dotted with humble towns sprouting out of the earth, the highway briefly becoming their main street: squares and clusters of stores glimmered in the sun; banks and churches rose up close to the center; a belfry whizzed by, silent as usual. Then the junk shops and gas stations at the outskirts said farewell without a word, and just like that, it was over. The town was gone, without having time to agitate or provoke interest. Again the road wound its way through the fields, its monotony wearing me down. I saw the peculiar people who swarmed over the countryside – for a fleeting moment they appeared amusing, but then I stopped noticing them, understanding how unexceptional they were measured against their surroundings. At times, locals waved to me from the curb or just followed me with their eyes, though more often than not, no one was distracted by my fleeting presence. Left behind, they merged with the streets as they withdrew to the side.

At last the fields disappeared, and real swamps engulfed the road – a damp, unhealthy moor. Clouds of insects smashed into the windshield; the air became heavy. Nature seemed to bear down on me, barely letting me breathe, but that didn't last long. Soon I drove up a hill; the swamps retreated to the east, to the invisible ocean. The trees grew dense, casting the illegible calligraphy of their shadows over the motorway, until, several miles ahead, the road became wider and a sign said I had crossed the city limits of M.

Everything I had heard was turning out to be true. I recognized not the details, but their essence: the frequently repaired pavement full of cracks and potholes, the impoverished projects, the industrial warehouses, and the unfinished Memorial with its useless, gleaming steel. Then the gold coating of a garish arch – a monument to Little Blue Birds – flashed and passed without a trace in the setting sun. Cars slowed; intersections interrupted the flow of traffic; trees gave way to cheap motels and antique shops. After reaching the inner city, I crawled through a traffic jam for half an hour and finally found myself downtown.

Instantly it all changed. The area around me contracted, and it became difficult to see in the congestion. Houses of different shapes and sizes surrounded me, their sides dilapidated, pockmarked with spots blackened by the moist climate. The architecture did not impress me, yet the buildings had a look of dignity and didn't need visitors to assess their value. The streets weren't empty at this afternoon hour, but the people on them didn't seem to be an important part of the area. The city would do just fine without them, for what could they give it – a beggar with an ashy gray beard and one white pupil, a crowd of bored youths by the movie theater, isolated groups of housewives, or a small cluster of strangers, me and my sedan? Nothing offered me a sign, neither an indication nor a clue; no one had noticed me among the utterly ordinary others. The world had not reacted to my appearance and wasn't interested in my intentions.

I told myself this was how it should be: real things don't reveal themselves right away. Nonetheless, the impatience made my chest ache, forcing me to twist my face and shake my head. Look at me, I wanted to cry out to the silent buildings, look, I didn't come empty-handed. I brought you a great intrigue, equal to your most formidable mysteries. I am capable of a lot, my scheme is pernicious and clever – what else do you need to breathe life into your daydreams? But the stone wouldn't reply, life resumed its normal course, and I began to have doubts: am I cheating by asking too high a price in advance? Certainly, ahead of time, I couldn't prove anything – neither to myself nor to others...

My thoughts spun with the web of streets, turns and alleys, road signs and store names. My route became unclear; I slowed down and began to block traffic. People honked and stuck their heads out the window as they passed. I tried to figure out where I was, then veered to the right without a goal in mind, just to get out of someone's way, and stopped short in a dead end.

That was the right thing to do – the city had already become a little too close to my heart. It's probably the same for a third of its visitors, and the remaining two-thirds are just hopeless fools. The dead end calmed me down. I climbed out of the car and took a seat on a bench next to a small apartment house. Sheets were drying on a line hung between trees, the courtyard was empty, and only an apparently stray cat gazed blankly at my car from a basement window. A vacant lot off to the side stretched down the hill. It was under construction: workers were digging a pit and puttering about with concrete blocks for the foundation; an excavator discharged a high-pitched screech, leaving behind a flawlessly leveled edge. "Good work," I thought ironically, feeling all of a sudden that the City of M. was losing its aura and turning into something conventional, even if I still knew almost nothing about it.

All at once a feeling of melancholy rose up in me. It seemed coming here was pointless: there was no hope of finding what I sought. But the whim passed quickly; I was now a different man and had almost forgotten how to pity myself. The uninspiring nature of M.'s welcome suited me just fine; I was not expecting an inspiration from without. My gaze turned inward – looking within, one can always find something to arrest the eye. I felt calm, forgetting the triviality of my surroundings, thinking about my own matters, going over and over the well-trodden paths – not like a traveler rushing to his last stop but like a flaneur out for a walk.

I drifted through fragments of my past although they were not worth much, especially when I returned to them time and again. Here they are in space: reverberating streets; a dim background; frozen groups of mute characters in backyards – pathetic pieces with no content. Then come the more distinct ones: an old park, trees packed close together with their branches intertwined, scratches and chipped paint on a bench – the echo of a place where I was once loved in my youth. No one lives there now, yet there's still more – a stadium and a boat stop, someone's tanned arm, the small puzzle of my first apartment divided into three unequal sections... But no, we're getting out of order. That's from the realm of Chronos: summer vacation and a pile of carefree plans, a time of big bumblebees buzzing through the air, then a time of wishes that were way too brave, and – a time when I suddenly grew up without realizing what I was sacrificing. Three unequal sections. With roommates and without. One woman. Another. Then – alone and no distractions...

As so many times before, I tried to imagine the exact shapes and vibrant paints, something I knew by heart, even if it was only the color of the leaves, the wallpaper, or the blanket on the narrow bed. But you can never alter the order of memories; the links are involuntary; you can't force one thought to freeze and stay as it is for a thorough scrutiny. You're always on the go – the glimmer of taxis, strange games of hide-and-seek in the rat race, the faces of people who are drawn to you, trying to find a connection, convinced there's something special in the union no one else knows about. Hopes deceived and deceiving. Mostly unintentionally.

It's easier with faces – you can remember them longer. You can feel touched or hate them all over again, or challenge them to a duel without wishing your opponent any harm. You can kick them out in disgust, knowing all the same that their memory will stay as long as you don't close the trap door. But it soon gets messy – everything drifts out of sync. You lose your way in wordless gestures, in a silent movie with no captions. And when you remember the dialogue, you romanticize and embellish; you improvise something new every time, for the temptation is too great.

That's how it was as I sat delving into the past, uttering names I hadn't heard in ages. Time and again I caught myself in an excessively bold lie. With some embarrassment I tried to worm my way out of it, feeling I wasn't able to, didn't want to, or that I'd almost run out of memories. Soon, I couldn't even distinguish between the images from the last few months and the last few years. They ran together, long and brief, and added up to a vision of my own gloomy self: waiting for a call, waiting for letters, waiting for bad news, receiving bad news, waiting for another call... Off you go – back around the loop. But the loop is unstable, if you aren't afraid to break it, if you make up your mind to rip it up abruptly, like taking a dive and resurfacing to: first self-pity, then inert apathy, later cold mockery, and finally a decision.

Yes, that was the crucial difference: the self-contained coil broke apart. I had something now, and I called it *my secret* – words add another dimension. You can live with this secret, believe me, and set off for the City of M. – which is exactly what I did. I severed my ties, all of them. Everyone'd think this was the road to despair, yet, in fact, it brought peace of mind. Again and again I thought it over from all sides, and every time my consciousness painted not a vicious circle, but something rational and almost real. It was my secret and the City of M., with me inside it, right in the middle – a spy who had passed through the body check, an undercover agent of an invisible army. Now everyone would say: yes, the distinction is unmistakable; he's a completely different person.

Let's take a closer look: a different man, an unfamiliar hero, an unemployed and reckless fugitive-pilgrim. He doesn't have a permanent address, doesn't currently live anywhere, except perhaps in his sports car, a five-year-old Alfa Romeo with stiff springs. This is who I am; the circumstances do not bother me; no attachments are holding me back. I have no one to worry about, and no one cares about my future. I do have Gretchen, but she doesn't count – I'll explain that later. Is it better this way? Let's compare the items on the list. The pluses and minuses come out equal. Then again, there's a lot I didn't take into account…

Having gotten carried away, I jumped to new episodes in the silent movie: the unfamiliar hero comes out of a dilapidated apartment building one sunny morning. He jerks as he walks, while a fleeting memory entrances his gaze. He'll never return there; he has said his last farewell to the concierge-gossiper. He has moved his belongings out and given them away. His keys have been handed over too – or discarded, or lost – and if he turns around now, he'll have to find a new home. He betrays not a hint of doubt, feels no regret. His car is already waiting at the entrance, its tank full of gas. All the bills have been paid – simply out of habit. He has no idea when he might return, has not given any thought to those who will forget him. All he's willing to do is imagine some scenes from a distant future that include:

A former resident of the capital steps out of his first-class coach at the main train station. He is tanned and somber, his gaze turned inward. No one is there to meet him, and he hardly has any luggage. His collar is raised – as protection against the dampness and fog. A taxi driver mistakes him for a vacationer and tries to cheat him but gets caught, takes offense, and falls silent. This is the welcome from his hometown – they are waiting for him here. Hello, you look so refreshed – like an entirely different man. Where are we going? To theater square? To the opera house? The streets are empty – who will suggest another address? The former resident of the capital touches his coarse wolf's hair and glances around, frowning. What did he do there, way off in the distance? What did he live through? He says nothing…

Images are just images, yet some of them almost come to life. Capital or no capital, returning is not crucial. Instead, you could go farther south, live in the sun among bleached houses, drink with expats, sleep with prostitutes. It's as enticing as a glittering dream. You can win easy money and build a mansion, acquire horses and servants, donate a lot to the local church... The opportunities are endless and most of them are awfully boring.

That's why you shouldn't think about the future, I told myself, stretching my arms. The City of M. and my secret are more alive than all fleeting images. I haven't yet had a chance to savor them to my heart's content, so I am hurrying now to show them my quick affection, despite the mustiness of the courtyard sheltering my temporary weakness. But this isn't the time to be weak – and there is nothing to hide. I can even take off my mask now. They don't catch spies here, and besides, I haven't come for mysteries.

My thoughts calmed down. Silent movie shots faded little by little, scattering like fine dust. Nearly an hour had passed, perhaps even more. The house regained consciousness after its afternoon siesta. Voices wafted through the air; a child's sobs spluttered out from the open window above me. By the lobby next door, a small group of men had gathered – I could imagine their wary words, the absence of curiosity, the usual aversion to strangers. To feel unwanted, it is enough to be ignored – but I couldn't have cared less. If anything, we were equally disinterested. Tired of sitting, I got up to move my legs. The screech of the excavator became louder, more high-pitched; the cat disappeared; evening was setting in. After dawdling a little, I started the engine and drove back to the main street.

Everything had become livelier: work was over, the city animated and alive. Even more cars packed the street, while people congregated on the sidewalks, their faces flowing together. No one was honking at me now. My car rolled along easily with the general flow and I wasn't suspected of being an outsider. Storefronts and entrances slipped by; traffic lights blinked, dictating the cars' rhythm and introducing an even tempo as the first sign of recognition. I reveled in my freedom; it was still new, not yet disturbing or obsolete. For the first time I was running not from something but toward something, which is completely different. Of course, what this something really was, I still needed to figure out, and I looked forward to long evenings without distractions, the blessed solitude of clarification, which can always be interrupted by going to a nearby pub. But the main components were there, on the tip of my tongue, ready to turn into phrases. They straightened out the curves and drew a thick line to the final dot, not at random but still ignoring the subtlety of the original outline. That, of course, was just an approximation, yet in my case it might work. I could refer to two genuine names: M. and Julian – they were each much more reliable than the usual marks, which one commonly makes do with. We'll get to Julian later, for the blood still pulsates wildly when I think of him. The City of M., however – here it is around me, so even the approximation might not be needed unless laziness gets in the way. But no – I'm not that lazy!

I turned off the avenue, following the fork in the road that sent my car into a tricky U-turn. Now I was circling through narrow cross streets, a pageant of small shops, cafés, and bars – some crowded, others half-empty. With cars parked on both sides, it wasn't easy to drive, and I slowed to a crawl, picking my way carefully like a man in a dense mechanical forest.

It would be easy to get seriously lost here, I imagined. To get lost and remain face-to-face with the urban ghosts, feeling their shadows slither along my clothes as they came out of the arches and alleyways. I could feel the tickle of excitement running down my spine – the city's magic was enveloping me. It became clear: everything here was for real. Every corner hid either an ally or an overt enemy, my secret victim. I even had to hold myself back in order not to succumb to the opiate and do something dumb – so I thought about cigarettes, deeming it a really good time for one. Yet I remembered I'd finished the last pack a while ago and began looking impatiently for a store.

One appeared on the very next corner. I bought my favorites and lingered a little before walking through the open door of an adjacent café. I was anticipating hot chocolate, or at least coffee with sugar and milk, but found only disappointment. An elderly waiter informed me gloomily that the only hot drink they had was tea. He then proceeded to stand stock-still with his arms folded over his belly, as if he were ready to be thrashed and humiliated but would not be forced back an inch. I nodded, peeking in exasperation at the cheap, fake gold on his ring finger. The waiter cast another glance at me, opened his pad, scribbled something down, and retreated, stooping and dropping his shoulders. As he shuffled across the room, I noticed several people turning to watch him.

I waited for my tea, lighting a cigarette and examining the locals. There weren't many of them – just a few homely fellows, the only interesting one being a scrawny man of about forty in wrinkled, soiled clothes, with disheveled hair and two-day-old stubble. But his gaze was astonishing – full of pure sadness that struggled through his dense eyebrows. Having noticed I was furtively watching him, he nodded to me and smiled so openly his wizened face became ten years younger while his eyes grew much older – although the sadness in them disappeared and gave way to passive melancholy. I was stunned by the change and turned away, just barely nodding in response, but the man, after fidgeting a little, got up and made his way toward me.

This was pointless and wasn't part of the plan. Annoyed, I berated myself and thought I'd have to leave without getting my tea. But the stranger didn't make an attempt to sit down and talk. He asked for a cigarette, received it, and then swiftly dug a small harmonica out of the recesses of his raincoat. Taking two steps back and turning to the side, he started playing an excerpt from something unfamiliar, filling the room at once with the sound of sobbing violins. It was unexpectedly good – it seemed the air even rang, soot fell from the walls, and the dim lanterns on the ceiling turned into a sparkling crystal chandelier. Yet a moment later it all ended – he stopped as abruptly as he'd begun and awkwardly bowed his head before returning to his chair. Someone laughed, someone applauded jokingly. It was obvious they had gotten used to him long ago and such episodes surprised no one. I felt a strange sense of uneasiness and tried not to look at him anymore as

I hurried to finish my cigarette and gulp down the hot and almost tasteless tea that had appeared on the table out of nowhere.

Suddenly I heard loud steps resonating as if steel were banging on concrete. Another visitor burst into the café: a tall man, a bit over thirty, with slicked-back, raven hair, dressed in an expensive black suit and an elegant scarf. He walked without regarding anyone, his entire appearance in absolute contrast to the rest of the crowd. His arrival quieted them down and made them cringe. Only my random acquaintance, the man with the harmonica, jumped to his feet and dashed to meet the newcomer, his face lighting up with joy when he realized who it was. His expression was totally out of place for everyone, including the man in the expensive suit, who barely turned his head as he put out his arm and gave the musician a jolt in the chest. The other nearly fell and had to grab a table at the last minute, his harmonica flying to the corner. There were chuckles all around, but he wasn't discouraged in the least, scrambling to his feet and smiling benignly at those who were laughing. At the far end of the room, the tall man sat down and began reading something with his back to everyone and his head propped on his palm. "Good work," I thought again, yet it didn't turn out ironically. Something had sobered me up. The city was showing its unfamiliar side, agitating me and hitting a sore spot. Interfering still crossed my mind for some time, but I was unsure how and just cursed my stupidity, chucked some change in the saucer, and walked off.

It was already getting dark, and the lights came on. A sharp gust of wind made me shiver. The first encounter is over, I thought somewhat sadly, I'm ready to get used to the new place and forget my fantasies. In fact, they had already retreated into the darkness and hid in the corners with all their demons, supplanted by a tedious list of mundane trifles. My recent revival faded; I was alone in a strange city, completely preoccupied with itself, and I had yet to determine my role in its life.

My car was waiting for me, its bumper shimmering reassuringly. It was time to find where to spend the night. I started the engine, went around an obelisk that rose up in front of me, and drove in search of a store where I could buy a tourist guide. But a guide wasn't needed: a hotel soon appeared with a neon vacancy sign. Then came another and subsequently a third, where I stopped and secured a single with a bathroom and windows looking out onto the courtyard. I haphazardly unpacked a few things and lay down on the bed, dozing off quickly.

CHAPTER 2

It wasn't long before someone woke me by knocking politely at the door. I opened it and found myself standing face to face with an elderly man in a uniform consisting of a jacket with a carnation in the buttonhole and wide pants with stripes on the sides. He introduced himself as Piolin, an innkeeper who had been in business for many years and was getting up there in years himself. The man greeted me with a nod and walked in slowly, taking a seat in the room's only chair. As he made himself comfortable, I went over to the window and stood there with my arms crossed. His presence irked me, and I was waiting for him to leave.

Piolin was in no rush however. He asked about my trip, wondered if the room wasn't too hot, and inquired into what I disliked more – the heat or the cold. When I snapped back I couldn't stand either one, he informed me the air conditioner was at its highest setting and the room wouldn't get any cooler under any circumstances.

"Under any circumstances," he repeated with gusto. Then he became interested in the size of the shoes I wear and the ties and shirts I prefer. He gave me a detailed description of the hotel's laundry and ironing services – completely standard ones – and asked which soap, shampoo, and shaving cream I liked to use. After going into the bathroom to get a bar of the hotel's soap, he was about to give it to me for a sniff but sniffed it himself instead, bending his head so I could see the round bald spot on his crown. Smelling it, he said it reeked something wretched, then broke the bar in two, tossing both halves into the trash can, and went to sit on the bed.

The conversation moved on to cologne. Piolin described minutely the three brands of cologne he had preferred in the course of his conscious life as a man, also mentioning various incidental types he had not gotten accustomed to and thus did not deserve in-depth consideration. He asked me to describe the cologne I used, and when I simply offered him to try it, he screwed up his face and said he hadn't meant that at all. A scent, he added, was rather easy to characterize. A color, for instance, would be simply impossible to explicate in words, but with a scent it was quite doable, wasn't it?

"All the more so, young man, when someone has talents like yours," Piolin went on authoritatively. In his hand I saw the registration card I'd filled out, putting *journalist* into the *occupation* field. This was a lie and it made me feel ashamed. Piolin, however, wrapped up the conversation on cologne, apologizing for his insistence and explaining he was generally interested in smells: they had occupied a significant place in his life and had always been very important, just like women – things that were closely related indeed.

I decided to get rid of him or at least change the subject, which was irrelevant and dull. Besides, I was hungry and told him this, yet Piolin only mumbled distractedly, "Yes, yes, hungry, that's not good…" and started talking about his niece Mary, who ate quite a lot yet was incredibly skinny. "Here, you can see for yourself," he suggested, pulling a threadbare notebook out of his breast pocket and plucking an old photo from its pages. Before holding it out to me, though, he glanced at it, frowned, slipped it back in, and pulled out another. He probably has a lot of nieces, I thought with a smile. Mary turned out to be an unattractive girl with a long, thin face and bulging eyes. She didn't resemble Piolin in the least, and I told him that just to say something.

Piolin replied with genuine curiosity, "Really?" and added, "But everyone says we look alike. Well, it's hard to say from the photo. The lighting, you know, the focus – there's no life on paper." He held the photograph in his hands a bit longer, peering at it suspiciously, then lifted his eyes to me and smirked slyly. "By the way, she lives in your part of the world now. You haven't met her by any chance, have you?"

"No, not that I recall," I responded in the same tone – and a moment later I found myself hearing the story of how Mary got involved with a teacher from the capital. He had come to M. for a three-month job but took off after a month or so because of the unprecedented heat wave that had tormented the city that summer. "And this dimwitted floozy ran away with him, without even saying good-bye," Piolin confided in a whisper. "At first she was indifferent and treated him coldly, but soon you wouldn't have recognized her. She went crazy and got pregnant at once, like a cat. The guy brushed her aside of course, but she's still there; she wasn't going come back," he complained and added they could've crippled Mary's seducer for life, even in the capital, yet it was no longer relevant because she was pregnant again – and this time it wasn't the teacher.

"Uh huh," I drawled, not knowing what else to say. "It's interesting indeed. Well, thanks for stopping by. I suppose I'm going to go have some dinner now, if you don't mind. I've been on the road all day and haven't eaten anything substantial."

At this, I resolutely walked across the room to demonstrate I was ready to leave, but that didn't make much of an impression on Piolin.

"Well, sure, you need to have dinner. You and I can eat together," he said contemplatively, looking off to the side before transferring his gaze to me and adding with some irritation, "But why are you in such a hurry, why can't you sit still? We need to get to know each other first, have a talk like human beings."

"Actually, I was planning to eat alone," I objected, a bit bewildered.

Piolin casually dismissed me, "Eat alone? Nonsense, nonsense." He raised his finger and repeated, "You've got to act like a human being!"

Then he closed his eyes and admitted he wasn't there just to chat. That is, he was there to chat too, why not, but he also had some business to discuss. He needed to ask me a question – "a completely formal one; nothing personal" – and there was no way to avoid it, because the city laws required it, and all innkeepers were obliged to obey the law, like other residents of M. As for me, I was not one, and its laws did not apply to me, so I was completely within my rights not to give an answer. But even if the laws had applied to me, I still could have refused to respond, because first of all, there was no law requiring me to do so, and then there was no one who would ask me such a question in this case.

After reasoning along these lines for several more minutes, Piolin fell silent, assumed a dignified air, and inquired in a soft, ingratiating voice, "Tell me please, what is the purpose of your visit to the City of M.?" And with this, something swiftly changed: he exuded a sense of threat, becoming a sly and unpleasant man. I sensed he was uptight and even a little anxious, as if he were getting to something he'd been expecting for a while and had now almost reached.

There was nothing bad about his question. And though I'm not fond of idle curiosity, there was no reason not to reply to it – that is, for anyone other than me, because just then I did have reasons and couldn't tell the truth to the first person I met. That caused me to feel offended: it was as if someone were obstinately prying into my soul, trying to penetrate its most private places.

My cheeks started burning. I realized I was blushing and saw that the expression on Piolin's face reflected poorly concealed excitement. He knew he'd nailed me on something – and I needed to pull myself together. It wasn't worth arguing with the man, yet I was totally confused: what could I say without saying anything? How could I possibly pretend to be nonchalant when my nerves began to tremble at the very first thought of Julian and my secret plan? So I just stood there baffled for a few seconds and didn't say a word. Then, at last, I came to myself and mumbled that I wanted to leave the question unanswered, as I had a fairly personal reason.

Piolin continued to look at me expectantly, not giving the slightest impression we had concluded the matter. I grew irritated and told him more brusquely that the question itself surprised me somewhat. This made me angry at myself – I was saying something unnecessary and losing my temper – but irritation got the better of me again, and I added that the very article in the civil code of M. seemed strange, smelling of restrictions on personal freedom and causing some unpleasant habits in innkeepers. This upset my companion tremendously – though I'm not sure which disturbed him more, my refusal to answer or my chaotic accusations.

As he remained seated on the bed with his head tilted to the side, Piolin began to explain tediously that there were no restrictions on freedom here since the law didn't forbid anyone from doing anything. It also didn't force anyone to take any actions – well, almost – and if it did, it was only to inquire about trivial matters. Furthermore, he went on, it forced an insignificantly small group of people to do this – just innkeepers and no one else. You could certainly talk about restricting the freedom of innkeepers, he said, but it's not worth it because they don't feel their liberties have been violated or circumscribed. Give them the right to act as they please and the first thing they'll do is ask their guests the very same question, as anyone else would, because – and here Piolin raised his finger – because how else can these guests interest the residents of M., if not by telling us why they came to the city? And especially out of season, this takes on a rather unhealthy form: as soon as a new guest appears, everyone keeps trying to squeeze the reason out of him, digging and digging until he finally loses his temper. So the law was passed to help regulate all that and – what's more – to protect innkeepers just a bit. And if it doesn't protect them, then at least it provides moral support, since they are usually among the first people to meet a visitor, and consequently it is even more difficult for them to restrain their curiosity. On top of that, Piolin continued, you have to consider the neighbors' inquisitiveness – and innkeepers are well aware of this. It excites them, drives them to extract the truth hastily, leaving them confused and embarrassed afterward. So now they do it in compliance with the law, as if others require it, and they are only subject to a small fraction of the embarrassment, an insignificant amount of it, which can't really be called that – it's just a little awkwardness, nothing more.

He went on in this vein until I interrupted him and proceeded to expound just as tediously that everything appeared in a different light now and I was not insulted in the least. And the law itself, I added, seems quite natural and even somewhat logical, especially if you consider the remarkable curiosity of the residents of M., and so on and so forth.

The minutes went by. Piolin sat on the bed, shaking his head from time to time. When I finished, it became clear I might well understand the situation, but, nonetheless, did not intend to answer his question.

He then sighed and tried to persuade me. He explained that this collective curiosity, the City of M.'s little weakness, was not something humiliating for its visitors – you should consider it as simply part of the local color, which is one of the main attractions anyway for everyone who's dying to come here. Moreover, Piolin added, no one is interested in the crafty phraseology that seems to roll off some people's tongues. No, he continued, visitors can't get away with lame excuses; they're expected to give real answers, not those clichés like "to do some sightseeing" or, even worse, "to swim in the ocean." In these instances, the asker simply feels hurt; and hurting your hosts, even slightly, is never a good way to begin a stay in an unfamiliar place!

Once again, I felt something unpleasant emanate from Piolin and a shudder ran involuntarily through my body. With a scowl on my face, I noted it was easy to imagine the kind of people who came here for precisely the reasons Piolin had suggested – and, moreover, those visitors probably made up the vast majority. At this moment I remembered I was very hungry and decided I just couldn't take it any longer.

Instantly, as if he were reading my mind, Piolin turned into the man who had entered my room an hour before – an elderly, polite, and very ordinary innkeeper. He apologized for his talkativeness and said with a wink he wouldn't mind getting a bite to eat too, proceeding further to beg my pardon for his forgetfulness. "You must be dying of hunger, while I'm harassing you with conversation," he said. "It's already high time to expand the scope of your knowledge about the hotel and the City of M. in general, and the best way to do that is to go to the restaurant downstairs and have a proper meal."

He headed for the door but stopped halfway and started to describe the roast rabbit in red wine with a local plum sauce we were going to enjoy. I certainly should have refused with the utmost firmness, yet the useless discussion had depleted my energy so much I could no longer argue. I said I was ready to go, yet Piolin held me up with a cautious gesture and intoned gently, gazing into my eyes, "The only problem is that I have a little question for you, one about the affinity of souls, so to speak. Tell me..." and he again inquired about the purpose of my visit to the City of M., as if we hadn't just spent a torturous half hour squabbling over precisely that subject. I dropped down on the bed in despair, sitting in the place he had occupied earlier, while Piolin just kept going. He passionately explained he didn't want to torment me. On the contrary, he wanted to be as hospitable as possible, but still there was no avoiding the matter. He wouldn't even insist on a complete description of all my motives and surreptitious reasons, but he did expect at least a hint, at least a tiny clue.

Because every hint is true in its own way, Piolin was saying. If you try, it's possible to find a compromise that's acceptable on all sides. But some effort is needed, and a little goodwill as well – after all, a compromise doesn't come out of nowhere. It was all up to me now, he said, after he had told me so much – about M. and the weaknesses of its residents. He had been candid with me, to say the least, and was now presuming I wouldn't just slip away and slam the door in his face without making any attempt to help.

"Okay," I sighed. "You win, Piolin. I'll answer your question with the utmost sincerity, because I've got no more energy." Then I went to the window, looked spitefully into the street, and divulged I had come there to find a certain person, an acquaintance who, as far as I had heard, had already been living in M. for six months.

Piolin's face took on an expression of interest, and he asked about the name of my acquaintance – if, of course, I could tell him; that is, if there was no reason for me to conceal it.

I interrupted him quite harshly with my tongue not obeying me as I enunciated the name Julian, and added, "Now, if you don't mind, I would finally like to eat."

Then I took a step away from the window, but Piolin appeared next to the door with surprising agility, his arms extended toward me as if to hold me in the room. I could tell he was going to keep me inside until he had obtained everything he wanted. And he knew that I knew this.

"Just one sec, though," he said. "Just one short second, because you misunderstood something, and we need to clear it up right away. This mix-up is so obvious it's a little bit strange even to talk about it," and Piolin really did stop speaking for a moment, as if to give me a chance to intervene and clear up the problem on my own. But I was silent, and he continued, embarking on a long speech.

"No one comes to M. looking for a specific person," he pontificated sadly. "It's impossible to find a certain person in M., the one you've come for and knew before. You have no hope of finding someone here, even an old friend, even if you remember his face and the details from his former life. You may repeat his name over and over again, write it down somewhere and keep it in your pocket; you may be on good terms with your memory and armed to the hilt, yet in reality you are absolutely unarmed, because there's no such person in the City of M. You have to understand this," he poked his finger at me. "Understand and not give in to delusion. It's certainly easier to lie to yourself than it is to look the truth in the eye, but I'll tell you the truth because I see you're worthy of it. You won't find anyone here, not your friend, not a woman if you need a woman, not compassion if you deserve compassion, and you'll leave the city without resolving its riddles because your misunderstanding won't let you open your eyes. Your goal isn't clear to me, but I can see your confusion a mile away. Give it up, abandon the useless, and M. will come to your aid. Otherwise... otherwise, you will remain a stranger, and those who you come across here will view you as a stranger and respond with indifference."

Piolin became agitated. His jacket puckered and his carnation bent sadly over to the side as it wilted away. Even his face transformed: his cheeks sagged over his chin, where a deep wrinkle or scar slit the skin; his eyes sank into their sockets and looked out from deep pits, like those of a hermit who had lost track of time.

I was surprised by his pompousness and tried to slow him down with objections, but there was no stopping Piolin: he stood his ground, becoming deaf to the words of others.

"Certainly anything can happen," he was saying. "You can run into the person you're searching for on the street, and you'll recognize him from the photo in your wallet. You'll be sure he's in front of you, sure you can't be mistaken. He may even respond to the name you know and agree he's the one you're so unceremoniously trying to find, perhaps against his will. And you'll think you've accomplished your goal, yet that's hardly the case, because the chances are minimal – minimal to no end. The City of M. isn't as small as it might seem at first sight. If you enter on the main road, then you're downtown in a flash, and it looks like the whole city is right there, half of it left behind, but no, there's a lot more to M., things that don't reveal themselves immediately. One glance isn't enough to take it all in while hoping to capture the face you need. If you look at the map – and I'll bring you a map – you'll see how confusing it is, what intricate lines can be drawn by tracing one single street with a pencil. And there isn't just one street here, but hundreds, hundreds… Furthermore, there are also quite a few people, each one different from the others; you can live here all your life and fail to understand who's who. That's what happens to the majority, and not all of them are dumb. Here, many are searching for many, and some of the many who were once very visible. Well, just try and unearth them now – you won't find a thing!"

"Your acquaintance may be someone extraordinary," Piolin continued, calming down a little. "Yet there are always others who are no worse. It's useless to ask everyone where you can find so-and-so who's like this and that. At best, they'll just go their own way, though they might laugh behind your back, or even in your face. And allegories won't help: every hint has a cost, but the cost usually isn't high and the white stitches always stick out, betraying a fake... Of course, if you don't want to talk, don't." He shrugged. "My job is simply to warn you. My amicable sentiments as well as my official duty require it – because I don't even know how long you'll stay here. Be it long or short, it's better to spend your time beneficially – for your benefit, of course, not mine. Remember, sometimes you act with the best of intentions, but run up against a wall, and those intentions get you nowhere. The least you can do is not act deviously." He tilted his head, enticing me toward the door and letting me go first. "It would be best if you said right away you didn't want to answer, although it's your business, of course."

As we walked down the corridor of the hotel, Piolin's face didn't show any sign of emotion. He appeared just as he had at the very beginning of our acquaintance, and even the carnation in his buttonhole freshened up and acquired its original spiffy look. Politely directing me to the elevator, Piolin drew my attention to the new carpet and ornate chandeliers – signs of the hotel's prosperity. He thanked me on behalf of the entire staff for deciding to stay there, and assured me the service was excellent, the staff well-trained, and the maids gentle and modest, with some being very cute. And he noted that the oceanside was windy at the moment, which was why most of the rooms were unoccupied, although it's difficult to find a place there during the holiday season.

"It's all full, young man; it really is," Piolin said and, becoming somewhat distracted, pushed the wrong elevator button, then turned away and started humming some melody.

Suddenly he swiveled around again and thanked me in the most official tone for the understanding I had shown. He appreciated my cooperation in the formal procedure he was obliged to follow, which had been demonstrated by the fact that I, in full compliance with the rules for visitors, had refused to respond to his enquiry while stating this in a clear and intelligible manner. It was delightful, because sometimes people try to be sly and elusive, which leads to mutual exhaustion and even dissatisfaction with the other party. That's why one couldn't help but rejoice when the whole matter goes quickly and smoothly because, in truth, it's not worth a damn.

As for my request, Piolin continued when we were in the elevator, my request for help with the search for my acquaintance, a certain Julian, a person, it seems, with enviable gifts and qualities, he was sure the entire hotel staff would be glad to help a visitor, or better yet, a guest, with whatever he was doing there. They would, for example, provide useful advice or offer topographical materials for a decent price – and Piolin again turned away and started humming under his nose. The elevator crawled so slowly one could hardly say it was moving, and it seemed like a very long time before the doors opened and we proceeded down a large, bright passageway.

"But I have to warn you right off the bat," Piolin livened up. "Have to warn you: there's no guarantee this help will produce any results. It's generally hard to find anything here, even an inanimate object, let alone a human being. Furthermore, sometimes, while looking for a thing, you come across a totally different one. Instead of finding person X, you find Y, and only then do you realize you needed Z. It's the same now: you might think you're searching for Julian, but end up finding someone named Gibbs, for instance – and it's easier to find Gibbs because it's he who manages the restaurant where we're going. So we'll certainly achieve our goal here – at least to some degree." Piolin chuckled shrilly at his own joke. "And there's no need to wince and be upset, because Gibbs is in fact an expert on the ocean Dunes, a local trailblazer, so to say, and if he can't help us find something in M., then nobody can. But even if the matter comes to nothing, it's not that bad either, because Gibbs will surely give us something to munch on. That's why it's clear none other than Gibbs is our man at the moment," and again Piolin turned away, continuing to hum to himself as if he'd completely lost interest in me.

CHAPTER 3

This is how we entered the restaurant – without looking at each other. The staff addressed us respectfully, took us to our table in the middle, and a few minutes later Gibbs came over. I didn't like him right away, although there was something appealing that would not let me go. Of course, I remembered Piolin's comment about the ocean Dunes, and while we sat alone, he added even more, telling me confidentially that Gibbs, on top of everything else, had actually seen the black pelicans – and didn't hide it in spite of decorum. This excited me at once, and I no longer regretted having dinner with them rather than alone as I had been planning initially.

"He's a very tricky guy," Piolin whispered to me before Gibbs joined us. "He's complicated and makes a strange impression – if not to say worse. Wherever he is, he always runs into trouble, leaving others speechless from the how and what of it all. Take this story with the black pelicans – when he lost half his face..." Piolin chewed his lip and glanced to the side for a few seconds before adding, "Yes, half his face was gone; there's nothing else to say."

"What do you mean?" I asked, not feeling quite at ease.

"Just that," Piolin cut me off roughly, before elaborating in a gentler tone, "you'll see for yourself when he comes. However, don't start enquiring – he doesn't like to be questioned. He's never spoken of them to me, but people prattle away – maybe some of them have heard something, although you never tell a fact from a fable. Any idiot knows: even when they come one by one, you need to keep your guard up. No, 'keep it up' is understating it a bit; you have to be very, very careful. Yet he ran into an entire flock and went right up to them for no reason. I don't know what was going through his head – some whim or simply sunstroke – but he strode on up to them just like that, as if they had him by a leash. He wasn't alone, no, he had a companion who understood everything instantly – that there was a whole host of them and that Gibbs was walking right there. The man was no blockhead: he threw himself facedown on the sand and lay there without moving, holding back his screams. When Gibbs got back, the man was already out of sight: he had waited and waited, and then shuffled away – but, in all honesty, you don't return from the black pelicans quickly. So Gibbs wandered about by himself, traipsed over all the northern Dunes and didn't meet anybody. The season at that point was also over, and that was for the better – he had time to get used to himself, which must not be easy without half your face. When he emerged in public again, nobody paid much attention to him: he had long since ceased to be a novelty, and folks almost forgot him – despite his being well known here, if not to say famous. And, as far as he saw it, he hadn't become anything new to himself either, even if he did change a lot…"

At that very moment Gibbs approached us in person. When we shook hands, I sensed somewhat bitterly that I was expecting too much and probably wouldn't get what I hoped for. He was fussy and ostentatious and looked at me surreptitiously – at first with a rather unfriendly gaze, but then, after Piolin introduced me, with exaggerated joy. I couldn't completely believe his pose – as I would doubt a shoddy masquerade – and the disappointment wouldn't leave me in peace.

I regarded him initially with a little fear, although I didn't see anything terrible. Of course, if you look at him from the lost side, it seemed a little strange – like he had no face at all, even if all the parts were in place – and from the front it was also unconventional in some way, but from the other side there was nothing remarkable – a profile like any other.

We were introduced and took our seats, then the waiter appeared, and we all began to discuss the menu. As soon as we finished, the two of them moved directly to the subject of me. Piolin was especially zealous – spoke nonstop, told jokes, and made rather blunt wisecracks, eyeing me furtively. Gibbs mostly agreed and cleared his throat, though he also tossed in a truism here and there. Still, neither let me get a word in edgewise.

I had no clue what brought me to the very center of their attention, and listened with some surprise to the story of my past, which they had concocted on the spot from the scanty information on my registration card. Gibbs immediately guessed I had studied at UU; a good university, he said, and the students there were generally bright. No wonder some of them became journalists – though, personally, he didn't think highly of media people. Then they pursued the question of whether I had graduated or not, and came to the conclusion that I had – "because he's more obsessed with himself than with girls," said Piolin, summing it up. Gibbs speculated on various activities that could have entertained me in my free time, distracting me from the acquisition of knowledge and even muddling my thoughts for some days or months, and Piolin considered each one before accepting or rejecting it: costly motorcycle racing (dismissed by Piolin), different games with balls (retained with some doubt), playing music (supported enthusiastically), and even mild political extremism – which made Piolin yawn. At this, Gibbs stopped the game, turned away from me, and started to ask Piolin questions like, "How has the young man settled in here?" to which Piolin replied that I was doing very well; or, "Does the young man know that the elevator doesn't work at night?" and Piolin said yes, I was aware of that, despite the fact that I wasn't – nobody had told me about it. Then Gibbs started to recount a long story about him being trapped in an elevator with two chambermaids, but he didn't manage to wrap it up because the appetizers appeared and everybody became preoccupied with his food.

The starters weren't bad, and the rabbit they served afterward was very good indeed. We barely exchanged a word as we ate, with only Gibbs mumbling something now and then. When we finished the main course, Piolin inquired about my preference for dessert, but I turned him down, since I was full and already craving sleep. With a wave of the hand, Piolin sent the waiter away and declared it was finally time to talk business.

Frankly, my greatest wish was just to pay and leave. I didn't need any help and didn't want anything to do with them; their clumsy hospitality and continuous pressure rather annoyed me. We hardly knew each other, and I wasn't used to trusting anybody after the very first dinner, which I was about to mention, yet Piolin's face took on such a purposeful expression and Gibbs tensed up so much that I became diffident and surrendered. Piolin turned formal and pompous, called Gibbs "my esteemed friend" and me nothing other than "our guest" or "our dear guest," while I listened to them obediently, as if entranced.

"So, my esteemed friend," said Piolin authoritatively to Gibbs, "our guest, you know, is searching for someone in M. That is, he still hasn't set out – he's only looking around – but rest assured, he will certainly begin soon. It's a difficult matter, as you are aware, and it would be better for him to scratch his plan right here, at once. However, our guest is not easily frightened," – Gibbs regarded me quickly and acutely – "and doesn't wish to renounce his intentions. No, sir, he doesn't..." Piolin became silent for a few seconds and Gibbs didn't speak either, waiting for him to continue.

Then Piolin loudly slurped a sip of water and started to talk about fellowship, trust, and some agreement we had made which I did not recall. For his part, Gibbs nodded absentmindedly the whole time, as if he, too, didn't completely understand. Only once did his face convey sympathy mixed with slight astonishment, but he abruptly turned the blank half to me and began scratching his neck violently. Piolin stopped, waiting for this to end, and Gibbs settled down, listening to Piolin and sitting as before – though with all expression having vanished from the normal part of his face.

I knew I should interrupt them and object. Piolin was again weaving some yarn, speaking all sorts of drivel and sneakily prodding me. Yet I was tired and just waited lethargically to see how it would play out.

"Yes, he dragged us into this, he did, but there's no calling him a con man," continued Piolin, threatening me jokingly with his finger. "No, he pulled me into it openly, without any craftiness whatsoever. But how he knew about you, my esteemed friend, I can't imagine for the life of me. That is, I'm aware of how he found out – I told him about you myself; but how he managed to force my hand – that's a mystery, all right. Nevertheless, he got what he wanted, and for us, Gibbs, there's nowhere else to go. So I'd say it'd be better to begin now, because it's a little late to waffle, and it's easier to take care of it quickly. Delays just do damage – faces, you know, get forgotten, names erased, and, worse still, people die inadvertently from time to time. So I would suggest," – Piolin grew even more somber – "I suggest putting aside the jokes and getting right down to business!"

Gibbs laid his elbows on the table, turned to me, and again became tense all over. His muscles bulged under his jacket and the veins on his neck stood out, but he asked in a fairly benevolent voice, "Name?"

"July," Piolin butted in, answering for me. Then he corrected himself, "That is, almost July... Julian, not July... July-Julian, what's the difference?" and he looked at me encouragingly with a wry half smile.

I didn't say a word, merely gazed ahead with a dissatisfied air, as Gibbs contemplated a short while, then crawled under the table and pulled out a small travel bag. He had probably brought it with him and I simply hadn't noticed – however, I could have sworn there had been nothing in his hands.

Riddles, riddles, I thought irritably while Gibbs rummaged, coming up with a photo that he lay on the table. It was a picture of an elderly man standing and leaning slightly to the side as he smiled sickly into the camera.

"Him?" Piolin asked me, turning it to himself and regarding it rapaciously.

"No, no resemblance whatsoever," I replied, shrugging my

shoulders. Piolin instantly lost interest in the photo and sat back in his chair while Gibbs nodded in satisfaction before picking up his bag and leaving.

At this, Piolin leaned toward me and, breathing into my face, began to explain at length that Gibbs was definitely a master in his field and indeed a trailblazer, but I shouldn't expect any results from him right away. It wasn't an easy task, even for Gibbs – and then I needed to keep in mind he wasn't famous for grasping the essence quickly. He spent a lot of time vacillating, so it could seem like he's just pulling your leg. Still, Piolin said, one shouldn't underestimate Gibbs – he was very dangerous, above all when he wasn't taken seriously. So we'd have to muster up a good deal of patience and wait a little – he'd come round now.

Soon, Gibbs approached us with a bundle of papers in his hands, sat down, beckoned to the waiter, and ordered coffee. We followed his example. The bundle turned out to be a huge map of the city folded up a few times. Gibbs tried to spread it out on the table, but there was no way the thing would fit, so it was impossible for me to see M. in its entirety.

The map was divided into squares. Piolin and Gibbs began to count them and found there were one hundred and eighty – twelve lines across and fifteen lengthwise. Each square, according to Gibbs, contained a few quarters, so they were rather big and their delineation had to be reworked – the present one having been done for another purpose and was thus too large. Piolin proposed increasing the frequency of the lines by one and a half, but Gibbs argued this would still be inconvenient and advocated even more – one point seven five. On that they agreed, took up a blunt pencil, and started to redraw the grid, the new, fat lines coinciding only rarely with the old ones. The result was such a confusing pattern of new and old streaks that, in my opinion, you couldn't make out a thing. Yet Gibbs was content and said the map was now divided just right, and Piolin also regarded their work with complete satisfaction.

Then Gibbs laid out his plan, warning us beforehand: he would begin with the very simple. He proposed to investigate every quarter thoroughly and completely – initially on the map, then "in the field." This way we would inevitably zero in on Julian and leave him no place to go – if he really was in the city. And if he wasn't here, which we'll know for sure after covering the last quarter, then the second part of the plan would go into effect, which was actually only a repetition of the first: we'd start over again with square number one and move progressively forward as before, because if Julian wasn't in town at the moment, there was nothing to stop him from appearing here any minute. Certainly, there was also nothing to prevent him from clearing out till the end of our search, and then we'd be in the same place we began, but we couldn't control this. Moreover, he could just as easily flit from quarter to quarter, and his path wouldn't necessarily cross ours. These considerations – was Julian living in M. or did he leave long ago, and, if he left, would he come back again and when – didn't change our plan in the least, and didn't make it any better or worse. That was what he, Gibbs, considered the fundamental virtue of his scheme: hardly anything in the world could interfere with its implementation.

All that remained, said Gibbs, was discussing the details, that is, the actual method. And here he suggested tried-and-true approaches such as continual surveillance in traditionally crowded places like bars, movie theaters, and tram stops, as well as talking with the locals who permanently resided in each quarter – possibly using some material encouragement to help untie their tongues. Although, he added with doubt, we should not overdo it as we didn't want our informants to fabricate something imaginary in a burst of zeal.

In this manner, Gibbs continued, acting methodically and persistently, we would keep moving ahead, which would be reflected on the map by the path of crossed-off quarters or, even better, by gluing pieces of adhesive paper over them – because no quarter, as long as one didn't lead to complete success, could be dismissed from consideration forever. After all, we might return to any given one later, retracing the same course a few times. And we most probably would return, since, between us, the chances of finding Julian on the first go-round or, more accurately, the first go-rounds were infinitesimally small. Nonetheless, gluing the squares would at least show us we weren't standing still but, quite the opposite, doing everything we could. And this, in turn, would give us an occasion not to hang our heads or spread our hands – which was important, since despondency was precisely the reason for failure in all complicated initiatives.

Gibbs stopped talking, visibly satisfied with himself. Piolin – murmuring "trailblazer, trailblazer" – looked at me, then Gibbs, with his hands shaking. It was clear I couldn't expect anything else worthwhile and had to leave right then and there. In a few words I thanked them both for their help and, with Gibbs eyeing me thoughtfully, I pulled out my wallet, laid a few bills on the table, and prepared to get up.

But I didn't get far. A stone hand came down on my elbow and pinned me effortlessly to the table. I felt like an insect, a butterfly affixed to a spreading board; I was so surprised that the light above me flipped over, then swung about and returned to its place, yet the hand on my elbow remained, though its grip did relax a bit.

"There's no need to hurry, my dear guest," said Piolin in a gentle voice, finally letting go of my arm. "What's the rush? We still haven't finished. You see, Gibbs is sitting patiently, and I'm not heading anywhere, and we're dealing with your affairs after all, not mine or Gibbs's. We should stick together, as partners do – since that's what we are, in effect. And moreover, Gibbs and I have already expended so much energy on this friend of yours, on our plan, and on you in general that there's no turning around now. Nobody likes it when one retreats after only going halfway, and Gibbs and I are no different: we're not used to backing off. Is that right, my esteemed friend?" And Gibbs nodded energetically.

"As for this plan of ours, it's crap!" continued Piolin unexpectedly, addressing Gibbs and ignoring me, although I sensed the alertness of the hand lying a few inches from my elbow. "It's nonsense because there are too many quarters, and no patience will be enough if you try to comb through them all. We have to forget that plan, and we should stop thinking about the city altogether – it's useless to search for Julian here. We must go to the Dunes; there's no better place for hunting something down anyway, and, in all likelihood, we'll find him there – since where else should he be?"

"That," drawled Gibbs, "is also an idea."

And I thought to myself, the Dunes – again the Dunes. Is it a coincidence or indeed something meaningful?

Things had been happening much too quickly; I felt thoroughly confused. As recently as yesterday, I had known M. only from hearsay, not to mention those places I had never even dreamed of reaching. Everyone preferred to keep quiet about them, as if to avoid straying into treacherous territory, but Piolin didn't hesitate at all. Dunes or no Dunes, he babbled away without batting an eye. It was strange: it looked like he was discussing a routine trip to the countryside while actually preparing to go recklessly to the very edge of the world, having no doubts whatsoever.

Expecting clarification, I glanced at Piolin, then Gibbs, but they were occupied with each other, enthusiastically outlining a concrete route, as if we had already agreed to embark on the expedition. No, I thought, this won't do, now you've gone too far – making decisions on my behalf, dictating where I will and won't go. You can take off yourself for all I care, just don't count on me – thank you very much. Julian is a matter for me alone, and I'll deal with him – no later than tomorrow!

At the same time I was listening to names, ominous and strange, regretting to the depths of my soul it was all in vain, and my unexpected companions certainly weren't taking me seriously. But what if they were? Anything was possible with these two. What an adventure it would be! It's a pity I have to go my own way…

"They probably think I can't turn them down," I whispered inaudibly to myself. "They're sure I've surrendered and agreed. Most people in my place would acquiesce, but I'm busy, busy, do you understand? Of course, it would be great to get ahead of Julian – yes, he's managed to come here before me, but if, let's say, I were the first to make it to the Dunes, that would tip the scales. Or would it not change a thing? And who will I prove it to? And what if it actually ends up he's already been in the Dunes too?"

The last thought was very unpleasant. I squirmed in my seat, and Gibbs turned and looked into my eyes. This passed in a flash, and he shifted his gaze, but it was still enough for me to start convincing myself – why not? Why shouldn't I go with them, even if just out of stubbornness, just out of independence or curiosity, even if no trace of Julian is there to be found? I was surprised at myself and this sudden shift of attitude but couldn't come up with a decent objection. Gibbs's expression hovered over my eyes like a shadow, and Piolin, as if to add to my confusion, began insisting this plan was the one we needed and infinitely outweighed the other.

"You'll get a good look at the ocean, my dear guest, and, who knows, maybe we'll really find your guy..." He gibbered on and on – about Julian, about the trailblazer Gibbs, then again about the new scheme, which was nothing like the earlier one, a hundred times better. So that he, Piolin, was even sorry he couldn't join us. He had too much work – running a hotel, after all, is no joke. "But it's not a problem," he quickly reassured me. "Other people will be going with you, friends of ours, good friends – when you set out for the Dunes, you know, the more people the better." And at this very moment a dead octopus came flying from a distant part of the room, hitting Gibbs in the shoulder. There was a scream, we jumped up, and mayhem broke out.

Everything happened so fast I didn't even notice the emergence of two tanned men in black jackets who seemed to exude a swamplike smell and a whole gang of thugs behind them – no fewer than eight. When I lifted my eyes, the swarthy men were hanging back against the wall to the right of us while the striplings were advancing from the corner to our left – where the exit was – loudly cursing and chucking in their path all the junk they could grab off the bar counter and the tables as they moved forward. We had landed in the center, and I was very anxious: the cocky boys were walking straight toward us.

I glanced over at the two guys being pursued. They were looking every which way but appeared quite calm on the whole, although they had nowhere to go, and their position seemed thoroughly unenviable. A second passed – no more – yet, when I turned back, I saw the boys were already there, at our table. Piolin was surveying them from top to bottom, his mouth opened idiotically, while Gibbs was saying something as he stood in front of them. The one close by, a stocky blond, hopped to the side and tried to deliver a whistling blow with something black, which Gibbs dodged like a cat. After that, everything spun in circles, as if I were having a disorderly dream. I remember Piolin holding the blond's throat in his iron grasp and thrusting a knee into his backbone. The youngster croaked and Piolin squinted at him with bloodshot eyes, saying contentedly, "I'll teach you something now, watch this..." The two men in black jackets emerged right in the thick of it and landed a series of vicious punches. Instantly, the floor became splattered with blood; a few boys were lying face down, completely still, while the rest were being thrashed and driven toward the door. I flung myself at Piolin to save the blond, for I thought he was going to strangle him, but someone forced me back and we fell to the floor, right onto the slimy octopus – my face smashing down in the middle of it. The person holding me whispered in my ear, "Wait, wait, let the fun go on!" I jerked about in his hands yet couldn't turn around, and when I finally broke free, the light went out and everything vanished into darkness.

Someone gave a terrible shriek – no doubt the blond, because when the light flipped back on, the boy sat in a chair, raising up his arms to shield himself from Piolin, who towered over him. One of his ears had almost been ripped off and dangled by a flap of skin. He moaned and howled sickly, then spit a bloody glob at Piolin, who grabbed a chair, grunted, and shattered it over the youngster's head. Everyone froze and in the silence you could hear Gibbs cursing bluntly. Then he appeared close at hand, obliquely looked at the crushed skull, and pushed Piolin toward the door.

I ran to the restroom and barely made it before I vomited convulsively. Afterward, I stood next to the sink for a long time, washing the remains of the octopus off my face and the blood off my sleeve. Some serious, absorbed men came in, but nobody paid any attention to me until I had the courage to ask one of them, "Excuse me, have they already cleaned everything up out there?" Yet he just approached me, stared in my face attentively, and left without saying a word. I stood in front of the mirror for a few more minutes and then headed back to the room, walking unsteadily.

The place showed no signs of a fight. Gibbs sat alone at our table and smoked. "Where's Piolin?" I asked and was astonished at my foolishness.

Gibbs, however, wasn't surprised in the least and replied in a bored tone that Piolin probably had business to take care of – he was always busy, day and night, since an innkeeper has to look into everything. I agreed, "Yes, of course," and sat down. Gibbs handed me a cigarette.

"I have to go now," he said. "It's unfortunate we didn't have time to discuss the details, but you got the gist of it, didn't you?"

"The gist?" I asked distractedly.

"Well, yes." Gibbs nodded. "The Dunes and all that. Think about it at leisure, mull it over. When the day comes to set out, we'll let you know. And don't worry about the bill for dinner – it's on me." He stood up, gave a short bow, and prepared to leave.

"Tell me," I entreated him, "who were those kids? Why did they get beaten up so badly? And who were those two guys?" I cast a glance at the wall to my right where the men in black jackets had been earlier. "And I also wanted to ask: are you sure Piolin won't be going with us – that is, if you really head out and I agree to join you?"

Gibbs turned, regarded me with a penetrating, serious look – and went away without a word.

CHAPTER 4

That was my first evening in the City of M. It seemed I wouldn't be able to fall asleep after everything I'd been through, but I slept soundly, in a dark abyss. By morning, yesterday's events had receded into the distant past, getting all mixed up with my uneasy dreams, and by noon it was clear the surrounding world had forgotten and would hardly remember me anytime soon. For breakfast, I didn't go to the hotel restaurant, heading instead to a café on the corner, and I didn't meet one familiar face then or later. I already presumed I wouldn't see either Piolin or Gibbs again, yet it turned out I was wrong. The next day I ran into Piolin in the hotel lobby, though we didn't exchange a word and bowed in a manner that was almost impolite. Gibbs also emerged in time as promised, but for now I remained free of everyone. I was left on my own, and my secret rose up and spread its wings, enveloping my being.

I wanted to do something without delay – however, a certain haziness lingered in my head and no good ideas came to mind. Of course I should have contemplated in peace, yet I couldn't sit still. As I walked around the area by the hotel, I looked closely at advertising columns covered with messages, hoping to find some foothold right away. But this didn't lead to anything, and I had to go back empty handed. To make the trip not utterly useless, I procured a colorful booklet filled with items for sale or purchase as well as other personal ads, from which, with scissors from the concierge, I carefully cut out an insertion card.

There was a hint of cowardice in this – getting into contact with the outside world by calling someone anonymously. Yet I told myself I had to begin with something small. Furthermore, anonymity may be different. In my case it even resembled an open challenge. And doubting no longer, I started concocting short, pithy lines that would build a rickety but enduring bridge to my target. After wasting two hours and growing thoroughly exhausted, I settled on the simplest, "Looking for Julian. Controversial legacy. Reward for quickness." Then I added my room telephone number and, considering the job done, slipped the coupon into a hotel envelope.

We'll see, we'll see, I said to myself, descending the stairs and buying a stamp in the kiosk by the entrance. Something was happening – my plan was getting off the ground, if only slightly, and this excited and warmed my blood. Simultaneously, it occurred to me I should also try the yellow pages. I spent an hour searching for them and finally managed to find an outdated version in a phone booth almost a mile from the hotel – without any tangible benefit. Then my enthusiasm died out. The initial fervor almost vanished and I instructed myself to relax, stop fussing, and get my affairs in some sort of order.

First, I needed to know more about the geography of M. – to be precise, its topological configuration. Gibbs and his map with thick pencil lines immediately came to mind. I thought about it enviously but realized there was no reason to be bitter. His map was too oversized, and markings by others were hardly suited for me. It would probably be easy to buy something similar – and I did exactly that in the evening. Moreover, after milling around by the counter, I purchased two maps at once: a large one and another much smaller, which I squeezed into the pocket of my pants. Then I studied deep into the night, memorizing the names of the streets, the locations of important intersections, parking garages, and other noteworthy places. This was useless, but I couldn't stop, agitated by the feeling that somewhere there, in some nook among the map symbols, Julian was hiding. And that night I only dozed off as the first cars honked in the morning.

The next two days I devoted to grueling walks, criss-crossing the city jungle, treating my memory to the new network of routes I could race about without being afraid of getting lost. M. had been constructed simply. At its center lay a cobblestone plaza bordered by the city's government buildings – the mayor's house, the police headquarters, and gray administrative blocks. Avenues beamed out from it like rays – a few main ones that extended in straight lines to the outskirts and others that soon began darting here and forking there. It would be hard to call the planning well-conceived or rigid – you only had to go a mile or so from the center until you arrived at a maze of narrow streets, forming real labyrinths at times, especially in the northern low-income quarters. Next to the main plaza, where naked stone reigned bleakly, sat the marketplace, and not far from it – a large, tree-lined square. Urban life teemed there, news and rumors were hatched, visitors and locals milled about the open space. And I, too, spent quite a bit of time on this common, observing, watching or simply basking in the sun.

On the whole, if you look from above, the City of M. resembles an assiduously woven spiderweb – with bald patches along the edges, but a strong interlaced structure. It's not easy to check its strength, yet we know it's reliable enough – too many strangers have gotten trapped there, and too many others have become entangled, unable to free themselves or promptly call for help. Not large by European standards and hopelessly provincial in general, M. long ago turned into a refuge for uninvited visitors hardly capable of explaining what attracted them there. A legend persisted: the world was designed differently here, more irrational and complex, as if its invisible trajectories veered off the straight path and retreated into kinks, passing through themselves, getting reflected, like in a curved mirror, running off and meeting back where no one expected them. It's not a picture you can easily imagine, and I doubt anyone would say in all honesty they knew what I was talking about.

Still, the legend lives on, and most agree this is the place where you can learn more about yourself than anywhere else. However, learning is a complicated subject. Only a few manage to deal with it properly – yet, turning to the facts, you can't help but notice that many people who cannot sit still land in M. sooner or later, either voluntarily or by a random series of events. Of course, no one has tried to assess this seriously, and you can claim any fact is fantasy and have a perfectly good reason to distrust it. That's how it was with all the lore about what happened here from time to time – it seemed to be way too unusual, so you race to M. to see for yourself, and once you've arrived, you look at its actual life and wonder: where are the secrets, where are the keys? Have I already been privy to them? Or was I just mesmerized by the idea arising from slander and gossip?

Well, I thought, the geography is simple, yet when exploring the place further a newcomer wouldn't always know where to begin. At least it was clear I should put aside the myths – I didn't need any more riddles at the moment. But all the same, the notions were leading me astray, as the images from the surroundings bear down – I would so like to line them up in a row and examine at my leisure, hoping to penetrate into the depths. If, of course, they really have a false bottom.

Who told me about the City of M. in the first place? I no longer remember, as I cannot recall the origin of other knowledge that became indispensable and whose inception I wanted to attribute to my own mind. Was it one of my friends from the university or a girlfriend who wished to appear wiser than she was? The truth wasn't really important now – I've already identified myself with the idea, no less than anyone else I knew who was capable of independent thinking. What's essential is to imagine the details you've never seen and, hitting upon them, to feel your pulse fluttering the instant your finger traces the route on a map and reaches the yellow dot denoting the city. It's essential to go there, whether or not you destroy all the bridges behind you. You may not be the first and you're even a follower in a certain sense – a follower in a way you cannot contemplate without protesting with all your heart. Still, you're here, and that alone overrides all the reasons to belittle yourself, especially since you could always find plenty of them.

As for me, I'm not inclined to belittling – it's hard to address small things anyway, for they tend to just slip through your fingers. But if to divide one general belief among everyone, will a lot be left in one's hands? Maybe that's why the very myth about the City of M. is depressingly indistinct, and those who visit it, or maybe just talk about its mystic spell, cannot be truly proud, although they try with all their might. Furthermore, there are many who don't try in the least – so you can't figure out who was actually there, who was not and may never be, and who passed through, yet decided to hold their tongue. "Congratulations, You Have Reached the Place of Everyone's Aspirations" states a roadside billboard at the city line. But declaring is easy, you admit to yourself – despite being somewhat confused by such directness. Then you change course in pursuit of reassurance and shudder from awkwardness as you stumble on a lacerated fissure resembling a question mark in concrete, or the pitiless gaze of a paperboy, or even the terrible frankness of "The City of M. is the Black Pelican," painted on a wall in a dreary back alleyway. It's easy to become dejected then and withdraw into yourself, risking no further disappointment – although the unknown graffitist probably reckoned on the reverse. You admit: either you didn't get the meaning or he was unable to explain it clearly. You circle through doubts, cursing his negligence, and uneasy thoughts gnaw at your insides: What if there's nothing more to it? Why are the local legends so vague? Who are their sibyls and prophets? And whoever you ask, they just shake their head and drop the subject right away. Only a few might say dubiously: Maybe the Little Blue Birds? It's too bad no one's seen them for a while…

I wandered the streets until nightfall, getting used to the city. Like someone yielding to its power, I milled about its labyrinthine lanes and inspected the gray stone of the surrounding buildings as if looking for advice. Then, on the third day, I decided the new territory had been well-explored – and suddenly felt down as I grasped this had brought me no closer to my goal.

More importantly, I couldn't think what else to do. For a moment it seemed I had gotten good news: my legacy ad was published and I lit up with hope. But it turned out to be a farce: only one person reacted to my signal – a young-looking vagabond with an emaciated face. I met him near the hotel entrance and he wasted a whole half-hour trying to sell me a trashy book with therapeutic tips and then some dark liquid possessing curative properties. When I asked him directly about Julian, he muttered something inarticulate and I went away filled with frustration as the doorman watched me intently.

No one else responded and soon it became clear my plan was heading up a blind alley. Drifting through the city, I just couldn't regain my confidence. The hunt for Julian appeared to be quite a difficult matter – almost as hopeless as Piolin had warned me.

Recalling Piolin made me furious. I cursed out loud, standing spellbound in the middle of the street – cursed and glanced about, my brow puckering with uneasiness. Nobody heard me, however, or they simply didn't show it; they were all busy with their own things, hurrying – from the tram stop to the dairy, from the pharmacy to the grocery store, from the bank building... Wait!

It was as if a bolt of lightning flashed in front of my eyes and a whirlwind swept through my chest. I was sure that, coming out of the bank, was none other than Julian himself. He exited the building and was now bustling away. I took a deep breath, then another, and rushed after him, examining and comparing on the go. It was unfortunate I couldn't see his face, but his gait and the swaying of his shoulders were enough to recognize him without a doubt. His raincoat was out of place though – what's that, I thought, a camouflage? And he's got a bag on his shoulder, a fairly roomy one – so I wondered, what could be inside it?

Julian or his double walked unconcerned, clearly not suspecting he was being trailed. His long strides forced me to increase my pace and I trotted clumsily at times, almost at an outright jog. What a dumb chase, whizzed through my head – straight out of a bad movie. We probably looked pretty funny from another perspective – two strangers bound by an invisible thread, moving in synchrony, harmony in everything. But it wasn't funny for us – especially me.

Julian stopped abruptly at a shop window and I sprang into the shadows, behind a newspaper stand, nearly knocking someone over and blurting out my apologies. He had his back to me as before, scrutinizing something behind the glass, and I strained to guess – was it him or not – and clenched my fists, trying to master my agitation and calm my nerves. Then we started moving again, one after the other, twenty feet between us – while I continued to think about what I should do, how not to lose him if he suddenly hailed a taxi and was off. Some course of action was called for. I began to close the gap, getting progressively nearer, and caught up to him at the light, maneuvering my way between people. A few meters back, doubt had stolen over me – something wasn't right: he had never worn his raincoat like that, and his trousers hadn't bubbled up that much as he walked. Maybe Julian has become provincial far from the capital, and his taste simpler in accordance with the local tradition? Or perhaps that was his true identity and his former fashionable self had been contrived? But no, soon it became apparent: this man with his coat and gray training bag belonged to the surrounding crowd. He's local, I thought glumly, although the smallest grain of hope impelled me to walk up and bump into him, as if by accident. Apologizing, I peered into his face and turned away in despair – no resemblance whatsoever. And what was I to expect? The chance was ridiculously small. The unfamiliar man hurried across at the green light, while I, still following him with my eyes, was surprised at myself – he and Julian didn't look even remotely similar. What kind of strange obsession had this been?

It was humiliating, and my cheeks became flushed from shame. The incident, though, was not for nothing. I understood I wasn't ready to meet my target and didn't know what I would do if we really ended up face to face. How should I behave, what script should I choose – act surprised and postpone the rest till later or resolve it all right away, using the suddenness of the moment? Moreover, I didn't have the required tools in my possession – I had left everything in the hotel room. And could I really carry out my plan just like that, on the spot, in front of everyone? Yes, my secret might be simple, but it wasn't harmless, and my courage had its limits… In any case, I needed to pull myself together and tune back into serious matters – right away.

It's time to clarify a bit: I was planning a murder. It sounds wild, but there's no reason to hide it: I wanted to find and kill Julian, as if that would make something clear once and for all. The essence isn't important – what will come of it and why. You can't always unscramble and put things together like a jigsaw puzzle. Sometimes you have to trust your instinct, although it, too, had betrayed me not just once. But you follow your intuition not because it won't trick you – you submit to it because it won't let you go. That's how it was back then in the capital when I woke up in my apartment and realized: enough is enough. I have to cross the border with no going back. Wild or not, Julian must cease to exist.

I remember I wandered from room to room, like a sleepwalker, my bathrobe half open, a bachelor's odds and ends all over the place. I neglected my morning rituals, not letting myself be distracted. I was getting used to my decision, and the more it pleased me, the more cautiously I considered it, afraid someone would penetrate my thoughts to reveal and interfere with them. It was then I named it *my secret*, so even the formal label wouldn't allow my lips to be pried apart. I assigned it a place in a narrow row of subjects I could not utter aloud, had to keep out of sight in case anybody was nearby – so they wouldn't guess from the shadows on my face or my nebulous gaze. Then the phone rang and I recoiled in horror, afraid that spies were already on to me, but I immediately forced myself to calm down and pick up the receiver as if nothing were the matter. And how easy it was to lie when I knew the space I was safeguarding wasn't empty. I agreed to a meeting and promised all sorts of nonsense, paid compliments and listened to drivel in response, bearing in mind every second that I might say whatever I liked and still no one would see through me, infiltrating the inner depths. And when my interlocutor disintegrated in the noise of static as if he were tired of his attempts and acknowledged the futility of his spying, I ran to the kitchen and poured out two fingers of gin, saluting my own craftiness, feeling larger and more prodigious. Something grew inside me, was settling in for years, shielded from others, from their silly curiosity and trite phrases.

I didn't go to the office, called in sick, and celebrated by myself. It seemed like the iron lock on my cell had crumbled to dust and the freedom was even more intoxicating than the gin, though I had to learn how to handle it without getting confused. I then decided every dead end has a hidden door – only discovering later that was not true, but the City of M. was still in the future, as a reality which is far from a dream. For the time being, I only experienced the events in my imagination, having no obstacles to keep me from seeing straight.

Those were the halcyon days, the honeymoon of the idea. Myriad details gripped my mind and I needed to consider them all. Nonetheless, I was surprised by the extremity of my intentions: I had never been inclined to violence, so what had happened, how could I explain it? Yet, I don't recall any hesitancy or fear, just feverish contemplation of the plan itself, as well as the recurring sense of liberty: nothing was holding me back.

The particulars of my scheme had not been worked out – I had only managed to clarify its general features. But what else to expect from someone who is taking on such an aim for the first time? No sooner do you ponder it than your nerves begin to dance and your head burns. Horrifying images emerge before your eyes; cries ring in your ears and feed your fantasy. You can't record anything concisely – the episodes collapse in a chaotic heap. I tried again and again – yet it always turned out badly. Still, I didn't have time for regrets: my life had already changed to the point of unrecognizability. The excitement of pursuit consumed my days, although I still wasn't rushing anywhere. Friends started to regard me with respect, seeing something new in my face, and my co-workers soon spread rumors that I was about to quit. I obtained a strange sort of power over the surrounding world – a power which I had never possessed before and which would have embarrassed me somewhat if I had considered it seriously. But other concerns overran me, not letting me sleep, troubling me like a horror movie in childhood.

What I had to deal with right away was the appropriate weapon. I mentally scrolled back and forth through the names of friends who could help me procure one without asking questions. For a while, I became obsessed with guns: they surfaced in my dreams, emerging in different sizes and shapes. They were black or iron gray, with engravings in bronze, wooden, and ivory grips, rotating barrels and loaded hammers presaging the coming explosion, smoke, and fire. After two weeks of cautious searches, fortune smiled upon me. A childhood friend, a slippery car dealer, promised to help. Before long, he hooked me up with three somber men who dumped such a mountain of weapons on the table that I was totally dazzled. I decided on a simple and reliable Colt – although the price seemed insane. Nonetheless, I didn't want to backtrack now and we completed the transaction, parting without a smile, like true conspirators. Unable to resist, I tested it out that very evening, driving way off into the countryside. At first, the bang was so unpleasant it staggered me. I even thought about a silencer, yet the ugly long barrel totally ruined the image. After a few more shots, however, I got so used to the sound and the recoil of corrugated metal that the Colt came to exemplify perfection itself.

I had an even harder time with the rest of the arrangements. Weighing how to slip away scot-free, I tossed over dozens of scenarios in my head, sensing in despair that I was a hopeless amateur, ineffectual in the face of real danger. There was nobody to go to for advice and badly written detective stories did not look reliable in the least. But I couldn't think of any other sources: my own imagination didn't get me beyond wigs, false beards, and heels with surprises that make you limp. Ultimately I had to bet on luck, the effect of unexpectedness and my own cleverness, although I did stock up on several props – if only to make me feel better. Excessive self-confidence is not one of my traits, and I knew I was risking a lot, yet my secret entailed some risk – otherwise the glory of the achievement would evaporate and the operation would lose all meaning.

Actually, regarding the meaning, I was walking on very thin ice. It's not that there wasn't any – on the contrary, I could think of a whole bunch of versions and untangling them was no easy task. Only one thing was certain: all the events of past years, all the insults and misfortunes point at him, Julian – or others similar to him, which doesn't actually change the matter. That said, I need to correct myself: all these *others* aren't entirely *similar*. He represents both a rule and an exception – the rarest of rare exceptions, which again justifies what I'm intending to do: the case is unique, which means anything goes.

This is how it happens – time after time you gather junk but then chance on a gold mine and stare in astonishment: here's the solution, all the pieces fall in place! That's how Julian, nonchalantly entering my life, stunned me right away with the completeness of the picture. He embodied everything that alienated me from the normal, from the world of my acquaintances and co-workers, their joys and arguments, their family squabbles, their wishes and fears. He personified the reality where all of them wandered blindfolded, running into sharp branches, not understanding sounds, not differing between day and night, and not recognizing their paths. It was as if substances that made up their core had gathered in Julian, smoothly interwoven, selecting him as their coryphaeus, endowing him with invisible buoyancy and confidence in himself. I was stunned at first as I observed his knack for pleasing everyone, only realizing later it was not because he was smarter than others and didn't have blinkers on his eyes. No, the blinkers were there; he was also confused, he stumbled and got offended and gnashed his teeth in response. His life was not cloud-free and was not altogether different from the majority of our colleagues. However, no one had less doubts than this man that the real world was precisely the way he, Julian, saw it – which made it, in his eyes, perfectly harmonious, proper, and unshakeable.

Blindness is blindness, but taken to the point of absurdity, it's a formidable strength. Looking at him, any average guy could lift up his head. Julian was comfortable in any group, and even if badly concealed artifice shimmered in his openness, it didn't bother anyone. Yes, that's who I am, but we are all like that, his entire image said – and his assertive voice confirmed it, resonating in everyone's heart and forcing them to forgive his base tricks. After all, he himself was quick to forgive, smiling broadly in your face. He wasn't stupid but coped easily with the stupidity of others, which opens many iron doors no less surely than a magic word. He knew his strength and used it; he exuded mental health and a sense of integrity that attracted both friends and women. He was a rare integral being, this Julian. It was even difficult to believe – though I did believe and grew to hate him, but eventually I matured to the point of renouncing my emotion, descrying in him an object not for feelings but for actions that would be taken dispassionately, with the cold-hearted decisiveness I was pretending to possess. There was no sense in trying to look brave or decent – it'd hardly deceive anyone. All the more so since the case was not one that can bear scrutiny – I couldn't even share it with my closest confidant, assuming I had one. And there surely was nothing to show off in front of myself or others, which was also good, for I didn't want admiring remarks – they weren't of any use. I was just looking for one thing – to be relieved of my burden; and I was only sorry no one could help me – I had to do it myself.

Everyone would ask: why such extremes? The answer is simple: what other options would I have? It's not just revenge – it's more complicated. My vigilant gaze became so accustomed to Julian, who was everywhere, that he turned into a symbol, the abstract but most important reason for my discomfort, which I couldn't endure anymore. And my agitated conscience, responding to the hint, agreed: yes, remove that and you'll be better off. Since it probably can't be otherwise.

Certainly one could detect a weak spot here too – for the discomfort issue was always present, whereas Julian appeared just recently. The heart of the problem, like the cavity of a whirlpool, retained doubt and annoying questions, but still: those doubts receded long ago, while Julian – Julian remained. He should pardon the way it turned out: perhaps he just wasn't lucky, yet I had nowhere else to direct my hostility. It seemed he became a barrier, severing me from the ordinary world, from everyday pleasures and wishes. Might it be that without Julian something changed subtly, the flimsy equilibrium was disturbed, and the world shifted the smallest bit? Not much, yes, but I didn't need a lot.

It's not worth searching for glitches in what had already been decided, and if someone said my impulse was too petty, like a ripple in a glass of water, then I'd just turn away, pretending I didn't hear. Petty or not, I saw there a great depth, a bottomless chasm. Others wouldn't even perceive what the trick was, but I – I was settling a score with the universe for readily apparent distortion. It would certainly feign to have not noticed a thing – however I wouldn't buy it. That's why I chose Julian – to make it impossible not to notice. He had everything in excess – he was an exception, I repeat, of the rarest kind. Cat and mouse games no longer confused me, even if the universe exuded all its potency, imposed its opinion without any hope of revision, refusing to admit I was special and had a right to be that. I don't need esteem, perhaps I'm looking for the opposite, but acknowledge I have the right – and I'll agree we're even. However insignificant my efforts are, no matter how absurd my challenges seem, please, write down my bet. I'll wipe Julian out, even if those who peer from the above laugh at me loudly, criticizing the awkwardness of the plan. Let's agree, at least, that reality, if you don't close your eyes, is too disgusting for the most part – and who else but Julian constantly reminds me of this? Could this be a reason? For me, this is the reason all right – a tenacious, inexhaustible and completely satisfactory one!

That's how I encouraged myself as I headed to the hotel after the fruitless chase, which rounded out yet another day without bringing me one step closer to what I had conceived. The words were familiar – I had repeated them a number of times – but they rarely helped, for they, too, hid a lie that wasn't so easily hushed up. It began to drizzle, and the city seemed to hunch over and turn its face away. My thoughts, like gloomy strangers, scurried their own way, not noticing each other and not coalescing. What was today's failure, I wondered – more mockery from the universe? Or was it a sign, hint, atonement – but for what? It appeared I was neglecting the main thing, overlooking something lying right in front of my face, and this irritated me to no end. I sighed, walked into the hotel, looked doubtfully at the elevator, where a crowd of people had gathered, and began to trudge up the stairs.

If you fall in a trap, says one ancient Eastern game, turn your attention to the simplest of things and don't make abrupt moves. Let's go back to the start, I mumbled to myself as I surmounted the steps one by one. Let's go back and put everything in order – maybe the next maneuver will become clear on its own.

Yes, to the start, I confirmed aloud after reaching the right floor. Then I caught my breath and continued to my room. On the way I ran into a giggling chambermaid and we bowed formally as we passed each other. I lingered just a moment, looking after her pensively, and, as if tallying something up, I slammed the door that clicked shut with its automatic bolt.

CHAPTER 5

Putting things in order meant returning to the starting point. I had to go way back, to the vanilla crème memories from my childhood – the real beginning of everything. It wasn't difficult or tricky, though I lingered nonetheless, circling the room and then doing something strange: I plopped down on the chair next to the phone, propped my chin on the palm of my hand, and sat like that for half an hour, knowing I had no one to call. Eventually, I even began to dial a number but immediately slammed the receiver on the cradle and didn't pick it up again, as if I'd burnt my fingers and developed reflexes – like a muscle spasm – to protect myself from such obvious silliness.

My only real friend had become unapproachable – and she had stopped thinking of me long ago. This didn't change the starting point; it just added a bitter almond aftertaste to the vanilla crème image I had memorized. I still had no trouble calling it to life, like an all-powerful genie, from whom there was nothing to solicit, and it didn't fade as I grew up: here I was, a twelve-year-old boy, with my darling Gretchen, my sister, who was thought to be a year older, though I knew eons lay between us. In truth, a lot of things seemed like eons back then. We jetted through time by leaps and bounds, from one juncture to another, and between them were countless weeks that got hopelessly lost and left gulfs and gaps. But that one day I still remembered distinctly, which was certainly to her credit.

The day itself passed as usual, and in the evening we had a party in our house. That was nothing new, but for some reason we decided to hide under the large table with the dessert dishes in the back room. We climbed in, ensconcing ourselves behind the flaps of the long tablecloth, our hearts thumping in anticipation of the rush we would get from the new game. People entered, and we froze with bated breath and peered through the patterned lace as they closed the door, thinking it would save them from stray glances.

I remember Dr. Roberts and his scary black beard. He stood in the middle of the room for a long time, picking at his nose and slightly swaying on his heels. It was so funny we almost burst out laughing – and then the door swung open, letting in our housekeeper, who stopped in her tracks, pressed her palm to her lips, and ran off at once, tossing over her shoulder something like, "You're everywhere! It's awful, truly awful," and we realized the black beard frightened her too. As for the doctor, he remained another minute, with a wistful smile on his face, then mumbled smugly, "Dirty witch," and walked out, his enormous boots creaking with every step.

In his place, the door admitted Herr and Frau Larsen, who had barely crossed the threshold before they started awkwardly poking and telling each other off in undertones. Frau Larsen belittled Herr Larsen with a word I'd never heard, and Gretchen grabbed hold of my elbow as Herr Larsen raised his hand as if to slap her. Yet we knew he couldn't harm a fly – it was a pity Frau Larsen wasn't aware of that. She shrank back in terror, shielded herself with both arms, hissed something indecipherable, and marched out with an overwrought face. And he, in turn, struggled to calm down, making loops around the room, shrugging his shoulders and occasionally munching on a goodie from the table – probably cherries or strawberries.

Eventually he was frightened off – by one of our uncle's friends, I think. Then another woman stared at herself in the cheval glass, moving right up to it, and withdrew, saying loudly, "That's what I thought!" as if blaming someone invisible. Afterward, our parents noticed we were missing; we heard their voices calling throughout the house, "Vitus, Gretchen," and, in pursuit of them, the cry of the hysterical madam Eloisa, "Virginia!" – though nothing new could happen to her peevish Virginia, which was confirmed when a yell came from one of the far-off rooms. Ultimately they found us, yet we didn't leave our spot, that cozy dark haven. We stayed, clutching each other, joined like an organic whole. Then my mother came with a glass of champagne and bent down, a wave of perfume cascading over us, but that, too, didn't bring us out of hiding. When they finally called her and she left, Gretchen hugged and kissed me insatiably, her lips tasting of vanilla crème, and I didn't turn away, understanding I shouldn't, because she and I were one.

Later, in our bedroom, while we were lying under the covers, listening to the murmuring voices and music on the other side of the wall, Gretchen jumped up, ran over, and climbed under my blanket, her whole body nestling up to mine like a warm little animal. "Don't be scared, nobody will see us," she whispered, but I wasn't afraid, for I also knew they never broke their evening ritual and no one would bother us till morning. And that's how it should be, since we have to grow up, as Miss Greenwich said before we were exposed. Only small and very dumb children believe in nighttime goblins, she added, not ones like Gretchen and me. Yes, that's right, we agreed, yet I imagine both she and our gullible parents would have been floored to find out how grown up we had quietly become, how we judged them with childish frankness, how we aped their words and habits, ruthlessly mocking everything that seemed insincere, not yet knowing what real insincerity was and what waited for us in the world we had just started to explore. And that night Gretchen opened another secret door, smashing the shackles that held us back, those taboos that are so terrible you never speak of them aloud. We went through that door more and more frequently – at first in the fiery confusion of our illicit union and later with the assurance of unexplainable righteousness, not asking "Why?" but perceiving we already had the answer.

That time, in the darkness of the children's' room, though we may have been sure no one would catch us by surprise, we were awkward and clumsy. But there is no one more daring than my dear Gretchen, my beloved sister, my little Teddy bear – and there is no one more resourceful when it comes to naughtiness. She touched me with increasing openness, and in that touch there was neither passion nor pitiful lust, which we weren't capable of back then. It was just a confirmation of our closeness, which had been overwhelming us as the bizarre life outside came to seem progressively stranger. And to discover a way out or acknowledge it entirely, you could do anything without being embarrassed. Gretchen showered us both with caresses, immersing me in a sweet game where I did whatever she wanted, shaking with innocent excitement, not knowing what was happening to me and frightened of myself almost to the point of tears. But she always found an infallible word to calm me, as if to dissuade the nighttime goblins, and we forged ahead into our labyrinth, exploring each turn one by one, understanding more and more clearly what we had hazily felt before: that she and I were one, nearly indivisible.

"No one will love you as much as you love yourself," she once said to me. And however dumb I might have been, I had a hunch she was talking about her own fears. Eventually, I knew this for sure, but that was much later, when she no longer took cover and cried on my shoulder, breaking down with revelations which weren't anything new. "No one, no one can love me as much as I love myself," she repeated, and I knew what she meant – as much as I loved her and she loved me, because she and I were one, and everyone else was immensely different.

Anyway, those words were found when we were already past twenty and had learned to get along with reality separately. By then we only rarely reunited in gloomy tenderness and were not jealous of each other – sensing what seemed to be our fate: the disappointments and countless bitter pricks, intensified by the fact that our outer shells didn't want to become any harder after being softened by our happy childhood. I had thought it would always be that nice and no one would take away my vanilla crème image, but wise Gretchen knew our crooked life couldn't continue forever. Afterward I too grew reluctantly aware of this, so our forays into outer territories, short at first, became more extensive and frequent, ultimately evolving into a tolerable form of existence. I went as far as to befriend her lovers, some of whom received the temporary status of fiancée, even if they didn't retain it for long – until Brett appeared, but that's another story. I had no trouble with them, being the obvious victor and disdainfully observing a game where they had no chance no matter how aggressively they framed their bold attacks. We simply looked at the gameboard from different angles – and from mine the view was much clearer. Moreover, there was no invisible clock ticking over my head, forcing me to hurry. I merely watched someone else's time expire, urging acts that deceitfully led nowhere. Gretchen also met my girlfriends, but women aren't that naïve, and I regularly had to hear the disingenuous, "Look how close they are, this brother and sister." Nonetheless, while it reeked of vague ambiguity, the words were lost on us; we dismissed them without a thought.

And really: no one caught us in the act, except unlucky Miss Greenwich, who paid for it afterward, though I have to admit I panicked when she flung open the door to our room at a most unfortunate moment. Gretchen, however, reckoned shrewdly our governess wouldn't be able to sleep peacefully that night. Later she confessed some oddities had made her suspicious of Miss Greenwich for a while, but then, in the middle of the night, she explained nothing. She just woke me up, took me by the arm, and led me to our governess's suite. Not a sound could be heard coming from it. I fidgeted in bewilderment and didn't understand what she was planning to do. It was all cleared up in a minute when Gretchen turned the doorknob and we saw Miss Greenwich in such an indecent position I automatically averted my eyes – only to survey various objects tossed across the bed, dully gleaming in the weak light of her night lamp.

"Small packages from London," said Gretchen quietly, and everyone was silent for a few seconds, as if paralyzed. Then a grimace distorted Miss Greenwich's face, and Gretchen rushed up and hugged her tightly, signaling for me to disappear, which I did with an inexpressible feeling of relief. We never mentioned those incidents again, although Miss Greenwich blushed at first when she met us in the morning. Otherwise, no one else came close to peeping behind the curtain – and the further we went, the more careful we became, realizing better and better the perniciousness of intrusive glances capable of penetrating our cryptic world.

Yes, cryptic is what you would call this oblong cocoon, irreproachable in shape and still impermeable for others. Shielded from the storms outside, much was developed and nurtured there: my muddled dreams, my partiality for timid rhymes that never turned into a passion, mutual fantasies full of brashness and affection, figures and signs, serving us as ciphers. Only with Gretchen did I share the enthusiasm of my boyish discoveries. It was to her I brought my first poem, which became our joint secret, imbued with allegorical meaning. I had composed a sad ballad about Malvinus, The Little One, though I've now forgotten almost all of it, since it was she who saved it for us, knowing my reluctance to put anything down on paper. There was something about a dusty courtyard, a house similar to ours and occupied by invisible beings. It began very cheerfully:

> *Malvinus The Little One*
> *and Ratcatcher his friend*
> *sang their song heedlessly –*
> *la-la, la-la, la-la.*

Then, however, the fun faded, and life got worse and worse for Malvinus. He, like all his invisible chums, bounced from corner to corner – because no one wanted to notice him. And when he finally found a way to take on a physical form, a rapacious bird flew down and whisked Malvinus away to some unknown place. The poem ended like this:

> *And who will ever cry for him –*
> *la-la, la-la, la-la –*
> *in the midst of white winter,*
> *in the December gloom? –*

and Gretchen's eyes always filled with tears, and I consoled her with a note of patronage so rare in our relationship she ruled covertly, but firmly.

Afterward, there were other rhymes and other secrets, yet it wasn't just them that created the cocoon's content – though discerning the exact content hasn't been easy. Nevertheless, none of the trifles in our world vanished in vain, none were thrown out in haste or rejected for a lack of patience. Patience we had in abundance – and curiosity as well. Any detail could develop into something big – while the cocoon was able to accommodate this. We were never bored together; our inventions, piled up in rows, always remained welcome. Every hint could turn into a whole story; the quietest sound could resonate like a chord and foreshadow distant thunder, falling rock or terrifying creatures. It was so easy to think things up on our own, knowing no one would challenge or cut us down to size. It was so tempting to look at the goldmines of glass pieces shimmering far off in the distance. Each of them, up close, might turn into a precious coin, since we had no reason to doubt the reality of the unreal – and there was no need to convince anyone else of it.

Looking back, I see under the cocoon the first signs of my careless intention to search for complexity everywhere, a tendency that mushroomed later – in me alone. Gretchen went her own way, but back then no misery hovered on the horizon. We frolicked like children, imagining and altering names and shapes, consequences and reasons. Of course, our judgment was superficial and, while we complicated things in a certain sense, they were getting simplified in another, more mercilessly proper one, since we didn't seek paths back from our fantasies to the dull daily life outside the window. Yet that world didn't disturb us and meant much less to us than the giggly, childish pleasure we found in our ingenious games.

It didn't disturb us until a certain time, however. Insularity is fraught with its own anxiety, and invincibility sometimes turns to paranoia: it seems something crucial you cannot do without waits outside. It's no one's fault; you just begin to languish in the constraints of the hardening walls, you knock, rap, bang – wishing to get out. It's dangerous out there, they admonish you, it's miserable and terrible – but you don't pay attention, continue to try stubbornly, and the partitions get broken down, quite easily sometimes. That is what happened to us – although our universe was almost real. Almost, it turned out, but not quite. As we grew older, each of us felt the threat more acutely, as if sensing the fragility of the incantations keeping our fairytale castle intact. Something wasn't quite right with us and the others. Signals, even sent according to rules, were broken off somewhere on the way. We had the impression no one heard us, no one even wanted to hear us, and we were just being told nonsense we had no way of replying to. The best intentions got bogged down in a quagmire of misunderstanding, and sharp little fingernails no longer scratched like children's, which called for more caution and care.

Why was it like that? Each of us could identify hundreds of reasons. Yet we didn't wish to scrutinize the subject, so we simply dismissed it. The fairytale castle, the moment in space and time, slid to the side, creating aberrations in the lenses of our squinted sight. It became clearer that every new disappointment proved the need to reconsider the limits, either quickly reconciling ourselves with ordinary life or rejecting it, which was probably not better. We honestly tried to be like everyone else, making friends and lovers, switching from one activity to the other, doing our best to seek out the reliable safe havens we were allowed to approach with all our suspicious belongings. Gretchen worried for both of us, insisting we couldn't survive in isolation, yet I only laughed, being more flippant. She would get upset at first, then wave it off and accept my carelessness, but soon she again attacked the invisible barricades, rushing to erect bridges between our shaky island and the immovable mainland.

Everything ended in complete confusion. As always, in the aftermath, it would be easy to blame our blindness, yet that would hardly makes sense. Words that ripened into speech needed a way out, conveying the lurking peril. It's only surprising that Gretchen, not I, turned out to be the weak link, although, on the other hand, that's quite logical as well. It was she who was doing the hardest work, assessing and calculating, discarding and affirming. Obediently, I followed at a distance, and this was much safer – at least I began to think so when Brett appeared and our paths diverged. As for Gretchen, she had no one to warn her when the navigation system failed. She lost the ability to question the course of things, as if she had forgotten the general hostility of the universe or assumed this hostility had changed to kindness.

Yes, wise Gretchen made a blunder – though it was not naïvety that provoked her, but rather a desire to prove by contradiction. I have to admit it was easy to be deceived – the man of her life, as she enthusiastically called him, was devilishly good looking and ready to worship her to no end, anticipating her wishes and fulfilling her every whim. This was a precious find indeed. He had a formidable appearance and seemed as solid as a rock, despite his tenacious, languishing gaze that disturbed me at times and hinted at grief cached deep down inside. His manliness, maybe slightly for show, turned into gentle docility in the presence of my sister. That even reached the point of ridiculousness, and our friends occasionally shrugged their shoulders in disbelief. But he, Brett, didn't seem to notice the astonished eyes as he sprung up to pull on her boots or blow off nonexistent specks of dust from her clothes, and ultimately we all became accustomed to it and concluded it was not our concern to judge the peculiarities of others.

Gretchen changed a lot afterward. In a flash, she adopted a patronizing tone, learned to be capricious, and we grew apart, to my querulous disappointment. Nonetheless, even feeling deprived of my share, I admitted I should accept that and agreed she was right in her way. Who, if not her, should be admired by the most enviable of all machos around – the one who had everything you could want from a man and was ready to serve without objections? Their idyll picked up steam. She was devoted to her new role, only infrequently freezing up in silence, as if she were scrutinizing herself in incredulous bewilderment, before livening up again and ruling indefatigably from her fortuitously found throne.

"It's not right, no, and I'm not that kind of person. Neither he is," she complained to me sometimes in infrequent minutes of candor. But this soon passed and her tone altered. "I see how he worships me," she said pensively. "I see it and can't believe it at first, but then I force myself and I do come to believe it. Why not? I'm no worse than others and I need that kind of happiness!"

I only nodded, a little embarrassed by the banality of the subject, not understanding what had to be reasoned out with such seriousness. Discussing ordinary felicity carried a scent of insincerity, but Gretchen was clearly placing every penny on that appealing card and was playing without any compromises.

"I'm going to turn him into an ideal husband, and I'll also become perfect – that's quite an achievement, and a real one," she claimed, contracting her brow and then vehemently trying to convince me, "How can you not understand? It'll almost be like what we had – you and me. Brett, Brett – who would have thought… Well, when one lands in our nets and goes astray in our labyrinths, it's not that easy to escape," and she laughed in her familiar way. Then a shadow again glided over her face and she yanked and pulled at my sleeve as she impatiently asked, "Just one thing… Is there nothing in me that could frighten somebody away unintentionally? Sometimes I look at myself and think: aren't others scared of me?" And again, I had nothing to say in response and carefully dismissed the subject with a joke.

One way or the other, the story was headed for a happy ending, and only a little time remained until their wedding when a clap of thunder sounded. Initially, Brett disappeared for a whole week, and then even stranger things happened – an anonymous letter, giggling on the phone, and finally another missive from an unknown well-wisher. Its deliberate brevity made it offensive: there was nothing more than an address and some mocking sign in the corner. Gretchen instantly became furious. She rushed out to hail a taxi and I followed in her footsteps, realizing we wouldn't find anything good there.

The scene awaiting us was vile indeed. Brett turned out to enjoy homosexual games, including a clearly risky kind. To Gretchen he declared that even thinking about her made him sick and added something that drove my sister really crazy. A disgusting quarrel ensued, with the two of us and Brett's bald partners, who didn't smell very pleasant. Finally, we ended up outside, where Gretchen fainted and passersby glanced at us before I took her home. She cried a little and then sent me back to my place – I was already living alone at the time, renting a room near the stadium.

"This is how it should be," she said in a dull tone at the doorway. "Only abnormality can be drawn to our abnormality, nothing else. No one can love us, they can only use us – this is the kind of 'love' allowed out there." And pushing me into the stairwell, she tacked on, "Those who already know that don't cry. So I won't either."

The next day I was prepared to show patient compassion when I went to see her, but Gretchen met me with dry eyes. She was lively yet distant, not concealing her aloofness. We chatted about trivial matters, and I just mentioned Brett once, like something that was long gone and forgotten – merely to make sure my dear sister wasn't suffering too much. Imperturbably, she interrupted me in midsentence, and with bitterness I sensed some rift was opening between us, increasing with every passing minute. It had taken only a night for us to become different, and it was no longer easy for our thoughts to fight through to each other.

"Who is Brett to us? He appeared and disappeared. If it hadn't been him, it would've been someone else," she said absentmindedly. "Forget about him – I, for example, have already forgotten. He was needed to prove what could never be proven…" And after falling silent for a moment, she burst out, wounded to the quick, "All our labyrinths, all our nets – what drivel! I'm such an idiot – and you are too, just like me. No one wants to adapt, they'll just try to play us, like amusing toys. They'll have fun and throw us away, like a useless thing constructed too complexly, flimsy, poorly. But we, too, are always ready to force someone away – so we're even, aren't we? I only need to pretend to be brainless and go with the flow. And as far as men are concerned – I no longer give a fuck!"

Something stuck inside like a splinter prevented her from being completely honest, but she didn't want to share it – with me or anyone else. I saw our unity was evanescing forever. The past was fading and the world was disintegrating into a myriad of separate parts. It was painful, but the right words didn't occur to me. The only thing I could do back then was read her my last poem, which I had composed mostly for her, though deep inside it was already harboring an allusion to frailty, the inevitability of parting, and pity for myself.

> *Late one night a cricket*
> *hangs on a hooklet*
> *a wooden bracelet*
> *and comical pantalets,*
>
> *twisted of bark –*
> *all his things are stark…*

I blurted out, looking askance, sensing the helpless offense gnawing at me, but not at deceived Gretchen. She didn't say a thing, just ruffled my hair and smiled thoughtfully. Then she started talking about something else, as if nothing had happened, and I understood I would never read her a line again.

We hardly ever saw each other after that. She soon moved to the countryside to teach in a private boarding school, only rarely coming to the capital and on even fewer occasions disturbing me with a late-night call. I didn't forget her – as she was before – and I have no one who is closer to me. But she doesn't want to remember anything; her calls are infrequent and the empathy depressingly shallow. I know I've lost her forever, but I can still evoke the image with the tinge of vanilla cream, and she is probably worse off, having discarded everything without regret. In any case, complaints are in vain. I just grin and accept, and as for the phone nearby – let it remain silent.

The apparatus on the table obediently followed my thoughts

and didn't give any sign of life. My mind was in ferment; vague figures came and went – bunching together, shouting, making up strange patterns I reached out for without being able to discern their meaning. Gretchen flashed by and vanished, waving one last goodbye and whispering something in my ear. I saw the other years – when we were already separated – and the other women in whom I had sought sympathy and warmth. Upon them I thrust my strangeness, which was absurdly alien to the instincts of ordinary females. The relationships were limited to short romances – except for two or three stoic attempts at living together – and they ended easily, with both sides relieved, at least until Vera appeared and demanded almost everything of me, occupying a greater part of my soul. That was later, however; before her, having learned to keep on the lookout, guarding steadfastly against the responsibilities they tried to impose on me, I accepted the rules of the game. I regarded the transience of my flings as a consequence of insufficient time and energy, dismissing my sister's bitter words, which occasionally entered my head at night.

Yes, compared to dear Gretchen, I didn't pay much attention to the romantic side of life. What flustered me much more was a strange sensation of congestion and overcrowding I saw everywhere. It appeared most people gathered in a very small part of the world, behind an impenetrable border, while the remaining free space had been given to loners like me. Clever Gretchen recognized this earlier and suffered more, trying to repulse the oppressive realization in whatever way she could, which probably explained her hasty quests that ended in complete failure. Yet I was fortunate enough to have thicker skin, and, if I dreamed of something seriously – inventing a means of proving what can't be proven – then it was far less tangible things, such as achieving worldwide fame in the shortest time or exhibiting heroism on a global scale. Fruitless fantasies excited my imagination, only occasionally being supplanted by an acute feeling of embarrassment and demoralizing powerlessness. As for the shortcomings in my personal life, I brushed them aside, relating the torments of love to the destiny of those who confined themselves to the small part and had nothing meaningful to do.

"No one will love you as much as you love yourself," my dear Gretchen repeated over and over, meaning, of course, something else, something more significant than what the words said. But I was blind and just took them literally and didn't actually believe in them, cherishing in the depths of my heart the hope of meeting some bright-eyed beauty who would belie the despondency of my precipitous discoveries. The hope was quite vague yet persistent enough to brush off my lack of success and my disappointments with the spurious mysteries of the female – antics and grace, dyes and feathers, all the features of harmony which you want to think are fathomless, although they are only there to serve the fulfillment of a simple program, common to all, as in an ant colony or beehive.

Certainly, the further it went, the more uneasy I became – especially when Gretchen voluntarily opted for exile. I was astonished to observe how even the brightest of my friends quickly found suitable partners, copulated, propagated, and settled into the routine of their breeding ground. Let them be, I thought as I turned away swiftly. They are only bad examples, not appropriate for broadening the view. "Everything's still ahead – just give me some time," I whispered to myself and let my imagination run wild: to chase ostrich feathers – the elegant attributes of sophisticated manners; or muskets and powerful harquebuses, attacks on the fortress walls, insane for their daring; or else a dazzling magnesium flash, illuminating a library or laboratory, writing table with a bluish lamp, a discovery changing the fate of millions, closely followed by applause in the stands, black robes and white wigs, plus some kind of satin ribbon on my shoulder… Sometimes the pragmatic present suppressed the romantic past, and my senses were pleased with more modest images, not going beyond selfless literary work, culminating somehow in an indisputable masterpiece. Soon, however, I got excited, lost my discretion, and was again carried away into the areas of worldwide recognition, imagining myself a fearless pioneer or, say, a genial actor forcing the masses to cry and exult. At this point, bright-eyed beauties came to mind as well, although I didn't have an idea what I really needed them for. I only wanted to avoid that strange feeling – the feeling of the ground slipping out from under my feet – like an augury of danger, haunting me with increased frequency.

"The world is neither good nor bad, it's just what it is. What waits for you ahead is not the fulfillment of wishes – but the City of M. and the Black Pelican," I could have said to anyone now, even if some of them knew this without me – while all the others didn't care at all, renouncing in advance the truths I had to agonize over. Back then though the future seemed to promise much more – and how deceitful it was turning out, time and again and again! How rashly it morphed into a dreary routine, losing its tinsel and revealing the same dull places and depressing spirit…

The only exception was my short career in the game of Dzhan, which gained popularity in the capital, developing into such a craze that clubs popped up everywhere to cultivate the most difficult version with one hundred and forty-four fields. And I proved to be no pretender. Together with other relentless warriors, I spent long evenings engaged in battles for money, tenacious and full of despair, filled with the utmost loneliness in front of a silent crowd – loneliness that was benign because of its shortness. Each of us, gladiators in a contemporary circus, was in it for ourself, and there was no way to object to genuine talent. You couldn't shift the white lines drawn in exact rectangles on black to please somebody's frame of mind, even if all the spectators would give a thumbs-down. And any glib bluffer inevitably surrendered to the quiet but completely incontestable words, "*Dzhan kkhat!*" – knowing at once his illusive game plan had led to nothing.

I really enjoyed the stages flooded with light; I felt protected from every vulgarity in the world, but my body cunningly set a trap, revealing its ineptitude for excessive burdens, unavoidable in a serious game. I regretted it much more than the collapses of my short romances, yet there was nothing to be done and I had to seek solace in the other spheres I was beginning to see as my youthful blinkers were being removed. Chaotically I raced from one activity to the next, changing friends and habits. With unprecedented insistence I tried to cling to the handrail connecting me to my compatriots, striving to demonstrate I was worth a lot that was not to be swapped for ordinary happiness. But it looked like my only talent – except the game of Dzhan, of course – was a well-developed hostility for the established order. I followed the well-trodden paths, joining various public groups and leaving in disgust, inventing absurd mechanical toys and losing interest in the middle, attempting to surprise the world with this or that, and noticing disappointedly that my efforts failed every time.

I didn't complain and didn't search for someone to blame, but I was deeply dissatisfied with my surroundings. As I looked around with increasing puzzlement I began to forget what it meant to be at peace with myself. It seemed the universe was taking its revenge for my tendency to look for complexity even in simple matters – which developed while Gretchen and I were happily isolated from everyone. Now nobody had the patience to hear out as much as half of what I wanted to say. My perception of events was impaired by the number of dimensions, which were so excessive I couldn't keep up myself. It was impossible to think about like-minded comrades, and the very idea of *like-minded* echoed of mockery and mean parody. So I remained in compulsory solitude – and batted about in the endless space of false reflections, sensing more and more some deficiency in myself or the outer world, which was taking me further away from comprehending the ordinary things others understood with such naturalness.

Lyubomir Lyubomirov, my devoted Dzhan partner, an ardent ironist and extremely cynical man, loved to say I possessed a unique ability to believe I could soar to the ceiling while pulling my own hair. He added he was incapable of grasping how I could combine such candid idiocy with my tenacious hold while pursuing some "reverse clinch," when the majority of our opponent's chips were lured to free fields on a very attractive section of the board – before they were cut off with two or three unanticipated sacrifices – and when the slightest imprecision could spoil everything and precipitate a loss. Flying up to the ceiling or not, I could seriously argue where pulling out one's hair could lead, especially if performed with enough energy. I tried to point this out to him more than once, but he just amused himself, laughing at me, although I'm still certain that in some sense we viewed things similarly. After all, it meant something that a quick glance above the one hundred and forty-four spaces was enough for us to understand each other. And if I was getting such a reaction from him, what could I expect from the rest?

So, a thoroughly dubious picture emerged from the wealth of evidence. I was getting increasingly upset and snapped back with less and less restraint. From hated high school to the very end of my university drudgery, I passed through different phases of fighting the efforts of my peers, who wanted to affirm me as a fifth column, a foreign agent, a symbol of hubris and uselessness, incapable of getting along or entering into a mutually profitable affair. Incidentally, when my studies were behind me, I began to rise quite quickly through the ranks at work, which was fairly surprising and even enthralled me for some time. The agility of my mind clearly played its role, and my imagination lit up in a strange way at the sight of multi-ton steel constructions and concrete blocks, at a distance reminding me of the delicate creations produced by ancient sculptors. My colleagues valued and tolerated me; my youthful rage, finding no outlet, felt confined; and the wolf's hair started to bristle little by little. I rapidly reached the next level, receiving my own office, the right to an assistant and relative freedom, which I shamelessly took advantage of until my first secretary, the beautiful Alina, put a knife to my throat, demanding I marry her right away and frightening me with all sorts of threats and the disclosure of "everything," as she put it. I didn't entirely understand my guilt, but I handled the situation with the utmost care, placating Alina and her brazen brothers and removing the reminders of this unpleasant event from my workplace.

Afterward, I never overstepped the limits, trying not to mix work with my private affairs – until Vera appeared, but Vera, of course, was an entirely different matter. Life rolled along with its ups and downs; they stopped promoting me and generally forgot about my existence, although occasionally noting my enviable usefulness. I didn't care: my separate office with its solid walls suited me just fine, and gradually I figured out how to get along with the secretaries without igniting an explosion. Any thought about my future career called forth unbearable boredom and even made me writhe, as if from a toothache. Gradually, everyone got used to my perennial limitations, but then Julian appeared at the same time as a position opened up on the floor above mine – one that I was inarguably entitled to.

Yes, Julian... Remembering his face, I shivered and couldn't hold back a suffocating wave, making my throat contract. My misfortune and my hate were concentrated in him, but nobody could have predicted that back then. He wasn't different from anyone around and behaved like every one of them would – that is, he rolled up his sleeves and, dispensing pristine smiles, plunged into the fray. As for me, I just observed it calmly, trying not to succumb to the prodding that came from different directions. As a result, contrary to logic, they promoted Julian ahead of me. With childish forwardness he informed me of this himself and was not even surprised by my sneer, which he considered a long-repressed grievance according to his code of reality, whose correctness he had never doubted. We became enemies then – or, rather, gossip in the company made us that after their thorough disappointment with our listless derby. Julian took this seriously, attacking me on every occasion, although he did it with a perfect smile, as the rules of corporate culture dictated. And something shifted inside me at the time; my youthful rage broke through the levee and began to seep out, turning into cold, shrewd aversion.

Certainly, the misfortunes in my career were only a screen, a background upon which the universe finally revealed something similar to its true face. I started to recognize it, even if, frankly speaking, it wasn't right to use Julian, like an obedient joker, any time I wanted to build links between diverse facts. His involvement in my fate was no more than a chain of accidents caused by a general paucity of events and an insufficient number of characters. Yet I preferred chasing this dull thought away – otherwise having started to doubt there wouldn't be anyone to blame. Every form of randomness is different, I told myself, and someone invisible nodded encouragement: yes, indeed. Sometimes random events just cannot help but occur – as if everything that happened earlier prepared the ground for their appearance, clearing the stage and producing the entourage. So, when they finally emerge, you greet them like old friends, or at least beckon understandingly – yes, we've been waiting, waiting…

Picking out explanations with deep roots is not as absurd as it might seem to many, and using them to patch up the breaches is also acceptable – more often than not. So Julian, after he came into view, never disappeared from the foreground. The longer it lasted, the more I considered him a symbol of the gray masses that didn't allow me to breathe. I saw in him a dotted contour, an abstract category containing everything vile that elbowed me out of the way, so I couldn't find reliable ground and felt all handrails slipping out of my hands. The carousel rolled faster and faster; I slid down and out – clenching my jaw, trying to pick myself up, but feeling more and more acutely some hidden trick, a well-disguised trap lying not far off, so it was possible to reach out and touch it. And then I discerned it with my own eyes – either in a dream, or in the brief madness of contemplation. The trap lay not in Julian but in the damn questions: "Is this it? Is there nothing else in the world?" They crept ahead and doubted the absence of limits; they established these limits in places I least expected them, still believing in some indistinct limitless future, however comical it is to admit. Yet in the terrifying "Is this it?" the question mark had already begun to quiver, even hinting at an answer, occasionally bringing horror or despair, which I chased off with hasty acts, summoning fantasies to help me out, to protect me from the intrusive, blazing letters in my head. But the decision did not come to me back then, and my secret hadn't been born. Only my friends started to squint with caution, and women didn't offer themselves as willingly, shunning me and being overly cautious, as if they perceived the alien vibrations from a mile away. And I grinned, betraying grimaces behind my smile, trying not to strain too much my facial muscles – avoiding traces which I was unable to shed and which would let anyone see something shameful, secret, shrouded.

CHAPTER 6

Agitated by flashbacks, I again slept poorly till a phone call woke me up – it was another disappointing response to my announcement in the local newspaper. I flung down the receiver, pulled the blanket up to my chin, and wallowed like this for some time, adjusting to the new day. Then I smoked a cigarette, glanced scornfully at the ashtray full of yesterday's butts, and felt something about the day was wrong from the start, and the need to take action depressed me like a habit that had grown tiresome long ago. All the same, upon leaving the hotel, I decided I had to come up with something productive, but soon sadly admitted I couldn't concentrate on my goal. So I resigned myself to the pointlessness of the walk and just wandered about the streets, observing the passersby and scrutinizing their gazes with no purpose at all.

A few days passed like this. My intentions remained in oblivion while former phantoms rose and reared their heads, sensing their impunity. And indeed, I was obedient and listless, as if entangled in the spider's web of city streets, not allowing quick dashes or darts to the side – from one sunny spot to another, from shades and shadows to crevices in the pavement, which may look perplexing enough to attune your thoughts to a new wave. Time ran through my fingers and I didn't regret it, looking back more than trying to descry what the future would bring.

Toward evening the city grew sullen. It became chilly; street rustlings made me edgy, and the twilight severed by flashing advertisements called up oppressive thoughts. I longed to take shelter in some place full of people, went to a café, and sat in the corner for a long time, sipping light beer and observing my neighbors. I only left when my eyes began to tear up from the smoke hovering in the air or when acute hunger whisked me out of my seat in search of a more or less respectable restaurant. The locals didn't speak to me, just saying an occasional hello, and I was tacitly thankful for that, withdrawing into myself as if meditating in the dim light under the steady din of voices.

Then morning would come again, and after a leisurely breakfast I would ramble to the marketplace to sit in the garden or stroll down one of the adjacent avenues. Occasionally I swerved into unfamiliar courtyards or darted into alleyways without any purpose. I stopped random people and asked them something that was often thoroughly off the mark. A few times I spoke with women and even accompanied one to her door and awkwardly kissed her warm, elusive lips. She gave me her phone number and was trusting and nice; her hair smelled like autumn and wet grass; but I never called her, not wanting to surrender to the resuscitating past, denying that she reminded me of Vera – of her manner of laughing, her habit of flipping back her bangs, her bold swagger and reckless youthfulness…

Cities you don't know are alike. You search for a secret path leading out of the cell; you run from loneliness and smash into a wall, wiping the blood from your forehead. And afterward, you hate yourself and listen to old words of consolation – believing and not believing but rushing to be deceived. The buildings and trees whisper them, the billboards suggest them, and the advertising bills foist them upon you, with an occasional distortion. Women say them too, all resembling each other. You endeavor to pinpoint one from the past, if you still remember, or one from the future, if you manage to concoct her, anticipating imminent treason, sordid artifice, indifference, and ignorance. You want to flee but don't; then you see tenderness and beauty – and you murmur affectionate words, revel in loving warmth, then become the first to betray it, then forget everything, not wishing to start all over…

Like a well-known dream, the days brought one and the same sequence of impressions. I saw familiar faces – paperboys, grocers, bakers. They recognized me in turn – the post office clerk in his official blue jacket, the elderly woman with her fox terrier, the policeman on the corner. And there, nodding to them as if taking up the baton, I would catch a glimpse of Vera – getting out of a taxi, coming out of a building across the street, exiting the bakery, turning her face away as if saying, "No, that's not me."

At the marketplace, hawkers screamed hoarsely, crying over the honking autos. I bought pink grapes and ate them on the spot, spitting out the pits. Then I walked on, to the avenue where street artists painted portraits – in a matter of minutes, with lavish and flattering brush strokes. I glanced over someone's shoulder – no, not quite, her mouth is larger, her gaze more mischievous, the curl not there. That's not her, you unskilled painter, this isn't a job for you. A buffoon rolled up his sash, threw and caught sharp blades without looking – under the bright sun, his leotard stained with sweat. His assistant, a limping boy, stared with open mouth before going around the group of spectators with an upside-down hat. I chucked in some change and went to sit on a shaded bench, smoking, looking at the women, fighting recollections and driving them away, then clinging to them with all my might, almost beseeching them: do not leave me behind, please, stay!

Vera, you lively child, I haven't forgotten you. I ran not from you, and I'm not here for you, yet I remember you very well. I love my dear Gretchen, but Gretchen is something different, something one can't talk about since it's too embarrassing to put in words. I don't think about her now, I recognize you here, as in any place, once I begin to get used to it. You don't respond to me, and what's the point of castigating myself, it doesn't change a thing. I've already gone through that, flown between the slimy walls, died, been born again, become a different man. Would you like him now?

I can hardly believe it. Do you recall who he was before? How he attracted you, what names he called you, why he chased you away?

The reality in front of me – an alien city: sun, moist wind, sticky grapes. The reality inside me – my office in an old brick building: the refuge of boredom, the beginning of our story. Vera was sent to us as a temporary replacement for Julia, who was on sick leave. I regarded her with brief interest but dismissed it right away – you can't expect much from a newlywed, all aglow in fresh happiness. She had no need for me, and I was rather indifferent, only once crossing the barrier of perfunctory amiable words. The evening and exhaustion were the guilty parties, not my passionate insistence: I wanted her, of course, as I wanted every woman, but you don't wrangle with fresh happiness, so I didn't make any plans. Yet that day, as if by someone's trick, we remained in the office till deep into the night. The late hour and weariness blunted our vigilance, and the naïve romanticism of the circumstances teased me more and more. We sat on the floor in the midst of papers covered with scribbles. I could smell her and desired her like never before. Then she tossed off her shoes and suddenly I patted her thin ankle and the instep of her foot, slightly clenching it in my hand and letting go – without a look, still talking business. And she didn't even turn around in surprise, didn't recoil, as if she had already known, and that told us everything, making it useless to pretend afterward. We didn't get any closer till the end of her two-week temp term, and it seemed the newlywed image hadn't faded. Nonetheless, I saw a question in her step, on her lips, in her smile. The question was "When?" – and that *when* soon arrived, put an end to her fresh happiness, whisked away my peace and confidence, but did not make me sorry, no, it did not.

For a while she wasn't telling her husband, shielding him or simply unable to decide. But he guessed, of course – for you always know such things when you're in love. To my embarrassment, I made fun of him, sending him silent greetings with a sneer of condescension, sometimes thinking about him for hours with some kind of unhealthy curiosity. I imagined his frail figure slipping among the shadows of their large house – from room to room, from the hall to the library, garden, patio. I saw him treading quietly in soft slippers, examining the backs of books, throwing up his small hands, tilting his head to the side: something wasn't right. Up and down the stairs, time and again – he couldn't sit still, something impelled him to keep walking. He put on a warm jacket – shivered for some reason, was uncomfortable, had no peace of mind. Picked up a magazine from the table, paged through it thoughtlessly, left it on the chair. Took his favorite novel off the shelf, made an effort to read a paragraph or two, closed and laid it aside with a bookmark, which was irrelevant – he wouldn't find the same place anyway, a return is impossible. He walked off, stared into the darkness: the happy newlywed – everything's ahead of you, forget about doubts, you're just not used to it yet. But something wasn't right and he had no one to ask. No one and nothing: no object revealed the secret or helped with either a gesture or hint. He went over to the phone – yet who could he call? Nobody would give him a clue to the riddle. All he could do was wander from one corner to the other: an indefinite trip, a never-ending trail.

And we, in the meantime, surrendered to passion in my attic apartment, feeling neither guilt nor pity, knowing life was only possible the way we had it – in and under the damp sheet, with struggles, caresses, resentment and reconciliation, hugging and cautious biting, spasms and absentminded dreams. We indulged in our ardor, drank cold wine, talked a lot of nonsense, raised improbable theories, lived lives imagined right then and there – a house on the ocean, a few servants, three children, a dog... We were jealous of the past and blamed each other lightheartedly; Vera sometimes cried a bit – though not for real. Then caresses and cautious biting came again; the reproaches were forgotten, we were back together – shameless voluptuaries finding our way to a place where the tastiest things are kept hidden from the uninitiated. There was no force able to expel us, and those watching us – from nowhere, from the air itself – remained perplexed, not hearing a sound, not discerning a single suspicious movement or silhouette behind the solid curtains. That spot in time and space was only open to us, not admitting anything foreign, not existing for outsiders and their eyes. And now we can lament it endlessly, without dreading the charm will vanish with careless words – for you can't scare away what has died, however false the grief seems. Mine, usually, is naïve and short – and I doubt anyone else mourns that death at all.

Vera, Vera, my affliction, my anguish, don't haunt me now. Our story is over, and I'm roaming in no one's land, among collapsed houses whose debris is weather beaten, not spared by time. Centuries and centuries have passed – how joyful for a rascal archaeologist. Let him rummage in the fragments, imagine the past. We left this place, and our descendants didn't return. The language was forgotten, the books burned. I'm wandering down the deserted roads, meeting the wayfarers of other tribes – they speak our speech, laugh your laugh, but their blood is different and their faces get erased as soon as their steps subside behind my back. I arrive in unfamiliar cities, get used to its boulevards and squares, recognize the streets by their corner cafés, but wherever I am, I can't escape recollections, they enter my head, ravaging like a typhoon, and retreat slowly, reluctantly, carrying the trunks of palms and the wreckage of wooden roofs in their wake.

Vera-Veritas… It is difficult to say why it was she who brought that turmoil into my life, eliciting grim passion and sweet torments, which I thought I had been deprived of forever. This shouldn't have happened, yet it came upon me and her without asking either of us. Nothing forced me to stay on guard; I believed the entire story – believed and hoped. I was ready to reject all the warnings from all the ghostly shadows, retaining only a tiny pretext, the thinnest lifeline in case something didn't go quite right. Despite putting a lot on the line, I still concealed a few bits and pieces unabashedly. After all, my Vera must have also kept something in reserve. Later, heading off to our opposite poles, we discovered with relief what we had set aside was still safe and sound – she while curling up on her favorite sofa, I while balancing on a thin wire. My nature remained unaffected, and my fantasies continued to run wild. Only the last obscuring blinkers had slipped off, no longer refracting the light from the dingy pieces of glass to turn them into precious stones, not freshening up the dreary colors, not blurring the outlines with a benevolent hint at the clandestine depths. I learned to see plainly and realized what my Gretchen had wanted to tell me as she dressed her meaning in flaccid verbal formulas – out of pity or excessive caution. I understood and finally admitted the time of indecisive attempts was over and wouldn't return.

Can I believe now in Vera-Veritas? Ask something easier. It all began so happily and ended so dismally. Every day brought a profusion of novelties – only to mutate into many weeks of misery. No, I'm not rushing to wipe it out, to discard and disown those long hours, that passionate expectation and excitement. I keep them in a safe place, just as she probably still preserves that slightly shabby baggage – an indoor scene in a box, a splendid courtyard under a glass in the room that is closed forever. But it's true that the bungled ending is what etches itself into your memory and the ugly images rush ahead of the monotone happy landscape. Now I squeezed my eyes shut but saw even more clearly how the passion waned and the fear emerged, how her nervousness replaced initial courage and her judgmental gaze froze occasionally on my face. I fought with all my might, but my strengths were in words alone, and they couldn't set the matter straight, only frightening her unnecessarily or confirming something she had already begun to realize herself.

Yes, we got what was promised, everything was for real: racy scents and soft lips, an attic to shelter us from the glances of others – a perfect setting for a twisted play with so many entwined threads. But now it felt as if someone invisible stripped away the top layer, like old wallpaper, and exposed the chipped plaster. Plagiarists with a false idea of their own importance – that's how he would probably label us right away. And we couldn't raise an objection vainly trying to prove otherwise; there's never a way to respond to the multitude of those who want to judge. How do you force them to look closely at the fuzzy shadow concealing the essence?

How do you name an imperceptible something that flung us from one universe to another, sent us soaring over the roofs and calling out to each other in an unknown language? No one would take the trouble – they'd just see a young newlywed slipping into the arms of a lover three weeks after her wedding. They'd see it and point it out to us, thoughtlessly ripping off the top layer. And we'd believe it too.

Vera, Vera... The image gets distorted even if you just blow off the dust. She might have been full of pride, but she was also guilty – and she felt guilty despite our extensive efforts to view the story as sublimely as possible. Whatever efforts we made, each of us understood the simple rationale for what had occurred, which was persistently hushed up, as if we dreaded harsh words – or just out of ordinary awkwardness. That was the reason for her fury whenever I suggested, almost always half-jokingly, that she leave her husband and live with me for good. That was the cause of her startled gaze and her rush of kindness toward him – whom she had previously badmouthed in the most offensive way. She was terrified of losing that serene harbor where she could return at any time from her exhausting pirate raids in foreign seas, from her nibbling lust, hastily covered by a heap of euphemisms and epithets. Yes, we constructed a life out of thin air, nurtured our fantasies, and lied to each other. And no sooner had we dug a little deeper than we found ourselves in different corners, ready to attack – especially since the lust had abated and a new object had appeared on the horizon. Unfortunately – not on mine.

Now a spasm still distorts my face, but the image cannot be driven away. Here he is in front of me – and I must say, congratulations to those who have already guessed, although it isn't that hard. Connecting the lines is always tempting, and this plot unfolds in the most compact way. Yes, it was Julian again – he and his pristine smile. Julian crossing my path over and over; the mediocre clown snatching the lead role right out from under my nose; the resilient, ever-present, omnipotent figure.

I could have blamed myself – I played along involuntarily,

helping them to meet for the first time. Who knows how it would have evolved if I hadn't dragged Vera to the corporate picnic, an annual event of the official sort where not showing up was considered poor conduct. So everyone came and was getting bored – you couldn't think up anything duller than discussing the same subjects for the thousandth time with people who just wanted a break from each other. Now and then, some unfamiliar beauty flitted by – someone's wife, friend, or even a daughter who has grown up quickly. Yet that was also hopeless – the setting was by no means appropriate – so all one could do was look on with regret, leaning against the tree and crumpling a paper cup.

On that occasion I talked Vera into accompanying me so it wouldn't be so tedious. No one seemed to notice us, only Julian jumped in like a setter, but I ignored it, which was a mistake. I even aided him a little: after getting upset with Vera for something, I walked off and intentionally avoided her, as if clearing the way. And then everything took its course: a few quick glances at the end to sow subconscious anxiety in my soul; her abrupt disappearance from my view in a week or so; silent phones and irrational lies; and finally –my shadowing, disbelief and confusion, the helplessness of a loser.

I could have undertaken a lot, but that was just too much. My mind refused to believe it and, having finally done so, insisted on immediate revenge, yet I kept it all inside, let nothing out, afraid to appear ridiculous or humiliated, as if something still remained which made it worthwhile to preserve my dignity. I even met with Vera without betraying what I knew, sensing I had a strange power over her, now being more myopic than me. At some point, however, my defense mechanisms could no longer bear it and – like a balloon poked by a pin – I exploded at her artificial smile or excessively careless gesture. And the world slipped into darkness, stunned by my hatred and nasty words.

I admit, I was abominable at that time – abominable and intolerable. And Vera heaped all her contempt on me, although no one promised her I would be different. "You should instead despise your husband," I advised her, "or despise this Julian who doesn't mind using second-hand goodies." It wasn't completely fair, and she took advantage of my weakness, prolonging the squabble with pleasure, like the loudest of street vendors. I heard a lot about myself – and there's no more biased judge than a woman you've annoyed. Yet what really staggered me were those new notes in her voice, not a trace of which I had detected before.

It was bizarre and strange, as if everything had been flipped head over heels. Vera, my proud accomplice, swiftly moved to the other camp. I suddenly saw we were not two against everyone else, but rather I was alone – as it turned out after Gretchen had left and as it would now be forever. "You have no soul," she said, and her eyes sparkled with true fervor. "Your soul isn't here, it's floating who knows where and only looks down with disdain, completely preoccupied with itself. Everything around you is bad, but who are you to be dissatisfied? Just because you can't live doesn't mean you have the right to envy those who can!"

A different face peeped through the makeup – one I didn't know – and unfamiliar lips moved with the desire to hurt me as much as possible. "Do you think I was happy with you?" she asked. "You have no idea how tired I am of you and your whims. You're like a strange place where dead ends lie at every corner and one always has to step carefully to avoid the trap... And Jules is so pleasant," she added with a sigh, her eyes boring into me. "I just relax with him. And don't you dare to touch my husband!" she screamed. "He's a saint, he suffers, but he'll never leave me. You, of course, would have already kicked me out, without a second thought..."

It continued like this for a while before she finally went away. I was left among the ruins and burnt-out slums and wandered aimlessly through them. And afterward, something clenched my throat so it became difficult to breathe, and I tumbled into a well with slimy walls. I thought I'd never come back to myself, but it turned out if your wolf hair has already begun to bristle, you'll haul yourself out sooner or later – with a blackened face and a wasted gaze, though relatively whole nonetheless.

Mine bristled, yes, but what was the point of it? I looked in the mirror and wanted to break it. When I saw my reflection in the glass doors, terrible curses flew from my lips. Only one thing imprinted itself on my retina: those familiar letters. Although something about them had changed, exposing the vulnerable spot, the most unreliable flank. "Leave me alone," I whispered harshly. "Get out of here. I don't need that now." But the letters blazed before my eyes and didn't recede.

"Is this it?" the words asked. And I clearly saw what was wrong with them, and what had vanished without a trace, fading away as superfluous. Yes, I felt with a shiver the words change their order, and there was no longer a question mark at the end, however much I practiced the intonation, futilely straining my vocal chords. "This is it," my consciousness confirmed; the mark of a question, resembling a crooked key, upon which I had placed all my hopes, had disappeared, as if unable to bear the burden, vanquished by the righteousness of the majority.

It may still become terrifying, at night or even during the day, when my gaze freezes, directed within, and I see something that doesn't have a name. The name isn't important though – what's important is that sooner or later you lose your ability to doubt the stubborn hints. And you tell yourself terrible things you've been chasing off for years: you're an outsider, hopes are illusory, death is real. The words appear in different guises. Anything you can think of may reveal the same ruthless nature, to which you surrender, admitting with some relief: I can't take any more. But as I surrendered, I nonetheless clung to fading reality, inventing artificial bridges. And here the laws of Dzhan came in very handy – and reality made concessions, offering illusionary rope ladders so I could climb out time and again, occasionally covered in cold sweat, and then – then came unexpected solace. This image was easy to bring to light, in any place I found myself. And here, on the avenue by the marketplace, it hovered before my eyes time and again, eclipsing the preceding memories and dazzling me with the sharpness of the details. It's a sunny morning and I'm enlivened by a sudden idea capable of turning everything upside down, that is, putting it all in its proper order, if you looked at it my way. Reality swiftly gained new meaning – if not a whole new dimension, mischievous or not. Me and my decision, my secret – of course, what could be simpler: take up full authority and get even for all the loners deprived of hope and not given anything in return. No one asked me to settle their scores, but I have my own and that's enough. If others don't understand or don't believe it, that's their problem, since I – I'm tired of explanations.

But here the camera angle changed, responding to my bravado, and everything appeared in a different light again. I still tried to concentrate on the question mark that had vanished, but I had to admit: my secret wasn't born in the wake of the damn questions. It followed a night of drinking, full of painful contemplation – after I learned Julian had left for the City of M.

It was inconceivable, it was more incredible than Julian and Vera, although after Vera I thought I was ready for anything. One should never forget that reality can play the cruelest of jokes – and indeed, what could *he* be doing *there*? That should be me – a man plagued by the paroxysms of the quest, the asker of questions that shouldn't be voiced – or my dear Gretchen, overwhelmed by distress. But what did hated Julian need M. for – he, who was so far removed from uncertainty and inquiries of an unreliable sort? How did he end up beating me to the punch again, as if winning another tender for the next vacant spot?

There were so many meanings they made my head spin. Maybe that's why I didn't make any headway. After spending a week in M. and not getting anywhere with my search, I began to seriously suspect something was fundamentally erroneous with my plans. It made me angry, but I still remained in a strange stupor, yielding to memories, as if that justified my idleness.

I was already recalling the capital little by little, and the perfidious thought of an early inglorious return flickered through my head. However, everything changed suddenly. The action was set in motion: back in my room, I found a note from Gibbs inviting me to meet him in the same restaurant where we ate the first evening. An odd tingling passed through my whole body. I realized the prelude had ended and the main part was about to start. The capital and pointless contemplations flew out of my mind; the phantoms, whimpering, dove into the furthest hole. I quickly shaved and headed to the restaurant – hoping only that Piolin would not be there.

CHAPTER 7

The restaurant glittered and pulsated with life – a party was underway. On the brightly lit stage, a loud band played; a dozen dancers weaved intricate patterns; waiters bustled about; drunken voices and laughter rang out. I tried to find Gibbs, but it was hard to make anything out in the commotion. The maitre d' only frowned when I hollered my name in his ear. Shortly after, however, he showed interest and led me to an empty table on the periphery. I sat alone for half an hour until Gibbs appeared and immediately came over to me, not paying attention to the noise and tumult.

We greeted each other formally, and I caught myself thinking his features no longer surprised me, as if we had been acquainted for years. "You look exactly the same," Gibbs said in turn. "At your age people don't change all that quickly. And at mine even less so." He groaned as he seated himself, then fixed his eyes on me and added, "Nonetheless, you haven't run away, so you must like it here."

"Why, actually…" I began, offended and startled by his unceremonious tone, but Gibbs jumped up, grabbed the arm of a passing staff member in uniform and ushered him to the side, where he whispered with his back to me – so I couldn't hear. The man just blinked as he stood erect and still, then nodded zealously and trotted off. Gibbs returned to his chair, briefly apologized, smoked a thin cigar, and spoke quite sternly as he stared at the bridge of my nose.

"Actually, not why – I'm joking," he clarified with strange

coldness. "Not that many people leave this place willingly anyway. And let's get down to business. I came for an answer. Do you catch my drift? Do you know what I'm talking about?"

"What is there to miss?" I shrugged my shoulders. "It means you're still going? And the invitation is still in place?"

"But of course," replied Gibbs with a surprised look on his face. Then he repeated impatiently, "I came for an answer. For now, everything's in place – so let's decide. I'm meeting people in a moment; we're gathering here to discuss the trip and address the nitty-gritty. So I'll either introduce you or I won't – and a *no* will be forever; we'll find someone else."

He fell silent for a second, apparently contemplating, before grinning at me across the table and continuing, "Only I'm not used to making a fool of myself. If you agree, please don't waffle afterward. Sometimes, you know, people get frightened but are embarrassed to show it. We'll be better off if you forget embarrassment – confess your fears, and we'll part ways. However, if you've made up your mind, then you can go with us – and no one will dare to object. I've promised, and I'll keep my word," he added pathetically, then leaned back in his chair and puffed out clouds of smoke, looking at me expectantly.

"This is odd," I drawled. "Why do you mention frightened first? Maybe I'll refuse to go because of my own affairs and different plans. But I understand completely: if you shake hands on something, there's no going back. And you have to admit you called me rather suddenly and are almost holding a knife to my throat..."

"You understand nothing," Gibbs interrupted me, "but you speak quite bravely: the knife, my throat..." He sighed, stubbed out his hardly begun cigar, and held his hand in front of him.

"First of all," he bent his index finger, "everyone wants to go to the Dunes. Except those, of course, who aren't even aware of them, but we'll exclude them from the outset. Second," he crooked another finger, "if you aren't frightened, that means..." Gibbs thought for a moment, gazed in his palm and turned down one more finger, "that means you're scared shitless – which is number three – and then we just have to part ways. And finally," he made a fist, "finally, points four and five, what are those different plans of yours – are you trying to dupe me? You're searching for someone here, right?" – I nodded. – "And you haven't found him in the city so far, correct?" – I nodded again. – "Well, you see," Gibbs waved his hand, "no doubt you don't even know where to look – neither where nor how. So start with the Dunes; we'll hunt together, I promise. Moreover, if he's there, then it's pretty idiotic to prowl about the city." He made a sympathetic grimace.

"That's true," I agreed gloomily, "everything's been pretty idiotic so far, I just don't know what makes sense. And you, Gibbs, you're a stranger, as well as all your people..."

"Nonsense, I'll introduce you," Gibbs interrupted me again. "That's not a problem. The problem is: are you going to give me an answer at last? You've already had long enough to contemplate, and please remember, they're waiting for me!"

He stared right into my pupils without blinking – and I couldn't hold his gaze. My lips curled into an involuntary smile and I drooped my head like a boy who's been caught by the teacher. I wanted to tell him a lot – explain many things and ask others – but as always, there was no time, and he wouldn't have listened to them anyway.

"I'll go with you," I said, raising my eyes to his face and nodding.

"That's good," replied Gibbs in absolute calmness and even with a touch of laziness. All expression vanished from his countenance, and his eyes drifted off somewhere above me, focusing on nothing. "Good," he repeated. "Wait here for a quarter of an hour. I'll bring them over." He shook my hand firmly and hurried to the door while I sat motionless, feeling incomprehensible exhaustion and pondering what had actually just happened. Had I acted as I subconsciously desired or had I succumbed to pressure, after letting myself get rattled and thoroughly confused?

In any case, it was too late for regrets. "It's better like this," I told myself. "One less thorn in my side. I'll see the odd and inaccessible Dunes, ticking another item off the list. The number of variables will decrease and some things may finally be cleared up. And I wonder: could Julian indeed be there?"

Gibbs brought his companions over after only a short absence – they must have been waiting nearby. It was a colorful group, attracting a lot of attention as they wriggled through the crowd. Gibbs walked in front, confidently carving a path. He was followed by two young men, and in their trail, falling behind and glancing around, were two women, the older one wrapped in a long, dark scarf like a gypsy. Catching sight of me, Gibbs expressed his enthusiasm boisterously, as if it had not been him and me who had just parted, while his entourage huddled together, looking at us intently. After some brief confusion, we got acquainted. The woman in the scarf said her name was Silvia and nudged her friend Stella to the front, who was much younger and appeared flummoxed. She clumsily dropped something similar to a curtsey and again stared at the floor. Gibbs introduced the men.

"Christopher," he said, pointing at the first one. Turning to the second, he repeated, "Christopher," grinning broadly as he spoke, and making both Christophers burst out laughing. Silvia took the second by the arm, forced open his hand, and softly intoned, "Christopher Two, don't get confused," and the men guffawed again – for a fat two had actually been drawn in ink on his palm. When they settled down, everyone seated themselves and adopted a serious expression, although the second Christopher showed the first his palm a few more times, and both chuckled silently, giving me a glimpse of a large gold tooth in Christopher One's mouth.

While we were ordering dinner, I sized them up. The Christophers looked like genuine farm boys. They were large, had chubby cheeks, thick necks, and big arms. The first was wearing a knitted purple jacket and a blue shirt; the second, an extra-wide coat with rigid shoulders and a black sweater underneath. Both had short, raven hair, were primitive and inattentive, and fidgeted in their chairs, swiveling their heads back and forth. The women sat calmly, their hands on their knees, staring across the table. Silvia, the older one, about forty or so, took off her scarf and revealed a dark wool dress, assuaging her plump, somewhat senescing curves. At one point she had probably been gorgeous, and her fading beauty still showed traces of this past – sensuous lips, large black eyes, stylish hair in a shade of red, and not one gray wisp to be found. A lot about her said she had seen better days and better people but had bowed to inexorable time, though she didn't forgive it and harbored resentment. Stella, sitting next to her, looked like a simpleton. Yet there was something attractive in her face with its high cheekbones – some cold northern charm, a perennial glacier, a ground-down snowy crust. Her fair hair was disheveled, her grayish blue eyes were glazed over, and her mouth compressed into a line, as if drawn by pencil. Nevertheless, a kind of embedded strength could be divined from her plain appearance, and while I was lost in contemplation, I missed a question Gibbs directed at me.

Apologizing, I asked him to repeat it, but Gibbs just looked at me derisively. Then they brought our appetizers and we stopped talking altogether. Stella ate very little, only picking at her plate sporadically; and Silvia, sitting next to Gibbs, spoke into his ear, whispered and whispered, occasionally glancing at me until he knit his brow in dissatisfaction and turned away. After drinking coffee, Gibbs signaled to the waiter, and we were led to an adjacent room that was a lot quieter and almost empty. We sat down again, and Gibbs ordered brandy.

"We're leaving tomorrow," he informed us authoritatively. "You need to be ready early in the morning – I don't know the exact time yet. Tell him what he needs; if he forgets something, put it in for him," he said to the Christophers.

They, snickering and exchanging glances, began to recite the list quite lucidly: soap, matches, cigarettes, bug repellent, tinea spray – don't have it? – a warm jacket, warm sweater – don't have it? – how could you not have that? – well, alright, we'll get it – and so on. I tried to remember everything, taking it down in pencil on a napkin, but felt ashamed in front of the women and stopped. By this point the Christophers had become even more serious: now they were again speaking with Gibbs, discussing the route and talking in a concise and sensible way. Everything sounded very legit. I believed every phrase and became imbued with respect for my future companions – despite the naïvety of their countenance and the comical nature of their manners. Imperceptibly, I was getting used to the thought I was really heading somewhere with them, these confident and strong people, trusting them in matters I didn't understand myself. And who were they in fact – outsiders who couldn't find a place for themselves, who keenly sensed their alienation and made an effort to support each other? Then they were right to choose me – it was at random, but on the mark. Or maybe, on the contrary, they were simple and ordinary, no different from the masses, even if at times they got bored at home. But no, I shouldn't doubt it – there was a reason we're headed somewhere the average person never got. That meant something was different about them, these five. They weren't ordinary and not average. Could we become friends, could I be integrated into their little group and be accepted as one of them? No matter how much bravado I mustered, celebrating my tiresome independence, that's what I wanted – what I kept wanting, even if disappointment was always lurking around the corner. Would everything work now? Would they value me as they should?

This way or that, the event was beginning to crystallize. I wished to make a good impression – sat and listened with unremitting attention and even nodded at a few questions not intended for me at all. One of the Christophers – the one with the gold tooth – watched me slyly, a spiteful grin slithering across his face. I didn't get upset though, for none of them had a reason yet to take me seriously and regard me as authentic. But they would, I thought, the opportunity would present itself, and, no less than others, I could put mockers in their place. Moreover, it was pointless to start out by squabbling over nothing and show an inclination to argue – even peacefully.

A bored Silvia turned to me and asked quietly, "What's your name, honey? I forgot."

I told her, somewhat confused; she took my hand in hers, saying gently, "Let's be friends, I like you." Then she stared at me for a few seconds and I held her gaze, feeling her warm fingers and contemplating whether I could seduce her during our trip.

By the way, how long will we be out there? No one had told me – and I extracted my hand from hers, awkwardly mumbling some excuse. Silvia sneered knowingly, aware of her power, and I looked at Gibbs and interrupted one of the Christophers by asking how many days we would be out of the city. Gibbs, however, didn't pay any attention to me, preoccupied with his companions, who were drawing some kind of diagram on a scrap of paper.

Another map – they really like maps here, I thought. Silvia again took me by the hand and said soothingly, "Not very long, don't worry, just a week or so." I didn't want to withdraw it this time, but she lay it on the table, studied it, ran her finger over the lines on my wrist and said something to Stella, who turned away without interest.

"What did you want?" asked Gibbs, having settled the matter with the Christophers, who again began to fidget and exchange looks. I repeated my question, though Silvia butted in impatiently, "A week or so, I already told him." I noticed I was still holding my unclenched hand on the table and shoved it in the pocket of my trousers.

"Well," said Christopher One, surveying the entire group, "let's sum it up, as they say. Don't bring anything unnecessary – we have a lot to carry, as always. Everyone has to help out. Those who don't like to get their hands dirty will have to endure."

He glanced at Stella and winked. She cursed him out brutally in a calm, yet scornful tone of voice.

"Well, yes, as I said, they'll have to endure," Christopher confirmed, not disconcerted in the least. "Right, boss?"

Gibbs just nodded half-heartedly, thinking about something else. Everyone quieted down. The Christophers looked dully into their shot glasses, their crude features blurred, while Two scratched his unshaven cheek. I noticed they had different colored eyes: the first had brown ones, the second – blue, brighter than Stella's, with a slight squint.

"The cognac isn't bad," said Christopher Two lazily through his teeth, after he'd finished scratching his face. "Are you spoiling us, boss?"

Gibbs grinned in silence, but Stella declared the brandy was crap and I regarded her with respect, even though she still didn't look in my direction.

Who cares about her? I thought crossly. What does she understand? She's a country girl, with the looks and blood of a fish. Anyway, I was preoccupied with Silvia, not Stella, whose soft hands and large breasts wouldn't leave me in peace. I watched her furtively, and she avoided my gaze, but certainly knew I was eying her, and that alone excited me, like an amusing joust that no one observes, despite it unfolding in plain view.

Then, that night, I had an embarrassing dream, with Silvia in it, yet till then I had to forget about her – a more powerful force abruptly interfered with my thoughts. Tired of silence, I went to the restroom, and Christopher Two came with me. He stood by the urinal, muttering something under his breath, then bent over the sink, his jacket lifting up slightly to reveal the grip of a pistol gleaming on his waist. Christopher, realizing what I was looking at, turned around and grinned. Both Silvia and Gibbs flew out of my head – and not because the gun frightened me. My secret regained life all of a sudden, reminding me why I was there and what was lying at the bottom of my suitcase, under my shirts and underwear.

"You like this baby?" Christopher pulled the pistol out and held it in his palm, his finger on the trigger guard. "Don't be afraid, the safety's on." He laughed, walked off to the high frosted-glass window, and waved me over.

I approached him unwillingly, trying to remain as independent as possible, and said in the tone of an expert, "Yeah, not bad, however revolvers are more along my lines." Then I thought it would be rather short-sighted to voice my own modest knowledge, and added, "Either way, though, I don't really know. I don't have any use for one."

Christopher cast a glance over me and agreed sarcastically,

"Right, what's it to you?" Then he raised the pistol a little closer to the light and offered, "Look."

I obediently stretched my neck. It was a first-class Austrian Glock, a fairly new model, judging by the trigger type. I had also wanted that kind of gun, but it would've cost me a fortune. Furthermore, my Colt wasn't any less reliable – at least that's what the heaps of authoritative publications I had read and reread assured me.

"Nice," I confirmed with a nod. "Is it powerful? Is it accurate?"

"It's so damn powerful you can't even imagine it," said Christopher, and he again snickered idiotically. "Read here."

At the base of the grip I saw the stamped brand of the manufacturer, and above that were the etched letters "NVG" – which could be nothing other than the initials of some ambitious owner.

"It has a real signature," drawled Christopher respectfully. "The signed ones – they're valued to the skies."

"So you bought it with this name?" I asked coldly, wishing to cut him down to size. He was grandstanding over nothing with too much self-satisfaction, and the categorical "what's it to you?" tossed at me after just one quick look piqued me more than it seemed at first. Christopher grinned and calmly said, "I didn't buy it, I took it. But I can sell it to you if you've got the dough. No go? Okay, whatever." He took the pistol by both hands, aimed it at the opposite wall, and ludicrously exclaimed, "Ba-boom!" Then he slipped it back into his belt and we returned to the main room. My ears were on fire; my head was spinning with something bold and courageous resembling a military march.

The rest were getting ready to leave, only waiting for us. Gibbs said a few more things, looked into my eyes inquisitively as he shook my hand, and we parted – without words, though conveying significance and emotion. Silvia grazed me with her broad hip and smirked as she passed. The second Christopher again slyly showed me his palm with its two, and I smiled out of politeness and raised my eyebrows knowingly, feeling at home in this new group, even if this was still based on transient, flimsy grounds.

That evening, behind the locked door of my room, I dug the Colt out of my suitcase, inspected it, lubricated the parts generously, and lay it in my travel bag along with the reserve clip. Around midnight, a courier from the Christophers knocked at the door and handed me a bulky package containing a coarse wool sweater, a waterproof jacket, and two cans of spray. The preparations were finished. I saw myself as an intrepid pioneer on the brink of a journey. My thoughts were all jumbled up; the question mark was back shimmering before my eyes, having now migrated to a different place. Some force was compelling me toward the inevitable – a formidable power with no end or limit, which I knew was connected to both the question mark and my secret. And I rushed there, longing to play with fire, knowing I should have been more cautious.

Night bestowed emptiness, and the phantoms came into their own under the cover of darkness. Two brutish Christophers in tufts of tangled wool were bending over me, while Gibbs with a goatee was urging them on, playing with a whip. I didn't feel any hostility; I wanted to speak with them or give them a sign, yet they just flashed their sharp fangs and I turned away indignantly. Then, rising from my slumber, I walked to the bathroom, swallowed tap water with a metallic taste, and stared out the window, in the direction of the ocean, trying to understand what was waiting for me there. The next few hours I kept falling asleep and waking up in a sweat until a large soft woman with a familiar face entered one of my chaotic dreams, and I melted away for the rest of the night.

CHAPTER 8

Gibbs knocked on my door in the middle of the morning – about nine o'clock. By then I had been ready for a while and was loafing about the room in boredom. I kept worrying they had changed their mind and decided not to take me – it was insulting, and I felt dejected. When I saw Gibbs, however, I was struck by the thought it would be better to stay in M. and not to go with him anywhere. But it was too late to back down now; I couldn't renege on my promise and greeted him with an affected, maybe somewhat forced smirk.

We headed out in two large Land Rovers. Gibbs got behind the wheel of the first, with Christopher One in the passenger seat and a heap of luggage in the back. Christopher Two drove the second car with the rest of us piled in. I offered to switch off with him if he got tired, but he just looked at me amusedly and didn't say a thing, so I became a bit offended and decided to ignore him in turn. Looking like sleepy birds, Silvia and Stella were silent too. We rode in this dull stillness – like complete strangers to each other.

Soon, we left the downtown area and were tearing along the wide roads full of expensive private homes, each enclosed by a high fence and hedge – safe, not a single hole, impossible to guess what was going on within. I twisted my head around, trying to catch a glimpse inside the rapidly passing grounds, yet it was fruitless – there were no peepholes; those who wanted to shield themselves from idle curiosity made a point of doing it right. I told myself I understand them very well.

Suddenly, to the right of me, from an aperture with a silently opening gate, something black and low to the ground glided out. Christopher cursed and jerked the wheel to the left; the women in the back screamed, yet the black car, paying no attention to the swerving Rover, darted ahead and disappeared around the bend. "Asshole," said Christopher through his teeth, with more jealous respect than any particular hostility. And I recalled a similar vehicle sitting in my courtyard in the capital, spending hours below my window, not having anything directly to do with me but etching itself in my memory, like a shameful weakness or an opportunity carelessly thrown away.

Actually, the window under which that car sat belonged to Katarina Polonsky, who lived three stories above me. Everyone knew her as jovial Kate who called on her neighbors every day for odds and ends, happily admitting her own helplessness when it came to common things. She did not, however, irritate anyone – for she had an outgoing character and was always ready to share with others. I didn't know who she was, where she came from, or where she spent her days. On no occasion did we exchange more than a few words about trivial subjects, and the gossip about her I happened to hear was only related to the lovers she consistently replaced from one month to the next. Other aspects of Katarina's existence didn't interest the devoted busybodies. Moreover, her busy private life, with its absence of intrigue, disappointed them too. Men emerged and evanesced one after the other, never two at a time. So even in the prejudiced eyes of the residents, Kate was considered virtuous in her own way, but perhaps confusing them a little with her excessive sense of liberty.

The sleek black car appeared under our windows three years ago, before I met Vera and while Julian was passing his days in other areas that didn't cross mine. I often lurked behind the curtain and scrutinized it stealthily for no short time. Something irrepressible attracted me – and then, by chance, only slightly engineered by my own efforts, I got to know the owner, Mr. McCarthy.

We ran into each other at the entrance to the building, and I intentionally tarried by pulling out a cigarette and pretending I didn't have a lighter. When he handed me his own, I let my eye rest on it and discerned the sign of a familiar investment firm printed on its side.

"You and I have the same broker," I said casually, trying to seem older than I was – which could hardly have fooled his steely gray eyes. Mr. McCarthy, however, gave a half-smile and informed me even more casually this was not so. He simply ran the main part of that corporate vulture, which he was thinking of liquidating, while his personal financial needs were handled by other companies.

"Here you go, just in case," he said, offering me his business card, and, with his hand already on the front door, absentmindedly slipped mine into his pocket. I soon forgot about the episode, but there was a surprising continuation. Mr. McCarthy called and invited me to lunch, although it happened when his car, to my great disappointment, had already moved on to other places and stopped appearing in our courtyard. In the restaurant, skipping formalities, he proposed a completely illegal and thoroughly tempting scheme. The details are not important, but, in brief, it involved secretly obtaining – stealing, to put it bluntly – some inside information about our company and its major competitors. This could throw light on the future actions of these sluggish giants and the forthcoming zigzags in the mysterious world of securities. Simple and old-fashioned, not even risky, stressed Mr. McCarthy as he tediously explained how and why the shadow of suspicion wouldn't fall on me. We talked until late in the afternoon, and I probably went a little overboard with my questions, trying the patience of the imperturbable Scotsman. I requested time to think it over and called him a few days later to reject the offer. Mr. McCarthy responded with an indifferent "okay," and hung up. Yet, for another week or two, I cherished the idea of the completely unfeasible scenario with a seduced CEO's assistant, a locked safe cracked open, white gloves, and a hypersensitive miniature camera.

Afterward, curiosity prompted me to follow the stock market news attentively, and I soon noted a whole network of new brokerage firms that appeared out of nowhere and started buying up millions of shares in one of the giants mentioned by the Scotsman. I had no doubt whose hand was at work there – and, I must admit, I delighted in the scandal that suddenly took place. It was publicized everywhere in the press: the president of the aforementioned company ran away, fled the country, and headed somewhere close to the equator, taking a golden-haired accountant and a solid pile of cash with him, while the corporation itself was placed under the microscope of the government and soon went bankrupt. I could only guess how much the stunned holders lost – I just hope Mr. McCarthy didn't have to give up his glamorous car.

Soon he receded into the depths of my memory; the only thing I recalled quite often besides the car and its glistening sheen were his words about the world of business. I was somewhat dumbfounded, as if being caught off guard by a familiar scene in a place I didn't expect to see it. And what's more, I was amazed by the hint at the causality of my own efforts, not to mention the unwritten tenets of Dzhan.

"There are ignoramuses," said McCarthy, "and there are idiots. In general, they're similar; the only difference is that the former don't know the rules, and the latter stubbornly follow them everywhere. That's why they both lose money – either by smashing their heads into a rule as hard as iron or by falling into the sudden trap of an exception without which any rule is inconceivable."

"The exceptions are countless," he added. "They're so frequent, you can almost consider them unspoken rules. Consequently, almost nobody wins constantly, and, in general, virtually everyone loses, except for those who cash in on other people's stupidity and don't reveal their own. And you never know what'll happen. You plot the charts, predicting the future, and they behave well, obediently rising and falling, until you buy something big – for a million, or two, or five. That evening you drink a lot, then you can't sleep, and in the morning, the sun barely up, you run to find out the latest news, and see – just as you intuited – it's crashed, a hundred points or more, gone for good, and you can't do a damn thing about it. Every temporary success is illusory and a downfall's unavoidable. That's the only rule that applies everywhere, but how can you use it to your own advantage? That's why the winners are those who risk what others have and keep their own deeply hidden and safe, but that isn't easy!"

I agreed with unexpected ardor, surprising the Scotsman and myself, as his conceited maxims tied together what I felt so acutely – even if unwittingly and in an entirely different light. Yeah, I said to myself, every rise is a mirage however much you try to convince others the victory is yours. And in the game of Dzhan, it's not difficult to move everything ahead, yet you won't achieve what you want: the opponent will push you aside and your enthusiasm will wane. It's easy to create a deceptive net, passing through two to three and alternating the right and left brackets – that's repeated in every textbook and advised by all the veterans – but in the same net you soon lose your own way, and that's what no one likes to mention. As soon as hope vanishes, so do all your chances – and how dare you remain hopeful when deadlocks are everywhere you look? The moment you take the right spot, it becomes unmercifully useless – so you think sometimes that life itself may be created according to the eastern game. Though, of course, Lyubomir Lyubomirov would have laughed at this reasoning, ripping it to shreds.

The black car was long gone now, after blinking contemptuously with its brake lights. More than an hour had passed, and our Rovers were still whirling past fences and mansions, briefly building up speed but slowing at intersections, so we were all constantly tossed back and forth. Silvia and Stella didn't complain, but I was getting pretty tired of it. I could have spoken to Christopher Two, yet I didn't want to. Instead, I reached into the pocket of my jacket, pulled out the map of the city I had bought recently, and buried my head in it. Let them know: I also have a map – I was proud of myself, and even Stella, it seemed, looked at me with interest for the first time. Christopher Two also glanced out of the corner of his eye, produced some indistinct sound, but didn't utter a word.

To my embarrassment, I didn't get far. I checked the intricate web of streets and couldn't find any flaw in our route. When we finally reached the outskirts of the city, villas were replaced with old barracks, and the layout became even more complex. For some reason, Christopher Two didn't head east, as he should have, but in the other direction, as if we were intending to go round the city clockwise. I noticed it and didn't understand the maneuver, yet hesitated to ask, especially since he was eying me with sarcastic caginess. Do they cover up their tracks, I wondered uncertainly, or do they want to confuse me so I can't find the way myself? Both the former and the latter sounded absurd, but no other explanations came to mind. Shrugging my shoulders, I folded up the useless map and testily shoved it back into my pocket.

The sun was already high in the sky, and it was stuffy inside. Christopher opened his window and the wind blustered in, whipping up our hair. Simultaneously, Silvia and Stella covered their heads with identical pink scarves, making them look like sisters. One – older, unloved, slutty, and cunning; the other – younger, unloved, cold, and proud. Which one do I like better? Both aren't bad.

I dozed off and only woke up when our Land Rover stopped. The city behind us, the sides of the road were now engulfed by marshlands with scant vegetation, and clouds of insects buzzed in the air. Gibbs and Christopher One had jumped out of the lead car standing on the shoulder and were walking over to us.

"Break time," said Gibbs cheerfully. "Let's eat and keep going."

The women began to bustle about the bags. I climbed out and slowly wandered to the nearest bushes. It was hot and humid; my clothes stuck to my body. I already wanted to go back to the city, but there could be no talk of returning now. The ground yielded below my feet, and I lethargically thought I could sink into it.

"Hey, tourist," one of the Christophers yelled, "don't go far."

Without turning around, I waved my hand at him and immediately sensed a voracious stare fixed on me. I froze and looked about cautiously. Right in front of me, just ten yards away, sat some strange creature on its hind legs – a small animal with a fair chest, round, slightly tilted head, and a piercing gaze that bore into my pupils. Its purple eyes were wide open, yet there was no fear in them: they expressed the sorrow and startling passivity of omniscience. Not far from it was another, and on the sides – still more. I stood at the conjunction of steady looks studying me without restraint, but also without curiosity, as if they knew in advance what I was capable of and had long since given up hope of surprises. I narrowed my eyes and stared back intently, yet it was like peering into a cold glass. Then, to overcome my confusion, I sighed deeply and strode up to the closest one, ready for anything.

The critter vanished at once. I approached another – it disappeared too. I paused, staggered by such agility, and then resolutely headed back to the place where the latter had been sitting. In the grayish brown soil I discovered a small burrow, bent over it, and tried to peek inside. It was dark there, but I peered more and more intently into the hole, picturing their refuge with its underground passageways and impervious secret niches. Then something squished traitorously below me and the boggy ground gave way. I slammed my palm down to brace myself and screamed – an agonizing pain shot up my arm, as if I had been jabbed by a red-hot poker that was being driven in further and further. I jerked my hand back and jumped up, noticing out of the corner of my eye something vile and shaggy, the size of a matchbox, scurrying off toward the shrubs. The stinging increased, my eyes popped out, I saw nothing around me and just sensed that Gibbs had appeared next to me, grabbed my uninjured arm, and dragged me to the cars, cursing through his teeth.

Help came quickly: Gibbs pressed down on some point near my elbow, and the pain eased, with merely a dull ache remaining. Then they applied a pungent salve to the spot of the bite and covered it with a clean bandage. My arm became numb, yet no longer hurt. The Christophers just laughed. One of them imitated a marsh spider with his fingers spread and demonstrated how it scuttles sideways. Gibbs, however, was very angry, repeating over and over that we were losing time. On top of that, an injured arm was the last thing we needed in the Dunes, he said. Only better than a broken leg, especially since we had so much to carry and each of us had been apportioned a full load.

"Everyone needs a nanny," he summarized acidly, and I couldn't say anything in response. Silvia looked at me compassionately, yet I saw I was becoming a burden from the very start.

Whatever, I consoled myself, It was their idea to drag me along. But that didn't help much – certainly no one expected me to blunder right away. Gibbs stopped talking and there were no more reproaches, though I continued to feel fairly wretched.

The rest of the trip I remember foggily. My head spun and I occasionally drifted off. Outside the window I saw just brown peat bogs, haze in the humid air, moss, and rare shrubs. The road again seemed longer than the map indicated. According to my calculations, the Dunes should have appeared ages ago, yet there was no hint of them. A clearly irritated Christopher Two, still sitting behind the wheel, now gave my topographic efforts a hostile look and said unkindly, "You should fold up your papers, tourist." He wasn't joking, and I nearly flared up, but decided not to get involved and simply shrugged my shoulders. The women didn't say a word, sitting like indifferent, obtuse sisters. Stella smoked a lot and looked out the window, her back to everyone.

When I woke up again, it was already getting dark. With its motor off, our Rover stood five yards from the other one, where three armed guards tramped about in uniform with portable radios. An instant later, Gibbs appeared next to them and spent a few minutes arguing persuasively. Then they flung open the cargo door and rummaged through our bags. Gibbs and one of the men walked off to the side, into the thickening twilight. I became nervous, yet Christopher sat tranquilly, as if knowing there was nothing to fear.

"What's going on?" I asked without really expecting a response.

However, he readily explained this was the Ocean Patrol, a special police force with a mandate to snag fugitives and smugglers.

"A small bribe normally does the trick. Although, if they find nets, they may get nasty," added Christopher, and Silvia sighed restlessly.

"Amateurs!" said Stella, lighting another cigarette.

"Retard," Christopher replied, yet it ended there – Gibbs returned with the policeman, and each was visibly satisfied with the other. The uniformed guards receded into the darkness, a dog barked somewhere, as if giving a signal, and we again set out behind Gibbs' car.

My head had stopped spinning, however I couldn't see anything outside. It became chilly, the windows had been closed, and the persistent smell of tobacco smoke hung in the air. Sitting in the car for hours had made all my muscles grow numb. I longed to get out and stretch my legs, yet had no clue where we were located or headed – the map was useless, and I didn't want to ask.

"Half an hour to go," said Christopher cheerfully, and I nodded with gratitude. He towered over the wheel, resembling a crude sphinx in the night, and I envied his stamina, aware I could never compete with him. The road became flatter; our Land Rovers picked up speed. The women rustled in their seats, fussing impatiently, as if aroused from a reverie. Then on both sides twinkled the lamps of farms in the distance, and we soon drove up to a lit space in front of a clunky gray building. Oasis Motel, I read in slanted letters, and my body rejoiced in anticipation of the break. Still we had to stay seated for a while – since our driver wouldn't let us out, as Gibbs and Christopher One had gone somewhere. Finally they returned and we began to unload the luggage.

It was a strange motel, not similar to those I had seen before. From outside, it looked rather like a warehouse, with a high staircase leading up to the entrance on the second floor, which was odd for a place with all its rooms on the first. The entrance door opened to a large lounge you had to go through, passing the reception desk to the right, while your gaze became transfixed by the abundance of bear skins and silver goblets, antique candleholders and daggers that hung on the walls and stood in the corners. In addition, the room had a real hearth with a fire, burning day and night.

The lounge was also used as a dining room, with a massive oak table and benches in the center. When we entered, dragging our bags and breathing heavily from the walk up, we met the owner right inside the door – a small, roly-poly fellow with deranged eyes who was writing something quickly at a desk. Hearing us, he waved his hand without lifting his head, and only came up a few minutes later after rapidly reading what he had written. Gibbs was very angry about this negligence – he became rude and caustic, and didn't calm down until we got our keys.

My room was ordinary but clean. I fell on the sagging bed and wasn't planning to get up till morning, yet soon my head cleared and the haze before my eyes disappeared – the bite from the swamp spider stopped affecting me. I stayed in bed a bit longer – recalling the endless day, the jolting in the car, and the animals with purple eyes – then jumped up full of energy and headed out for a walk.

Obviously, I wasn't planning to go far after the day's events, but my legs carried me around the building, past a pavilion and a dried-up fountain, and along a deserted alley lit up by infrequent lamps. It turned into a barely visible path with lonely trees and plants on both sides. The lanterns came to an end, although the bright moon shed enough light to discern the way, and I wandered further, enjoying the fresh air after the suffocating ride, as well as the solitude and peace. The path hit a split trunk, hardly visible in the darkness, veered sharply to the right, and ended. A plain stretched out before me; there was no trail, no road, not even one single shrub. Only patches of moonlight lived a whimsical life there: flaring up in strict order, moving and changing places, solving their eternal mysteries.

Spellbound, I watched the animate images – they never repeated, pulsating with their own rhythm, indifferent to the rest of the universe. This was the most flawless thing I had ever seen. It was better than the kaleidoscope of my memory, better than all the words on a sheet of paper or an intrusive melody in my head. Convulsively, I hid my secret in the furrows of my consciousness, not letting it out for an uneven duel, so the completeness of foreign harmony wouldn't destroy its essence. What I saw in front of me was stricter and more convincing – sharper than burnished steel, louder than a sudden shot. Music rose up and drew me in, and I, unaware of what I was doing, wanted to go there, to the glimmerings and glows – to trace their contours with my uncertain hand, feel the icy beams with my palm, lie down and swim in the murmuring waves. I was about to take a step when a gruff scream rang in my ears, crushing the magic and making me shiver and look back, retaining my balance with difficulty.

"Are you crazy?" Gibbs asked coldly, coming out of nowhere. In the moonlight, his face had a rapacious silver hue, and his tenacious eyes flashed. "Quicksand is no joke. You take a few steps – and nothing will save you, not your prayers or mine."

He leaned over and picked up a big, dry branch. "Watch!" – and he flung it onto a bright patch. The branch stuck in the sand, sketched in the air something vertical and broken, like ink on a silvery pale-gray film, congealed for a minute or two, then became shorter, swung, shook, and disappeared without a trace. It seemed to me that an oily surface shimmered and a slight ripple ran over it – but my naïvety may be the reason for that.

"Do you understand?" asked Gibbs, and I didn't say a word. For some time we stood and looked at the fickle patterns, yet they no longer inspired me with the same abandon – now they concealed a trap that couldn't be ignored.

"Many secrets were hidden underneath," said Gibbs. I glanced at him. He was different here, far from the city – he had squared his shoulders and tossed off a few years. His loose limbs had turned taut, and invisible springs were tensed – he was ready to jump, fight, and I wouldn't have envied a predator who decided to pick a quarrel with him.

"Many secrets die out here," he explained, puckering his brow.

"There's nothing less visible than what has been buried like that branch. It can be very handy, you know."

He regarded me archly and winked. I cleared my throat and asked in a voice not quite my own, "As a hiding place, you mean?"

"Well, yes, as a hiding place, you put it well." Gibbs grinned, and again I sensed a whiff of irony. "Hiding places come in many forms. Some of them you don't even want to return to, so it's better to forget where they are."

He took two steps off to the side, loudly unzipped his pants and began to whistle and relieve himself. A bird flew up not far from him, squawking anxiously a few times. Something swished at my feet, and I glanced down, afraid of a snake.

"I know this place like the back of my hand," Gibbs continued, returning to me. "I grew up close to here," and he waved in some direction. "We searched out every nook and cranny, came here now and then, played games, laid in wait, watched. Strange people would arrive and bury all sorts of stuff. Sometimes it wasn't funny: they would bring someone, stick a gun in his back and say – go, go yourself. And he would go – what else could he do – and just scream when it was too late..." Gibbs grew silent. "My father is also resting there," he added abruptly. "Well, let's go, they must be waiting," – and he set out in front, heading for the motel.

Indeed, dinner was ready. The owner sat at the head of the table with his hands nervously tapping the tablecloth and a smile glued to his face. Our whole group was there. The women, who had changed clothes and combed their hair, sat upright, somewhat formally, while the Christophers prattled away in an undertone. Serving us was some skinny girl of no particular age – the owner's niece, as we learned later.

When Gibbs arrived, everyone livened up. The Christophers met him with loud exclamations, and the owner immediately calmed down and reached for a large flask of wine. "It's local. Don't pass up the chance to try some," he said while pouring it out.

We ate and drank for three. I don't know what hit us – but I felt devilishly hungry, rapidly devouring my plate of food. The meal wasn't bad – pâté from wild fowl, stewed duck, crudely cut vegetables, and an enormous saddle of roasted lamb, dominating the center. Wine was served, time and again, and we consumed everything at such a staggering pace that the girl-waitress could hardly keep up. The owner seemed to be very satisfied – he was flush, his cheeks became flabby, a greasy lock fell on his forehead and remained there like an incongruous stain. He poured wine continually, singling out Gibbs above all, and smiled still more contentedly.

Finally everyone was full. The girl gathered up the dishes and dragged over an old-fashioned metal kettle with an herbal drink. I pulled out a cigarette and walked off to the open window, a little ways from the table – for I wanted to be alone. The alcohol roared in my head; I gazed into the darkness and remembered the quicksand, knowing I wouldn't want to go there again. In the distance, thunder rumbled – a late autumn storm was gathering. A cloud shrouded the moon and the night became more impenetrable.

A gentle voice called me back from my thoughts, "Do you need a light?"

The owner of the motel had come up soundlessly and was handing me a box of matches, blinking, his unhealthy pupils peering into my face as he shifted from one foot to the other. I shrugged my shoulders and said no, flicking my own lighter. Instead of going away, however, he faced the window and contemplated the invisible with me.

"Thank God," I heard him whisper. "Thank God everything turned out okay. I didn't know what to think – when they told me he had gone after you, my heart skipped a beat. Why, I said to myself, why does it always happen here?"

I stared at him, raising my eyebrows inquiringly, yet he paid no attention and just whispered away. "Sometimes, a whole year passes quietly. Only hunters pull in or policemen visit occasionally: they just eat, drink, grope Hannah now and then, and leave – and I say, 'Good riddance.' But he – every time he passes by, the devil knows who arrives afterward. They come and ask – when was he here, and how long, and with whom? What did they do, where did they go

– and what do I know, it's not my business. Though I sense it: a terrible, terrible guy. And his face… There are reasons he's a marked man, no doubt. Yet I never say a thing, I keep quiet as a mouse and just ask myself sadly – why can't everything be peaceful? And today I was distressed for you – however, now it's over, unlike the last time, when…"

I turned away without listening to the end, stubbed out my cigarette, and walked back to the table. He was grubby and unpleasant, his gaze strayed and danced around, his murmuring gave me the creeps. As for the rumors, I didn't want to listen to anyone, knowing well: everybody's a liar.

After sitting down, I furtively watched Gibbs. It seemed he smiled sarcastically, but then he shifted the blank part of his face to me, so it was no longer possible to guess what it reflected. Someone offered me more wine, and I drank the whole glass in one gulp, knowing it would affect me and desiring that. I really needed to chase off the marsh spider, the armed men on the road, and the crazy host with his unctuous smile. Flickers of quicksand, its surface illuminated by the moonlight, still beckoned me time and again, yet I was not afraid anymore and didn't acknowledge the threat.

We went off to our rooms way after midnight. I was drunk, and fantasies induced by alcohol swirled in my head, unleashing carnal instincts. I recalled Gretchen – her small body, insatiable to candid caresses, the uneasiness of Miss Greenwich, ending up an unwelcome witness, and the slick way my sister saved us, paying her back in kind and surprising me with her mature sagacity. Strange: imagining Gretchen behind the closed curtains of my eyelids, I came instead to ponder Miss Greenwich, who I had secretly dreamed about for a year or two – until she was dismissed and left. She probably found my sighs and lusty looks funny, but she still noticed me, her pale-pink, fair-haired figure openly tantalizing me on occasion. She resembled a Rubens nymph – driving me crazy with peignoirs in the evening before bed, open dressing-gown flaps and revealing nightshirts.

My mother forced her to leave, thinking she was having an affair with my father. It was a lie, although my father did try to flirt with her more than once. But she rebuffed him every time, the unforgettable Miss Greenwich, the prim coquette with a British accent – and I was secretly proud of her, imagining she was preserving her fidelity for me. I cooed silent, ardent words to her through the walls that divided our bedrooms, and when Gretchen told me the truth about her, I wasn't let down. On the contrary, something made me want her even more, and I cried sincerely when she came to say goodbye, pale and serious, with her funny blue eyes where she carefully concealed her suppressed vice. She kissed me on the lips, swiftly pressing her adult body against mine so I caught a whiff of her scent through the cheap perfume, and for a long time I turned red at the thought of this memory, both then and later, when I was completely grown up.

Now I was thinking of her while wrestling with sleep, envisioning her in my bed. Then I heard a squeak of the door and light footsteps, and suddenly I felt her – large and soft and shameless, just as I fantasized in my childhood daydreams. I opened my eyes – no, it wasn't Miss Greenwich, but Silvia who came in through the unlocked door. I plunged my face into her breasts, as if saving myself from the visions of the long day. She smelled of wine and guided me impetuously and imperiously, demanding rather than promising, even if afterward she resigned herself to the unavoidable and no longer wanted anything in return. Concealing her weakness, she didn't request protection – as if, on the contrary, I needed comfort, and she had come voluntarily to help me. I tried to ask her something, but she merely laughed, drawing me to her, and fondled me playfully.

Later she became serious, looked silently in my eyes – and turned away indifferently, as if discovering a mistake, though in a minute she was back to amusing herself. I settled down into her sighs and dropped off into a quick, drunken sleep from which I was again rescued by unambiguous stroking. Then I woke up alone and saw only a mauled pillow and a beam of sunlight on the floor. A new day had begun – I thought about it and winced at my headache and dry throat.

CHAPTER 9

A few hours later, my shoulder was also throbbing – from the strap of the bulky backpack digging into it. We were walking along a barely visible trail, like a group of fugitives who had long ago severed all ties to their homeland. I recalled yesterday's dinner uneasily and the night after appeared lost in the distant past, as if it were only a blur. In the morning at breakfast, Silvia had met my gaze calmly and smiled coolly, greeting me without any hint of intimacy. Now I was mindlessly counting steps, with no more inspiration for fantasies. It seemed we had been wandering for an eternity, yet the sun was still at its zenith, and the day was not even close to winding down.

Gibbs led the way, glancing back every so often but not saying a word. All morning he had been silent and gazed in irritation as we got ready near our heap of things by the entrance. He quickly showed us who should take what, and we strode away from the motel toward the underbrush surrounding the gently sloping hillock. I felt terrible – yesterday's drinking bout came back to haunt me, and the bite from the marsh spider pulsated dreadfully, shooting into my spine at the smallest of movements. As Gibbs had predicted, I couldn't lift anything substantial, so on my other shoulder they hoisted the notorious backpack that didn't seem heavy at first but made all my muscles stiff in an hour.

The Christophers carried the main portion of our load. Silvia and Stella also took something – without arguing or grumbling, although

I saw they suffered a lot. Gibbs had less than everyone else – and he set a brisk pace, tapping away with his wooden walking stick. Initially, such unfairness surprised me, yet then I decided it was necessary. Here and there, he halted abruptly, signaling for us to stop, darted fifty feet off the trail, carefully inspected something on the ground, then ran in the other direction, and only after this did he lead us onward, turning almost imperceptibly and again guessing the elusive way with its myriad forks.

After we had emerged from the motel, I swiveled my head in search of our Land Rovers, but they were nowhere to be seen. Then it became clear we would be going the rest of the way by foot, and that disconcerted me considerably. I even asked Christopher Two whether everything was okay with the cars, and where they were, and, most importantly, why we were leaving them behind today. I didn't want to reveal my weakness, yet I wasn't excited about the prospect of walking, especially since the road by no means ended at the motel, but rather headed to the east – what seemed to me like the right direction. When I looked back, I actually saw a car traveling down it, although I didn't manage to get the model. Christopher Two grinned, called over Christopher One and repeated my question, which made the latter grin in exactly the same way. They began to mock me, fully aware of their superiority and speaking in dumb riddles. I didn't hear anything worthwhile; the catch to all their jokes was that you could definitely drive on the road, though it wouldn't take you where you wanted to go. That, of course, I couldn't know, they said, all the more so since it wasn't depicted on any map, because the maps of this area had been strictly forbidden. They reiterated this idea a few different ways, so I started to suspect they were referring to my recent topographical efforts. And indeed, they smirked quite disgustingly, so I was itching to put them in their place.

I also had something to say – and about the Dunes too. I could have easily quoted the Blonkhet travel guide as well as another two or three reliable sources. All of them may have lost the aplomb of eyewitnesses as soon as they started to talk about the Ocean Zones, yet they still candidly tried to enlighten a stranger about the place each unanimously agreed you shouldn't visit. Regarding maps – or, more precisely, their absence – they mentioned something as well, although old, crudely sketched plans still existed. One of the books offered an illustrated replica – and honestly warned you not to believe it because in all likelihood it hadn't been done correctly from the very beginning, and moreover, the whole area had changed considerably, and not just once. "In accordance with local geographic peculiarities," Blonkhet explained obscurely, and the same phrase kept turning up here and there, like a helpless conveyer of ignorance, only sometimes switching, with dry straightforwardness, to something categorical. It proclaimed, for example, "The local flora and fauna have been poorly studied!" – as if saying: if you go there, it's all your own fault, don't even think of blaming Blonkhet.

This all ran through my head, and I knew I could have responded to the Christophers so they wouldn't have put on such airs, but I didn't want to descend to their level, especially after the incident with the spider. I just calmly said, "Yes, I know there are no maps." And added as casually as possible, "In accordance with local geographic peculiarities," – making a mistake I instantly regretted.

"What sorts of peculiarities?" asked Christopher One with interest. "Tell us, you tourist. We, you know, have been living here for ages and haven't a clue."

"Well, the sudden changes in the terrain," I strained to remember. "Various kinds of atmospheric occurrences of an extreme nature…" I intentionally yawned. "A number of aspects are involved. It's not that easy to explain."

"Yeah, if you've never been to the Dunes, nothing's easy to explain, you're right," said Christopher derisively. "Reading books won't help you with explanations. But if you'd ramble around here for a few days, then, for sure, you'd be able to explain a lot – if, of course, you still wanted to."

"Speak for yourself, not for me," I retorted coldly, and we again strode on in silence, gazing now at our feet, now at Gibbs indefatigably searching out the right way. Here the trail was wide; I walked alongside the Christophers as before, and then Silvia joined us, asking one of them something. Only Stella continued to follow behind Gibbs, and I wondered if I should give her some company, getting to know her a little better. Yet, at that moment, the bored Christophers started arguing at the top of their lungs and I began involuntarily to listen to them. Silvia also jumped in, which animated them still more. Gibbs even glanced back and cast a strange look at the whole group, making the arguers quiet down and shift to fierce whispering.

Christopher One got quite excited. The second replied with a drawl, yet stood his ground with the stubbornness of a bull. They were talking about a man named Jim who, according to Christopher One, was not worth a fig, whereas Christopher Two considered him a thoroughly resourceful guy who wasn't to be messed with. The main confusion and the subject of their dispute concerned Jim's nickname, and here both were intransigent in their own way, which led to other differences I was incapable of judging.

Almost foaming at the mouth, the first claimed Wild Jim was capable of nothing but picking a fight with whoever came his way. He got beaten quite often – nonetheless, he still hung around the taverns in search of a quarrel or simply a dirty glance. He was a tough guy, that's right, but there are always enough even tougher ones, only not all of them have brains. The second Christopher maintained in turn that wasn't Wild Jim, but no other than Jim the Wild, whose obscure glory came from where drunkards and bullies had no chance of settling down – in no time they would be found in the swamp with busted heads. Jim the Wild, strong and deliberate, with a heavy reptilian gaze, passed his time somewhere among fugitives who didn't fiddle with trifles, and none of the rabble monkeyed around with them. And it was among the rabble, added Christopher II, that Wild Jim would have found a place for himself if he'd actually existed – with a whiskered, broad-shouldered and short-legged appearance. As for Jim the Wild, he was for real, all right. He exuded the power petty folks couldn't even dream of, all the more so since the Dunes were different at that time – quite different and full of things, all sorts of things...

In this way, they insisted on their own, yet the last thought struck a chord in Christopher One as well, so the argument lost steam and the fervor of both ebbed away. Ultimately they made up, coming to the consensus that the Dunes today were nothing like before. Now, as Christopher One expressed it, "There's almost no life here – just a trick and not much else." Announcing this, he instantly exhausted every cause of dissension, and the conversation took a different turn, much more interesting in my opinion.

"Yeah, at one time, some pretty serious fellows wandered there," the second Christopher echoed. "Now, of course, that's no longer the case: the people in general have become pettier. Back then the majority was also rubbish, although there were quite a few fugitives as well – the real ones, not like today's. No one dared to mess with them, and the police didn't come here either. They just wrote in their reports: everybody has died, all of them, drowned in the swamps or somewhere else. One of the younger cops would sign off thoughtlessly, like a witness, and the case was closed – but those folks, no, they didn't die, they ended up here in the Dunes, among the others who were written off. That's why they had such confusion with the monikers: there weren't enough; the survivors outnumbered the list of possibilities. So now those still visible are getting all the credit, like heroes or the likes, although everyone understands they'll never find out who did what and who tried harder."

"Well, that's okay," interrupted Christopher One, waving his hand. "That's their life, and that's not the point. What I'm trying to say is: the Dunes were *different*. All sorts of people swarmed over them, and it was even possible to drive there – on dirt roads, of course, since they didn't lay asphalt for no reason at that time. Murky gangs roamed about – some on horseback, some in cars. And the government wasn't overzealous: its power didn't extend to the Dunes and the coast."

The Christophers nodded in unison, having achieved mutual agreement. Obviously, the government and its efforts had become a common subject. They even came close to marching in step, swinging their arms and legs identically.

"The city wasn't big at that time," the first went on, glancing patronizingly in my direction. "No advertisements, no tourists, plains all around, and just two or three little factories. It was a joke, not a city – and the authorities had little influence and no faith in themselves. Only later did they start to build up everything, even deciding to tackle the Dunes so the area wouldn't remain useless – and that's when the trouble began. The reformers were coming fast; they rushed them in from the capital and brought some foreigners too. My grandfather told me right away: if they dragged in so many strangers, then the locals will be soon deprived of their due!"

He cursed and spit, and we continued moving ahead in silence. Insects whirred; something crackled in the thicket that alternated with uneven bald patches, overgrown with long, flowing grass. The bumpy ground made it difficult to walk – we had to look down the whole time to keep from stumbling. Once Stella tripped anyway, but it wasn't serious – she just turned her ankle slightly and went on, limping a little after receiving a harsh rebuke from Gibbs. Silvia breathed heavily, and I also found it tough, again recalling our Land Rovers by the motel.

"Listen, why are we on foot, anyway?" I asked Christopher Two. "I don't get it. It wouldn't be hard for an SUV..."

"You don't get it, that's right," he said lazily. "But don't worry, you're not the only one. There are others who are even denser than you."

"And are you one of the whizzes or what?" I inquired, unwilling to tolerate their goading anymore. "You don't look much like it to me."

Christopher squinted at me, thought a little, and replied quite genially, "Whether I look like it or not, I've been in the Dunes since childhood. You don't need to understand here – you only have to open your eyes. You have to look patiently and just take in everything as it happens – then at some point it all becomes as clear as day. And don't try to get on my nerves, *tourist*. We are on foot because of a lack of roads; and roads aren't there because the sanatorium isn't there either. It's obvious – as I said, as clear as day."

"And why isn't there a sanatorium?" I inquired dumbly.

"Take a wild guess," laughed Christopher Two. "I told you: because there aren't any roads. How stupid can you be? The thing with the roads is that they started with the sanatorium... Did you know that?" he asked Silvia, who shook her head. The second Christopher chuckled again, exchanged looks with Christopher One as usual, and began to tell the story as he patted his thigh to the beat of his feet.

"All reformers are different," he said didactically, conveying the significance of his words. "Some languish in their idiocy from the outset, and the others a little later, when the first burst comes to nothing. Well, ours proved to be the bright ones – they decided to build a health resort at the ocean for people who had lost their minds. They chose a good place, you couldn't argue with that. Everybody laughed – the only thing the place was missing was the lunatics, they said, although maybe it would really do some good for lunatics," – and Christopher Two twirled his finger in the air, a wry smile contorting his face.

"The project began with the road, as you would expect," he continued after a pause, enjoying the attention. "They started to pave the highway – wide and smooth. There was a lot of noise in the press, and big guns invested heaps of money. However, just after finishing, the road crumpled right in the middle. It was like in a movie: a festive procession, the governor and his main architect in a limo, two motorcycles with flashing blinkers in front of them. Everyone's in a celebratory mood, looking forward to speeches, picnics, the full program. Only they didn't make it to the ocean: ten miles in, they climbed a hill and on the backside was a pit. The chauffeur of the limo managed to slam on the brakes – giving the architect a bloody nose – but the bikers rolled right in. One kicked the bucket, but the other was fine. They dragged him out, brought him back to life, then whacked him one for not being sufficiently attentive – you must keep your eyes open, they said, you almost put the governor in his grave. Still, search as they might for the guilty party, fifty yards of road had vanished into a deep cavity and lay there covered with water. The ground sunk, the architect explained, although he was no longer in charge. It's an unanticipated movement of the shifting substrata, he insisted – but who would listen to him after that? They began the repairs right away, built a bridge, poured gravel in here and there. And just after they finished, two other parts of the road collapsed, though without any victims that time: the people had become smarter and no longer recklessly raced down it on motorcycles. That's how they ended up dumping the plan. No highway – no sanatorium. One to one."

"Not exactly," Christopher One objected. "It wasn't that simple. They still wanted a health resort, but they didn't have enough guts, and the Dunes were in serious turmoil. It was no longer possible to drive on the former trails: every car broke down, whether it was old or new. Horses stopped obeying – sat silently, didn't move an inch, and could only be turned back. Folks were leaving their cars right there – and nobody wanted to drive out for them, no matter how much money was offered. Bad rumors spread and the people were unhappy, but nothing serious would have happened anyway if there hadn't been a new chief of police. My granddad worked as a detective, and, when they appointed that man, he retired voluntarily, with just a half-pension. All his faculties told him, the old fart, that everything would go awry. He said right off the bat: the city had never seen a chief as hard-headed as this guy – only problems and pomp come from such mules, not profits. And the police started to take action right away – they destroyed the flea market, and drugs disappeared off the streets. The chief could crack down indeed, there's no arguing about that..."

He suddenly stopped talking, froze, and began to inspect something at his feet, then whistled and waved to Gibbs. The latter came over and they sat on their haunches, twirling some stones that lay next to the trail. A few minutes passed; I wanted to sit and toss down my backpack. But the others stood without moving, patiently waiting until they finished. Finally, Gibbs shook his head and we went on while Christopher stood, looked around, and chucked the rock into the distant bushes, frightening a large gray bird.

"Well, what did the boss do next?" Silvia asked when he caught up and was walking alongside us.

"Ha," Christopher One chuckled. "The point was in what he *had*, not what he *did*. He just wallowed in his success for a while, but he had an idiot for a son. A well-known dimwit, who hung out with punks, smoked grass, and loved to bully others – until he came to his senses and made himself the pride of the city. The chief's kiddo became a student at the National Academy, where rumor had it even his father hadn't been able to get accepted in his time, despite trying with all his might. Who knows how he managed to pull it off, but afterward the kid became a celebrity. In the local newspaper they printed an article on two pages, then hung a medal with gold plating around his neck when he got here for summer holidays, and Dad was so pleased he gave him a new car – a convertible, glittering all over in silver. We never saw something so luxurious on the streets; it was certainly not for a student. But no one wanted to count the chief's money – he had everybody under his thumb. So his son drove about the city, honked at dogs, and everything was fine until he began to think too much of himself and started to look for risky ventures. And, you know, if you want to get your ass in trouble, the trouble will find you in no time."

Christopher One stopped to chug some water, and the second Christopher quickly butted in. "The car was a Morgan," he said with a knowing look. "Expensive, of course, but he didn't go easy on it: revved the motor and scared pedestrians, his buddies at his side the whole time – whooping it up, cackling, ashamed of nothing. One day they decided to try a different game and the whole team headed off to the Dunes – to hear how the ocean owls cried. This was common among local dumbbells – cruising to the Dunes for 'a night in nature.' The screams were terrifying, they made your skin crawl – and it was impossible to get used to them – yet the boys wanted to play heroes. They took some chicks, wine, and vodka, piled into the brand-new Morgan, and drove away at dusk. By foot would have been better, but no, stubbornness overpowered them, and that, you know, never leads to anything good. When they'd reached the remotest of areas, their Morgan broke down: an axle split in two or the engine died – things happen in the Dunes, yeah, even with the priciest of cars. Terrified, they stumbled and bumbled their way back – one girl, a professor's daughter, was hysterical for days afterwards – however they all made it out alive in the morning. They should have forgotten it then and kept their mouths shut, but that son ran right to Daddy and complained like a baby, and Daddy lost his mind right away. Whether he hated to lose the Morgan or something else, he turned completely red, stamped his feet, and locked himself in his room till evening, and the next day the local newspaper published an article which alarmed the whole city. Enough is enough, wrote the chief of police, we're declaring war on all these conjectures. We'll bring order to the Dunes so that everybody can drive there without fear, either in a Morgan or in a horse cart, and come back unharmed, knowing for sure nothing absurd can occur anymore."

"Yes, I remember that," said Silvia, "he had a name that sounded foreign – Sullivan or Sallivan. Or, maybe, Fakir or Fukker?"

"Fukker is good, yeah," Christopher grinned, clearly feeling superior. "Actually, his name was Salmon Fuchs and he was a former Navy lieutenant, if they aren't lying, of course, though I think they are. Lieutenant or not, he declared war and took charge himself. And where there's a war, there are spoils and trophies – so the first thing they did was go drag out the abandoned Morgan with a police van. However, as you can imagine, the van got one flat, then another, and after bending the springs, they found themselves stuck in sand. Then the real problems began: the boss decided to walk, but a sandstorm rose up – everything became invisible, and he got totally lost. They began to search with a helicopter and almost killed themselves: fog, wind, sand whipping about – nothing to do but return and wait. So they sat and waited for almost three days, until the chief showed up after wandering in circles. His clothing was tattered, his eyes were popping out of his head, yet the stubborn man wouldn't throw in the towel. Moreover, while he was drifting about there, his wife cuckolded him – running off with a journalist and leaving a farewell letter behind. 'I no longer want to live with a despot. I desire personal happiness and beautiful physical love,' she wrote. The housekeeper found the note first, and soon the whole city was gossiping about 'beautiful love' and stuff. They badgered the chief of police endlessly – everybody smirked behind his back, so all he could do was devote himself heart and soul to his quixotic war." Christopher Two shook his head, obviously not envying unlucky Salmon Fuchs.

"Yeah," Christopher One continued. "The Dunes got under his skin. But he wasn't a complete idiot. He decided to act systematically, without rushing ahead. Furthermore, there was no hurry. Neither his wife nor the new-fangled Morgan would return. He employed a whole host of surveyors, and they combed every inch of the Dunes – preparing detailed maps of the terrain: here higher, there lower, now wet, now dry, this place is reachable with ease, that one should be avoided, and so forth. Then they sent builders – to section the Dunes into districts and fence off each one for practical use in the future. Only they didn't get far: wherever they had marked an area arid, it turned into a swamp; wherever there was level ground, it gave way to a ravine. And no one could figure it out: the builders blamed the mapmakers and vice versa, yet you could commiserate with the former, since they risked their skin, not someone else's, and suffered a lot for nothing.

Finally, they rewrote the maps – but everything started moving again. This time, however, entire villages disappeared, slipping into wetlands and quicksand, and canyons came dangerously close to the urban homes nearby. At this, they all flat-out lost courage. The chief of police was dismissed for health reasons and a special commission was appointed – to review, as they said, the disconcerting circumstances. They spent two months checking the facts, scratching the backs of their necks, and then passed a resolution: maps were forbidden – with the threat of a jail term for violators – as was traveling to the Dunes by motorized means of transportation. In connection with local geographic peculiarities, as you, tourist, put it. And those who disagreed with the new rules, it said, would be deported from the city within twenty-four hours – since such residents were not good for anything except committing sabotage and causing misfortune.

But the latter was pointless: the people themselves caught a whiff of the danger. Nobody headed out there anymore, only the most reckless ones, though they too received dirty looks from their neighbors. As for the fugitives and exiles, they went from the Dunes in the other direction, to the plains. There, anyway, it was calmer and not swampy – with no gnats to pester you in the summer."

"And what happened to the chief?" Silvia inquired.

"He went off his rocker," said Christopher One cheerfully. "Took off for the Dunes and disappeared. No one saw him again – not in the city or elsewhere. And," he added, "they only allowed roads along the edge, for visitors, to show them the place from afar – though you can't see the Dunes from afar, there's nothing to look at, it's all just senseless. And, yes, some villages remain in the south, and there are roads going to them, but that's not for us – they're out of the way, and besides, the police hassle you all the time." And he grinned again as he regarded us mischievously, his gold tooth sparkling.

Gibbs ordered the group to stop sometime after noon. Behind us were ascents and descents along the uneven paths, prickly shrubs, and the marsh that began beyond them. We had come out into a dry, fairly hilly place. My shoulder was about to break, my neck and back were numb and had lost feeling. The others were also exhausted – both the women and the Christophers fell into the grass with brief sighs. Gibbs, alone, looked around, ran off to the side, and disappeared beyond the knolls.

"Are these the Dunes already?" I asked the closest Christopher, and he nodded indifferently.

"You can wander about, tourist. There aren't any spiders here, just lizards," said the other Christopher, though I didn't deign to answer or consider him.

Tough dark grass and coniferous shrubs grew thickly on the sand hills. In some places, bald patches were visible and masses of lizards really did scamper along the ground, tracing quick trajectories on the light sand. A few basked in the sun, motionless, thinking the same thoughts they had a million years ago, with enough patience for the next million. It seemed time stood still here, and any sort of commotion was inappropriate, like a fake reason for getting distracted from the essence. Occasionally unfamiliar birds swept by, some landed close to us, sitting down nearby, unafraid, maybe not even noticing us or not wanting to, like something unnecessary, which you try not to ponder, secretly hoping it will vanish by itself.

"The Dunes!" I thought. "I'd hardly gotten used to the idea, yet here I am already. Rash, it's all rather rash. This way I won't have time to digest anything."

"If there's something to digest," another thought interfered right away. "How many times you have deceived yourself that emptiness isn't empty? Here, too, it all might turn out to be just props…"

Yet I knew: props aren't this integral, this self-sufficient and indifferent to observers. "Wait, wait," the hills seemed to say, "though you probably won't ever get an answer."

It was senseless to argue. I could only submit, become accustomed to waiting and not nurse grievances. The sand and shrubs looked completely innocent; the grass occasionally stirred, conforming to the weak wind. A ripple ran through it, like muscles quivering under skin, and lizards darted off to the side, as if clearing the way for something the eye cannot behold.

Gibbs returned a half hour later. From the bags appeared our meager victuals, which we quickly ate before sprawling in the grass to smoke cigarettes and enjoy the peace and quiet. Silvia and Gibbs sat a little way off, discussing something in private. Silvia's hair was disheveled, her clothes wrinkled. Now I didn't find her attractive, but knew I'd be longing for her again at night. Stella, on the contrary, looked relaxed but distant and thoughtful. She moved away from the Christophers, who tried to tease her, and regarded something on the horizon, drifting off there as if she had no need for us. Her detachment startled me – the walls of that universe she inhabited at the moment seemed painfully impenetrable. What if everyone decided to fashion an invisible shell for themselves? A strange, muffled sense of melancholy bore down on me. I wanted a human voice or laughter, something that would anchor and extend a thread of life – so I got up and went over to Stella, still not knowing what I would say.

She watched me blankly, slightly narrowing one eye. "Are you bored?" I inquired as casually as possible. "You might say so," she replied after a short pause, as if grudgingly, though I saw my approach had succeeded.

We made small talk, sizing each other up, then I asked, "Have you been here before?" and I was dumbfounded by the spiteful grimace that distorted her face. Quickly, however, Stella got a hold of herself, squinted, maybe regarding me in earnest for the first time, and quietly said, "Well, you don't dally around, you ask things right away. Yeah, I've come with them. Did they tell you? What's it matter to you?" Her voice shook, and she added, "How about you? Is it your first trip? A clueless novice?" But her defense was naïve and couldn't fool anyone.

I sat down next to her and took a cigarette from her pack. She moved closer and peered into my face. At once something brought us together, like accomplices who didn't know the content of the conspiracy but were ready to protect it from the others. The thread I had just been dreaming of turned out to be tense, like a violin string.

"No, I haven't heard anything about you," I said plainly, aware she knew I was on her side – a random stranger, a temporary ally who hadn't yet given her a reason to be disappointed.

"I've gone with them – I had no choice," she began, leaning forward and wrapping her arms around her knees. I watched her thin neck and long, locked fingers, the thin wrist and tanned forearms, painting in my mind a picture of everything concealed from my eye. My desire hadn't been aroused yet; however I felt its dormancy was not for long.

"My brother..." Stella cautiously sought the right words. "My brother owed those two money." She nodded at the Christophers. "And we didn't have any way of paying them. They offered to let us work off the debt, but he couldn't, so I had to."

"So you came here instead of him?" I asked in order to say something.

"No, no," she shook her head. "What do they need him for here? They wanted to involve him in their business as a decoy, but he tried it once and said – no, I can't take it anymore, do as you like with me, but I can't. So I replaced him, although I owe him nothing. He always takes advantage of me, for some reason or other!"

Stella's face became angry and withdrawn. She tore off a blade of grass and began to chew it intently. "He's not that bad in general," she added. "Not bad, just useless."

I remembered Gretchen and desperately wanted to pose an impossible question, but chased it away and asked instead about the Christophers and what they did to make her brother so scared.

"Cards," Stella dropped the word succinctly. "They needed my brother as bait." She sighed and, maybe to change the subject, started talking about her childhood: how she, her brother, and older sister had played in the forest on the family estate – and how they had to sell everything later and move into a cheap condo. Her mother quickly withered away, unable to endure the change, while her father married another woman, rough and quarrelsome, whom they drove crazy with their haughty hostility. Her sister wedded a young doctor, but the devilishly bad luck that kept following them showed up there as well. Soon the doctor ended up making a wrong diagnosis for a rich manufacturer, lost his license, and drank himself into oblivion. Her sister went abroad without any connections or money, and they fell out of touch.

"From the start, each of us was too good at imagining the future, so it was hard to admit later it wasn't coming true," said Stella with an unhappy smile. "We lived in what had not yet come and were surprised at the wretched present, which didn't befit us in the least. My brother and I couldn't even go to college – we had to earn money to live on. I managed to make more, while he got annoyed and angry. Then rich men began to appear, yet I was rude to them, and that period quickly passed. Now my lovers are poor and unsettled. I'm better than them and harder; I'm tougher than my brother, and I like that. I'm a thousand times stronger than my father, and I despise him. However I'm not even close to that girl who was in my future

– and I won't become her no matter what I do. I try not to think about it – it's quite possible to live with myself as I am now. I know how, I have my secrets. And I can love this self no less than that one – I just have to try a little harder."

Stella nibbled on the blade of grass and gazed absently into the distance, then broke out of her cataleptic fit, laughed, and playfully jabbed me in the shoulder. "Don't be distressed. It's not all that bad. This is my second-to-last trip here – one more, and that's it. I'll be free of them and probably of my brother too. I've figured it all out, I've already decided."

She gave me another sly look and didn't say any more, despite my prodding. Then, after a brief silence, she added, "You shouldn't know too much about me – wait a little, you'll understand why." And suddenly admitted with passion, "I hate the Dunes!"

Soon Gibbs signaled for us to rise, and in a couple minutes we were again hiking down the narrow trail, stretched out single file. The heat had abated, and it was easier to walk. An hour later, I noted the Christophers were sniffing the air – which had, in fact, changed. It now tasted of anticipation and anxiety, forcing me to forget about exhaustion. We climbed another unimposing hill, and at the top, the smell of salt and algae hit me in the face. My mind cleared – the indistinct roar I had been noticing for a while now turned into the rumble of surf. An endless expanse extended far and wide before our eyes: we had reached the ocean.

It breathed evenly, like an enormous animal, obeying its own rhythm and casting a spell as its surface oscillated in time to myriad dreams. The crashing waves, the deliberate commotion let you first guess at the imperious design and then confirmed it, leaving no room for doubt. It seemed every movement was subordinate to a general plan unknown to the uninitiated – and none of the weak-minded would get it anyway. You could brush it off and reject it vociferously, you could choose not to believe and struggle to deride it, but the essence wouldn't change: the design existed; only not everyone had been allotted a place in it.

It was ebb tide, and we walked on the wet sand by the foam of the receding waves. Initially, it was pleasant – easier than the trail through the Dunes – but soon we faced a headwind, flinging sand and spray into our eyes. A gently rising bluff of sand, licked by gray ripples, stretched as far as we could see, with no lighthouse, no pier, and no sign of human existence. I soon lost track of time. It seemed we had been wandering for hours, even days, but still just an instant of our lives had elapsed, a tiny insignificant part in comparison with the never-ending coast and the roar of the waves, hinting at an eternity of every kind.

The sun set into the Dunes and twilight approached quickly. We walked, hunched over, countering the wind we didn't dare get annoyed at. Everyone was tired, Silvia limped noticeably, Gibbs took almost everything she was carrying and strode in front, like the bulky flagman of a small retinue battered heftily by a storm. My thoughts were a muddle and didn't want to calm down. Heaps of stories got knotted up in my head and disappeared before I could catch the gist of them. Images from the past alternated with brief shots from the future that I didn't envisage, as opposed to Stella, who had such faith in what was destined for her. I looked at my fellow travelers and fantasized, feeling affection for every one of them.

Each was worthy of admiration, each was ready to be a hero and didn't expect praise or rewards. Yes, I thought, we gave a secret pledge, and our order doesn't tolerate defectors. We know our fate – even if it seems unattractive to some, our belief will let them believe too, and our courage will make their strength ten times greater. Cynics will take swipes at us and the laurel wreaths will go to others, yet we will laugh with the insight of insiders, we will retain our focus and think about the new hardships and new campaigns. Many will remember our figures in light-colored raincoats and hair whipping about in the wind, however no one can understand us from their comfortable lawn chair, never taking a step beyond the hedge separating the chosen from the rest. Our women will remain a mystery for them – returning again and again in disturbing memories, taking away their peace and sleep. And all the treasures of the world won't console those who couldn't gain access to our secrets. We don't pity them, those who couldn't gain access, but we understand them – and instantly forget, having ceased long ago to remember strangers whom we don't need in the least…

A flash of light blinded me and I returned to reality – Gibbs bathed our group in the beam of a powerful lamp, checking if everyone was there. One of the Christophers cursed and Gibbs shouted at him. It became totally dark. I had trouble discerning the sand below my feet, with only the undulating waves gleaming dimly in the starlight. "We're almost there," said Silvia, who appeared at my side and shivered in the chilly air.

Gibbs turned in the direction of the Dunes, lighting up the ground. For five minutes we trudged through loose sand, and then, out of the darkness, appeared the dim silhouettes of two shapeless buildings. The end of today's trip, I thought – and indeed it was. Christopher One slid two fingers into his mouth and whistled loudly, as if informing the invisible owners of our arrival. The second Christopher was going to do the same, but a terrible, gnashing sound came from nowhere, growing and intensifying, tearing the membranes and bearing down on the brain itself. I stopped in my tracks, stunned; the rattling in my head shook me, its crazy rhythm increasing in frequency. Then everything abated, just as abruptly, as if I had stuck cotton balls in my ears through which I could just indistinctly hear Gibbs' swearing and the quiet wheezes of one of the women.

CHAPTER 10

I only managed to see the outside of our new refuge in the morning. With puffy eyes and an aching body, I bumbled out of my room, fumbled with the rusty latch at the entrance, and then breathed in the moist air full of salt and seaweed. The ocean roared steadily a hundred yards away. I strolled toward it, shuffling my feet through the light gray sand mixed with fragments of shells, walked right up to the edge of the surf, and glanced back. Two houses stood behind me – one that had burned down, leaving a gloomy charcoal skeleton, and the second, built recently and freshly painted, stood glowing like a twin who had found better luck. Both of them were typical southern bungalows – long, one-story structures. Yet if the first one hinted at a dash of sophistication in its lines, the second appeared totally plain and crude, as if taking revenge for its own frailty, which you didn't have to go far to witness.

I was alone on the shore. The strip of sandy coast sloped evenly up from the water until it reached the dunes, overgrown with grass, that began almost right behind the charred carcass. Far off to the south, a large shoal shot boldly into the ocean, its contours shifting constantly, so every minute I wanted to ask myself whether I was just imagining it or not. I shook my head, avidly inhaled another lungful of ocean air, and ambled back.

The night before, after somehow collecting ourselves, we unpacked our gear and sat down to eat an ad-hoc dinner. Gibbs wasn't with us. After coming inside and seeing that everything was okay, he took a short-barreled carbine from the cupboard and vanished into the darkness. I glanced inquiringly at Christopher One, whose cheek twitched from time to time.

"Went to shoot the owl," he said crossly, searching for something in his pockets and not looking at us.

"Does he really want to kill it?" asked Stella incredulously.

"Or else he's going to destroy its nest. What's it matter to you?" He turned to her, and Stella gave him a guilty look and stopped talking.

"Forget it, calm down," grumbled Christopher Two in a conciliatory tone. "Everyone's uneasy, not just you. We're not in the city, after all. People are edgy here." And then he babbled away, not addressing anyone in particular: it – the owl – has no further choices. As soon as its nest is ruined, it'll fly onward to find another, prepared in advance. It won't build a new one here – it's clear this isn't a peaceful place... I listened to him, envisioning a large white owl, startled and horrified at its devastated perch, just as we were by the hooting that caught us off guard. It seemed to me I was about to understand the depressing logic of this world: no one's insured against surprises, so it's better to have your own ready – to stay one step ahead and not end up confused by unanticipated developments that pop up everywhere and could never be evaded. When you stumble upon them, you can't help but get trapped, yet you can tyrannize others with your own in revenge, as if playing the game of who will fall first. It's hard to say how you identify the winner, but one thing is clear: how pitiful they are – those who don't know how to trick the others!

We didn't talk much at dinner – everyone was tired and lost in their own thoughts. The women bustled about in the kitchen and brought us a skimpy meal, while the Christophers leaned back in their chairs as if they owned the place. No longer did they cover up their pistols – the black handles stuck out of the holsters hanging from their belts and gave them an intimidating look despite their good-natured, rural faces. Weapons always mean a lot – and I was proud to recall my Colt and my secret, feeling a burning wave on the back of my neck. In my mind I even momentarily towered over my fellow travelers, naïvely assuming they saw through me, not knowing and not wishing to know the false bottom, my menacing and scary plan. It's so easy to get deceived when you just look at the surface, I thought as I scrutinized myself from a different perspective, mentally narrowing my eyes down the length of the pointed barrel, tracking an unsuspecting Julian. Then I cut short my incessant bragging, remembering that others – including those sitting next to me – might also be full of tricks. You can't dismiss anyone – moreover, I'm now in their hands, and no one knows why they brought me here. So it's unclear who's in charge, I whispered inaudibly, chasing off excessive self-confidence and glaring at the Christophers. They chewed tranquilly and seemed to be incapable of any craftiness, yet I remained on the alert and promised myself one more time to stay watchful and not talk too much.

Silvia came to my room again that night. I didn't expect her, presuming she would have no interest in me after the exhausting hike, and I myself just wanted to sleep soundly till the following afternoon, but something rejoiced inside me when I felt her heavy body by my side. Silvia, though, was preoccupied and pensive, as if she didn't know where we were and why she was with me. After some quick sex, she asked for a cigarette and sat off on the edge of the bed, wrapped in the blanket, like a large bird with a somberly tilted head and messy hair. Far from each other, we smoked in silence until she began to talk monotonously about insignificant things – unveiling her domain, but not letting me over the unwelcoming threshold, just allowing me to gaze from a distance and not worrying about the pleasantness of the view.

It turned out she ran a small restaurant on the outskirts of town, along the main road, which I must have seen and ignored when I drove into M. The restaurant was always full, but the food was bad: they saved money on the chefs, and the patrons were just visitors. What's more, the staff stole – Silvia occasionally caught the especially brazen ones, but they did it anyway, time after time. That was common in this city, she said, as in other places too, at least in those she had been in. She needed a companion, she added, but where could she find a good one? She might have considered Stella, yet she'd only known her for a few days – and you could never be sure with these conceited girls who suddenly become impoverished…

I wanted her again, wanted to possess her body, forget myself in embraces and ardent ecstasy, but words erected a barrier, shifting us both from the liberating darkness to the dull realm of daily worries, and in anguish I thought I wouldn't get another chance to touch her that night. Finally, I became bored and interrupted her with a senseless question, and she stopped speaking and looked askance at me through the cigarette smoke. Time stood still, as if it were uncertain whether to go forward or backward, and it seemed we couldn't move without its command.

"Do you like me?" Silvia asked after finishing her cigarette, and I nodded yes.

"Why don't you say it? Are you frightened?" she inquired, and I couldn't think of an answer.

"Yeah, you're a shy one," she drawled derisively. "You're unable to rule, only able to request, although you probably view yourself differently…" She chuckled. "Admit it. Do you see yourself as a conqueror? Did you seduce me? And make dumb me incapable of resisting you?"

I wanted to reply honestly, but Silvia dismissed the subject carelessly. "Well, whatever. Let's not waste our breath. Don't you realize you can't compete with me? You don't need a woman, you need a friend, and I'm not suitable, to tell the truth."

"Friend?" I blurted out, yet Silvia just laughed. "What would you do with a woman?" she asked archly. "Please her with lovemaking? That's short-lived, and you're not capable of even approaching the rest. How would you shut her up when she starts quarreling? Where would you get the strength to grab her arms and throw her down on the mattress when she's hostile and doesn't want anything to do with you? Could you turn your back to her when she pesters you with questions and doesn't understand you don't want to talk?

No, you're not that kind of guy, you give in right away. You squirm and hesitate; you're unable to hold your ground like those men who women are attracted to, who they cling to... Am I right? Admit it."

I was annoyed and didn't speak. Silvia studied me, her eyes glittering in the darkness. "I offended you," she said absent-mindedly. "Though there's no reason to take offense. I'm older and wiser, I'm teaching you. You're just a boy for me – still wet behind the ears."

She tossed off the blanket, stood up from the bed, and walked across the room naked. In the darkness of the night, she was hardly visible – only a barely perceptible shimmer of light came from the window, making it difficult to see much. However, a silhouette was enough to stir my crude instincts again. I jumped up and rushed over to her, yet she slipped away evasively as I grabbed at a void.

"The bird's in a cage, yet the bird's gone. The trap is empty." I heard her laugh somewhere behind me. "Are we going to play games? Okay, come over here..." And she drew me over to the bed, threw herself on top of me, catching me unawares, assailing and forcing me to surrender. Later, while I was still recovering, she moved away, as if nothing had happened, fixed her hair and started smoking again.

"You want to know why else women aren't attracted to you?" she asked in a business-like tone.

"No," I shook my head. "What's it matter to me?"

"Good," agreed Silvia. "Actually, some of them should like you – those who are sick of the vulgar for the moment. One look behind the façade and it's clear: you're a softie, a gullible and innocent boy. Women can convince you of anything, fabricating a whole heap of lies. They can arouse your pity and then complain endlessly. They can tell absurd tales all night long, and you'll listen – no wonder it appeals to those who've had it up to here with the others. Friends... But don't delude yourself: they run off too – if your 'romance' doesn't end earlier by itself. A real woman lives in every woman friend; don't forget, you can't force back the juices that flow inside her. Even the most faithful abandon you occasionally, suddenly becoming lustful kittens pawing left and right. Are you aware of who they go off with? Beware of smilers. Your 'friends' race off with smiling scoundrels who have nothing but moustaches and a tiger's gait."

The darkness pulsated softly with a beat of black blood. In it gently fell sounds whose merciful outer layers had been peeled off. Silvia sat on the edge of the bed as if isolated by a fortress wall.

"Who are you angry and upset at?" I asked her. "Do you believe everyone's to blame? That's nothing new, but don't get me involved."

I was tired of her and wanted to go to sleep, yet I couldn't kick her out just like that. In some way, she's right about me and women, I thought, disgruntled.

"I'm not angry in the least," Silvia shrugged her shoulders. "No one's guilty – but it's not my fault that all the crap is readily apparent. And as for me, I'm no better than others. Who do you think I am?" She finished another cigarette and turned her shaded face to me. "Why am I throwing myself at you – out of passion, fatality, the desire for something new? It's not easy for you to conceive I have none of the usual desires now. Some do exist – I can't pretend otherwise – yet I don't recognize their nature."

Her tone changed; I felt a whiff of tiredness in it, which made my eyelids droop down. But Silvia wasn't going to leave. She flung the sheet over her shoulders, swathed herself in it, like a snail in its shell, and instantly appeared defenseless and frail, though I realized it was an illusion, deceiving to no end.

"Bear with me," she said. "I can't sleep now, let's talk some more. I had men who resembled you, and other kinds – ones who used me, like an object, like a toy. Those like you, I wanted to cheat on secretly; as for the others, I made it painful for them, didn't bother to tell lies, didn't conceal anything in the least. I hurled my affairs in their faces, and they went buck wild in their helplessness. Sometimes they beat me, debased me as much as they could, but I sensed my power, and they saw it, though not admitting it openly... I'm not angry, I simply don't know what to think. What power can I sense in myself with you? There's no name for it, one could spend hours tediously explaining it, and I have no patience – that's why I always preferred roughness. Both my husbands were real bullies, self-satisfied and blunt. I belonged to them and saw through them; I was happy like that – the defiant slave, the secret mistress. I'd still be living with the second one today if he hadn't gone overboard in every game – which really was too much. It's all his fault: he got to love whips and bridles, forgetting that I'm not a horse. I wouldn't accept it; there are limits. That's why I'm alone now – and I don't regret it, even if it's difficult, which, of course, you also know very well. Yes, you know it, and I know that you do – you just won't confess it."

She lit another cigarette, thrusting her hand through her thick raven hair, brutal and beautiful, pitiful in her revelations and free from sympathy for others. A tense silence hung in the air, as if alerted by the allusion to loneliness. I became uneasy and didn't want to go any further into jungles where I knew there were no allies. But I had to say something, so I tossed out, "What about Gibbs, then?" By which I didn't mean a thing, simply taking a wild guess.

Silvia turned around and looked at me closely, as if searching for a catch, then extended her arm and squeezed my shoulder painfully, digging in with her fingernails. "Don't talk about what you don't know," she said. "Gibbs is from a space you'll never reach. That's there, where there's passion, savage craving, and no timid caresses. It's just unfortunate that most men are such assholes."

For a while, we didn't speak. "If you want, I'll tell you, of course," Silvia said a minute later. "Gibbs is an explosion, a volcano, a tornado. Do you know his whole name? Well, no, I can't reveal it. Actually, he's like his name, everything you hear in it."

I got the feeling she was inviting me to hear secrets which she hadn't planned to divulge. "Why does everything revolve around him?" The thought pricked me, but I could have answered it myself, all the more so since any jealousy would look inept. Nonetheless, I slid my hand over her smooth thigh, hastening to convince myself she was still there, but I didn't receive any response and rolled over to the wall, though the narrow bed didn't let me move far.

"Gibbs seduced me when I was a girl and he was still underage himself," said Silvia in the way you retell a story everyone knows.

"He took me with him everywhere; we went to the Dunes quite often and had sex on the beach. At first, he forced and defiled me, but then it was me who taught him what to do. Women always know better, and I was insolent and insatiable back then. He was almost stunned: I never got enough and wore him out… Afterward, I had many men – and then I found out there were more capable ones. Yet it was still a volcano because he was my first love, and you live a whole life in it. Later, there are only the remains of what you didn't fritter away back then. With him, I was in seventh heaven; though most of the time he just tolerated me – tolerated and used me a lot. I was the only really useful one; the others merely pestered and clung to him like unneeded baggage. Once he hid in the Dunes for a whole month, and lots of people went in search of him. I brought him food and nobody saw hide nor hair of me. He grew up quickly then – snuggled up to me when I came, yet spoke less and chased me off in the evening. I always wanted to stay with him, but he rejected me, saying, 'Go, that's enough.' And I couldn't argue, I'd wander back all out of sorts and knew whatever he said, I'd do it."

Silvia looked around and again reached for her pack of cigarettes. "You smoke a lot," I observed. She waved her hand, "It's just here. I don't smoke much in the city. The Dunes are oppressive – I'm ill at ease, as are the others. Except you-know-who, but he wouldn't admit it anyway."

"Well, what happened? Did they catch him?" I asked, returning her to the story about Gibbs.

"Eventually they found him, of course," she nodded. "Then they let him go, though he had to endure a great deal. That was when he began to become colder to me. I felt it immediately: he realized I too wouldn't bring him good luck, even if I tried as hard as I could. And I really tried – and never again I've made such an effort."

Silvia smiled with a touch of sadness, then jiggled my knee playfully and began to romp about like a pert schoolgirl. "Have I tired you out?" she asked sympathetically. "Be patient, be patient," and without waiting for my response, she kept right on going.

"Finally, I got too old for him – I turned twenty-three or so – and he ditched me for good. He didn't say much, just shouted at me and vanished. There was nothing to be done; my first life came to an end, and others began. Gibbs left the city and I didn't care what I did, so I got married for the first time and learned a lot about men, much more than when I was with him. I even gloated sometimes, but there was no point to it: he was gone and didn't witness it, so it was worthless. Occasionally rumors drifted my way, yet I couldn't bring back the past, so it didn't matter. Only when *that* occurred," – Silvia passed her hand over her face – "did I feel I should see him, that the time had come again, even if it was against my will. I was already with my second husband, tolerating all sorts of crap, having no idea how to escape – and then one day I just picked up and went to Gibbs, although I was terribly scared. Everyone steered clear of him then, but I showed up on my own. He was probably happy, even if he didn't look it. At least, he didn't shoot at me or banish me like before. I told him everything – about myself, about my husband – and Gibbs promised to speak with him, which he apparently did, since my second soon raced home in the middle of the day, grabbed some things without glancing at me, and disappeared forever. Admittedly, I was somewhat at a loss, but then thought it was just something between men. Let them work it out, I decided – and afterward Gibbs and I began to see each other again."

"What do you mean by 'see each other' – as lovers? Or did you just meet up?" I asked, confused.

Silvia didn't understand the question. "What do you mean by what do you mean? We saw each other, for lunch sometimes, or sometimes like lovers, what's the difference? Of course, he took possession of me again, but now he didn't waste me as he had in the past. He needed me less than in those days, and I no longer resembled a lucky star. The older we got, the calmer we became, anyway…"

She shifted her position and sat up, putting her legs on the floor and propping one elbow on her knee. "He had different women, and I slept around, but that doesn't mean much – I can laugh at other men, and none of them understand what they really *want* from me.

Gibbs is the one who always knows this. *That's* why I'll be with him forever."

"So, why are you in my bed now?" I asked sullenly. "Go and love him!"

Silvia dismissed me casually, "Don't be so stupid. I haven't been in love with him for years. He doesn't do anything for me, he just takes. Our love ended back then, when I was twenty-three... And you, don't you delude yourself either," she tossed her head. "I'm not here 'cause there aren't better guys. It's no big deal – I just wanted to find out what you're like without clothes on, and to hear how much you desire me. But you haven't even said anything nice."

"Well, what could I say?" I wondered to myself.

"So, do you like me after all? Are you satisfied with me?" she asked suddenly, a searching tinge in her voice.

I didn't know how to respond and gave her an affirmative uh-huh. Again Silvia burst out laughing and then goofed around with me carelessly, pressing her soft breasts against my body.

"I know you want Stella now," she whispered, her lips tickling me. "First it was me, now it's her – you're all like that. But I won't be jealous, I never am. It'll work out with Stella, too – don't worry!" And she slipped out of my arms and began to get dressed, rustling in the darkness.

"Will you come again?" I asked, yet she didn't say a word, as if she had forgotten me altogether, and merely gave me a fleeting kiss before she left.

In the morning I saw that only three of us remained – Gibbs and the Christophers had gone off somewhere. The women served me a hearty breakfast and headed back to their chambers after informing me everyone would soon return and the real business would begin. For the meantime, I had nothing to do and was bored. Moreover, the weather had changed: a misty rain fell outside the window and the day was unwelcoming and gloomy. I floundered about in my room for a while and then went to roam through the house without any particular goal.

It had just one story but was quite large, with a separate wing for the kitchen and dining room, numerous bedrooms along two symmetrical corridors, a lounge with a stone floor where a muffled echo came from all the sounds that had accidentally ended up there. Beginning at the lounge, the corridors culminated near some storage rooms and a creaky, yet strong staircase headed to the attic. After climbing up, however, I encountered nothing but dusty boards and laces of cobwebs that must not have been disturbed for months. Then, in one of the corners, I discovered a yellowing packet of newspapers tied together with twine – old editions of the local *Chronicler*, which covered public events and gossip. I started to untie one after another, fleetingly scanning the content and getting gradually carried away to distant lives outlined by reporters' pens.

It was quite captivating, and I sat there for hours, mulling over characters, hardships, and worries from someone else's past. The dated *Chroniclers* offered enough to fuel my imagination on almost every page: a girl who had lost her puppy and stole another from her happier neighbor; a fugitive swindler who spent a week in a pigeon house; or a conventional, humble clerk who ended up in an unexpected adventure. I only had to let my fantasies run wild, following the impassive phrases, digging out the tasty bits that would be good to scrutinize a little more closely.

Here, before my eyes, is Mr. P., a middle-aged bank teller. He has an unattractive wife, a modest salary, and ordinary interests: betting on horses, bridge on Tuesdays with cigars and port wine, chats about politics, and furtive glances at the cute secretaries without hope of something real. P. is shy and indecisive; he values his orderly life too much, and, moreover, he'd hardly be able to treat the girls right, anyway. He is younger than all his bridge partners, just as all the secretaries are younger than his ugly spouse. P. is forty-something; he's caught up in the middle of his life and doesn't notice how time is flying by. He'll think about it later, when he's bald and wrinkled, with a shortage of breath and creaky joints. At the moment he's still satisfied with himself and knows that everything is happening just as it should. To be sure, he just has to look around and doubt vanishes, zapped away by countless examples.

The image shifts – P. is on vacation at the ocean. The usual attributes shimmer rapidly by: yellow sand on the beach, a nice group of old friends, a pool in a local club, splashes in the warm waves. And suddenly there's something odd – a triangular black fin appears out of nowhere; P. is the last of the bathers to notice it as he takes a final dip before lunch. The movie slows – every detail is important now. A woman screams hysterically, triggering a general panic; the unlucky swimmers hurry to the shore; P. is the only one who doesn't get it – looking around in confusion with his feet just touching the sandy bottom. Someone probably drowned, flashes through his head. How terrible! Instantly, another thought comes to mind: thank goodness that wasn't him; he was right not to have swum out too far. And a second later – sudden fear, a triangular fin flickers a few feet from his face. What was that? He had read about it somewhere… He still refuses to believe, yet he knows, already knows it's a shark. Completely incredible – how could this have happened to him, such a regular, normal guy? He glances about spasmodically – no one's around, they've all swum off, gotten out, cowardly jerks. He hates them all. The beach and the cries are thirty yards away – like another world he can't reach. He's alone in this one, totally alone.

A wave splashes him in the face, his heart skips a beat, he coughs and spits, making an effort to inhale. Then something heavy and rough like a grater grazes his thigh, and he shrieks in terror with what's left of his breath, silencing the people on the beach, as if informing them the ending is near. And really, the black fin is already circling quite close. The water foams, and then – pain, jaws, complete darkness, a weak subsiding ring in his ears, someone's voice calling, falling, losing the thread…

Then he hears voices again, a bright light shines into his face, consciousness returning in a flash. P. is in the hospital, a local celebrity, a lucky guy, a rarity. Everyone wants to approach, touch, exchange a few words. They say he got off with nothing but a shock and a couple scratches. The shark hardly chewed at all, spit him out and swam off, and the rescuers arrived just in time, so he didn't choke. P. is a hot item – a television station even shows interest, though he's only an extra. The lead role goes to a fish specialist in wrinkled clothes with a crushed face who offers an in-depth analysis of the habits and behavior of aquatic predators. They by no means use their jaws just to eat their prey, he claims. Much more frequently, they collect all sorts of junk in their mouths for the purpose of gaining knowledge. Like children, the specialist insists, just like children, – and P. is offended, having viewed his role quite differently.

The day comes to return to his native city. Initially, they also make a fuss about him there, ask him all sorts of questions. For the first time in his life, P. is important and talkative. He willingly offers the figures he heard from the specialist with the crushed face, informing everyone, for instance, about the number of shark attacks on people in recent years (459) and how many of them ended fatally (only 65). He shares the feeling of having a shark's jaws close down on you and even tries some awkward jokes, but his listeners hear it all grudgingly, just gazing at this child of destiny who fortune has patted on the back. And once they have indulged their interest, they take off. Soon, P. becomes superfluous again. Only a skinny girl from the office next door rests her eyes on him whenever they collide in the corridor, yet he never finds the courage to strike up a conversation with her…

An informative story, I thought with a grin. The goofball is worth envying – and I went back to thinking about the terror of a sudden attack and the befuddling joy of resurrection afterwards, when you love everyone and are ready to forgive them all. And I wondered: would I forgive Julian, ever?

I smoked and blew rings that rose to the ceiling, coiling in hieroglyphics. They didn't offer any advice or opinion. After watching them for a while, I laughed at myself and returned to the old newspapers. This time, I didn't stumble upon much worthwhile material. The *Chronicler* had nothing but drivel – it seemed hopeless and I got upset, turning page after page. Yet finally I hit upon something useful – a short paragraph with a comical interwoven skein which my trained eye couldn't help but seize hold of.

The humming projector of my fantasies rolled on: Ms. LL is about twenty-five, I envisioned confidently. She's modest and efficient, myopic and somewhat corpulent. She knows she needs to go on a diet – and she's terribly unsure of herself in the company of men. Her last lover's ardor cooled quickly, which adds bitterness to her nighttime thoughts, and a new one is not on the horizon, so she's got a reason to be depressed. At work she's attentive and serious – they value her, recognizing rare dedication. There is certainly the envy of her co-workers as well: "Those are the ones that become spinsters," they whisper behind her back, yet she is oblivious to their caustic looks. Her thoughts are focused on greater things, even if they're still unclear. Some of them she has already achieved: her own apartment, a real refuge she can be proud of, as well as the new hatchback that was difficult to afford. They give her a sense of stability, visibly demonstrating she's doing well, especially if you forget about trifles.

The gray November day begins as always – coffee, toast and jam, quick sprucing up in the foyer. The morning routine is interrupted by a phone call: her old aunt wants to share a worrisome, unprecedented dream, but LL has no time for this. She's hardly listening, then excuses herself and breaks off the detailed monologue. Her aunt is offended, but there's nothing to be done. LL hangs up the receiver and bounds down the staircase – however, a surprise is awaiting her at the entryway. The parking place is empty; her glittering dark-blue Peugeot, the joy of her life, her favorite toy, has vanished without a trace, like her last lover. She darts from one building to the next in search of her lost car, hoping she just forgot where she parked the night before. But the further she goes, the more distinctly she senses that a true disaster has occurred. Soon, she's in despair. She calls a friend, calls the police, and, not knowing what else to do, she simply sits down on the stoop and covers her face in her hands, expecting someone to appear. A fat, dumb policeman arrives. A spark of momentary hope flames out in an instant. She begins sobbing in the middle of the conversation, so the officer mills about in embarrassment, adjusts the club on his belt unnecessarily, and takes off at the first chance.

A few days pass. The pain recedes, but she feels as if some tightly wound spring inside her has snapped, and her whole body has become loose and inert. LL doesn't want to see anyone, is irritated by pointless talk. Everything around her, in unison with the November weather, seems depressing, damp, grayish brown. The trolley bus attempts to spray her with dirt; unwelcoming faces drive her anguish deeper; life seems to be completely wretched. Nothing brings good news – but one evening, her gaze falls on an advertisement pinned to the building door. A certified magician helps with general everyday problems, like ailments or evil eyes, broken hearts or insomnia, and, among other services, offers to search for long-lost things and recovery of stolen objects. LL doesn't believe it, vacillates, struggles with doubt, but ultimately can't resist and makes the call. A low, smooth male voice promises assistance, inspiring incomprehensible confidence, and she surprises herself by quickly getting ready and going to the address.

The door is opened by a handsome man with black hair. They chat for a long time; he holds her hand in his strong, warm fingers. The meeting isn't cheap, but she's prepared to pay – she really wants her car to be found, and, also, their talk has aroused something in her heart. On the way home she feels she's rapidly losing her mind. The next day the magician calls and makes a second appointment. She can't sleep at night, dreams of him being with her, in her apartment, in her bed.

Not herself, she goes to see him again, gazes at his face with a defeated look, but now the man is cold and professional. He studies her thoughtfully for a minute, then takes her money – more than the first time – and hands over a paper with a hand-drawn map, where a careless cross marks the spot of her lost car. Tears rise to LL's eyes, she wants to explain, justify herself, but no words spring to mind, and he waits in silence for her to leave without offering any more help. She departs obediently. The car turns out to be exactly where he said it was, yet there's no joy – the gorgeous sorcerer has bound her by some mysterious spell, and she needs to see him, to look into his eyes, hear his voice. After three days of agony, she goes back to the familiar address, ready to debase herself, yet she finds nothing but a sealed door and two intimidating men who carry her off and interrogate her as a victim. The detectives explain they have been monitoring a gang of imposters who made a living stealing cars and exacting money to retrieve them. Soon they'll all be caught, don't worry, they say. However, LL is in deep distress and doesn't want to hear anything. Afterward, at home, she sits and stares at the wall, recalling her seducer with his smooth baritone and repeating to herself, "Life is a lie, one big lie!"

Of course, everything could be different. Examining something at a distance, it's easy to mess up the details. I stretched and straightened my back, put the pack of newspapers aside and picked up the next one. The day was winding down, but I didn't want to switch on the lights, as if my actions involved a shameful sin that had to be hidden. Sifting through the sheets distractedly, I hit upon another funny article, but all my fantasies faded when I turned the page. In the middle of the magazine lay an odd leaflet, quite old, judging by its yellowness. It was not the *Chronicler*, but something foreign, written in a language I didn't know. However, this was not what made my blood run cold – right in the middle was a large photograph of Piolin. I recognized him immediately, although he was much younger than now. Piolin was not looking in the camera, but off to the side, glaring and frowning spitefully. There could be no doubt he was being sought for something, yet I didn't understand a word, and, to tell the truth, I didn't really want to.

Suddenly, the *Chronicler* started to look utterly boring. I slowly straightened out my legs, which were numb from sitting so long, and headed to the dining room to see if the weather had improved.

CHAPTER 11

Outside the window was nothing but the same mist, wind, and cold. Nature seemed to have settled into a state of troubled anguish it was unable to wake up from. The whole autumn might go on like this, I thought, sitting down at the table and drawing senseless figures with my finger. The months would fly by and nothing would change – not the sand, not the weather, not the overcast sky.

My eyes glazed over and my finger came to a standstill. I felt like I could doze off right there in the chair, abandoned by everyone – nod off and sleep until spring. At that moment, however, I heard male voices outside, jumped toward the window, and peered through the glass. It was the Christophers – they stood nearby, two hundred yards from the house, lazily bickering with each other. In their hands they held shovels; on the sand lay a large pole and some ropes, though they were difficult to make out from afar. One of them walked off a little and put his hands on his hips; the other started to dig, raising a sandstorm and shouting raucously.

I raced to my bedroom, grabbed my raincoat, and ran over to them. Christopher One – who was dawdling a few yards away – whistled when he saw me, and the second Christopher stopped working and stared in my direction with a surprised grimace. For a few seconds, no one spoke. Then the first drawled, "Look, the tourist is paying us a visit. What? Did you come to help?"

"Uh-huh," I nodded, casting a crooked glance and suspecting a trick. "If you want it, of course."

"Yeah," Christopher One exclaimed, "help is exactly what we need. You can see how hard our friend here is working!" He pulled out a pack of cigarettes, smelled it, and again adopted his Superman pose, smugly asking, "What can you do, for example?"

"Almost anything," I replied cautiously. "I can help him dig if that's needed."

"Di-ig," he sneered. "Digging is good!" And he tossed the shovel so that it landed upright in the sand a yard from me. "There it is. Show us what you can do. Do you know how to hold it?"

I grasped the handle with two hands and looked around, the shovel angled downwards. Christopher Two spit at his feet and started giggling foolishly. "Where should I begin?" I asked. Their behavior irritated me immensely, and I already regretted offering them my assistance. "Where's the pole going to be? And what will it be for – something like a flag?"

"Yeah, a flag – you got it right," grinned Christopher One. "You're the smart aleck here. And where should you shovel? Come on, I'll show you."

He led me thirty paces to the right, stood, gazed around, walked off a little farther, and ground his heel into the sand. "Begin here. When you get tired, we'll switch up. I'll personally take over!" He pounded his chest with his fist, winked at me, repeated, "You're the smart aleck," and retreated to his former place, where Christopher Two had already resumed working, still screaming and flinging sand behind his back.

I sized it up, gripped the shovel and drove it in, time and again, without lifting my head – first slowly and tensely, then methodically and swiftly when I got into a rhythm. Soon, however, my back began to ache and blisters appeared on my hands, but I didn't give in, gritting my teeth and dismissing the sharp pain. After half an hour I had dug no small hole and took a breather, looking at the Christophers and wiping the sweat from my forehead.

Grunting and cursing, they were setting up the pole, which

had a tin can shining dully at the top of it. I thought a minute and went over to them, intending to help, but as soon as I approached, I heard the offensive, "Get out of here, tourist. You'll hurt yourself." This ticked me off again and I remained standing a few feet away, watching the process with cold dignity. Finally they erected the pole and Christopher One asked me sarcastically, "Well, you think you've done enough? Want a smoke break?"

"I was just going to ask how deep I should dig," I said crossly.

He changed his tone, "Well, that's another matter, you're right. Go back, climb in, and we'll measure."

I thought they were joking, but both of them looked completely serious, so I had no option but to actually scramble down into the pit, which caused a fairly large amount of sand to cascade to the bottom of it. "That's not much!" shouted Christopher One. "Keep digging. Up to here," he pointed to his chest, "and wider, wider!"

Glumly I nodded and picked up the shovel. My hands were burning, my back hurt; the work went much more slowly. I tortured myself for another half hour, expanding the shaft a good deal and descending to almost my waist, then I climbed out and sat on my folded-up raincoat – exhausted. The Christophers by now had thrown sand on the pole, strengthened it with supports, pounded in special stakes to hold it in place and were very satisfied, as they headed in my direction.

"Resting?" Christopher Two asked in a stentorian voice. "Taking it easy? Listen, those who don't work don't eat!" They laughed and Christopher One added something else – sardonic and nasty.

"I'll continue in a moment," I muttered with a sigh, but my partners turned to the ocean and slowly walked away, babbling about their own concerns. The other shovel lay idly by the pole, and right then a terrible suspicion crept up on me. "Hey!" I screamed. "What do you need this second pit for anyway? Are you going to bring something here or what?"

The Christophers stopped and looked back with serious, even severe expressions. "Keep digging," the first began. "We need a pit like we need air." But Christopher Two couldn't hold it anymore and doubled over, choking through his laughter, "Like the ocean air, for lunatics!" And the first one shrieked mirthfully through his sniveling and rasping.

"We'll bring something in a sec," cried Christopher Two. "We'll drag it over and slide it in if it fits. Come on, tourist, climb in, let's measure again," and they hooted and hollered, slapping each other on the back.

"At least you've warmed up – that's good anyway," said the first Christopher, wiping away tears. "As for the pit, it's a useful thing and will always come in handy." He briefly snickered one last time and they traipsed off while I just stared at them before chucking down the shovel and shuffling home.

I wasn't particularly angry; my senses had become numb. I wandered down the empty corridors till dusk – not switching on the light, sometimes only finding the path by groping, banging into ledges and doorframes, and cursing in undertones to avoid disturbing the sleeping things. Familiar voices spoke familiar words – I readily agreed and drove them off, but they didn't leave me that easily, reveling in their own righteousness.

When the night closed in, my thoughts became more troubled. The gray contours I peered at outside the windows slipped out of focus, faded, like an obscure script invisible to idle eyes. I recalled the photo of Piolin that had come into my hands at just the wrong time, and this increased my agitation – either like a subtle threat or simply an allusion to another life that surrounded me and would keep me out no matter how much I tried to find my way in. It seemed too hard to comprehend; its fabric intertwined with too many other people's fate, and I couldn't hope to hit upon the right point.

Finally, after spending a few pointless hours, I found myself in the kitchen and discovered dinner was already over. This didn't disturb me however – I still wasn't interested in seeing anyone. I tossed some ham and moldy cheese in my mouth, drank it all down with cold water, and retreated to my bedroom feeling lost and lonely.

I wasn't tired but got undressed, took a quick shower, and lay down, thinking Silvia might sneak over like yesterday. It would've been good timing, but no one appeared as I waited. I considered knocking at her door, yet something held me back – probably her cold indifference when she left last night.

The minutes turned to hours and didn't want to speed up, tangling my consciousness in their tenacious tentacles. Instead of soft and warm Silvia, I saw ethereal silhouettes settling down at ease in the darkness. My thoughts thrashed about in a restless rush; it seemed I would never fall asleep and the morning would never come. Finally, I did doze off, though only to wake up, startled by an unpleasant dream, which I instantly forgot except for the painful impression it left behind. Not wanting to repeat this, I began to think about Gretchen and Vera and then various other women I combined into one – a nonexistent, yet potentially real person who was probably waiting somewhere with increasing doubt about getting even a short message from me.

With her, I now conversed, whining and whimpering, boasting and promising. There was nothing carnal in it – I just wanted warmth and was ready to give it back. Words sought new depth, and lines composed themselves, rhymes linking them, as if helping each another emerge from a cocoon. Some were born freely and quickly found their place while others wiggled through warily, trying and losing faith.

> *Mesmerized again I stand*
> *drowning in acutest longing*
> *under spells of magic words*
> *like centuries ago I'd been…*

I was saying to my distant stranger, calling her quietly, testing my voice and suspecting I had heard this rhythm somewhere else, yet not worrying about that in the least. I caressed the quatrain with my tongue, then peeked ahead, at a new strophe:

> *startled by a hasty lure*
> *or by an elusive shadow…*

and suddenly my enthusiasm waned, for I had a hunch that the next rhyme would be dull, and I returned to the opening four lines without any desire to continue. The main thing was already clear, although the stranger I was addressing might miss the point anyway. That was a pity, of course, but nothing new.

The last thought upset me. I rolled over and sighed, then sat up in bed, shoving the pillow behind my back. You never know whether you should hope for sympathy. Everyone has their own sorrows and it's senseless to guess what will touch the right chord.

My eyelids lowered; in a quick dream I saw the Christophers with shovels in their hands, laughing at me as I fell for the cheap bait. Then I woke up again and stared out the dark window, chasing off the distasteful and glimpsing a different life. The "elusive shadow" took shape: I heard the swish of clothing that covered graceful figures, guessed the movements, the deep-rooted secret of the dance, impregnable elegance and eternal Eros. How should I put it? Who should I reveal it to? And what if no one listens?

With surprise, I noticed that my lyrical outburst had not dried up at all. It was alive within me, had taken hold firmly. Plenty of words came to mind, although they didn't always flow together as they should, and the lines became melancholic while the meter changed, with additional syllables allowing for an extra breath.

> In the distance ill forebodes
> a gloomy truth portends.
> Tempests rise to drive all sounds
> into the wayside dust.

> Their foliage stripped, the willows bare
> from breezes gusting until dawn
> that stray along the lanes and fare
> on city streets and windswept lawns...

I was telling the very same stranger who stood before my eyes with a serious, half-turned face – sympathizing, reproaching, recalling, or not remembering at all. That's from the remains of the past – the old one, without a doubt. I have no link to them, but my imagination chases them restlessly and doesn't want to stop. And stanzas stack up without any exertion, as if someone were reading from a book:

> *Pungent odors overwhelming*
> *with a sense of coming hardship.*
> *Weeds and brambles groping, trawling*
> *overgrow and hide the gardens.*

> *Like a weather-beaten canvas*
> *the scenery offends the eye.*
> *We are uninvited guests*
> *this feast is meant to be for others.*

And further:

> *The hard expanse, unkind and cold*
> *and here the joyless dawn*
> *without clemency nor pity*
> *send to us their blessing.*

> *We assemble at the quay*
> *on the silent river*
> *glumly wave to us goodbye*
> *someone else's women.*

> *Flowing endlessly away*
> *casting off from shore*
> *having found no refuge*
> *ships sail into twilight.*

> *Heavy heart confounds its beat*
> *taking my breath away:*
> *someone's youth will soon be over*
> *not another's – but mine.*

The last lines were clumsy and imbalanced, yet I liked them anyway. I stood up and paced about the room, yet it was too cold and I jumped back under the covers, feeling my pounding heart. Yes, the rhymes arouse me more than ardent flesh; they so overwhelm me I beg for a break sometimes, though if you think about it soberly, there's no logic to them – at least, for me. Moreover, you can't really impose much on grateful humanity – we know, yes we do, it turns up its nose. So it seems there's no reason to try and suffer, yet you don't disengage when you get in the mood – you tremble in anticipation, straining your internal ear…

I rolled over on my stomach and covered my head with the pillow. Yes, the internal ear cannot be fooled easily. I can't order it about, even if I want variety in what I hear. Where does the bright side of things hide in general? Not in wonderland, where my ambassadors, the heirs of ruins, are stalking. But maybe it's worth trying anyway.

I flipped from one side to the other and tried to get into an optimistic frame of mind. Even half-lines surged up instantly: "… why castigate myself?" – the little hammers tapped out, and I rushed back to the quest but ran up against a wall. The question mark at the end was probably at fault – I could never deal with them properly. One way or the other, I had to answer the question, and I couldn't find a response circling around the cheerful surface, so my consciousness began to grope about, seizing neighboring territory. Suddenly a subtle rhyme emerged and didn't want to give up its spot. Then the entire line unfolded, confirming something that was not cheery in the least. I looked back, to the very beginning, timidly agreeing with the banal generalization, and finally filled in the lifeless area between these two with some homely, polysyllabic material. Then I examined the whole quatrain, and the next, not expecting anything good:

We all will pay, why castigate myself
for warm compassion and neglect
that from affinity had sprung
and killed it halfway through.

We all will pay, I'm ready for that too
derisive nature gives a bitter verdict
the wasted years will rustle quickly by
like stubs of bills we rashly settled.

Nothing good turned out. To me, it didn't even resemble a poem, sounding far too somber and rolling awkwardly off my tongue. Yet if there are words that are born by themselves and fuse together, the result must mean something! Could it have possibly struck a response in someone? Where are you, my long-suffering judges? My optimism ebbs so easily – is even a trace of it apparent? Can I embolden someone, or is it all hopeless – is it destined for oblivion, for the trashcan?

Continuing did not make sense, only falling asleep did. Yet, I couldn't drift off. As if out of obstinacy, my imagination fuelled me with even more thoughts. I began to envision places where I had never been but would swear I recognize anyway. An old stone house – probably a lord's mansion; a large, deserted garden – hardly discernible in the late dusk; dim beams of light from the window; the muffled call of an eagle owl; the rustling and sobbing of invisible secrets… A different fate tantalized me from afar, only flickering in scattered patches, in flashes of events erased from my memory. How very difficult it is to fight my way through to them now, buried under prosaic normalcy; how unfortunate that many disappeared forever – not getting a chance to emerge – or emerged not here, not with me, as they found my double in their time – maybe the same one that I'm longing for, as my solitude asphyxiates me. But I can see with my own eyes and recognize the details – the forms and smells and diffuse light. My own rhymes abound in my head – this all did happen at some time, even if with another me, and I just have to recall him, that "other" who wrote:

…The wine imbibed, he goes outside.
An owl cries in the distance.
Plants grotesque cast mangled shadows
that sport at fairy-tale charades

and here epistles are composed
uniting words, whose many shades
had served him well his whole life long
to cure the gloom of nighttime madness

and using it to shape the fruits
which, to the shame of pain endured
depart indifferent, uninvolved
to leave no gladness in their wake…

And continuing:

Mist takes the garden in its shrouds.
The owl scornfully and haughty
blasphemes the night with senseless cries
not troubling itself with meanings.

The trees concealed by foggy haze
while under foot their shadows cast
as though they would deny the fraud
in which they have been justly caught…

or something like that. He wasn't bad – that other one – probably
better than me, more confident, stronger. The person I am today
might be able to like his poem, although not down to the last line…
And my imagination went on painting: the bottom of a garden –
leading to the lake; the view from the window – a hazy surface;
and also a creaking corridor, the shabby wing of a house where the
owner no longer resided. A few lives were lived there, including
mine and my double – or all my doubles, if there wasn't just one.
It's not hard to detect the essence: seclusion is the name for it, and
it shouldn't be confused with solitude. You run from solitude and
search for seclusion. You nurture and rear it, turn it into steadfast
customs, which neither women nor mortal fear are able to alter.
In seclusion you ponder your thoughts – make headway, move
forward, dig deeper, while constantly acknowledging the weakness

of ideas, the perfidy of words. But you can't escape your tenacious fate, as you can't sidestep onerous habits. You fight to flee and get a break, but an invisible force draws you back to the old house, where you can take your pick – a cabinet wainscoted with smoked oak, the lake shore, a dewy meadow or the very same garden where you can meet the shadows from the past, your voluntary inmates, sharing the cumbersome comfort of imprisonment, which, you know, is forever. You can scribble down thousands of pages and not get close to freedom; you can come up with an ocean of music, with the whole world of colors and paints – and still not alleviate the pain from the chains. There's no one to sympathize – those who are with you know the severity of the oath and don't even notice anyone's complaints. You and they don't have matters to discuss – everything was clarified long ago. Their faces just flicker occasionally in the aperture of the windows; their silhouettes can be sensed on the unlit porches, and here is one of them: a female figure, walking off down the alley – that's her, the stranger!

I understood I had to call her up, otherwise I wouldn't get any sleep and my mind would never be at peace. I must have her listen to me – she would glance over her shoulder, scrutinize me in the dim hope of detecting something she needed. Decisiveness came from nowhere. I took up the lines seriously, reworking them, shuffling, shifting, removing superfluous words – until it was no longer embarrassing to hear them tinkling in my ear. But I couldn't elude myself, at least that particular night, and the very first octave set the usual despondent tone:

> Beyond the oaken desk there lies
> black darkness your reproach to hide.
> Now scarce would you expect of me
> that I should with this paltry note
> enjoin such hardship to myself.
> So look, behold the slumb'ring lake,
> a spacious room with me inside.
> Absolute desolation. Not a single soul.

I didn't give up, however, and made attempt after attempt, peeking in from the other side, trying different approaches – some sinuous and long, some with good prospects, and still others that were deceptive from the start. The result was mixed:

> *A pair of open eyeballs, double-barrels.*
> *A mirror as unassailable as armor.*
> *Now scarce would you expect of me*
> *what you yourself once schemed in haste...*

and then, somewhere in the second strophe:

> *Trigger's pulled, the creature's leg is maim'd,*
> *with round deflected from the very armor.*
> *If a chimera comes close, believe it not;*
> *should it persist, just try to drive it hence...*

at which point a lump welled up in my larynx and I rushed to wrestle with it, submitting to the intractable poem, which had quickly taken shape up to the last assertion, to the indisputable finale:

> *I can admit you're right in all likelihood:*
> *what's behind masks, it's only deceit and lies.*
> *And my story here is nothing new –*
> *nothing but musings of a writing fool.*
> *Rapacious void dominates the scene.*
> *A feeble lamp. A table gashed and grazed.*
> *Do you want me to draw a circle freehand?*
> *That is my story. Reiteration. Loop.*
>
> *Do you recall the large room past the door?*
> *The ancient armchair, the off-cast keys?*
> *If a chimera comes close, believe it not;*
> *should it persist, just scream at the top of your lungs.*

Dim is the night, the curtains all painted black.
The desk and the paper. Utterly helpless words.
Do you perceive the dead man here beside you?
That would be me, someone you should meet at last.

Morning. A tranquil lake, some birch trees,
and light fog, which is rather the mist of decay.
The nauseating room – a dusty sign
of life repeated, life redone. Refrain.
Just a thoughtless whistle nurtured by my lips.
My view is plastered on the walls and proud of it.
There is nothing to grasp hold of, just paper and desk.
Absolute desolation. The nature morte.

Yes, it's really *the* still life, I thought wearily. *Adhuk vitam. Naturaleza muerta.* But in the lines, there is existential energy, even if they speak about death… I repeated the parts I liked, only wincing at the repulsive passage about the dead man. My heart stopped at a few of the combinations, and a proud shiver ran down my spine. I knew no stranger would remain indifferent – even if only for a moment, an instant – should she get the opportunity to actually hear me. Immediately I wanted more: to work on the poem seriously – a couple days, a week – to remove everything that wasn't perfect, make it simple and clean. Yes, I'm capable of a small masterpiece, I convinced myself in a near delirium. And my fantasies left the images from the past and took up the fictitious future: hours and hours at a desk, hordes of words, like enormous blocks of salt, and the thin chisel of an automatic pen, always beginning timidly, but then – thunder and smoke, dashed-off parts and a fine-tuned profile at the end. A new poem on thin paper hot off the printer – what can bring more pleasure, what can do more to set you on fire, inspire, motivate?

Yet afterward – afterward comes what alienates you and makes you discouraged. I wasn't afraid of a staggering effort, I could let my eyelids tremble and my eyes tear up, but my whole being rejected its lack of sense, opposed the uselessness, evident at a glance. Yeah, I wasn't born a creator – they, creators, wouldn't even understand what I'm talking about. I can only be envious from time to time – and then lament and get pointlessly annoyed with my own petty ambition. Yes, following the effort, I quickly wanted everything: well-deserved accolades and fame, and – ha, ha – money... Here I might laugh in my own face – though, of course, I'm not griping seriously, don't think I'm *that* stupid. What kind of glory is there when I'm unknown from the very start? It's better not to begin at all than to commence from absolute zero. The verses are so fragile and defenseless – and the indifference is so, so rife. You show them to someone, and he only nods; you tremble as you give him the page, and the reply – is a blank expression. No one will probably even read it, and those who do will forget it instantly, preoccupied with their usual routines. Friends will slap you on the back and switch the conversation to another subject, whereas the stranger – the stranger doesn't exist at all, I thought angrily, staring at the invisible ceiling with wide open eyes.

Here I became cunning – the stranger was real, and I even recognized her at last, but that didn't change the essence. Everything now seemed really petty. The misty garden and old mansion dissolved without a trace; I only spotted the female figure thanks to her narrow shoulders and her gait, which even her old-fashioned dress couldn't conceal. It was my university passion, a slender Jewish girl with slightly crooked legs and a serene, gentle smile, with whom I lived for about six months in that very same flat near the stadium. I don't remember why we broke up – I probably got tired of having someone around all the time. Her things were everywhere, as was her strange odor. And when she left, she gave me an ocean shell, fished out from the Promised Land – quite symbolical, if you assume such a place really exists and is not just some dumb joke.

I now recalled her hair and her shell, feeling sorry about all my aborted destinies, which are completely hopeless to mourn. Where are you, my double, and where are you, Lilia, you obedient and tender gal? What poem could reach you both?

And the last lyrics, calm and remorseful, rang in my head, like a pact with desperation that was accepted and became almost ordinary:

> *Behold you now my face*
> *As if through a prism*
> *through half-blinded days*
> *as if we're between them squeezed*
> *but not together – apart*
> *amid the scowls and frowns*
> *of fate outmaneuvering us*
> *twice as evident as now.*
>
> *Lying to us twice. Though your*
> *eyes're even kinder still…*

and something else, rhythmic and lulling me into a trance, something addressed to everyone who might still think about me.

The lines cast a spell. I wanted to keep listening, but had no more strength. Zigzags pulsated before my eyes, the carcasses of words swamped the room, and I could hardly make anything out through the hubbub. Thoroughly exhausted, with icy hands and burning temples, I rolled over to the wall and fell asleep, managing only to think I would remember almost nothing the next morning.

CHAPTER 12

And that's how it turned out. When I woke up with an ache in my neck, I didn't recall any of those zealous lines, although a few lost rhymes lingered in the vacuum, as if they didn't know where to alight. I didn't cling to them, knowing well I wouldn't be able to untangle the skein by pulling out random threads. It's all familiar – sudden fervor and a lyrical hangover. If I'd written them down, I probably wouldn't have wanted to look at them the next day. I wonder how it is with others who compose something for real? I've never had the opportunity to ask.

Slanting sheets of rain poured down outside the window. I ate breakfast alone, reluctantly consuming a couple of pieces of bread and butter with a cup of disgusting coffee. A long day laid ahead, its lack of content already irritating me.

After wallowing in bed and smoking, I forced myself to get up and go poke about the house. A quick inspection confirmed what was clear: the Christophers and Gibbs had again disappeared, their doors were locked tightly, and no one replied when I knocked. The women however were in their chambers. Silvia opened up but said she had work to do and had no clue where the others were while Stella didn't even respond, although I heard her steps and the clinking of some glass. Cursing, I began to aimlessly kill time. My legs again carried me to the attic stairs, and I climbed up, brushing aside the old cobwebs in disgust.

The *Chronicler* didn't inspire me in the least. The rest of the attic was almost empty, with only two covered chests in the far corner, both containing boxes that partially stuck out. Trying to walk as quietly as possible, though still making the rickety boards creak, I approached them and started to examine their content.

The round window was covered with dust and didn't provide much light, but it was possible to see something, and I apathetically rummaged through the odds and ends consigned to oblivion by their former owners. There was old navigation gear with rusty arrows, a whole heap of maps I swiftly laid aside, and pieces of cold russet rock with large pores. I slipped one in my pocket, but it chilled my thigh in an unpleasant way, so I returned it to the chest. Then I noticed a large photo album and, moving closer to the window, opened it in anticipation of new discoveries, but found only a few pictures of one and the same woman, sitting every time in a tense position, her eyes stubbornly riveted to the camera. She was young, and I thought it might be Silvia fifteen years ago, yet I didn't see any resemblance. Furthermore, the snapshot seemed to be taken much earlier, judging by the brown tarnish. Flipping through the album to the end, I discovered a clump of paper that had been roughly torn out of a lined notebook. Latin letters had been assiduously printed on one blank side: MEMENTO MORI, while faded, handwritten lines of an almost unreadable text swept across the other. I could only make out: "Let's consider the trajectory of one drop a little more carefully. A tear is born in the corner of your eye and runs down your cheek, smudging your dark-blue mascara…"

"Mascara – fascara," I babbled quietly and slipped the sheet back into the album. There was nothing else to study and nowhere else to go – crude beams hung over my head and walls enclosed me on all sides. I lay the album on the floor by the window and sat down next to it, leaning forward, subconsciously trying to occupy as little space as possible. The downpour had not stopped; a cloudy veil obfuscated the horizon, meekly absorbing both looks and thoughts. It was all so familiar, almost painful, repeating scenarios I had scrolled through a lot. My morning doubts surged up again, recalling the brusqueness and mockery, the Christophers and arrogant Gibbs, while the absurdity of what was taking place hit me in all its power. I couldn't lie to myself anymore – I realized I had fallen into a trap.

This is how you make turn after turn, assuming you still hold the whole picture in your head. And then, out of the blue, you crash into a barrier for which there is no sign, and the paths going in both directions veer back after a few steps. You need to ask for the right way, but you're alone, and even if you meet someone, you can't explain what you're looking for. The goal doesn't have a name, and it's terrible to confess you've gotten yourself into a muddle. All your weaknesses are put on display and you can't hide a thing...

"Caught, you sly cat," Lyubomir Lyubomirov probably would have said, winking maliciously, as he did more than once, sitting at my side by the board with one hundred forty four squares. Yes, playing Dzhan, we were experts at traps, but even we weren't always able to save ourselves from unexpected danger. Somewhere in the middle of a protracted game, your attention often wanes from excessive confidence, and then, in a little while, you suddenly realize you don't control the adjacent fields and have almost no moves to consider – someone has already thought for you. This time the thinkers skulked away, leaving me alone, but that didn't make the trap harmless. They're waiting till the mouse in the mousetrap exhausts itself, and, in my case, maybe they're anticipating the first signs of craziness to dispose of me once and for all. Not a bad idea, and it might work to perfection – here, among the silent rooms and persistent inclement weather!

I shook my head and, wishing to cut off the nagging, thought about the game of Dzhan again, replete with its perils and submerged rocks not apparent at first sight. Only later, when the combination becomes clear and there seem to be no good options left, every novice inevitably panics. And there's a legitimate reason: you stop moving the chips and you're doomed to a slow death – or a quick one if you're lucky. It can be quite a misfortune, especially if the beginning looked rather promising. Yet there's usually nothing to be done – you'll be inundated by a foreign will, like an avalanche that cannot be prevented.

"It's coming," drawled Lyubomir Lyubomirov, as if to himself, and his eyes blazed when he and I wrapped our claws around a pair of upstarts, brutally shoving them to the brink of a devastating loss. "Drive 'em out, blow the whistle," he said, scratching the bridge of his nose and watching the eyes of our dumbstruck opponents shoot from side to side as they tried to find a way out. And then, when it was over, he concluded with a repulsive grin, "This is their wet dream," or something of that sort, never failing to add a customary, "Perverts!" – his final verdict on the losers.

But if you tighten the noose, you need to stay alert – and when, in turn, they have you stuck in it, you should never succumb to despair. He and I knew this well, having assimilated from our youth the basic rule of Dzhan, the one around which all its complexity revolves. The first part reads, "Initiative is everything," which is right: only the one who makes the moves can hope to win. Yet there is a second, which isn't even a part of the rules, but rather an expression of its main philosophical principle. "In the game of Dzhan," it states, "you should not take an initiative if there's no clear need to do so," and that's even more right, for there's nothing more absurd than to knock at an open door and turn yourself into a laughingstock where it's worthwhile to think it over again and maybe even doubt how correct you are. In this is rooted the trap for those who set the traps; here glimmers redemption for others who have already been ensnared. These two cornerstones simply cannot be butted up against each other without a gap, so there's always a chance of slipping from the beaten path into a deserted space, where obscurity reigns and it's impossible to discern what's what. Things may change on the board quickly. You can always hope to find the one chip capable of the daring burst, make out the strongest nexus in the entangled multitude of single pieces and bet on it, no longer waffling, making a choice that seems strange to anyone except yourself…

That's what I pondered as I sat by the attic window until all my muscles lost feeling. Rain pattered against the dusty pane; the walls creaked quietly while I racked my brain, shuffling through different perspectives on my own position in the game. I thought about who was who and how the board had been drawn out, trying not to blunder with the choice of my strongest chip – whether it was the yellowed photograph of Piolin or my secret or the loaded Colt awaiting its hour in my travel bag. It was a pity I didn't have Lyubomir Lyubomirov with me. Yet it's doubtful he could have helped me now – even if I had been able to explain it all lucidly.

Then the pain in my back and pangs of hunger drove me downstairs. On my bedroom door I found a note informing me lunch, or actually dinner, would be at five in the afternoon. I quickly washed and bustled off to the dining room, where I couldn't hide a sigh of disappointment – only Silvia and Stella were seated at the table, and the other untouched plate was waiting for me. Apparently, the three of us would be eating alone.

I grumbled hello and sat down on the low stool. The trap was snapping shut – that much was clear. Maybe these women, too, would soon finish up what was left for them to do and disappear, slink off under the cover of nightfall without even saying goodbye. And the one who bestowed her caresses on me will just smile at the fleeting memory on her way to the next shelter… The image did not make me happy, and I again sighed heavily as I stared at the floor.

"Why are you so depressed?" asked Silvia absentmindedly. "Or did you remember something bad?"

"Nothing's going on," I complained, irritated. "Gibbs isn't here, and those two clowns have also gone somewhere."

"Well, and what are we – bad company?" inquired Silvia, smiling. "Why is it all Gibbs this and Gibbs that?"

I looked across the table at her. She sat with her arms folded and didn't touch the food. Her elusively seductive smile grated on my nerves – as if outlining the borders of desires one so desperately wanted to cross.

"Is there a signal there?" flashed through my head. "And Stella… Silvia probably had something in mind when she mentioned her that night!"

This thought was followed by another, then a third – and on it went. "They must be bored to the point of desperation, even more than I am," I asserted to myself. "In general, women are better than men – finer, friendlier, more perceptive. Why shouldn't these two be on my side? Perhaps we three can join together quite happily – it won't get me any closer to my goal, but it wouldn't be all that bad either. A small harem at the oceanside, at the very edge of the fearsome Dunes – it sounds romantic enough. They're so different; I wonder what they can pull off together?"

The prospect was tempting. The world suddenly sparkled. I felt a hunter's thrill run down my spine, though I only said, "Of course not. Your company's quite good, in fact." And I shifted in my seat in a relaxed and confident way – at least as much as was possible on a stool with no back.

Silvia nodded her encouragement, and I continued, "Yeah, your company's quite good, but all we're doing is sitting in our rooms. We could be having a more enjoyable time."

"How, for instance?" she asked gently, dropping her eyes.

"She gets it!" I thought admiringly, preparing for some subtle cat-and-mouse that could take us far. A few scenes flashed before my eyes, one more enticing than the next. I was already searching for something to say, something ambiguous and a bit risky, which would head the conversation in the right direction. But Stella interrupted us, casually declaring, "Where else should we hang out – in your bedroom looking at your sad face? Or in the attic, where you stomped about all morning? After knocking at my door," she added, glancing askance at Silvia, who nodded knowingly.

"Well, sorry for the noise. I can't flit about," I grumbled and sensed the end of a game that hadn't even begun. "The attic floor, it's shaky as hell. And if I languish in my room any longer, I'll lose my mind from boredom. Maybe you have a better idea – what did you do all day?"

"Dreamed," Stella cut me off and, turning to Silvia, spoke with her about some ribbon with a bobby pin and brooch. Silvia replied with hardly concealed irony, yet Stella didn't give up, and I started to feel like a third wheel again. They're all ganging up on me, even these two, I thought caustically. It's as if they're going out of their way to demonstrate it!

I intentionally inquired as slowly and insolently as I could, "What did you dream about? Not me, by chance?" Stella just looked at me in disbelief and turned back to Silvia, but I rudely butted in, "Or your fiancé? Do you have a fiancé? How do you manage your needs anyway – you understand what I mean, don't you?"

They both stopped talking and stared at me. I went on and on, saying all sorts of ridiculous things, clowning around and trying to get at least one chuckle out of them. It continued for a quarter of an hour or so, yet my efforts got me nowhere. Silvia gazed at me with mounting gloom, while Stella pouted, frowned and finally shouted, "Stop it! Don't make a fool of yourself – at least here and now. Who needs this?" And she added ruefully, "You have no idea what a woman is!"

I got quiet – seeing she was totally right. On the not quite clear "at least here and now," I didn't even want her to elaborate. We finished dinner in silence and left the table, hardly muttering our good nights.

I returned to my room but couldn't calm down. "Don't make a fool of yourself," I repeated over and over, upset at my own idiocy, too late as usual. Then I grew angry and barely overcame the desire to go find Stella and insult her.

I talk to these two about the timeless sorrow, about the intolerability of estrangement, but they – they can only imagine the most trivial of things, I thought in irritation, knowing all too well I had only myself to blame. I wanted to change the subject, recall something more engaging, the game of Dzhan for instance, but I couldn't control my mind. Compatriots, friends, colleagues, or simply strangers I didn't have any interest in knowing – all merged into one abstract form and didn't want to leave my head. What do they care for Dzhan? What do they care for me and my reflections?

Outside, twilight was closing in. The world shrunk to the size of my room, which had become intolerably confining. I asked aloud,

"Those who brought you here, what did they want from you?" And I answered, "Whatever the case may be, you should admit you've become unneeded. It's clear now – clearer than clear."

I dashed to the window and opened the casement. It was dark and windy, but the rain had almost ceased, turning into a misty drizzle. There it is, I thought, it's a good sign. Really, why am I wasting time?

I took a deep breath and began to get ready to go. Obviously, it would've been better to wait till the morning, but my impatience was tormenting me; I simply couldn't sit still. Moreover, I hoped the wind would soon blow away the clouds, and the moon, which was nearly full, would give me enough light.

It may be night, but I won't stray from the trail, I assured myself. Quickly throwing everything into my bag, I performed a check in my head and surmised the direction of the shortest road to the motel. A hand-made map would help a lot, but I remembered: no maps! I even refrained from running my finger through the dust on the windowsill to draw the two legs of the former route and the hypotenuse of my future one.

The preparations were finished, if you could call them that – I had almost no luggage and nothing to hold me back. After sitting on the bed for a few minutes and pondering whether I should say goodbye to Silvia, I switched off the light, went to the kitchen for some crackers and water, and silently slipped out the door.

A moist gust slammed into my face. I immediately wanted to go back inside, but overcame the weakness and strode over the sand, moving away from the house, abandoning my unfriendly companions and their unexplained riddles. The whistling wind and surf behind my back muted all the other sounds. I wasn't scared; there was only regret at failing to complete what was started. I drove it off, being full of determination, and muttered rough words, forestalling each and every doubt.

An hour later, however, it became clear that my plan exceeded my strength. Once I got beyond the crest of the first sand hill, the ocean quieted down. The steady crash of the waves changed into the sounds of the nighttime Dunes – squeaking and whizzing, quick running and plaintive crying, a jubilant scream in the distance, or a doomed sigh that seemed to confess the senselessness of any stubborn effort. The farther I went, the more anxious I became. I envisioned hidden monsters on all sides and walked with extreme care, darting this way and that to sidestep every dark spot, sometimes freezing in place and looking over my shoulder – to see whether something was creeping up behind me. I realized I had covered only the smallest bit and would take all night to reach my destination at this rate, but I couldn't do anything about it – my nerves were stretched taut and my head was ringing from the excess of adrenaline, not letting me think calmly.

Every call and every sigh became magnified to a deafening growl or an ear-splitting shriek. It seemed they were rushing to inform and warn me, but, halfway there, they were cut off and only signaled: too late, too late, you won't make it. There is nothing worse than incomprehensible hints: I pictured the ground quaking all around me on the brink of preordained disaster, though I couldn't figure out the epicenter of the danger – my eyes had been blindfolded, my mind forfeited. I knew my actions were fruitless and the worst was still to come, but where was it, what was it? Maybe they were trying to presage something, yet I couldn't believe the cries of invisible powers, originating in the darkness and having such an inhuman pitch. Why were there so many? It was impossible, it couldn't be – and that was more terrifying than anything else…

Fear this way or that, sooner or later I would have come to grips with myself, but the situation was all the more deplorable without a clear physical direction. The moon glided in and out of the clouds, and the whole landscape changed entirely each time it appeared. I was constantly consumed by doubts: is it that hill, is it that bush, which served as my reference point ten minutes ago? Was I in the same place at all? The shadows altered the contours and I couldn't recognize a thing. It was clear I wouldn't get far – I would probably wander off track and walk in circles. I had to return, however unpleasant the thought was. For the sake of appearances, I had a little argument with myself, then stopped and admitted I was about to get really lost and waited for the moon to re-emerge so I could figure out the path back.

This was no simple task. I gazed into the darkness so long, the outlines of everything swam together and made the area look thoroughly different when the silver moonlight flooded it again. Spasmodically, my eyes darted from hill to hill, ran to and fro in search of my footprints, but nothing could convince me the picture in my head was correct. I forced myself not to panic, squatted, and began to draw in the sand the Dunes and the ocean, my presumed route and the elusive moon, reckoning how it might shift and how the shadows should lie now. Finally I also recalled the direction of the whistling wind – although it didn't make much sense, since that could have changed in the meantime. Then it hit me like lightning: what am I doing, it's a complete sketch, almost a map! Perhaps I've broken the rule, and the Dunes will take revenge, transforming and moving, not sparing either a settlement or a lonely traveler. I quickly smoothed the sand over, wiping out all the lines, and moved as quickly as I could toward where I imagined the so dumbly abandoned house to be.

An hour later, worn out by uncertainty and subsequent fits of nighttime terror, I did reach the ocean. The inexpressible relief I felt at the sound of the waves was rapidly supplanted by new doubt: there was no trace of the house and no light shining from the windows. It was obvious I had wildly missed the mark and had to make another decision. I wavered a little and turned to the right, strolling along the water and shivering from the wind that puffed up my jacket.

The ocean roared angrily; the dark sky hung over me like an endless dome; all distances seemed enormous and impossible to cover. I was so insignificant and meant so little that I couldn't be surprised at the indifference of my surroundings – it wasn't in my power to amaze them. The City of M., the threatening legends, the Dunes from which I had just managed to escape, my travelers, and even slippery Julian – it all slid into the background and was continuing to shrink in size.

At that moment I understood how madness emerges – and was

almost able to envision the finest of lines, an elusive path, along which someone guarding my brain runs endlessly, not getting distracted, looking straight ahead – with a precipice on each side. He cannot stop – just as he cannot stand still. Even slowing down is frightening: the equilibrium gets instantly lost. He's running, breathing smoothly and deeply, vigorously working his elbows, at the same speed, in the same motion, year after year. But at times something unexpected happens – and his speed changes and the rhythm breaks…

I visualized: he's getting scared and picking up the pace, his thin legs scissoring so quickly you can't discern the details. That's how it always is: if you begin, then there's no going back; just cross the border – and you won't return to steadiness. First, it seems you just can't catch up: you're late and will never reach your mark. The frequency of the movements becomes intolerable, and then – then it happens: the subtle path becomes empty. It's desolated and vacant – and a scream rises from the abyss. All the previously muted voices now clamor to be heard; the chimeras climb out of the corners; the phantoms fill the void – and there's no fleeing, hiding, or restoring anything…

Ice-cold sweat ran down my spine. What are you doing, I screamed at myself, you may really go crazy with fantasies like that! My legs carried me on their own, my head throbbed from the exertion. I needed to get distracted, to grab onto something and calm my nerves.

"Let's consider the trajectory of one drop a little more carefully," I babbled. "A tear starts in the corner of your eye and rolls down your cheek…" It was irrational, but I muttered away, assiduously imagining rain on the glass and moisture on my face. Then I felt my own tears from the salty wind, and I settled down in a strange way, reconciling myself to the endlessness of the space and the inevitability of fate. The verbose clichés are really good, I admitted glumly, peering into the night. I've got to remember to keep one or two in store. It's especially true for those like me – who are designed too complexly, flimsy, poorly, as my dear Gretchen said.

Time passed; an absolute darkness stretched in front of me as before. The prospect of sleeping on the beach was not attractive at all. I cursed my idiocy but at that particular moment a weak glimmer appeared in the distance and I quickened my pace. Soon the familiar house rose up, its bulky contours submerged in the gloom and a rectangle of light shining from two windows.

I was reeling from exhaustion as I reached the entryway. All my emotions were left in the Dunes and on the coast, by the roaring ocean. I just wanted to fall into bed and the deepest sleep possible.

Trying not to make any noise, I walked through the dark foyer and saw a yellow stripe under the kitchen door – which meant someone had left the lights on there. Dying for something to drink, I threw my bag on the floor, entered the kitchen, and came to a halt: an unknown man sat at the dinner table.

He looked at me unceremoniously for a few seconds and then turned away toward the opposite wall. His face was weather-beaten, though young. Only his eyes seemed too hollow, as if he suffered from excessive strain. Something in his posture, in the swivel of his head and the lines of his shoulders, said he was older than he seemed at first. Maybe his hands would have betrayed his age, but he kept them in the pockets of his formless overalls, which were open at the neck.

I said hello with some hesitation, while the stranger just nodded dryly without glancing my way. Deciding we had fulfilled our social obligations, I poured myself some water, gulped it down and was about to leave when an unexpected thought hit me like a rocket: what if that isn't just a guest? What if that's some unwanted stranger sitting here for a reason? And then one after the other: where are Gibbs and the Christophers? And where are the women? Did something happen to them?

My blood ran cold. Maybe they left me to be the defender – of the house, of Silvia and Stella – and I ran away like a coward. And what if... I conjured up terrible images in the spirit of a movie about serial killers, one of whom – why not? – could be now staring daggers into my back!

Mindlessly picking at something on the shelf, I delayed the

moment I would have to meet his direct, bloodthirsty gaze. But what if the stranger was silently creeping up behind me and a devastating blow was about to rain down on my head? Or no, he probably keeps me in the gun's sight, expecting me to recognize the hopelessness of resistance, so that before he pulls the trigger, he can relish my helplessness and disgrace me. Anything is possible in this sick world. It's capable of atrocities I've never even hallucinated, yet I had to be ready for them. The question is *how*...

I couldn't drag it out any longer. Mustering up the remains of my strength, I turned around and faced him, trying to appear calm. No one was hiding behind my back. The man in overalls was sitting in the same position, staring off into space as before. However, there was a new wrinkle on his face, as if he had been concealing an omniscient grin.

"Let me introduce myself," I said – in the most casual way. I told him my name and yawned intentionally, looking strictly into the stranger's eyes.

"Yes, we know, we know..." replied Gibbs's voice, regarding me askance and winking. It was as if the veil had been torn from my eyes: I stood there and smiled goofily, blown away by my own blindness and puzzled as to why I hadn't recognized him straight away. There was nothing confusing – not his posture, not his figure nor his manner of sitting. Only his face – but how important is a face? Had I not seen enough shifting faces?

"Did you go for a walk?" asked Gibbs derisively, enjoying the effect. "The weather's welcoming, indeed."

"Yeah, I took a walk," I grumbled. "What else should I do? You left me here, alone."

"Not quite alone, and, furthermore, everything in its time," retorted Gibbs, shaking his head, and added instructively, "Walks need to be taken with a purpose. Did you have some purpose?"

"Yes, I did," I replied, not understanding what he was driving at.

"That's good," Gibbs praised me. "Since if you do it without a purpose, you might be prone to act senselessly. In general, when I look at you, I suspect more and more that acting senselessly is your defining trait. How did I guess?"

In response, I wanted to blurt out something rude, but exhaustion had overcome me, and, besides, he was right. "Maybe that's true," I shrugged my shoulders. "However, I can also do things that make perfect sense. You shouldn't write me off."

"Well, you know, writing somebody off..." Gibbs distractedly pattered his fingers on the table. "Writing you off isn't worthwhile, and it's disadvantageous – now everyone has to be on board. By the way, what actually brought you to M. in the first place?" he asked abruptly, his eyes flashing as he rotated his whole body toward me.

"I already told you: I have to find someone," I muttered, examining his new face, which I couldn't get used to.

"You'll be able to find him, but when you do, what then?" Gibbs kept at it.

I suddenly felt a strong urge to explain everything, and only fear of exposing myself to his ridicule prevented me from being completely candid. With satisfaction, Gibbs observed my inner struggle, and when I came out with the awkward, "Then I'll think about it," he grinned broadly as if he had achieved what he wanted.

"And what happened to you? Have you procured a new guise for yourself?" I asked somewhat belligerently. "I didn't recognize you at first."

"Oh, come on, it's just a mask. It can't deceive anyone," said Gibbs. "Here, watch this." He raised his hand, clicked something on his neck, and the face plopped down in his lap, folded in two, and flipped inside out. "I have a few of them. This is Swiss made – they can still produce quality things."

With some uncertainty I nodded, sullenly regarding the former Gibbs in his strange, but already familiar look. Then I dawdled a little, managed to say with the last of my strength, "Okay, I'm going to bed," and turned to the door but sensed his glare resting on me.

"What's that? Where have you been, anyway?" Gibbs looked at my feet. "It seems as if you stepped into gopher's crap."

I quickly lowered my eyes. On the outside of my right boot was a clear, bright-green stripe.

"That may bring you luck," drawled Gibbs derisively. "You see, I was right – you need to have a purpose when you take a walk!"

I nodded again, as if agreeing with his joke, but noticed he was staring at me very coldly as I left.

CHAPTER 13

The next few days passed flatly. Gibbs and the Christophers didn't pay any attention to me and weren't in the house most of the time. My pathetic escape attempt restrained my ardor, so I was left to reconcile myself to humbly waiting. I tried to talk with Silvia, but she behaved like a stranger – replying gently, yet aloofly, demonstrating in every possible way that only in my imagination had we briefly been intimate. I showed her the photograph of Piolin that agitated me so much, yet she was thoroughly disinterested, saying she couldn't read the language and had never seen that person. Then, despairing of the uselessly passing time, I dug out the amateur photo of Julian hidden at the bottom of my travel bag with the Colt, and casually laid it on the table after lunch. But neither the women, nor the Christophers, who ate with us that afternoon, recognized his face.

Christopher One just said nonchalantly, "Ask the neighbors," vaguely waving his hand, and both of them laughed. "When is Gibbs coming back?" I asked coldly, but got yet another sneer in response, "He'll be here soon; don't worry." And I couldn't do anything except stick my face in my plate, suppressing a sharp desire to shout something nasty.

Gibbs, by the way, appeared that evening, yet I didn't really manage to talk with him. He had no mask on, looked off to the side most of the time, and was dressed strangely – in rough boots and a wide poncho hanging from his shoulders to the floor. It occurred to me he had probably slept like that outdoors, but I didn't feel comfortable asking. Moreover, as soon as he came in, he holed up in a corner of the kitchen with Silvia, and I couldn't find any reason to interrupt their téte-â-téte. When I did finally catch him alone by the front door, it was readily apparent he was in a hurry and didn't have time for me. On top of that, Silvia sprang out of her room, intending to say something at the last minute, but became confused at the sight of me and stood there without uttering a word.

An awkward scene ensued and Gibbs grimaced in irritation, then opened the door and invited me outside with a nod. The wind made me shiver – I wasn't wearing any upper layers. Gibbs inquired crossly, "What's your deal? Why are you fussing around like a bimbo on a podium?" – and I couldn't find the right words. It was clear we wouldn't be able to have a serious talk in a rush. "Do you remember our agreement not to do anything dumb?" asked Gibbs in the same cold voice. "You were warned – I don't like to make a fool of myself!" To this, I had nothing to say and just glumly nodded, feeling guilty, as he enshrouded himself in his poncho and walked away from the house with a bounce in his step.

Obviously, this episode did not embolden me. I thought more and more often that our trip was a futile waste of time and the Dunes didn't conceal anything new for me. Then something different rolled in: I started to feel an unavoidable storm approaching, some invisible events thickening in the distance, picking up speed. The plain faces of the Christophers became cunning and spiteful; indistinct coarse voices infiltrated the nighttime sounds, and the seascape offered up its share – the weather did not improve, low black clouds raced across the sky, like battalions of ragged troops accustomed to never-ending retreat. The wind picked up, howling and hurling raindrops on the coast, then died down completely and the roar of the disgruntled ocean reigned, its waves lashing at the distant banks as if demonstrating their power to anyone who dared doubt.

Only one thing kept me going: my relationship with Stella progressed day by day. She was now quite a bit friendlier, although she seemed somewhat jittery at times. We frequently chatted about all sorts of subjects, and I got to know her better, liking her more and more. Not without some self-satisfaction, I convinced myself her abruptness at the beginning had been a result of shyness and jealousy. I even contemplated on occasion whether Stella was that strongest piece on the board, my lucky card, which I could place my bets on. Though I couldn't wrap my head around what that meant, I sensed it strongly, as if in spite of misgivings and anxiety. Something seemed to whisper in my ear, "Here, perhaps, is the real find. Don't miss the opportunity, don't frighten her off!"

One night a tempest raged, and I couldn't fall asleep till dawn, but in the morning the wind subsided. The sky cleared, becoming bluer with every passing minute, and Stella enjoined me to go for a walk. We wandered along the edge of the water, pondering the sand at our feet, the chaotic traces of the nighttime tumult left by the waves. Lifeless crabs and clams lay everywhere; dark, petrified splinters of wood were strewn across the beach. Here and there, we saw clusters of matted seaweed and collections of shells with strange forms, split in half and retaining their sharp edges, like razors, with their intact mother of pearl glistening in the sunshine. The shore had changed vastly but not lost its indifference – nameless barbarians emerged and evanesced, unable to make themselves at home, abandoning their belongings and mundane trash but not violating the solitude of these lands.

Stella didn't look very good: the features of her face became pointy; dark rings appeared under her eyes. I tried to engage her in conversation, but it didn't work – we were clumsy like complete strangers. So I stopped speaking and decided not to be intrusive, secretly regretting I wasn't alone.

Soon, however, Stella livened up and started a game with the shells she'd been assiduously extracting from the wet sand and collecting in her hand. "What do you think this is?" She showed me one with elongated ends and a narrow fissure wandering across the middle.

"A cracked plate," I replied, and Stella chided, "Primitive! How old are you – seventy? Don't be such a bore, use your head."

"Maybe a gorge trail?" I guessed randomly.

"Too simple," she disagreed again. "Anyone could come up with that. Let's think seriously and be inventive."

"All right. It's the wall of your room, with the plaster peeling along a seam. You gaze at it when you wake up and the day immediately seems depressing," I fantasized at length, secretly hoping she would praise me. Instead, Stella just said, "No, it's hopeless, you're not even looking at it right. I thought you were more observant, but actually you're as lazy as everyone else. Do you suppose both halves are identical? Can't you see – it's Gibbs!"

She thrust the shell in front of me and, as she turned it in the sunlight, I saw the fissure dividing two different sides – one covered by an opaque patina, as if hewn out of sand, the other glistening and untouched, faceless and smooth.

"Yeah, it does resemble him," I admitted earnestly, trying to retain my dignity. Yet by then, she was already twirling the next part of the charade before my eyes. This shell had been ground in the middle, like a Greek Omega, while its edges curled in round, asymmetrical ringlets.

"Let's see some imagination," Stella demanded as she peered into my face. And for some time, I really did mull it over, but without hitting upon anything ingenious.

"A wig on a nun," I proposed at last. Stella just shook her head. "Why a nun?" she muttered in a barely audible voice. "Who's a nun here?"

"Two waves in a row – one large, one a little smaller," I tried to convince her, insisting and illustrating it with gestures. She acknowledged it was close, but still not quite right.

"What connects your two waves?" she flared up. "Look at the ocean – can you choose those that resemble the shell? You can see for yourself: each one is detached and stands apart. You just don't want to try seriously."

"I don't know," I gave up, and she said in a confident voice, "It's the night between two days – the days are the same but not quite. And between them is a conduit, night, graceful and fragile. You can't stay there long: you glide into a dream, ending up in front, or into recollections, falling behind, as if the past day doesn't want to part. Has that ever happened to you?"

"Maybe," I replied, ready to defend myself as some combative feeling rose up inside me, though no one attacked me or searched for a soft spot. And again Stella offered me a shell; this one recalled an outstretched flipper, sharp and long, with a curving spiral on the other wide end. An ever-contracting image, winding down to a point.

"What's with this one?" she regarded me cunningly, and I felt as if something responded within me, stirring my stalled memory.

"That's how you dash away," I said, uncertain whether or not she'd understand me. "You gain enough courage to run – and bolt for the hills. That's the direct route, no time for turns, as if there's a maelstrom behind your back – where you whirl around and can't escape…"

Stella interrupted me, nodding, satisfied, "In some ways we aren't all that different. I was thinking about that too. However there, in the rear, is not only a maelstrom, but also someone's vigilant eye – watching closely so you can't get away!"

She said something else, but my head was already spinning. Gibbs-Night-Escape – was it accidental or not? I instantly remembered my recent, disgraceful attempt, and heard the spooky trilling of the nocturnal Dunes.

"Gibbs-Night-Escape," I was about to say out loud, yet Stella skipped ahead, rollicking and not listening to me. "We've played enough; now we're going swimming!" she cried. The ocean roared chillingly in the background and I realized it was worthless to question her – she wouldn't tell me more than she wanted anyway.

The idea of taking a dip didn't excite me – it wasn't warm, and the wind even penetrated my thick jacket. "Shame on you!" Stella hollered. "Watch," – and she tossed off her clothes without any hesitation. Goose bumps immediately covered her skinny, boyish body, yet she bravely waded into the water and was soon splashing away from the shore, diving under the undulating waves. I stood and looked, occasionally losing sight of her, being afraid for her, though I somehow knew the ocean wouldn't cause her any harm. "Come in!" Stella yelled, flipping over on her back, but I just waved my hand, feeling ridiculous and awkward.

After swimming for a long time, she got out and stood in the wind to dry off, grinning at how I averted my gaze, feeling shy about looking openly at her slim hips and small breasts. "If you'd got undressed," she said archly, "then you could have taken me in your arms, but you're a chicken and boring, so there won't be anything for you." I smiled, unsure, and she stuck out her tongue at me and began to slowly put on her clothes, shaking her wet hair.

We headed back. Color returned to Stella's face and her cheeks became red. It seemed as if all her troubles had vanished. She frolicked about, threw shells at me and squealed, dashing away from the excessively playful waves threatening to swamp the sand below her feet. As before, there was no one around. I even fantasized that people had never come here before – it was pleasant to feel like a pioneer. I was in total control of the shore, the saturnine waves and the happy savage with wet hair – if you know no one will take all this away, you can pay a lot in exchange. The capital and Gretchen? Maybe. Julian? Why not?

"Turn your back, I need to pee," Stella drawled in a childish voice. I did – and gazed at the ocean receding to a hardly visible horizon, where the scowling and again overcast sky met the never-ending surface of water. The wind picked up; patches of dark clouds floated in from the north, like messengers of future hardships arriving under a gray veil without a moment to rest. Futilely, I sought order in their ranks, trying to figure out the meaning from the conflicting signs so I could respond in turn. But the emissaries were not counting on me, and my lonely mind yielded to a hazy, alien will. A few times, it seemed to me some dark points flickered in the distance, now swarming together in a group, now fanning out. I peered at the space till my eyes hurt, yet again and again I got deceived by ocean ripple and dirty-gray tatters of saturated moisture.

"What are you looking at?" Stella asked, quietly coming up from behind and startling me. I spun around impulsively, remembering her with difficulty and returning to reality in a slow, inept way.

"The black pelicans," I joked in response. "It's like someone's hiding them from me, I haven't seen one yet."

The joke didn't go well. Stella recoiled as if I'd hit her, turned away, and frowned. Her shoulders dropped and her face shriveled up and aged instantly. Some kind of alarming despair flashed through her whole body. I felt like I'd said something very improper and touched her hand guiltily, but she withdrew it in anger and marched ahead without looking back. I followed along, a little bit behind her, cursing myself for something I couldn't name.

"You can't wait around for the black pelicans," said Stella after several minutes. "Everyone knows it's they who find you, if they want you. Do I really look incapable of understanding that?"

She stopped, pivoted, and glared at me. "You think you can say such things aloud, taunt me with your jokes, because no one will shut you up? Do as you like, but I don't need such hints, and furthermore – who are you to me, what are you to me? Go to hell with your grown-up rules, with all these games of yours. They really, I mean *really*, make me sick."

And again she stalked down the coast without glancing at me or saying a word.

Toward evening we patched things up. Stella came over to me in the kitchen, took my hand, and gazed off to the side, saying, "Alright, I know you didn't mean it. You don't understand anything, but that's not your fault." And looking in my eyes, she added, "Don't lock your door tonight."

I nodded, recalling her delicate figure on the shore, and wasn't even surprised at the sudden change. Silvia watched us sneakily, laughing to herself in all likelihood, yet I was annoyed with her and wasn't at all interested in her reaction. And more than anything else, I wanted Gibbs to return soon – so I could have a real talk with him.

Not long after evening had set in, my hopes were rewarded. Gibbs and both Christophers entered the house raucously, bringing in the aggressive roughness of owners and the smell of ocean salt. Christopher Two tossed down a plastic bag and dumped two large fish on the table. One of them was still alive and gazed dimly from a motionless, hostile eye, its gills twitching occasionally. The voracious mouth with its bent-down corners was slightly open and full of tiny teeth. In all its features you could divine boundless hatred for everything, including its tormentors and its own fate. It didn't expect mercy from us, as it never took pity on its own victims in the invisible ocean depths, and this was more honest than all the forced moral sufferings which two-legged creatures had accumulated over thousands of years. It was only evolution's trick that let them turn out more wily and cunning as they filled the land and now brutally encroached on the expanses of water, subjecting them to their laws so the former rulers could only submit and suffer. "We'll see who will rule after you and whether you'll then manage to die with dignity," said that indifferent eye, and I thought its silence was as valuable as the greatest of speeches.

"Well, tourist, they're impressive, huh? I caught them, no one else," said a satisfied Christopher Two as he chewed something loudly. "These two machos, they took a walk for nothing, it was me who reeled the monsters in. The second one fought hard – my goddamned hands were almost bleeding."

"Who took a walk for nothing, me?" Christopher One was offended. "Do you remember the one I had on the line? You don't even see that kind in your dreams – nothing like your puny ones. It's just that our tackle is crappy shit!"

"*Puny*," snorted the second Christopher with a victorious look. "These puny ones send a shiver down my spine. You probably caught a skate and it broke away. It would've been funny if you'd actually dragged it in. Now you're just jealous…" – and for a long time they couldn't calm down, bickering and jabbing each other, until Silvia chased them out of the kitchen.

The women quickly chopped and fried the fish. Everyone sat down at the table, but I didn't feel like eating. When I went to my room before dinner, I grabbed something that, if it didn't shock Gibbs, should at least cut him down to size, show him that others also have some value – and now I was waiting for the right opportunity to set my trap. Unexpectedly, I was aided by Christopher Two, who still hadn't gotten over his success and was heckling the rest of us.

"Tell us, tourist, what did you do all day?" he asked.

"Me? Well… I read the newspaper," I replied calmly as I mentally prepared myself for the moment.

"That's good! And what are they writing?" he continued, clearly planning to pester me.

"Different things," I said vaguely. "For instance, I found this yesterday…"

I pulled out the folded-up piece of yellowish paper with the photograph of Piolin and carefully spread it out next to Gibbs. Continuing to chew his food, he scanned the cutout and looked away without uttering a word.

"What's there?" Christopher Two would have snatched the excerpt, but Gibbs quickly covered it with his hand.

"It's not for you," he sneered. "It's Tyrolean, you won't understand it."

Everyone stopped talking and then I said quietly, with insolent laziness, emulating someone, perhaps the Christophers themselves, "So, Gibbs, one way or the other, you know that man, right? Where is he, in the Alps? He wandered far away."

Gibbs winced and looked at me attentively, almost as he had in the hotel restaurant that first evening. I didn't avert my eyes.

"Some may know him and some may not," he said sternly. "I couldn't care less about this man."

He was clearly disgruntled and now seemed to be calculating something in his head. But I didn't let up, "How can that be? We ate dinner together – that's Piolin from the hotel, don't you see? You and he are friends, I recall."

Hearing the name Piolin, the first Christopher whistled and shifted his gaze to Gibbs. The women didn't say a word and just stared at their plates and preoccupied themselves with the fish.

Gibbs thought a second, then, clearly having decided something, sighed and reclined in his chair.

"You thought that up," he said dully, took a toothpick off the table, and began to play with it in his mouth. "That's not any Piolin, that's," he pointed at the lines, "that's Jurgen, Jurgen Morse. It's written there, read it." He took the piece of paper between his two fingers squeamishly and turned it in my direction.

"No, no – that is, yes, of course... I don't understand the language, but that's not important. Maybe that was some Jurgen, but now it's Piolin, it's clear," I muttered, feeling like I was losing my initiative. And then Gibbs slammed his fist down on the table with all his might, causing the dishes to rattle, and said in an iron voice, "You don't understand, so don't pry where you aren't wanted!" He quickly folded up the article and slipped it into his pocket. "Don't pry," he repeated just as coldly and leaned toward his plate.

Christopher One stared at me point blank and declared threateningly, "He's a spy!" Silence reigned in the room again. You could hear Gibbs working his jaws while Christopher One kept at it, "Yes, a spy. Well, boss, did you slip a spy in among us?" And he made a movement, as if preparing to get up from the table. I tensed, ready to defend myself by any means possible. Although my chances against him were minimal, I wasn't about to capitulate voluntarily.

"I don't like spies. I've personally sunk a few of them in the toilet," Christopher One asserted, shaking his shoulders menacingly, his eyes boring into the bridge of my nose. But here the second Christopher exclaimed loudly, "What kind of spy can he be – he's simply a tourist. What does a tourist know – he's as blind as a fly. A fly, not a spy!" He winked at me and laughed at his own joke. Christopher One chuckled repulsively, still looking at me darkly, but not with his former hostility.

The tension eased. The men ate while Silvia and Stella talked women's talk in an undertone as evening swept over us smoothly and peacefully. I didn't know whether to feel insulted or not and decided I shouldn't – there was no point in taking these childish morons seriously. Unexpectedly, Gibbs stood up and left but soon returned, carrying something behind his back. "Surprise, surprise," he said, placing a bottle of real scotch on the table, and everyone livened up, completely forgetting what had happened.

He brought the liquor at just the right time. Everyone was apportioned their fair share, and we quickly polished it off. After loosening up, we prattled on and looked around lazily.

I tried not to linger on anyone in particular and shifted my gaze from one companion to the next, thinking about how I had deluded myself at the outset: merged them into one, thoughtlessly viewed them as similar, judging by insufficient signs and not wishing to notice the differences apparent if you examined them closely. Take the Christophers, for instance. They were doubles during those first few days, but now they became two completely different people, only ending up together by chance. One was a nasty wolf, while the other resembled a trained watchdog that would rashly paw at the thigh of any careless intruder...

My mind was going around in circles. Christopher One, I conjectured, had never learned how to behave, had been constantly chased away and often beaten. He could easily have drowned in a gutter and had just managed to stay out of it thanks to his physical strength and enviable decisiveness, the root of which was loneliness and despair. Loved by no one, he grew up as an undesirable stepson who had no trouble instilling fear in even the strongest of people, a helper who would serve you for no small piece of the pie while always remembering his own interests.

Yes, it was probably tough for those who used him as an accomplice, I continued. They'd have to keep an eye on him and a whistling whip on hand, yet it was worth tolerating him for his contempt of everything that suppressed the feeling of danger and occasionally plunged him into the very whirlwind. One day it would smother him and he'd land in something really terrible – I felt sorry for those who happened to be nearby. For now he was under control and reasonable enough, but he was always surrounded by an aura of lifelessness that you're scared to touch, not knowing for sure whether it was contagious or not. Women shunned guys like him, foreseeing their sick future, and they themselves were incapable of forcing open the rusty shutters of their souls that have become stiffer as they grew older. That's why he, the first, was hostile and morose, envious and as dangerous as a snake, although you couldn't distinguish him from the second when they were sitting next to each other. But the latter was a different story and actually resembled a normal man – if you didn't bully him for no reason...

He grew up a cheerful fellow, I fantasized enthusiastically as I switched to Christopher Two. This was a boy who classmates revered for his recklessness, someone who spent his entire childhood in wild groups, which he was fond of recalling somewhat haughtily, considering himself a mature adult now. His street code of honor had its rules; you could rely on him when there was serious danger, but he was less dependable in lulls and dull periods – being prone to doing dumb things out of idleness. He had an amicable appearance, yet when you scrutinized him, it was easy to notice something dark inside, something capable of overflowing in impulsive cruelty, which would surprise even himself. In fights, he was very dangerous, since he never loses his composure, and was valued by leaders, since he's unflappable and fearless. However, don't even try to involve him in something hopeless from the start – his peasant slyness, passed down from his ancestors, keeps him from bumbling into a place with no escape route. That's why he has good luck – in his own special way. It's too bad I can't learn to be like him!

The two Christophers in the meantime had reignited the fish argument and were tossing out accusations of lies and unjustified boasting. Now and then Gibbs yelled in their direction and they obediently quieted down until one of them reverted to the dreary dispute again. Looking at all this, it would be hard to believe the complexities of the portrait I'd created, but I didn't give in – who said surroundings are always as straightforward as they seem? What, then, was the purpose of the efforts of those who ceaselessly tried to look deeper and deeper into the core of things? No, the iceberg of reality must contain hidden parts, which were inaccessible to the blunderers and concealed an essence that can only be guessed at by the barely noticeable traces on the surface…

I let my gaze wander to the women. Silvia and Stella sat facing one another, engrossed in a conversation that didn't pause for a second. The bright lamp callously emphasized details but wasn't marring their contented faces. It seemed they had found a place for themselves where peace was merciful and the souls revealed themselves, softening external features. The two offered a striking contrast – passion and restraint, darkness and light – but they were still similar in some way, like two different versions of the same idea concocted with a few years of searches and doubts in between.

It was the disparity, though, that I liked better. I envisioned one of them as a disappointed favorite, always searching for more than she could hope to find and never tiring of condemning her lousy fate. The envy of others wouldn't bring her relief – there was no value in the grumpy voices of hawkers who don't see farther than their own counter at a fair where there should really be more attractive goods. Insults and slander would encourage her to proudly raise her head. Excusing the dirty tricks of others, she would think about herself sadly and notice more acutely the ruthless progression of years marked by hopes that didn't come true. I'd be able to interest her for some time. Not that she'd see us as equal, even in her moments of weakness, but she'd probably descended to my level, admitting that sometimes one had to be satisfied with variety, if not quality. So intrigue would be possible – and even likely for many reasons – yet it would be a flimsy union: I wouldn't be able to tolerate her persistent, silent reproach for long, all the more apparent in her sweet words. I'd rebel, certain I was right, and she'd be astonished, crying at night, asking herself why the world was so blind and men were so stubborn – what was their damn problem? The matter would head toward a pathetic finale: I foresaw my moments of infidelity, the chaotic and awkward expressions of protest – and her infidelity in return, doing no less damage, behind which the despondent, never uttered "Why?" would lurk in all its glory. Finally we would separate, led to different corners of the ring, stunned by the sound of the gong, confirming we could stop driving each other crazy. For a long time, however, we wouldn't be able to escape the lingering memories that left both of us feeling victorious, yet acknowledging we didn't manage to discern enough in each other, and the mutual attraction still remained unfulfilled, even after turning into its opposite. She would be more offended – it was she, after all, who tried harder – and I, with an extra layer of skin, would avoid women similar to her, only, at times, getting exasperated I no longer ran into any of them.

The exasperation is easy to moderate though. You just have to change the focus – it always more or less helps. That I knew very well – and I shifted my eyes to another target promising much more. There were enough reasons – her thin neck, for instance, begging for a touch, or the reminder of the age of innocence in her appearance, although in her gait everyone would recognize that those days had passed. I imagined her, innocent or not, bewitching me with a satisfied smile, testing her strengths on me, maybe realizing them for the very first time. I would teach her different things – she would be a good student. She would hate her failures, never admitting her ineptitude and being eager to practice the same routine countless times. I would possess her, the restive and wild one, but strangely obedient to a firm voice exuding confidence – even if it wasn't always genuine. Gradually her thoughtful gaze would learn to penetrate me to the very depths of my being, searching there for something cached away from myself, as if demonstrating that her bet had been placed correctly. She would become more and more tolerant of me; she would find the right words in my moments of despair, binding me to her, winning me over with a naïve faith in my uniqueness. "No, it's not naïve," I would assure myself, "she knows it, she is wise like no other!"

In time our roles would change. She would mature from a student to the mistress of my moods, not embarrassed to inform me of this, requiring recognition for her feats – and deservingly so: all the energy of her heart was focused on me alone. We would argue, sometimes seriously, when my obstinacy would confront her intentions. She, however, wouldn't let the arguments cross the line where it came to scratches that didn't disappear quickly, so the dangers threatening us would remain slight. Little by little she would spoil me but wouldn't be able to live without the power she had acquired over years of persistent effort. She would lose her peace of mind, become more jealous and hide it, suffering in secret. The longer it went on, the more she would get tied up in chains she herself had created, but her northern face wouldn't reveal anything. Only her eyes would glitter more and more brightly – blue, so piercingly blue I would've been astonished sometimes, shrugging at my inability to find a sufficient explanation...

I broke off, noticing Stella staring at me, obviously surprised I didn't avert my eyes from her. I grinned guiltily, winked, and turned to Gibbs. Everything indicated we would be heading off to our rooms soon, and I still hadn't come close to obtaining any clarity regarding our plans. Maybe I should have waited for everything to work out on its own, but the days spent paging through old newspapers, in boredom and wearisome idleness, added to my impatience.

"Here's one more photo, Gibbs," I said loudly, pulling a picture of Julian from my pocket and shoving it toward him. "This time it's my friend, not yours."

Gibbs, sitting with a relaxed, thoughtful look, fixed his eyes on it with clear dissatisfaction, probably expecting another trick.

"No, no, I'm not hinting at anything," I quickly added. "You don't know this man and probably wouldn't want to. But remember, we talked about him in the restaurant, and you brought me here to find him. I realize you have your own business, but you've got to agree I can't simply sit here in complete obscurity, in the middle of nowhere. Could you finally tell me when we'll begin and what's ahead for us?" I concluded somewhat crossly.

While I spoke, stumbling and gradually getting angry at myself, Gibbs watched me more and more serenely and then nodded. "But of course," he began ingratiatingly, almost gently. "I'm aware of that, but we simply got caught up in other concerns – we should've told you already. It happened all at once: first the owl, then something else, and the damn weather's been terrible!" He sighed.

"Yeah..." one of the Christophers added ambiguously.

"But you timed your question well," continued Gibbs, again livening up. "It's just the right moment – in fact, I was actually planning to talk with you anyway. We'll get started tomorrow." He paused for a loaded silence. "Tomorrow we're moving to another place – and largely because of your 'target.' He went there today," Gibbs nodded at the second Christopher. "Take a look. Did you see anyone like this?" And he tossed the photo to him.

Christopher Two stared at the snapshot, holding it at a distance, like a dangerous toy, and at last said uncertainly, "Nah, I don't know. Maybe he was there, maybe not. There were a lot of people, and they all looked alike. Can I keep it?" he asked innocuously. I shook my head and Christopher threw the photo back, no longer interested.

"Well, you see," said Gibbs, "he may have caught a glimpse. And if he didn't, we'll track that guy down tomorrow – and find him for sure, if he's there."

"What kind of place is it?" I inquired, deliberately disinterestedly.

"The place?" repeated Gibbs. "The place is well-known – it's called White Beach. Various settlements are there, consisting mostly of volunteers – those who are helping develop the oceanside. At first they got lured by lucrative one-year contracts, but many then stay longer. Life on the coast is odd; you may even find it appealing, if you get used to it. And they aren't paid badly either," Gibbs yawned. "In short, you'll see tomorrow. Now, I think, it's time to hit the sack."

And he pushed his chair back noisily, setting everyone else in motion too, as if the evening lost its content with his departure, and there was nothing else to do but follow his example.

CHAPTER 14

I lay awake in bed, both hands behind my head, and waited for Stella. The bone-chilling north wind now came from the west and whistled in a different key. The sky had cleared and stars appeared, with only a few wisps of defeated clouds eclipsing them here and there. The moon hung heavily over the waves, basking the bank in treacherous light and letting me see the outlines of things in the darkness of the bedroom. The ghosts, which had been hiding in the house, rose from their slumber, anticipating the departure of the unwanted guests, and started an intimate talk, not muted by the crashing surf or the howling wind.

Time passed. I was listening to the sounds and trying to guess why Stella was taking so long when the door finally screeched and I recognized her light steps. A moment later I felt her beside me. Strong and limber, she knew what she needed better than I did. Her body got used to me quickly; it confidently found its way in the labyrinth, and I followed, endeavoring not to fall behind and get lost. Her fingers intertwined themselves with my own; her hands clasped my neck, pulling me up, or thrust in my chest, pushing me away with dishonest strength. Her aroma was everywhere – the aroma of impatience and boldness, which made me forget patience and embrace boldness in turn. Her face was serious in the cold light, her eyes closed, lips firmly drawn. She didn't say a word, just sighed impetuously and emitted muffled moans when convulsions shook her. Then she dropped on her back, lay there, just as sternly, drifting inside herself. Yet she had already come a thousand miles nearer, though I had to admit, upon closer inspection, I still hadn't totally reached her.

Soon she became insatiate again – it went on like this for an eternity, and I was ready to appeal for mercy when she abruptly calmed down. I wanted her to stay until morning, wanted to wake with her at my side, but I was too shy to say so. Actually, we didn't have energy for words and lay silently for a long time, peering at each other with fresh interest, as though we had converted to another form and were gradually growing accustomed to it.

Stella spoke first. "You're better than I thought," she informed me gratefully. "I questioned Silvia, who you were so willing to get in bed with – one might think you're attracted to oldies. But she didn't tell me anything, though I like to know ahead of time."

"Ahead of time? Why?" I asked, somewhat thrown off by her tone. "As for me, I don't like to know anything in advance. It's much better to discover for yourself."

"Discover what – is there anything new?" Stella inquired derisively. "Or, as they preached to us in school, 'everyone's interesting in their own way?' Really? Not at all. That's not for me – all this's so deadly dull!"

She flipped over on her back and continued, "I understand. You, like everyone else, consider yourself the center of the world. You believe that, yes, you are *you*, not something boring and obscure, and everyone should be fascinated by what's inside you – since what you have inside is so special to you. And I'm not special for you, I'm ordinary, but do you know me? Do you know what am I for real?"

In her voice was a note of offense. I wrapped my arm around her to comfort her like a child, but Stella removed it right away. "No, don't try to convince me of the opposite, I don't need it. I'm better off this way," she said with slightly insolent hoarseness. "I also don't want to know about you or the rest, so we're even. Only one thing is amusing: observing my own self when I'm with others – it's quite funny sometimes. And I do observe – me and my own self; as for the others, they don't concern me. Although you, of course, are a special case," she added, smiling craftily and again snuggling up to me like a cat. "With you, I have to admit, everything is different. And don't think I have to tell you this – I can leave right now and not say a thing. But you've won me over somehow, made me want to take care of you, maybe even protect you, although it's not my style. After all, I'm a woman – you men should look after me, shouldn't you?"

We stopped talking. I wanted to think about her but couldn't find the right key, was unable to open the box. Then, in irritation, without knowing why, I began to speak about my secret, telling Stella what I had never shared with anyone. I said that tomorrow I'd again get back in action – maybe I'd catch some luck and we'd really find Julian at White Beach. Lowering my voice, I asked her if Gibbs had been telling the truth, but then, not waiting for her answer, said surely that Gibbs and I would come to terms sooner or later, so she shouldn't worry about me. I even pulled out my Colt and showed it to her, getting excited by the cool heaviness of the steel. Stella touched it with her fragile hand and wanted to hold it and take aim. I didn't give it to her, however, explaining a gun was no joke, and she got upset but then cheered up again and requested some water. I slid the Colt back in my bag and went to the kitchen, groping my way down the corridor and scaring away the pitch black darkness lodged in the corners.

When I returned, Stella was sitting wrapped in the blanket, almost exactly like Silvia a few days before. She drank down the water and – still resembling Silvia – began to talk about Gibbs, scowling and wrinkling her forehead in distress. It was odd to see her struggling with words, and even her voice became gloomy and muffled.

"I hate people like him," said Stella, "those self-confident, pretentious men. They're all so arrogant – and Gibbs is full of arrogance, and on top of that he always knows what he needs from others. I can't even disobey him – when he looks at you, his gaze forces your subordination, and, besides, he has an answer to every question. You can't outsmart him: it's as if he can see into the future – sees all your sly maneuvers and is ready for them in advance. Even when he errs, he gives you the feeling he knew he was going to slip up and already has – actually, always had – a solution, even better than the previous one…"

Stella spoke unclearly, I didn't really understand her. "Gibbs," she claimed, "is clairvoyant or something like that. He never doubts everything will work out according to his rules, or, rather, he doesn't want to think about any other rules than his own. If some blunder occurs, then it means a new rule is coming from his reserve for every occasion. And if others think he's totally wrong, then that's their problem. He's always right, that's his main trait. When someone has such authority, how can you not be jealous?"

"Just like Julian," I said sullenly, but then thought – no, the comparison isn't legitimate. They aren't even close; Julian can't live by himself, he needs the world around him so he can unite with it and dissolve into the crowd, while Gibbs… Where could one find a crowd of people similar to Gibbs?

"No, my Julian is different," I admitted aloud.

Stella just shrugged her shoulders. "I don't know your Julian," she replied indifferently. "But I do know Gibbs, and he's way out of your league."

"I feel sorry for him," she said. "He's even more of a loner than you since he's much more daring. But I'm also afraid of him – as Silvia is – and it can't be otherwise. He's probably the only man that inspires fear in me – he's incomprehensible, I don't know what to expect or what he's capable of. That is I know he's capable of greater and more terrible things than I can imagine, since I can't imagine I'd willingly go where he once went – you know what I mean. Everyone I see around me would not even consider it in their right mind. There's no road back, and furthermore, no one can predict what happens to you *after*, as no one knows what happens after death, which is why everyone is so terrified of death, even if life isn't always pleasant, it's quite abominable, more often than not. But when you pass through that – the reason for his mark – you also can't return, and who knows what he feels now, whether he remembers what it was like up to then, or whether his current life is even more hopeless…

I can't call myself happy, but to go further may be even worse. I'll never take such a step – and I'm terrified to watch those who have, although they're appealing of course, in their own strange way. So I listen to him unquestioningly, even if he's crude and rough, and I'll never puzzle out his horrifying secret. I can only pretend, lying to myself that those…" – she wanted to say the word but stuttered and couldn't – "well, as if they, you understand, did not exist at all. As if they were invented by hypocrites – to have a reason for feeling superior. Yet self-deceit doesn't change anything, especially when you have a living reminder in front of you."

"Did you sleep with him?" I asked, feeling an acute shot of jealousy, and added in embarrassment, "If you don't want to tell me, that's okay, of course."

Stella laughed and playfully nudged me with her foot. "That's what worries you more than anything else? No, I didn't sleep with him. I don't like him, and he's too old for me. But he didn't suggest it either," she divulged with an incomprehensible snicker. I frowned, not really believing her, and she looked at me mockingly. "My God, you men are capable of letting such nonsense bother you. What's the difference? You need to worry about other things at the moment."

"Why?" I pricked up my ears. Stella sighed and turned her back to me. It became darker in the room – the moon probably hid behind the clouds. Now I could only discern her thin profile in which I saw, with no apparent reason, insincerity and stubbornness.

"Why?" I repeated insistently, taking her by the arm.

"Why, why," Stella imitated me with surprising sadness. "I can't tell you. They won't forgive me for it later."

"Please," I pleaded, clenching her submissive fingers. "Is it the Gibbs-Night-Escape? Say something. Is it that?"

Stella sighed again, withdrew her hand, tossed the blanket off her shoulder, and stretched out beside me. "Promise not to snitch on me," she whispered in my ear, tickling me with her breath. "If you do, I'll be in trouble. You don't want anything bad to happen to me, right?"

"Of course not. I promise," I said with impatience. "Tell me. What are they planning? What's the next move going to be?"

Stella began to explain, stumbling and picking the right words. The longer she spoke, the more I wanted to laugh at myself, acknowledging my own blindness. Yet I listened in silence, afraid of scattering her thoughts and interrupting her erratic murmuring since I knew I wouldn't be able to wrangle anything else out of her afterward. Gradually she told me the whole story – or, more precisely, the part she and Silvia knew.

"Gibbs and those two traffic in sleepy herb," said Stella softly. "Other people smuggle it in here, I don't even want to know about that, but these three collect the stuff and bring it to the city. For sleepy herb, as you know, they can give you many years in prison, and M. is full of undercover cops. Of course, Gibbs doesn't work in the city itself; the police there aren't any threat to him, but they are also detailed here, to the Dunes. Many areas are under observation, especially those where large schooners can dock – the grass is delivered in fishing boats and unloaded on the coast. Then the local dealers move it on – Gibbs or others who are in on it. Since the police are in pursuit, everyone contrives their own ruses, however they can, and this is where Gibbs is so different from the rest. He's more ingenious than all of them put together, and he knows the coast better than anyone else. So the smugglers prefer to work with him – others are envious, of course, but he's no idiot. He lets everyone earn some money, and no one complains very much. The detectives went all out, but the grass just keeps coming. No one can do anything and won't… But I haven't tried it myself, don't think that." She became uncomfortable. "That's not who I am. I just need the money, and there's my brother…"

"Okay, but where do I fit in?" I interrupted her. "I don't even need money – why are they messing around with me? And what if I chickened out or, let's say, wanted a share of the profits or ratted on them?"

Stella smirked. "You dumbbell, who's going to let you have a share?" And she stopped talking again, and I didn't butt in, patiently waiting for explanation.

"You're here because what they need can't be done without you," she said finally. "I mean, not you personally, but some novice like you – who can easily be fooled. That's why Gibbs keeps everything in his own hands – the grass is picked up where no one else would risk going. There are places where the police don't buzz about since not a soul goes there anyway. Docking a boat is easier than easy, and nobody's in sight... You've probably figured out why. Yes, *they* either live there or feed there. In general, it's their land for a few miles, and everyone walks around it, takes a lengthy detour to avoid stumbling onto them. The locals know the place, and with Gibbs they know it's better to keep their distance so they don't get roped in either. That's why Gibbs finds people like you, curious tourists, and drags them along in order to have this entertainment for the..." Stella brought her lips right up to my ear and said in a hardly audible voice, "... black pelicans, while he deals with business. Gibbs says if someone ends up alone with them, they won't touch the others under any circumstances. Everyone has their chance, he says, or their hour, but every time only one has it, just one person. If you find such a person to send ahead, then the road is clear for everyone else – so they're sending you. That's why you're here!"

Stella rolled over, felt for her cigarettes below the bed, and began to smoke. I lay in silence without moving, processing what I had heard.

"Okay, I get the point of the Christophers: they transport the stuff. But what are you and Silvia here for?" I asked, also taking a cigarette and puffing on it.

"You're really slow," said Stella in amazement, throwing up her arms. "We're here for your sake, so you'll play along and won't rebel. You can't be brought there by force; what if you just lie face down in the sand and say, 'Kill me, I won't go'? Then that's it, you're useless, and the entire plan is ruined – and, frankly, that's definitely what I would do if I were you. So, Gibbs and Silvia, they masterminded this trick: the men will leave you with us. It's obvious, you won't slip away – after all, *they* have to catch someone…" – and Stella named *them* again in a barely audible voice. "And if it isn't you, then it has to be one of us, and Gibbs is quite sure people like you can't let weak women suffer. He always says: men like you will voluntarily rip off their shirt and run on their wobbly legs right into the face of the threat. Although, he adds, if you think about it, what kind of defense can they provide? Except in our concrete case, of course. So we're here as a sort of a guarantee, to ensure you don't disappear, having understood you're in deep shit. That's why we've been jumping into bed with you – to complete the picture, so when it's time to make a choice, you won't have a sudden insight. Here Gibbs's assessment was correct," she added with incomprehensible malice. "These men with ideas, he said, won't leave you alone in danger no matter what. They'll always play the hero, thinking you've really fallen for them and considering having sex with you to be the proof of that. I didn't believe this nonsense at first, but then I saw for myself – it works, he's right. And it would've worked with you," she contracted her eyes, moving out of the darkness with the flame of her lighter as she lit another cigarette. "It would have worked as smooth as butter – if it hadn't suddenly become so distasteful to me. Now I don't know what you're going to do. Just don't tell on me, I don't deserve that."

"I don't know either," I said conciliatorily. "We'll see tomorrow," – and I wanted to hug her, to shield myself from everything with this body that smelled of almonds, sweetness, and agitation, but Stella slid away fitfully.

"What's this 'we'll see?'" She was sincerely wounded. "You just think for yourself. Don't involve me; I have enough problems as it is!"

I didn't argue with her and closed my eyes, suddenly feeling very tired. Within a minute I was dreaming of enormous monkeys dancing around, climbing on top of each other. There was no Gibbs, no Julian. They had disappeared from my life forever. Instead, there was an island with tall palm trees, a thin coastline along the sea, the smooth surface of a bay, and yellow sand that glittered more and more intensely, irritating my retina and not letting me concentrate on one thought.

I woke up late, alone. A bright beam of sunlight, reflecting off the nickel-plated coffee pot, shone right in my face. The wind whistled wildly outside the window, instantly returning me from the world of phantoms to a crude commotion with no mercy for slackers. I lay on my back for a long time, listening to it and recalling Stella and her admiration for this scoundrel Gibbs – admiration he didn't deserve and was, at the same time, more worthy of than anyone else. My thoughts skipped from the capital and Gretchen to the ocean and the Dunes, from Julian to Gibbs, from my plan to their sly secret that had entangled me in its cobweb. The longer I thought, the more inconceivable appeared the very essence of turning back. It wasn't Gibbs who lured me into coming here where obscurity reigns and is capable of splitting any life in two – all of my past had been steadily preparing the same trap. It was masked as a question mark at the end of a seemingly innocuous phrase, provoking me with inanity in which I wanted to see myriad meanings, inflaming my imagination and concealing the boundaries beyond which its release was harmful. If I had known in advance, I could have kept my guard up, but it was too late now. I had to make a move, and rules – rules are merciless.

Soon, I felt a simple and clear plan emerging in my head. Everything's developing rather well, I convinced myself, chasing away the wearisome whispers of uncertainty. Those who would like to use me, only viewing me as an instrument, don't even suspect they're playing into my hands. Let them drag me wherever they want, but when it comes down to the decisive step, they'll have to admit, in astonishment, that I have hatched something too, and have a scheme allotting the others just a side role.

They want me to protect them from danger – okay, I'll protect them from danger. Just not alone: someone else has to share the assignment – let him be afraid of the uncertainty along with me. He understands it better than me, will be able to reconcile me with it – by example or simply by being at my side. I need someone at hand who is like me: who is frightened when it's frightening, who only laughs when it's pointless to be afraid, who seeks an escape when the mission becomes intolerable, who sticks to my elbow when everyone wants to cling to somebody, knowing, yes, I'm doing terribly, but I'm not on my own…

In a word, I decided to force Gibbs to go with me. The details appeared vague – I was aware that forcing him wouldn't be easy. "Gibbs is way out of your league," Stella had said the night before, and I knew she was right, but I also assumed nothing was impossible if I really wanted it and acted decisively, all the more so since no one expected this of me.

As in the case of Julian, when I created my secret, which had now lost its primacy, I couldn't think out all the minor aspects, so I just imagined myself with a revolver aimed at Gibbs's chest and my brief but audible monologue, which I'd compel him to listen to and which should settle everything right away. Ultimately, no one would lose, I proved to them all in my mind. Gibbs and I would return together, and I'd help them with the luggage or just head my own way, forgetting about them and not interfering anymore. We would be even – no one would feel offended and seek a convenient moment for revenge. And if they didn't get it, I'd persuade them – trying my best.

Regarding persuasion, my intentions were not particularly clear – I was uncertain whether firing in the air or a threatening scream with the veins popping out of my neck would help. Neither the Christophers nor Gibbs looked like they were easy to frighten and were probably able to scream even more threateningly, not to mention their pistols and obvious experience in carrying out negotiations of this kind. But I didn't let that discourage me – since I had no other plan and there wasn't much time left. Moreover, on my side there might be advantages as well – from the resourcefulness of my brain to a support from unexpected direction. And here, not daring to hope outright, I secretly thought about Stella, recalling her caresses and her whispers, almost believing in our mutual passion. I wanted to forget about the Christophers and Gibbs, remembering only the slender, limber girl with a northern face and fair hair who decided to warn me, putting her own fate on the line. I pitied and loved her with fleeting fondness; I fantasized about how she would act when I rose up against the group. Would she not do anything foolish? Could I save her from danger if it came to that?

With these thoughts I went to breakfast. The others were already sitting at their places, eating eggs with bacon. Silvia gave me a friendly smile, and Christopher Two saluted me with his fork, mooing good-morning through his full mouth. It seemed like a thoroughly cordial team had been waiting for the one who had overslept. They now welcomed my entrance, but I knew what lay at the bottom of these pseudo-pleasantries. Glimpses of falsity and concealed alertness slipped out everywhere; words were distorted by secret meaning and hints of the imminent conclusion toward which we had been patiently progressing. Only Stella sat without looking at me, silently studying something on her plate. I didn't glance at her either, thrilled to sense the fragile alliance connecting us to spite the others' intentions – like a conductor that transmits the signals, knowing someone will catch them on the other side.

"Power up," said Gibbs affably. "Today will be hard going. Silvia, give him some more coffee." He sat at the head of the table, surveying his small army and evidently certain everything would work out exactly as he had planned it.

"When are we heading out?" I inquired.

"We'll eat and then go," muttered Christopher One. "We were waiting for you, not someone else."

"You could have woken me up," I shrugged my shoulders and yawned. "I sleep well here by the ocean."

"It's no problem," Gibbs reassured me. "It's not late; you came at just the right moment. And, hopefully, the wind will calm down soon."

"Are we walking into the wind?" I asked with interest, as if that was worrying me.

"Yes, into the wind," replied Gibbs absently. "Into the wind and into the sun... All right, let's get ready," he commanded the Christophers, got up, and left the table.

The others stood up after him. I shoveled down my eggs and returned to my room. It now seemed so familiar and cozy that I sat down on the bed, glanced at the walls with a bewildered gaze, as if asking myself whether I was actually leaving them forever. I imagined activities I could enjoy in the house, the staircase to the attic, and the yellow packages of the *Chronicler.* I recalled Silvia and Stella sharing my bed, and the whistling wind outside the window, which met me in the morning, promising vastness and infinity, other mainlands and other countries. I didn't want to leave, but as almost always, it wasn't up to me. Another reality awaited me, probably worse than what I had experienced so far.

I sighed and began to pack my bag. Julian's photo was sent to the bottom – something told me I wouldn't need it in the near future – and the heavy Colt with its cold grip found a place right at the top, barely covered by clothing. I held it in my hand before slipping it under a carefully folded sweater, and my heart thumped loudly. A shiver of panic overcame me and my eyes dimmed, but I gained control of myself, not having time for weakness. Then I finished collecting my things, smoked a cigarette, and just stared blankly out the window.

Soon we were walking along the ocean, right into the wind, which had abated a little as Gibbs had predicted, though it was still persistent and gusty, making the going more difficult and not letting us talk. I noticed the luggage had decreased by almost half – clearly, a portion had been left in the house where they were going to return. The women were hiking without any backpacks at all, each carrying only a small bag, while the rucksack I had been assigned at the beginning of our trip now weighed heavily on Gibbs's shoulders. The Christophers hung a little behind, so the whole time I was between them and Gibbs, who led our band as always. "They're guarding me," I thought with a grin, remembering the attentive eye in the center of the shell curled out in spirals. "As if I had somewhere to run."

After hiking a few miles, we turned toward the Dunes. There was almost no wind there and the temperature rose immediately, although the sun barely shone through the cloud cover. Drops of sweat dripped down my spine but I ignored them, glancing around as if trying to commit the path to memory. This was senseless; the barren, nearly lunar, slightly hilly landscape didn't offer any signs, and I didn't understand how Gibbs could find the right way. We traipsed between the hills without a hint of any trail, getting further and further from the coast or perhaps approaching it again – I had lost my sense of direction long ago in the many turns. The sun stood right over our heads and didn't help with orientation, so I simply regarded the area, making a fruitless attempt to find a trace of something living.

The Dunes were silent. Looking around, I could hardly recall my recent escape nightmare, the discordance of the bizarre sounds, and the turmoil of horrors. The surroundings remained aloof, repelling me with gloomy apathy, almost intentionally, as if saying, "We warned you. You have only yourself to blame."

Beyond one of the hills, we stumbled upon the burnt frame of a car, an SUV, similar to our Land Rovers and half-covered in sand. "Tourists," said Christopher Two, nodding at it and winking mischievously. "Went out for a ride without local guides, so to speak." He went a little closer to its body and was about to peer inside when he recoiled and almost fell, cursing briefly. From the heap of iron, a prairie hare with long back legs skipped out, dizzily swiveling its head and hopping away, its spotted back bouncing up and down, its ears pressed back. All of us burst out laughing, and someone hooted – probably Christopher himself. He raised his fist in the air yet didn't return to the vehicle, and we marched on.

My shirt was wet and stuck to my body; my legs were exhausted from walking over the uneven, pebbly ground. Still, I didn't ask questions to avoid giving the impression I was longing for a rest. Silvia was also suffering from the heat, but the others seemed not to notice it. Finally, the air became fresher, the smell of the ocean wafted in, and a few minutes later we again came out on the water, where the threatening boom of the surf mixed with the cries of a few lonely seagulls. Gibbs tossed his backpack on the sand, stretched with pleasure, and turned to us.

"Now, we'll have a bite to eat," he said cheerfully, with the satisfaction of a man who had just completed something major and was prepared for gratitude. We sat in a circle. Stella dug out our sandwiches and, looking at the ground, handed them to each of us. Intentionally, I plopped down next to Gibbs and placed my bag close by so it would be within reach at any moment. The Christophers were lying across from us, sprawled on the sand and using their loads as pillows, which gave me confidence.

They don't suspect anything, I thought as I slowly chewed without noticing the taste. They're regular village boys who are used to just carrying out uncomplicated orders. I'll outsmart them. The main problem will be overcoming Gibbs!

The latter, in the meantime, was declaiming about something trivial, picking on Silvia, who was replying quietly without sharing his animation. This didn't bother him; he gesticulated a lot, letting crumbs drop in the sand, but the absent half of his face was turned to me so I couldn't see what was on it – a victorious smirk or perhaps a shadow of tense expectation similar to mine.

When he finished his food, Gibbs brushed his hands off and cast a glance over us, stopping at me. "Things look like this now," he said in an efficient manner. "We have a small matter to deal with – so these two and I will be gone for a couple hours," and he nodded at the Christophers, who were already on their feet with their backpacks ready. They are quick, I thought, and Gibbs continued, still not taking his eyes off me, "You guys rest here for a while, inhale the ocean air. Silvia will be in charge, and we'll come back quite soon."

Trying to maintain an indifferent expression, I dragged over my bag, slid my hand under the sweater and felt for the ribbed handle. Gibbs didn't rush to stand up and kept staring at me point blank, from time to time scratching his cheek.

"What do you mean – 'a small matter'?" I drawled without pulling out my hand. "We didn't discuss any other small matters. You said we were going to White Beach, that's why I consented to come. What's happening now – are you putting it off? The sun's already going down, you won't return until evening – what will we do then, just go back to where we started? That's not why I walked for half a day in this heat."

I mumbled on drearily, feeling furious doubts ripping me to shreds – Is it time? Is it not yet? – almost despairing I had already missed the moment and lost the initiative. "Have you heard? 'The sun's going down.' He's a real trailblazer," laughed Christopher One, jabbing his elbow into the side of the second Christopher. Devilish fires were glittering in Gibbs's irises. He stopped scratching himself and looked at me curiously.

"What's this about? Do you want to be the boss now?" he inquired seriously. "Well, all right, lead us then to that White – what's it called – Beach!"

Silence ensued. Only the Christophers sniffled and snorted, expecting a continuation. "Why aren't you saying anything?" Gibbs persisted. "You want to be in control, so lead the way!"

His curiosity vanished and his eyes narrowed unkindly. On the part of his face where there was nothing, I saw deep lines that wouldn't vanish with either a smile or sleep.

"Or are you scared?" He was getting more and more wound up. "Maybe you only have courage to fling photos around and annoy busy people?"

Gibbs spoke loudly with unconcealed malice. He felt all his power over me and reveled in it, even if still half-heartedly, inviting others to feel the same. "You're just a gabber. You think way too highly of yourself, but it would take nothing to put you in your place!" He made an undefinable movement with his fingers and looked at silent, confused Silvia and Stella. "Here, give them commands – but you can't even do *that*. I warned you yesterday: don't pry! But you keep prying like a nosy child."

At that moment, my fear vanished and doubt disappeared. I grabbed the Colt and, holding it with two hands, aimed it at Gibbs's chest. Everything was instantly still. The space around us became enormous and empty, with only the ocean rolling evenly in the distance.

"I'm not prying," I broke the silence – and my voice shook traitorously. "I don't pry," I repeated more firmly. "It's you who came into my life and wanted to rule it like your own. But I won't allow that – no way!"

Gibbs froze and stared in disbelief at my revolver. Then he slowly lifted his gaze and looked at me with interest, as if being surprised by an unexpected discovery. From the corner of my eye I noticed the Christophers stirring on the side and screamed with all my might, "Everyone stand still or I'll shoot him! Do you hear me, you two?"

"Why the uproar?" asked Gibbs calmly. "If you want to shoot, then shoot. Nobody's stopping you."

"I don't want to shoot, but I will if it's necessary," I snapped, glancing at the Christophers and trying to give my words a threatening and convincing ring. "You want to play me, but I won't let you – or, better, let's play together. Let's go together, you and me!"

"And where do you want us to go?" Gibbs inquired.

"You know where!" I screamed again. "Don't make a fool of yourself – you told me you don't like that. We're heading where you wanted to send me alone; I figured it all out. And I'll go there, all right, though not on my own. I'll go with you, Gibbs – do you understand?"

"Now I understand," Gibbs nodded, a stern expression on his face. "Only I have other plans, so don't count on me."

Somehow he ended up on his feet, his eyes still fixed on me, and I jumped up without lowering the revolver, watching him and the Christophers, one of whom had a dully glittering black object in his hand. "Tourist, throw down your toy," his wheezy, strained voice boomed, but in response I just flipped the trigger, sensing a drunken shiver run through my body.

"Okay, that's enough mischief," said Gibbs, his pupils boring into me. "The jokes are over. Now, my friend, put the gun down and be a good boy, otherwise they'll really shoot."

"And I'll really shoot you," I replied with hate, but Stella suddenly screamed, "Shut up, you idiot, you don't have any bullets! I took them out last night. They'll kill you, now!"

Like thunder, it crashed through my head: Stella was alone in my room when I went to get water. Stella and the revolver – that's it. I glanced at her: she sat upright, like a pale statue, showing me a few shining shells in her open palm. I shifted my gaze to Gibbs, who only laughed.

"That means, you knew..." I began, but the Christophers were closing in, approaching from two sides, while Gibbs also changed his position so I could no longer keep them all in sight. We moved around in a strange dance, crouching and gracefully shifting from place to place. I waved my useless Colt, frightening no one, realizing I had lost, yet not wanting to admit it, even if it would cost me my life. There, before me, twinkled our scattered things, Silvia and Stella, looking at us in despair, the concentrated faces of the men, who again became complete strangers to me, as if I were seeing them for the first time. One of the Christophers held his pistol ready, the other hid something behind his back, and I didn't know which was more dangerous. Slowly I retreated to the Dunes, taking a glance at one, then the other, spasmodically trying to follow them both and still keep Gibbs within view, but the circle was getting tighter and tighter. Then I sensed one of the three behind me and started to turn, but something crashed into my head. Balls of fire flared up and died down. Sound went silent. And I sunk into darkness.

CHAPTER 15

I don't know how much time passed until I regained consciousness. Gibbs and the Christophers were nowhere to be seen – they had gathered their belongings and left. My head rested on someone's rolled-up raincoat, and at my side sat Silvia, observing me silently. Stella also stood nearby, facing the ocean, her arms wrapped around her shoulders. After counting to ten, I sat up and carefully touched the back of my neck. A hot lump throbbed there, but otherwise I felt fairly okay. There was no blood and I wasn't dizzy – they hadn't wanted to do me any serious harm. Thanks, I thought bitterly, for your calculated humanism. I suppose it's better than nothing.

"How're you doing, cutie pie?" Silvia asked quietly. I glanced at her – she was composed and politely cold. She had no compassion for me whatsoever and was thinking about her own matters, yet I couldn't get angry at her, although I knew she, too, had been deceiving me from the start.

"Soon it'll heal. The ocean air cures," she added. "Do you want a wet bandage?"

I shook my head and gave her a crooked smile. My Colt lay five yards away in the sand. Upon seeing it, I remembered all the details of the recent scene, feeling awkwardness and then relief that it was all behind me and I had no one else to clash with.

I asked Silvia for a clean handkerchief, stood up, and took a few steps. With every passing minute I felt better. Only when I stooped down to pick up the revolver did blood rush to the painful spot and make me groan involuntarily, but even that was over quickly.

Spreading out my jacket on the sand, I disassembled the Colt and began to wipe down each part methodically, ensuring not one bit of sand remained. Occasionally I peeked at Stella, who still stood with her back to us, as if asking myself who she was to me now and what should I think of her. Every time I found no answer and rapidly shifted my gaze, afraid she would turn around and I would say something stupid. Then Silvia came over and sat down next to me, watching my hands meditatively. I didn't object – it was relaxing and better with her than alone.

"Don't get upset at Gibbs," she said in a low, guttural voice. "What else could he have done? Every other option would have ended up worse."

Aha, that means Gibbs knocked me out, I thought. But rather than speak out loud, I just nodded my head glumly and mumbled something in agreement, not wishing to argue.

"He's not as cruel as it may seem," Silvia continued. "Everyone has their own affairs, and whatever you do, it'll always be both good and bad. He asked me to tell you that – that everything is bad, but good at the same time. You can't say who it's worse for, and it's the only way it can be."

"Okay," I said, "you told me and I thank you. Pass on a message from me too: he and I will discuss the subject when we meet. Both what's good and what's bad and for whom in particular."

Here I stopped short, instantly recalling how easily Gibbs and the Christophers had checked my defiance. It obviously wasn't worth waving my fist in the air now, after a fight where I got beaten.

"No, it's not that I'll try to get even, but there's still something left unsaid, that's certain," I began to explain, looking off to the side. "It's convenient to talk through you, of course, yet he'll have to speak to me directly at some point."

Silvia nodded as you nod to an upset child, extended her hand, and casually stroked my cheek. "You'll work it out, I'm sure. Sometime later – the city is small; everyone bumps into each other," she said in a conciliatory tone. And she added more loudly than was necessary, obviously wanting Stella to hear, "Don't be angry at her either. She's still a girl – and doesn't know what she's doing."

Stella turned around impetuously and fixed her wide-open eyes on us. Her face was pale and plain, her thin lips curled and twitching. "You whore!" she screamed at Silvia. "I hate you all. You can go to hell with your beloved Gibbs. You think he's a hero – but he's not the only tough guy out there. There are others, tougher – you'll see!"

Silvia just smiled condescendingly, and Stella came closer and spun toward me. "You're pathetic too," she said angrily. "Nothing but a buffoon, not a man. You think I deceived you? Yes, I did, however what did you want me to do? I couldn't take any other risks. I kept trying to give you a hint, but you understood nothing. Now, they'll never take me with them again; where will I dig up the money – as a streetwalker?" And she added bitterly, "I'm the dumb-ass who decided to be generous. All was in vain – you just slept and dreamed."

Silvia shook her head and began to sift through some package lying next to her. In the meantime I had finished cleaning the Colt and peered thoughtfully at the empty clip. "Silvia, ask her where the bullets are," I requested. Stella came up silently, dumped a handful of shells on my jacket and, without uttering a word, walked off to the side. I loaded the revolver and laid it in my bag. Silvia looked at her watch.

"It's time to say goodbye," she said firmly. "We need to walk a long ways, cutie pie, and so do you." Then she gazed in my eyes, as if trying to read something there, but quickly turned away.

"Where am I to go?" I asked, standing and adjusting the bag on my shoulder.

"Toward the water and then to the right, along the shore," Silvia replied. "You'll see it soon. Go, and don't be scared…"

She wanted to add something, but hesitated and kept it to herself. I nodded, gave a little wave of the hand, and swiftly strode toward the onrushing waves. Some hundred steps later, I glanced back. Silvia and Stella lay facedown on the sand, two fragile figures on the endless yellow-gray canvas. Something pained me, but it lasted just an instant. I marched ahead and didn't turn around again.

On I tromped, muttering, frowning, talking to myself. My head was swarming with angry arguments I would have enjoyed throwing in the face of my recent companions – and Gibbs above all. I regretted with all my heart I hadn't voiced any of the vindictive words flying off my tongue now. I could have ridiculed all of them – the self-confidence of him, the main liar, the silliness of the Christophers, the shallowness of their wanton women... I tried to convince myself not everything had been lost and we would meet again someday thanks to the laws of greater justice, whose existence I wanted to believe in so often. But it didn't help – despair overwhelmed me like bitter bile.

Then something shifted inside me – dikes slammed shut and exasperation dried up without a trace. The farther I got, the further my thoughts drifted. Gibbs and the Christophers moved away; I recalled only Silvia, thinking about her with a slight melancholy, feeling I had wasted something I didn't have. No longer offended, I sensed a strange lightness; it seemed I had tossed a heavy burden off my shoulders, and my misfortunes had been replaced by long-awaited freedom – from everyone and almost everything.

I caught myself counting steps, trying to harmonize them with the crashing surf and its persistent, hypnotic rhythm. My head spun a little; my eyelids quivered. I sensed the smells and sounds intensely – as never before. The ocean music enraptured me, I even rapped out "one-two-three," or even better, "Ju-li-an," so I could firmly retain the beat. Then even that didn't seem like enough. I began to alternate the hated name with an entirely taboo word, as if laughing at the legend I might be urged to verify at any moment. "Pe-li-can," I chanted in an undertone, slightly astonished at my own boldness, forgetting my own secret for an instant and endlessly contemplating what kind of event was awaiting me. Does it measure up to the threatening rumors? Isn't it a lie like almost everything else?

"Well?" I asked, scanning the seascape. "I'm here – you got what you wanted. Where are those powers instilling terror? Where is the one that's not even mentioned out loud? I'm not hiding – the hiders are laying face-down now, afraid to raise their heads. And even if they're right, I don't need to be right. I'm sick of pointless rightness, I don't want it anymore. They chose me to be their bait, but I'm not bait – maybe I wanted to come here myself in spite of the others. They didn't have to lure me into traps; I'm here willingly! Voluntarily! Do you hear me, you tyrants of the shore, you cruelest of rulers?"

No one responded – with either a gesture or a sound. Time stopped, as if finding a shelter it couldn't leave. The scenery didn't change, nothing attracted my gaze. The sand to the right and the gray ocean to the left merging with the gray sky at the horizon constituted the scene, familiar down to the last grain, though still concealing more than I could grasp. I sought words I could draw on to name myself, yet all of them seemed inadequate – their lifetimes were measured in ridiculously small quantities. I knew they would pass away even earlier than I would fall from the surrounding world, not to mention this coast and these waves which might not be eternal but would live long enough to become an illustration of eternity, to provide a clue of what I was striving for, only slightly deceiving myself with assumptions. I sought a word or a name worthy of every single wave being born over and over again with such ease and faith in the continuity of its existence. "If it's impossible to put it all in one word," I said to I-didn't-know-who, "then let them tell it to me in as many as they like. I agree to be patient; I'm not rushing anywhere. To forget about the question mark, one finally needs to find answers. Why am I always swimming against the current? What can serve as a comparison, a contrast, to help find even one hint? If my fellow men, thronged together in a crowd, drive me off, closing the borders and denying admission, then give me something else – give me the sky and the ocean, yellow hills of sand and threatening storm clouds. I'm ready to stand in the same row and measure myself against all that, just show me the appropriate place!"

Then I stopped listening to the waves, wishing to liberate myself from their power, to break off and return to my familiar contemplations, which had rescued me more than once. My steps, however, fell into the rhythm they'd discovered, and the ocean didn't let go, gripping me with all its might. I listened alertly but in confusion – an unfamiliar voice in my head summoned without naming me, merely hinting it knew me. It trailed off to a whisper occasionally but was impossible to get rid of. It commanded my entire being and lived in my body, like a new owner who has chased out the temporary tenants. I shuffled my scattered thoughts, invoking piles of memories here and shy phantoms there, yet it all ended with nothing – my brain was quickly losing power, surrendering to something fearsome and unclear.

Soon the phantoms hid in the corners and the memories faded away, yet a voice inside rose up and gained strength, becoming increasingly distinct. I whipped my head from side to side, trying to find its source, yet the same gloomy reality surrounded me, offering neither a foothold nor a hint. I tried to blame the wind whistling in my ears, but it subsided, sighing and dying, while the voice continued to rise.

"What is that?" raced through my head. A quick shiver slithered down my spine. Terror of the unknown made my blood run cold and paralyzed my mind. I stopped involuntarily, not having the courage to go on as I examined the horizon and saw nothing.

Then the wind died, with one last blast feebly beating my chest, but the ocean pounded away even more forcefully, its waves rolling up the shore. Ashamed, I collected myself and moved on again, taking deep breaths of the motionless air. "Who's that?" I uttered aloud, and it seemed I'd never receive a reply. But then my pace switched back to the rhythm of the waves, the ocean got used to me, and the answer came: the Black Pelican.

It flew in from the south-southeast. At first it was just a point on the dull gray background, then black, a barely noticeable silhouette, yet I was already envisioning it as if I could discern its predatory profile with its sharply curving neck and disheveled tuft of hair, its massive, menacing beak and evenly flapping wings. Transfixed, I was unable to avert my gaze. I stood on the wet sand, unaware of the waves that occasionally doused me up to my ankles. My thoughts got all mixed up and my questions lost meaning. I couldn't describe what I saw or felt. I simply knew the event was unavoidable – and no fear, no despair would make me run away.

Soon a whole flock gathered. They chased down their prey not far from the coast, like a battalion of storm troopers adhering to the strict rules of rank, jetting ten meters up in the air, hovering vindictively for a moment or two, and then – plunging down, blasting through the surface of the water with a loud splash and returning with a fish in its mouth. There were a lot of them, all similar, all sharp angles and dashes of black ink, yet I was only aware of the one that selected me, made me out countless miles away. It reigned over my soul now without even turning my way – though I knew for sure it was constantly thinking about me, testing my pliant nature with the horrifying power of its spells. They may have been incomprehensible, yet were so oppressive and so capable of enslaving that even collecting all my strengths together, I couldn't brush them off like something superfluous, just as I couldn't question the existence of the ocean roaring in front of my eyes.

It was as if my mind had split in two and the world had splintered into its spectral colors. I knew who I was, remembered the Dunes and the City of M, could imagine to the last detail my recent fellow travelers and my oldest friends. Yet, at the same time, everything I'd ever experienced, even just a second ago, drifted into the distance and took the form of a fantasy or a dream. Only the dashes of the winged beasts and an unfamiliar, inflexible will made up the reality worth believing in. What was happening met with a clear response inside me, like a tuning fork or well-adjusted string; my wishes and ambitions, reservations and hopes now rang in unison with sounds coming from outside. We existed together and desired one thing – the Black Pelican and I, that is, a part of me, the new half, wanting to merge with the elements and discover something unknown to anybody else.

The pelicans hunted and leaden waves foamed, yet the voice in my head echoed more and more shrilly, becoming intolerable, like metal grinding against glass. Now I knew who its master was and

I no longer asked the dumb "Who is it?" as if finished with that once and for all. Instead, the perplexing "Who are you?" slid off my tongue, but I clamped my jaw shut, not letting out any unnecessary words.

Gnashing, the voice grew and strengthened. It called me somewhere, and I wanted to follow it, although the remains of stagnant prudence still tried to fight the inevitable. But I knew they wouldn't hold out for long, the powers were unequal – just a little while and I'll lower my head and go wherever the voice leads me. Here: my eyes are already closing. Here: something is poking me in the back... I'm extending my arm to grope onward, but it's falling helplessly, feeling only the spray and bareness. Yes, indeed, there's just an abyss, a craggy bottom and merciless waves...

Coming back to myself for a moment, in fear, almost in panic, I pried open my eyelids and saw I was still standing on the coast and hadn't moved an inch. But then, instantly, bright patches of reflected light blinded me and forced me to squint. The voice rose, roaring at an ear-splitting pitch. I managed to think of poisonous smoke and hypnotic fever, and then I strode on ahead, seeing nothing around me, as if following secret orders, no longer afraid of my destiny. The specter in me won; its nervous trembling obeyed the tuning fork and seemed stronger than the survival instinct. I had crossed the border and landed in the middle of an elaborate dream with me in the main role. Nothing remained except to follow in its trail, and I did so obediently, scorning all cautiousness. With my eyes shut, it seemed I was invisible and elusive and not a thing was capable of doing me harm. That was naïve and ridiculously dumb – my intoxicated mind attempted to cry out and forewarn me, but all its efforts came hopelessly late.

CHAPTER 16

The rest happened very quickly, although it took forever, as it should in a dream. But a dream it could hardly have been – no nightmare could imprint itself so profoundly in my consciousness, overturning my mind and tearing my thoughts to shreds. I lived a new life – the one I deserved. I could have envisaged it myself if I'd ever had the courage to see everything without frills or lies.

At first it was easy: I moved without effort; my feet didn't get stuck in the sand and the water didn't drown me. In the distant corners of my brain I realized I wasn't making any progress, though I was wandering toward the beckoning call I could feel even with my skin. The wind whistled again, dancing, rushing, and frightening. The surf roared and visions circled in my head, although their essence remained unclear. Long phrases lay on the tip of my tongue, muddled up, like scraps of multicolored ribbon.

Everything subsided a moment later. My eyes were open, my hands empty, my thoughts distracted and defenseless. I was in a large hall with rough stone pillars, an extremely high ceiling, and smooth marble floors. Walls surrounded me on three sides and in the back there was instead a gaping void that sent a murky chill to my heart. The voice almost died out, only allowing itself be heard in a barely audible cry, as if oozing from the gloomy walls and the vaulted ceiling. It no longer called after itself and didn't lure me anywhere – it felt like I had been abandoned and left on my own, and this offended me to the point of tears.

"Where are you, omnipotent ones?" I asked aloud, shamefully slipping into a falsetto and not receiving any answer. Then I screamed at the walls, "Dumb jokes!" and at the ceiling, "Dumb!"

My shouting stirred the air, echoing off the stone blocks – and something bubbled over and jabbed me in the chest, so I flew back a few feet, toward the abyss behind me. Whoa, I thought, I've got to be careful with these things. I need to expect all kinds of tricks, although there's no one around. Who trapped me here? Let him finally come out – if a fight awaits me, let the fight begin!

Someone emerged out of the wall to my right and trotted across the room. "Hey," I screamed, "hey, wait up." The man did not turn around, as if he hadn't heard me, and, for some reason, I didn't want to call him over again. An oddity, something I recognized too easily, shown through his entire physiognomy, something familiar, unsteady, elusively mortifying. In consternation I realized – yes, that's me, me or someone who's no different from me. I was about to yell to the well-known stranger again, but reconsidered – apparently he hadn't noticed my presence, as if I were transparent and ethereal. He's blind, I thought crossly. He's just a worthless copy. But no sooner had I turned away than a second double materialized out of another wall. Then more and more – before long the whole room was full of identical human beings, not paying attention to me or each other, as they scampered back and forth, reflecting off the uneven surfaces and tracing complicated trajectories, each with his own concealed goals. I found them unpleasant, something was lacking in each and every figure, and to look at them was onerous and awkward.

"Duplicates, duplicates," I said irritably. "It seems to be the best way to find a soulmate, but there's no one to befriend here." The figures continued to ignore me completely. It was shocking – I was still number one, and probably better than any of them. How rude, I thought as their number increased, crowding me out and forcing me back, toward the terrifying chasm that made goosebumps run down my spine.

A disturbing realization flickered through my mind: I can't stop them, I don't even know where they're coming from. The ground was slipping out from under my feet. The absurd was gathering steam, and my footholds were disappearing at a frightening rate. I shifted from leg to leg and gradually ceded space, not wanting to block someone's path, although this someone, a brazen phantasm, could probably pass through me with ease. This was precisely what I didn't want, so I had to stomp about on my miniscule patch of floor, dodging the quick elbows. Yet my pathetic copies kept coming, not only filling the place, but also, it seemed, breathing in all the air.

Just give them a bit of freedom and any place will get crowded in no time, I thought hatefully. These creatures, who are so similar to me, are no better than the others, the complete strangers. It's all the same everywhere: ungratefulness and enmity. Are they really intending to force me out?

Suddenly I felt I was choking for real. My head jerked up, my mouth opened, drawing in air spasmodically. I lost my sense of direction and took an incautious step, and then my foot shuffled along the edge. I stumbled and flew down, just managing to wave my hands and think in despair – it's all over!

But it wasn't over yet. I fell on something cold and solid; acute pain pierced my body. Beyond the abyss lay a step, not wide and slightly lopsided at the bottom. I fell no more than a yard, yet the blow took my breath away and stirred indistinct fears, like ancient sediment rising up from the depths of my soul, the cloudy particles making visibility poor. I half crawled to the base of the step, leaned against the smooth wall, and began to look around.

Twilight ruled the neverending space. All the boundaries vanished in the darkness, with only torches, hidden somewhere below, shining light and casting reddish patches. Over the edge yawned another chasm, and opposite it, fifty yards away, ascending tiers stretched in a semicircle, creating an enormous auditorium. Thousands of eyes stared down at me – some with interest, some clearly bored – and from the chasm came the smell of burning and musty smoke. I was confused and didn't understand what they wanted from me now.

"This is my castle!" screeched, clapped, clanged in my ears. "Mine, and you're in my hands. Take a look," the supernal voice thundered, speaking to everyone. "Take a look and welcome Mr. Arrogance!"

Listless claps cascaded down. I surveyed the rows of spectators, maybe even recognizing familiar faces, and trying harder and harder to shrink into the cold stone. This *is* the challenge I was waiting for, someone inside me boasted, but another, cowardly and pitiful, muttered instead about atonement and retaliation. As if with a third eye I looked at myself from the side, discerning the beads of sweat on my forehead and the grimace of agonized contemplation. Putting things together wasn't easy. I couldn't understand all these tricks, couldn't figure out the truth or its deluding antipode – someone's malicious invention, an insidious ploy. The decisiveness I'd flaunted before dissolved without a trace. And the cloudy particles didn't sink back down, muddling my thoughts.

"Defend yourself, Mr. Arrogance!" the voice screamed and laughed cruelly. "Defend yourself, and we'll see what you're capable of!"

I gulped convulsively, opening my eyes wide and clenching my fists. Obviously, the critical moment was approaching. A small firecracker shot up and drew a half circle, scattering sparks through the sky. It fizzed and fizzled out with stinking smoke, and some shades twinkled before my eyes as if obeying a sign, inching closer and occasionally grazing my clothing.

Here it is, it's begun, I thought, flustered, jumping to my feet and waving my arms in horror. This infuriated the attackers, ugly bats that were thrashing about more quickly now, assaulting and crying nastily as they moved in. I brushed them off as best I could, trying to stay on my feet and not slip to the edge. "Come on, come on!" spoke the triumphant voice, and the shades steadily increased in number, flittering down from above and diving right at me, assailing me fearlessly and thoughtlessly. A burning lump surged from my gut. I simply wanted to fall to the floor and howl in terror, but instead I gritted my teeth, raising my hands and elbows to shield myself.

"Look, look," the voice roared. "He got fooled, he bought it!" The spectators began to fidget in the rows. Their animation was palpable and their snickering could be heard, but I continued to repulse the bats aiming for my head. "Those are scarecrows, dummies. Only a child could fall for that," rumbled in the air, and a sigh of disappointment rolled through the tiers.

"What scarecrows?" I wanted to scream. "Everything's for real. They're attacking me, I have scratches and blood on my hands!" Yet the words stuck, as if I knew no one would believe me anyway. It was insulting and pitiful, unpleasant and nasty; I couldn't understand who conceived of this amusement and why. At that instant one of the bats grabbed hold of my collar – I ripped it off with a terrifying cry, which echoed off the walls, pushing me toward the precipice, to the vertical ledge. I screamed again, trying to grab on to something, but there was no support and no protection. The wings of the bats rustled about my face; horror and disgust swamped me in a stifling fog where I knew what awaited me: another fall, a swoon, and the intolerable pain.

That's how it turned out. The next step didn't differ from the previous one. The blow was just as strong and stabbed my whole body just as painfully. Groaning, breathing heavily, covered with sticky sweat, I sat with difficulty and snuggled against the wall. The spectators calmed down and stopped shouting; the faces across from me contained no expression except polite boredom. Here and there I saw condescending grins and badly concealed yawns.

It's intermission, I thought sadly. They probably know the entire program in advance, and the battle with the bats, however awful it was, may not mean a thing to them. From their seats they might not even be able to discern the shades properly. I'll never disprove the lie about scarecrows – I have no evidence, only scratches and dried-up blood. I can't convince anybody I didn't have them before...

"Unfair," I said gruffly and didn't hear myself. "I'm quitting," I pronounced distinctly, but nothing more than unclear gibberish broke the silence.

"What, what, what?" erupted inside the building. "Defend

yourself, Mr. Arrogance!" Suddenly, a small wooden arrow scratched my face, a plywood sword appeared in my hands, and I began to fight with a gang of rapacious gnomes attacking from two sides with bows and clubs.

This could be funny, but, believe me, it wasn't. Their sharp tips pricked for real, and I was frightened again – since my weapon couldn't inflict any harm. Even the audience seemed to grow quiet and hold their breath, but then the voice bubbled over, "Look, look, he's doing it again!" Sweat ran into my eyes. I wiped it away with my sleeve, brandished my useless sword and cursed through my teeth, turning from the arrows and blows, as thunderous roars poured down on me. "He's holding his ground," came from all sides, "but against whom? It seems, against those who are capable of nothing? And he thinks it's all for real! Let's laugh at him – ha, ha, ha!"

Ha, ha, ha, the obedient auditorium echoed back. The spectators shook their heads again and sighed in dissatisfaction. Some even stood up and disappeared or just turned to the side. I understood they would soon lose all interest and for some reason that frightened me immensely.

"They almost don't exist," the voice didn't abate. "They don't exist, but he fights like crazy. And when something real occurs – no doubt, he'll run right for the hills!"

Ha, ha, ha, the viewers joined in. I breathed heavily, my heart thumped like a hammer, and the villainous gnomes whacked me back toward the edge and wielded their clubs twice as forcefully. "They're real!" I cried in anguish, not wanting to condone this injustice, and here someone whacked me below the knee and others pushed me in the side. I again flew down, my head spinning, and was blinded with the same pain, lying on the slippery rock…

This continued for an eternity – falls and dizziness, unbearable suffering and cold stone. I was a toy, a helpless splinter that twisted and turned in accordance with their perverse whims. One new abomination after another drove me to the depths of misery, and occasionally it seemed my actual demise was near at hand. I fought with the last of my strength. The rows of spectators were gradually thinning out. But the voice rattled on and thundered like iron, deriding me and not wishing to believe in any of my cries.

My opponents became increasingly demanding – the unknown creators fantasized vigorously. Time flew by, entire centuries seemed to pass, yet there was no end in sight. One form of despair was supplanted by another, vanished, then returned again; thoughts leapt up in the turmoil, then hardly moved at all. At first I sought some meaning in the events, trying to grasp where the steps were leading and what would happen if I reached the very bottom. Maybe those who get to it were allowed into the rows across from me, and that was an honor, a reward, if not a victory? Or, at the bottom, was there only an inglorious finale, desolation, and oblivion? At rare moments of respite I peered at the faces barely visible in the darkness, endeavoring to catch someone's eye, arouse compassion if not support – but to no avail. My hopes wasted away; I lost any kind of belief and admitted the discouraging truth: those sitting in the tiers were a different sort and their apathy wasn't just a mask. Then I understood there wasn't any sense in what was happening; all the torment was futile and led to nowhere. Instantly I started to hate the crowd, as well as everything around me: the haughty Black Pelican, the voice ripping my soul to pieces, the malicious scum attacking me from all sides…

I was getting used to my weakness – feeling all sorts of stifling shame over and over again. They were making a laughingstock of me – right down to my utter core. I thought I had imagined all this in the past, yet now it was a hundred times worse, infinitely more agonizing and frustrating.

Having firmly resolved to hold out until the end, I struggled on, contesting every challenge. It was impossible to stop, though all the reasons for continuing the hopeless fight had vanished long ago. I admitted the eternity of distress and came to terms with it, although its senselessness hurt me more and more. Something like a gigantic abscess was growing inside me, and the public was dwindling – up and down the rows were gaping holes that resembled the blind eyes. Finally just a few remained in their seats and with the next fall my entire soul was knocked out of me, up to its last plaintive cry. Then something burst – burst and poured lead into my ossifying body. I lay on my back and stared upwards, into the darkness, into the invisible cupola, with no more strength or fear. I didn't even have room for hate – the final drops had been wrung out.

"He's ours. He's given up!" the voice rejoiced, and in response sparse applause could be heard, but I didn't listen. I can't take it anymore, swirled through my head. It's over, that's my limit. I got your joke about the copies, it's not that complicated, yet I had nothing left to prove or fight with. Your world is stronger than me; I've never believed that before, but now, now...

"Fourteen steps!" raged the voice, the muffled echo reverberating. "Fourteen steps – that's what he's worth. To put it bluntly – not much, useless, insignificant! What do you say, Mr. Arrogance – are you giving up forever? Or will you stand up, as befits a really courageous man?"

I lay without moving and didn't even turn my head. My lifeless body seemed to absorb the sepulchral dampness seeping out of the stone below me. My muscles stiffened, and my thoughts became paralyzed, as if frozen in eternal ice.

"Answer!" The voice did not let up. "Answer and don't walk away from retribution, you consummate coward!"

With great difficulty I unglued my lips and spoke indistinctly, "I'm not a coward. I'm not getting up. I curse you." The words were barely audible, even to myself, yet a cunning echo carried them in every direction. The sounds thrashed about, banging into each other, helpless like prayers.

"Ha, ha, ha," the entire hall broke out in laughter. The spectators were getting lively, awakening from boredom, as if they had finally witnessed something hilarious. "He's cursing us!" the voice mocked with inexpressible disdain. "He curses and pronounces an anathema! That's just like him; that's what he can do better than anything else. Well, enough with the chimeras. Let's check out what he really is!"

Somewhere above, invisible rattles began to chirp, gradually turning into a drumroll. Thousands of feet stamped in the tiers, beating triumphantly; the torches went out, casting everyone in complete darkness. "Open your eyes!" the voice shouted – and I understood my eyelids had been clenched shut. "Open your eyes and take the real weapon!"

I did as they told me and began to look around, blinking and getting used to the bright light. The familiar pillars from the uppermost hall rose up around me, with no pitiful copies of myself in sight. My strength returned bit by bit. I stood in the center, fairly far from the edge, and a glittering object lay at my feet.

"Is it possible?" I wondered, speechless, bending over, glancing from side to side as I picked it up. It was really a revolver – genuine, with a short barrel but a little larger and heavier than my Colt. There could be no doubt about its authenticity. I spun the cylinder, it was full of cartridges. A nervous shiver shook me again. Okay, let's get even, I thought feverishly. Let's get even or fight to the death. There's still a chance – they were laughing at me, but wasn't it too early?

It became clear everything was for real now, no tricks or jokes. I flicked the safety, gripped the handle with both hands, and began to turn cautiously as I sought my enemies.

From the same wall to my right they came. Two men in loose capes with hoods, indefinably similar to each other, leading a third with his hands tied behind his back and a blindfold over his eyes. I've certainly seen that one guy before – isn't that my next double, I asked myself in bewilderment, but then I noticed we were different heights, he being half a head taller. The drumroll that had abated now picked up again, became shriller and drier. They led the captive to a pillar five meters from me and placed his back against it.

"Let go of your fears and let your dreams come true!" thundered down from above. I took a good look and realized I knew the man standing in front of me. It was Julian, no doubt – I couldn't mistake him for anyone else.

"Shoot," said the voice plainly, without its usual intensity; the word resounded with hundreds of small echoes and died out in a parting "oo-oo-oo-tt."

"Shoot!" it repeated a few seconds later, though more threateningly. "Kill him. He's yours!"

Julian stood there, one knee slightly bent, grinning ironically, as if he had no idea what was going on. Yes, how could he? – He doesn't have enough imagination to conceive of himself like this, I thought fleetingly as I clenched the revolver with fingers that had lost feeling. Two sentries positioned themselves on each side of the captive, looking at me haughtily.

"Come on already!" the ruthless cry hit me in the face. The guards slowly opened their capes, pulled out crossbows, and aimed them at my chest. My mouth dried up. I understood everything would end in this moment – in the most terrible way. Thoughts flickered, flashed, floundered in a chaotic pile. The burning thirst for revenge washed over me. I wanted victory and justice, but the price of taking another's life choked me, and I didn't have the strength to overcome its grasp. Every nerve told me there was no more time to think; the last seconds were slipping away. Then there was a scream – it seemed I was hearing my own cry from outside.

"Run, Julian!" I yelled desperately and fired in the air and to the side, at the walls, the pillars, the soaring vaulted ceiling – anywhere to avoid hitting the victim or the guards with their crossbows. Bullets whistled and ricocheted off the stone, the drumroll reached an intolerable pitch, and then a distant rumble was heard, something burst in my brain, shuddered it and split it in two – but without causing any harm.

My eyes fluttered open. The echoing hall, the guards, and Julian vanished, like swooning ghosts. There was no gun in my hands, and the reflections of burning torches in the emptiness no longer enthralled me. I was back, standing on the ocean shore; my hallucinations receded little by little; my mind became clear and the shaking settled down. Everything remained as it was: the same waves doused my legs, the surf still roared, and the pelicans jumped in the water to hunt. Only the one that possessed me sat motionless and stared, as if trying to penetrate my soul with some torturing device I can't hide from.

I shifted from leg to leg, lost my balance, and almost fell. I felt sick – sick and terrified. It was apparent I wouldn't have to battle anyone else, but this didn't calm me – in fact it was the opposite. No blood or scratches were left on my hands, however I still remembered the recent pain in every inch of my wasted body, still recalled the humiliation and embarrassment, the confusion and scorn. Not one bullet had grazed me, though the ricocheting screech had been etched in my memory forever. It seemed I had aged ten years, been at war, and lost all my treasures. Completely different people were now wandering about my grounds – I probably had nothing more to command. And what would I need all the riches for if any second I might collide with an inexorable power capable of crushing, exhausting, annihilating?

"What? What was that?" I asked myself silently, and then voiced it out loud too, "What was that? What should I do now?"

"Have you curbed your hubris?" rang in my ears instead of an answer. The voice spoke to me again. I didn't say anything; I didn't want to reply. His question was an unscrupulous joke, like everything that happens on this coast, in the small part of the world populated by the majority that does not know mercy. Only the coast isn't small; it's enormous, and the horizon is endlessly far away – do they know that? I'm no longer in the castle, no longer locked up. I'm free – at the ocean, in the piercing wind. What does this mean – I've been pardoned, released? Or ostracized – dishonorably and eternally?

"Fourteen steps!" the voice roared sarcastically and then bleated, mocking my desperate cry, "Run, Julian!"

I was silent, my head lowered, and he repeated, becoming icier with every sound, "Have you curbed your hubris? Answer! Don't vacillate!"

Violent shivers covered me. I recalled how I walked there, full of eager expectations, naïve and unaware that all my efforts had been calculated in advance. The memories made me groan and cover my face with my hands. Useless copy, I thought, and my tormentor was glad to sum it up, "You're mute! You're mute and that's it. There are questions that don't need to be answered. But here's a different one for you: *now* do you know who I am?"

"No," I replied almost inaudibly, just so they wouldn't think I'd been struck dumb from embarrassment or fear. Everything grew silent again, and the silence hung over the shore, stretching for miles and miles. I thought the conversation was over, but the voice called out again and confirmed, "You don't know…" – elongating the ellipsis with a spooky hissing and cutting it short by asking with a concealed threat, "You don't know, but did you believe in my existence?"

"Yes!" I made haste to admit, not even giving myself time to think whether it was so or not. "Yes, yes, yes…" I repeated, but the voice rolled on incredulously, "Did you always believe? Always?"

"Yes," I said quietly once again, feeling like I was skating into a precipice, shriveling up inside, foreseeing my fall on the slippery stone, and then in my ears growled the accusation, "You're lying!"

It was true, and there were no objections to be made. I wanted to turn away and couldn't, again losing my ability to move. The pelican screamed shrilly, as if giving a signal, and something flickered in front of me like a carousel whizzing round. I shrunk and felt a chill as I thought about the bats, but no, this time it wasn't dirty grey, but a multicolored show that flitted past me. The images from my own life moved along, like the shots of a silent movie – from the present moment of my senseless struggle back to the "secret," a fruitless ploy leading to a dead end, then to triumphant Julian, to Vera's high, screeching tones, to the faces of colleagues gazing askance with reproving looks, and further – to the university and my room near the stadium, to some gloomy awkward figure, aimlessly wandering from one place to the next…

"Look, look, that's you," the voice grated in my head. "If you didn't lie, prove it to me. Where's your belief, where's your courageous knowledge?"

I saw I couldn't point my finger at anything. The film rolled again, spun ahead, and gradually slowed; in sequence came my spasmodic jumping from encounter to encounter, the mass of hindrances along the way and the conquering of them with enormous efforts, the angry gestures of onlookers and their stunned expressions… Immediately I recalled the abyss and the steps, rows of identical faces, mockery and indifferent eyes, but here the film stopped, having reached the beginning that had turned into the finale – my dear Gretchen, dumbfounded and perplexed, telling me her discovery as if surrendering to something we'd dismissed in our conceit, overestimating our strength and not thinking about consequences.

"Let's see, let's see," the voice was saying as the camera shifted to my sister, who soon filled the entire shot. We stood face to face, regarding and not regarding each other, feeling and not feeling one another, preoccupied with our own affairs, but mourning one and the same thing.

"No one will… as you… yourself…" she was whispering to me again.

"Fourteen steps… pain… shots in the air…" I whispered in reply, and there was nothing to add; the abyss yawned between us, and we both acknowledged the powerlessness of words.

"Let's see, let's see," the gnashing metal clanged inside me. "She knew, she just didn't reveal it to you, ignoramus. Where, where is your belief?"

The image finally changed, and the chasm disappeared. Gretchen was now with me. We seemed to be one indivisible whole, revolting against the entire world, against the voices and the callous spectators, against lies and foreign blood. The universe froze in place. A full second passed in peace and serenity, and then the brass gong struck again and everything dispersed and flew off in tatters.

"You lied to me!" the voice rumbled, crushing and pushing me down toward the earth. "You lied, and there will be no mercy. The weak will fall! What's not proven at the right moment will be forgotten! Fourteen steps – we'll leave the number as it is. See: you said everything yourself!"

Gathering my strength, I wanted to scream something, but my tongue didn't obey me. The mercurial light of the invisible projector started to flicker again and the shots glided away before my eyes, moved all at once, closed together first in familiar figures with an excessive number of sharp angles, as in black blotches on a grey-blue background, and then – in one common contour, in the uninterrupted, endless path. Now I knew why a whole flock of pelicans had flown in. I even became momentarily proud with the thought that darting from side to side might also let one attain something, at least if only to consider quantities. But my pride flared up and faded, supplanted by profound sadness. I recalled the stone steps, the humiliation and senseless pain, the despair and horror waiting in the vaulted hall with its cunning echo. I saw myself shooting in the air, away from my target, and realized how frail I was, how overconfident for no reason. All the deceptive lenses had been removed from my eyes: the outlines filled in; the objects returned to their normal size. Everyone had abandoned me, I was alone, and my secret had been derided and ridiculed, ground to dust and left in the gutter. Clear to the point of tears was the staggering number of murky plains I had to cross to reach the most minor of goals, and the countless misleading paths every step of the way, and the insignificance of what I had done so far…

Yes, I agreed with my tormentor. One shouldn't hope for any other logic. The dumb will fall; what hasn't been proven in time will be lost forever, and what has – even if not by you – simply cannot be disputed.

Yes, I wanted to scream to my dear Gretchen. Yes, you are right through and through. I have nothing to comfort you with, and others won't help us either. They see things in a way that's impossible to accept – but they accept them eagerly, they like what the world offers. It isn't their fault we alienated with impenetrable emptiness and our destiny is to spend a great effort getting even slightly, infinitesimally closer. Yet it must be spent – even though we despise their blindness and sleepy satiety – otherwise we'll spin out and our hands will get ripped from all the railings. Among the loners, the air is just too thin, it's frightening and not pleasant at all, so we doubt again and again – doubt and draw back, hoping the maneuver isn't visible from the outside. But now I know *how* visible we are – and how ridiculous, awkward, pitiful!

I looked through the gray light into the coal-black pupils of the one who has chosen me, and tears ran down my cheeks, bringing no relief. The pelicans hunted, rejoicing in their strange life, the ground was receding under my feet, and Gretchen turned her face to me again. I stroked her with forbidden caresses – now everything was permitted, the restrictive rules were conceived by those opposed to our souls, those happy with the absence of question marks. They don't need to take refuge in fantasies – everything suits them as it is. One day they entice you to the ocean shore, where your Black Pelican commands in a gnashing voice – and you discover the same knowledge that makes the others so strong. You discover it and toss it away – as if saving yourself after being burned – and you understand this is forever, there's no denial and never could be.

"Try this," they say. "Live according to someone else's will – either in a dream or for your entire being."

"This is your limit," they say. "You are incapable of more." And they add, "This is life. You simply didn't know it!"

And the chimeras wound you for real, although no one believes that and takes you for a liar. The solitude is boundless, and every step causes terrible, terrible pain... Others call it *growing up*, but we know this is just a trick to take our hope away. We cannot grow up as they do – after all, they're also unable to head down our path. They don't end up face to face with the violent waves, looking into the eyes of you-know-who. They may never arrive there, not until death, and I still have so long to live – so how can I live with this now?

The wind whistled a celebratory march, the drums pounded somewhere in the distance, and my distracted thoughts vanished, resulting in nothing. The light went out, eclipsed by an enormous shadow – the Black Pelican flew up and spread out prone above me, getting larger and larger. I gazed around, glancing in terror at the huge wings and the monstrous crooked bill ready to descend and crush. The pelican gave a warlike cry, hung for a moment, contracting into a spring prepared for flight – and I closed my eyes, unable to even scream. Then an invisible force ripped me from the earth and rolled me over in the air.

"Do you believe in my power now?" the clashing iron rang in my head, and I sought my last bits of strength to make my tongue admit it with a doomed "Yes." Yet I suddenly heard in disbelief how something or someone inside me recklessly persisted, "No, no, no!" – standing up to the last challenge, as if proving he'd never learned to surrender on any of the hundred and forty-four fields. And then I, against my own will, whispered aloud the ludicrous "No" with parched lips. Again thunderous laughter rang out, as if the stones were raining on a tin pipe; then something whistled through the air, its sizzling whip scorching my cheek, and I dove into a well – somersaulting, as in a Ferris wheel, and vainly clutching at the vanishing glimmer of one last thought that whispered something familiar, fanatical, far-off.

PART II

CHAPTER 1

Sharp fragments of shells scratched my palms; my fingers stung and lost feeling – I was digging in the sand not far from the water, sitting on my knees and anxiously working both hands. When I reached the moist levels, my progress slowed. I broke one nail, then another, and had to use my heel, loosening the intractable surface strip by strip. Finally, I got what I wanted – a deep, square pit.

Wincing from pain and trying not to get my already wet shoes completely soaked, I started to make the connecting canal – a passageway allowing the waves to gradually fill the artificial pool. Sand flew in all directions and salty water foamed in the trap, rewarding my ardor. Never before had I been so focused on the result, recognizing the meaningfulness of my actions with utmost clarity. It seemed all my doubts and failures were being expiated by the fervent desire to complete this job without taking a moment's rest. Soon, enough water had accumulated. I blocked off the canal and sat down, wiping sweat from my brow and blankly waiting until the silt settled.

The ocean heaved rhythmically. My miniature pond was clearing, a ripple quivering across it just occasionally, and soon it became transparent, gleaming like smooth isinglass. It was time to get down to my real task. I inhaled deeply and held my breath, not wanting to stir the surface by respiring. Over the water I leaned, prepared for the worst, catching an unsteady reflection in the motionless mirror.

A stranger's face gazed back at me, and instant confusion gripped my entire body. No, nothing terrible happened. Parts of it were intact and even fit together as before, but the overall picture has changed irreversibly, as if denying my attempts to imitate my former self. Perhaps others would hardly have noticed a difference, but to my own eyes it was obvious. Pretending to be unemotional, I looked and looked – trying to identify with the unwelcome novelty. I wanted to get used to it as quickly as possible – knowing there was no way back. Yet I couldn't – as if the surface concealed a collection of obscure signs blurred by the ripple. What was there – firmness and stubbornness, or merely bitterness and gloom? Would I ever truly grasp it? Why was it so hard to see here?

Blinking once, twice, I held my breath again and gazed intensely into the water. Something wasn't right; something spoiled the balance. As I swiveled my head back and forth, I finally figured it out: a mark had been imprinted on my left cheek, a fine spot resembling a monkey's hand, not large but visible even in this murky reflection. Yes, I thought sarcastically, I might have "said everything myself" as they were quick to point out, but they also left a sign for others – just in case. I might think it's a private matter, but no – it's on show for everyone, for the sake of clarity. Or is it for me – so I won't forget? But I won't forget anyway; they shouldn't worry that much. One thing is clear: even with a chaotic effort one can achieve something, attracting the world's attention. Yet this hardly makes any sense – nothing will change a bit. Only you change drastically, feeling it's far too late for justifications of any kind…

I touched the skin on my cheek – it was smooth, just inflamed a little. The other man looking back at me grinned and winked helplessly. Or I winked at him – it was difficult to tell, and moreover, that other was quite suited to be me. He was different, but I could get used to him, especially with no alternatives in sight.

The absence of the alternatives was really pitiful. I cursed my powerlessness and then recalled all that had happened the evening before. Erratically, I began to snatch at snippets of vengeful thoughts that flickered through my swollen head, endeavoring to challenge and decide something. Yet soon I had to admit it: everything's already been decided. The meaning of the verdict was unclear; only the humiliation was obvious to no end. And there'll be no changing, no adding. "Fourteen steps!" – the reminiscence tore through me. Anger made me groan, and I smashed my fist into the smooth surface, breaking it into hundreds of fragments as I screamed nonsense at the distant horizon, summoning someone and chasing someone off. A few minutes later, however, I calmed down and coldly grinned at both – myself and the other, who was again reflected in the improvised mirror.

The sun rose, its slanting rays cutting the coast into unequal parts. The aching of my body and the ringing in my ears reminded me of the night before. I remembered falling on the sand after my tormentors had flown off, then crawling away from the water and sleeping until morning under the open sky, wrapped in my jacket, with my sweater wound around my legs and my bag below my head. The cold woke me, and I was unable to warm up despite the pit I had dug. A shiver ran through my whole body, beginning at my feet, at my still-not-dry boots. My face tingled, and beads of sweat gathered on it like sticky pollen. Listlessly I thought I was getting sick, but forgot about that right away as I gazed at the horizon, a bright orange disk rising above it. The image was majestic and contained everything – hope and vastness and eternity. My memories faded, became ethereal and unsteady. What had happened yesterday, which seemed impossible to leave behind, receded and cringed in the farthest corner. An acute feeling of life seized me. I wanted everything at once, as in the most animated dream, and I burst out laughing, not even thinking that black dots might appear in the distance and grow into unwelcome judges.

I didn't care about judgments anymore – the worst was behind me, I convinced myself. I repeated this time and again, and the words became ingrained in solid crystal that could be whirled, tossed, and dropped without any danger of damaging the edges. And I realized I had found a reliable formula, like a spell created by a generation of alchemists, a formula that could explain the unexplainable and save me from insanity.

"The worst is left behind," I said with pleasure, clothed in invisible armor. And then something else tickled my tongue. The formula had another part, and my vocal cords, as if separate from me, sought it as they produced strange sounds. Finally, a flash of lightning pierced me, and I said quietly, "But silence still rules." And that completed my modest victory: I sat on the coast and laughed at the rest of the world that had caught me in its traps but failed to deliver the fatal blow and probably had no idea what to do with me at present. Do I know what I'm going to do with myself now? There'll be time to figure it out. And meanwhile: *Silence still rules!*

The horizon and rising sun, as well as the monkey's hand on my cheek, didn't leave me in peace for half an hour or so. Then I woke and realized the cold, the forsakenness of the area, and the necessity to do something. I had to get out of this desolate place, and, after vacillating briefly, I decided to walk south rather than go back. My artificial lake became shallow, the water seeping out the bottom and carrying away the unclaimed secret. I grinned, mentally parting with it, took a sip from my flask, which I fortunately found in my bag, and set out at a steady pace along the hard sand, leaving a curving chain of footprints that were quickly washed out by the surf.

Soon I was overcome by exhaustion – probably from illness that I now felt for real. I was so weak my head was spinning; my muscles shook and the bag hanging from my shoulder had become intolerably heavy. I traipsed on, absentmindedly acknowledging that the remains of my energy were running out fast. Like a scientist studying a dissected specimen, I observed my body, in which the malady was spreading, meeting little resistance. Some keys, unmelodious and abrupt, were clanging in my mind; the cold turned to heat and I was instantly covered in sweat, which soon dried in the wind that again made it chilly and unpleasant. When I sat down to take a rest and surrendered to immobility, I discovered the surrounding world continued to be in motion – everything trembled, with circles and colorful dots swimming before my eyes. Indifferently, I reasoned I

VADIM BABENKO

might soon collapse. Yet I stood up and stumbled on, reeling slightly and noticing in surprise I was actually progressing.

Not far off, a bridge rose up with one end projecting into the water and cars in various colors whizzing down it, right into the waves. I got agitated but soon grasped it was just an early-morning mirage, a pitiful vestige of yesterday's hallucination – inoffensive like everything that can be explained. The bridge and the vehicles, by the way, did appear real. It seemed I was hearing the noise of the tires and the roar of the motors through the crashing of the surf. I even managed to pick up my pace in the impatient desire to clear up the delusion or be deluded forever. Yet then I began to choke, stopped to catch my breath, and the bridge with the cars vanished into thin air.

It disappointed me – the narrow strip of sand and the smooth surface of the ocean were wearing me down with their monotony. My brain and even my memory appeared to be getting more used to them than any of the cities where I'd lived. But soon another group of harmless phantoms appeared in the distance, and I experienced one mirage after another, like the calming sighs of outer space, benevolent in their aloofness.

I plodded and stumbled, shuffling my feet with difficulty, first toward a cavalry galloping on malicious horses, prodding with their lances and dispersing into nothing, then toward a dressed-up scarecrow, hanging upside down, its feet moving in comical fashion, and finally to a flock of the Little Blue Birds, existing despite the fact no one wanted to believe in them anymore. All the figures were dummies, no doubt about it – created out of emptiness and ready to turn into nothingness. The game wasn't for real; I knew that without any intrusive voices. The mirages entertained me and that was enough; they appeared and disappeared without a trace, not agitating my mind or my memory. I only remembered the scarecrow – and also the bright yellow hot air balloon with a straw basket below it, hanging over the water's edge. A staircase stretched from the basket to a few yards above the ground, and the whole time I expected someone to descend, but I lost patience waiting. Then finally a fragile figure climbed down with his back to me, working his arms and legs furiously. It was a ludicrous little man who reminded me of a famous comedian, although there was nothing comical about his rash descent. He moved with a fateful sense of obedience, like he was tired of convincing others of the opposite. When he reached the last step, he glanced awkwardly into the emptiness, as if he hadn't noticed that the staircase ended there. I wanted to scream and warn him, but the cry got stuck in my dry throat, and I probably couldn't have helped him anyway. The absurd figure vanished without a splash, and the mirage began to recede, quickly dissolving in the air – the basket, the stairs and, last of all, the balloon, which was ridiculously similar to an egg yolk.

From the water to the Dunes now strode a family of sad giraffes. The last one, the youngest, kept looking back, but then I forgot him as a whole cluster of cacti blocked the way, making me almost get lost. There were lots of them – different sizes and shapes, tall and short, succulent green with widespread arms, or hard with shriveled spiky stems. Pale lilac flowers hung on some; it even seemed to me I could sense their deathly smell. Others curved oddly, extending their rapacious spines or defenseless young sprouts. And I carefully dodged them, circumventing the plants, like cunningly set traps, trying not to step on this or that specimen and not prick myself on the stem of the next one that suddenly rose up in my path.

The cacti were so diverting that when they ceased to exist, I didn't exactly recall where I was and what I was doing. The ocean roared to the left of me, and five hundred yards ahead a dark object emerged – a closer look confirmed it was a cabin by a streaked pole. Another phantom, I thought irritably. The useless fantasies were beginning to wear me down, and my eyes wanted rest. But something told me that no, this time it wasn't an illusion. I got closer and saw a barbed-wire fence stretching from the ocean into the Dunes. Behind it were the cabin and the pole from which a faded rag hung. A border post, I guessed, and sat down on the sand.

I didn't like it. First, it wasn't clear how the people in the cabin would react to my appearance in general. Second, I recalled my Colt

– such an object wouldn't look like a harmless toy no matter how much I pretended to be a nice, regular guy or simply a confused scatterbrain. I didn't have a permit for it and didn't even know what was allowed here and what wasn't – though I suspected the local laws were fairly strict. The idea of walking around it flashed through my mind, but the fence looked solid and might turn out to be too long for my dwindling strength. In any case, it was quite probable they'd noticed me already. I cursed, put the revolver and my papers at the very bottom of my bag, re-hid my money in the inside pocket, and headed straight for the cabin, slightly limping and dragging my feet.

As I approached, I detected the figure of a man, and then a dog appeared at his side, sniffing and breaking into a volley of blunt barks. Soon I was standing next to the fence itself, or – more precisely – by the locked gate. I silently looked at the youngish officer, who also examined me without saying a word. He was skinny, had fair hair and shrewd, roguish eyes. His police uniform, with sergeant's stripes, was wrinkled and hung awkwardly as it would on a badly made mannequin. Without shifting his gaze from me, he ordered the dog to be quiet. It instantly settled down and wagged its tail. Then, as if in doubt, he turned to the cabin and screamed, "Caspar!"

Nothing happened at first, but a minute later an unhappy, sluggish man in a white T-shirt looked out.

"What's the fuss?" he inquired grumpily.

"Someone's showed up," the sergeant explained, nodding in my direction.

The man gazed at me with blatant indifference and said to the sergeant, "Well, let him in." Then he went back inside and reappeared in a lieutenant's uniform shortly thereafter.

The sergeant opened the lock; I pushed the gate and walked in. The dog ran up to me, sniffed, and stood nearby, regarding me unkindly with its ears quivering. The man who the sergeant called Caspar had broad shoulders, a black moustache, and flabby cheeks. He surveyed me casually for some time and growled through his teeth, "Close the gate behind you."

"Do something about the dog," I said to no one in particular. The lieutenant whistled; the beast ran away and lay down in the sand, placing its muzzle on its front paws. I turned my back to the whole group and slowly closed the gate, chasing out a dumb thought about the cut-off roads and burnt bridges. The lock clicked back in place. To be sure, I jerked the handle and pushed the rusty bolt, although they hadn't asked me to.

When I was facing them again, I saw both the sergeant and Caspar were smiling at something. I also grinned in response. My legs were really failing me now; I wanted to sit, but no seat was available, so I just set my bag on the ground and stuffed my hands in the pockets of my jacket to make as independent an impression as possible.

"Well, what are we going to do? Write him up?" the sergeant asked Caspar, breaking the silence and turning away from me.

"We have to," the latter said irritably and spat.

The sergeant headed to the cabin and anxiety overcame me. Now it'll begin: inability to understand, threats and pressure, their self-satisfaction and my helplessness. I needed to do something, but what, what?

Maybe being rude would help, I thought fleetingly. But then they'll probably just wallop me... Yet I couldn't keep quiet any longer.

"Why do you have to write me up? Can't we work something out?" I said, trying to imitate a provincial manner. "It's so time-wasting, the paperwork."

The lieutenant peered at me. "What is there to work out?" he asked brusquely, without a trace of his recent grin.

"Well, if you don't write me up, I'll... I'll keep going and that's the end of it," I suggested.

"So, you're afraid of being written up?" the lieutenant inquired just as harshly.

I made some ambiguous sound and stopped talking, trying to regard him confidently and firmly.

"He's afraid," the lieutenant resumed. "That means it could be a serious matter. Alright, Fantik, prepare the forms and attend to his bag. And then we'll talk!"

My fears were justified; everything was only getting worse. I was suddenly gripped by impulsive fury. Blood ran to my head – either from my illness or from disgust for both of them.

"Dumbasses," I wanted to scream in their faces. "What do I have to talk about with you?" My arms were itching for a senseless fight, which obviously wouldn't lead to anything good. I needed to be more ingenious and a hundred times smarter than that. Everything was hanging by a thread. I knew: right now, this very second, I had to race at least one step ahead of them – otherwise, later, no ingenuity would help. Making a desperate effort, I gathered the remains of my strength to quiet the shaking in my voice. My head was spinning feverishly with combinations, variations, and unconnected images from my past. I was quickly becoming imbued with the spirit of that alien world where the fittest survive and teeth and elbows have the authority.

"Hey, Fantik, wait up," I said insolently to the sergeant, who had taken a step toward my bag. He froze and turned in astonishment to his partner, who stared at me with renewed interest. "The commander and I are going to have a chat, and you better stay here in the meantime. Any objections, Casper?" – I intentionally messed up the lieutenant's name, trying not to break out of the tone I had adopted.

"It's Caspar, not Casper," the lieutenant corrected me automatically while twirling his mustache. "So, that's what you want – to speak with the commander?"

A grin played on his lips again, though I couldn't say whether it was mockery or slight confusion. He paused, scratched his armpit, and said impartially, swiveling toward the cabin, "Okay, let's have a chat, as you put it. Fantik, wait here. I'll call you if need be." I tossed the bag over my shoulder and stumbled after him, secretly expecting it was an insidious trick and Fantik would now attack me from behind.

We entered cramped quarters, and the lieutenant made himself comfortable in the only free chair. The other surfaces were swamped with papers and various crap, so I had to stand, leaning against the doorpost.

"Well? What do you have to say?" Caspar asked, yawning. His eyelids were only half-open, yet I perceived the alertness in the dull luster of his pupils – alertness and a threat. He's probably very dangerous, almost like Gibbs, went awkwardly through my head.

"This is quite a desolate area," I said aloud. "In fact, it's straight-up terrifying. Are you from around here? Or where are you from?"

Caspar briefly named some place that didn't say anything to me and continued to regard me expectantly. It was time to get down to business.

"No, I haven't heard of it." I shook my head. "I'm from the capital, not a local. Looking after our guys here, you know..." – and I again stopped, gazing at Caspar with the calm look of a man who's aware of his worth.

"I see," said the lieutenant, nodding slightly. I was about to proffer an explanation, but the person I imagined myself to be at that moment wouldn't have begun explaining. He would have waited and waited until his interlocutor showed a weakness, got nervous, and revealed himself. This other would've had enough presence of mind to do it – and for some reason the three terse men who sold me the Colt popped to the surface of my thoughts. I knew I'd most probably fail at this, yet I kept my mouth shut, staring at Caspar as at a large, well-outlined target, narrowing my eyelids to match his, and intending to go all the way in this game – if only out of curiosity.

The lieutenant fidgeted and turned around. "What's this about your guys?" he asked querulously. "I didn't hear nothing about no guys." A fly flew through the room, back and forth, buzzing intrusively. He tried to catch it with his hand but couldn't and let out a stream of profanities.

"Just normal guys – ours, from the capital," I replied after a brief pause. "They're studying something here, in your ocean. And I'm making sure nothing bad happens." I grinned and winked.

"I didn't hear nothing about that," Caspar repeated stubbornly, chewing his lips in doubt. The fly didn't calm down, and he followed it with his eye.

"Well, if you didn't, you will soon. Don't worry," I assured him, trying to look right at his brow or the bridge of his nose. I really wanted to incinerate him with my gaze, like a laser beam, then polish off Fantik and leave without any hindrances.

A palpable silence hung in the room. Even the fly quieted down, hiding somewhere far away. Finally, Caspar began to fidget again and asked in a strange small voice, "Can you show me your papers then?"

I realized he wasn't certain about anything, almost like me, and worries were gnawing at him no less than myself. This might have been amusing at a different time, but now was not the moment.

"Ring up your bosses. They surely know something," I said, shrugging my shoulders and turning to the dusty window. "As for the papers, I doubt you'll understand them."

"I'll ring them up, I will," Caspar promised gravely, took a pad from the table and scribbled something down. "I'll ask about your guys, alright. But that doesn't change the matter. How'd you end up at our gate? There aren't any guys here, you know. The place is dangerous; random people don't go walking here. Or are you not a random one?" He looked at me sharply.

"Whether someone's random or not depends on how you see things," I snickered. "It depends on how and *what* you see." And what you remember, flashed through me. What you remember, wanting to forget forever... I cut off my laughing abruptly and glared at the lieutenant, telling him distinctly and strictly, "You know what? You'd be much better off not sticking your head into this for nothing. That's our business, not yours. I don't need the trouble, and you won't gain anything by it, trust me. Let's resolve it fairly: you get some greenbacks for your attention, and we'll part ways happily."

I dug in the pocket of my jacket, pulled out a few bills and picked out the largest, thinking rather indifferently that in all likelihood I'd overdone it with my pretense and he'd be on to me now. But Caspar looked at the money favorably. "There are two of us," he said. "You need to add something."

I peeled off another note. Suddenly, Caspar jumped out of his seat, coming close to me. "And don't bullshit me about your guys!" he said, breathing the stench of onions and wine in my face. Then he snatched the bills from my hand and began to nudge me toward the door. "Don't bullshit me," he whispered again before we ended up outside, where he turned his back and screamed, "Fantik, escort him out!"

The sergeant approached us, smirking with satisfaction. "Walk this way," he waved toward the south. "There's a village in three miles – it's easy to get out from there. Stay on the water's edge," he added with a sigh.

I nodded, took a glance in the direction of the prospective village, and said casually, still not believing they'd let me go, "Okay, take care." The guards were silent. I turned around and walked toward the water, heading south.

"What was that on his cheek?" I heard the sergeant's voice – and then the sound of a slap.

"Shut up, you turd!" the lieutenant hissed angrily.

"What's that for, Caspar?" whined Fantik.

Caspar whispered furiously, "What are you asking for? What's it to you? I teach, teach you all the time, but you're still like a puppy. You got to be careful here... All kinds of people here... Rotten stuff and footprints all over the place... You've only yourself to blame..." – and something else I couldn't make out.

The sun was at its peak. I had no more energy but traipsed on, clenching my teeth, not slowing my pace. "If you let up and take a break, you probably won't get back on your feet," I assured myself. "Three miles isn't that far..."

I had no more water in my bottle and was feeling worse and worse. The agitation from meeting with the policemen had passed, and my illness took to its course afresh. My heart pounded wildly; I knew I had a fever, but tried not to think about it. My head was empty, as if someone had wiped the blackboard with a wet sponge.

I could only count off the yards I had walked – one, two. One step, another – how terrible this is, how intolerable the pain!

The progression of things occurred to me in a strange way – as if an enormous screeching wheel were in motion, gloomily rolling on in dark rusty, brown, gray shades. It turned in one direction and its tempo didn't change; its pace was unvaried, yet elusive. It lifted you above the crowd and dropped you, independent of your personal efforts, and everything you requested came true at the wrong moment because you didn't have the power to comprehend the laws of its movement. I felt crushed and worthless, as if all my inner strength had been taken away yesterday. The stranger's face in the artificial pond rippled before my eyes, exuding despondency and fear. Who can it deceive? Only idiots, like Caspar. As for me, I won't be able to believe it – so what can I come up with every time I need to tell myself a merciful lie?

I cursed my wretched fate, anguished and overwhelmed by bitterness. Indeed, what prevented me yesterday from going back, lying down on the sand, and not asking for trouble? Again I heard the screeching of the enormous wheel that rotated impassively, carrying me from one fiasco toward another, just like everyone else. I might not be able to get back on my feet after more falls, the thought flashed through my mind and immediately called forth a new form of fear. Will my soul never be able to rise after all this? Or – forget the soul. Maybe my entire life was over, and the illness was no accident. The logic was simple: humiliation, a bitter outcome, and then what? Death?

The desire to live filled every cell in my body, but I felt more and more acutely I simply couldn't go on. Sweat was running down my face; my eyes refused to see. I was on the brink of giving up when, up ahead, I noticed some structures resembling homes, ugly and pitiful. I licked my dry lips and turned toward them, lurching and dragging my legs through the sand. If they give me shelter, I'll pay them whatever they ask. Where are you, my clear-eyed stranger with a cool hand? I don't have rhymes for you now, my girl. All that remains is resignation and exhaustion. But still I made it – look, I'm already here…

I went up to the first of the houses – sinking into the ground, with a half-dilapidated fence and a lopsided roof – and realized I couldn't continue. My heart was ready to jump out of my chest; my knees shook; I had the taste of iron in my mouth. I stopped, tossed my bag on the sand, and began to look around, squinting and blinking. A barely perceptible path headed toward the Dunes, and I saw other homes there. The one I stood next to was located out of the way, forming an advanced post or, on the contrary, a hopeless rearguard. Right in front of me, a hole had been cut in the fence, which created a gate without doors. Beyond it was a dark but strong façade, and a skinny old crone sat on the porch, regarding me silently and smoking a pipe.

I waved to her but didn't receive a reply. For a few seconds I just stood there and felt my pounding heart. Then I lifted my bag and walked up to her, barely able to move my legs. She didn't say anything; her face showed no surprise or compassion. I wanted to introduce myself, but my tongue didn't obey me, so I only nodded, sat down with difficulty, and snuggled up against the porch, dozing off into a restless nap.

Then a piercing sound ripped through my head, reminding me of something terrible. I opened my eyes and looked up. The crone had vanished; the porch was empty. I heard a sound again, a rough grinding, and a shiver ran down my spine. It was nothing however – just the front door screeching with the draft. How long had I dreamed? Had years passed, the old woman died, and others left these environs? Why did they leave me behind again?

A strong gust blew the door open, banging it against the wall and making it creak plaintively one last time. The woman came onto the porch and stopped in front of me, holding a shabby mat in her hands. I looked up at her, twisting my head awkwardly. Now I saw she was tall and straight, with wizened arms and a long, furrowed face. She called to mind an unsmiling giant, the strict master of some inaccessible realm, but with just one blink you'd notice that all her features, no matter how grand, shifted imperceptibly, creating broken lines, the contours of inveterate despair, assiduously concealed or so ancient its strength had already dried up. Her pupils bore into me coldly from under her bushy eyebrows and her lips were pressed together tightly. For a minute or two we gazed at each other, then she came closer and laid the mat on the porch.

"Take this and get out of here," she said, hardly cracking her lips. Her voice was prickly and dry. The words came out separately, almost unconnected to each other.

"I'm sick," I replied, trying to keep my teeth from chattering. "I'm sick and can't go on. Let me stay here."

"What do you mean?" the crone snorted. "This is my house. You have no business being here. Lots of people come – what's it got to do with me?"

I strained to lift my arm and pulled the rest of the money out of my jacket, saying awkwardly, "I have this. I'll pay."

The crone bowed her head and silently surveyed my hand with the crumpled bills. Then she sighed and said, "Okay. Hand it over. All of it – otherwise you'll lose it." And she added, seeing my doubts, "Whatever's left, I'll give back to you. What do you need it for now?"

I gave her everything, even rummaging through my pockets to make sure I hadn't forgotten any coins. "Wait here," she ordered and disappeared into the house. Soon she returned and led me down a dim corridor, walking confidently, not looking back. I traipsed after her, trying not to hit any objects. My eyes caught sight of old furniture projecting from all sides, a piano gleaming in the living room, and the worn runners on the floor. When we reached a guest bedroom with faded wallpaper, my head was spinning again. I sat down on the bed, gazed blankly ahead of me and didn't even listen to the old woman, who was muttering something in the same hostile tone. Eventually she went out, leaving the door slightly ajar. With difficulty I pulled off my shoes, stretched out on my back without getting undressed, and silently thanked my unknown protectors as I succumbed to sickness, knowing I had been saved.

CHAPTER 2

I lay in bed for some two weeks, only occasionally going out on the porch to bask in the sun. An acute attack of delirium broke out the first night. My body coped with it, but recovery was slow. It didn't bother me; I was in no hurry.

The owner – she was called Maria – attended to me with an intense persistence, despite voicing her disapproval at every opportunity. At first, I took it seriously, assuming she was annoyed at my intrusiveness, which just added to her troubles. I was even prepared to move somewhere more hospitable, but my half-hearted attempts were checked by a cold, adamant response: Maria swore she'd hide my clothes and lock the door and windows if I didn't stop this idiocy, so I had nothing to do but meekly accept what was happening. She washed my belongings and gave me a haircut, mumbling and grumbling in a low tone. And she worked tirelessly in the kitchen, boiling water for tea and herbs for drinks, chanting over the spicy-smelling brews and special sea salts. If I lost my appetite and a portion of her puritanical dishes – chicken, pumpkin kasha, or broth with croutons – remained on my plate, she lowered her head in offended silence, retreating behind the kitchen door and banging the pots and pans more loudly than usual. But I already knew she had the kindest heart. All her severity was only for show, and I even teased her sometimes, always ready to return to my usual respectful attitude.

Finally, my strength started to come back to me. I felt my sickness receding and began to be drawn from the cramped room to the wind and ocean, to the waves and dry sand – as if to old friends to whom you can tell everything, or former accomplices who you miss while in captivity. I started to leave the house, taking short walks on my still-weak legs. Soon I was strong enough to wander for hours, and the village became familiar to me.

It wasn't large – a few dozen log cabins scattered across a considerable space, with mounds of sand sloping between them, concealing the borders and making distances seem longer than they were. The homes roughly lined up in six rows, retreating into the Dunes and separated from the ocean by a wide strip of undeveloped coast. Some of them looked quite good, displayed carved shutters and new tile roofs; others were clearly falling into disrepair, with peeled paint and collapsed porches. In general, the place had the feeling of old age – but not one of death. Embers of life didn't burn, but they smoldered persistently – as if admitting a lack of fresh desires, yet not wishing to give back what they had won, no matter how minor it was.

A red cross was painted on one of the houses, and in the middle of the settlement stood a single store. It sold a mixture of things, ranging from bread to nails and aluminum basins, once a week receiving the residents' orders and other goods from the city. It was run by an elderly Turk – he could hardly speak the language, but I became friends with him by sharing my cigarettes, which were invaluable in the village. In return, with the look of a conspirator, he led me into a backroom and offered a collection of threadbare, pornographic postcards that had obviously been in a lot of hands. When I turned them down, he was perplexed and whispered behind me for a while, probably complaining about people's uppityness.

The village lived on fishing and the searock, which the same weekly truck transported to the city. On the coast, a little to the south, near a small bay and surrounded by high cliffs, lay boats pulled on the sand like the chins of lazy ocean creatures. There were also a few low, locked huts where the rock collectors stored their findings. When I regained my strength, I began to get up early and loved to go to that place around noon. The fishermen would haul in the fresh fish that glittered and sparkled in the sunlight, leaving the whole area replete with a pungent aroma. They sorted their catch right there on the shore, filling large homemade baskets woven from chaparral sprouts, and I spent hours with them, looking at the curiosities the nets brought in – shells and crabs, black mussels and grey shrimps, twisted balls of seaweed strongly smelling of iodine and resembling a mermaid's hair, and sometimes oysters that were probably concealing real pearls. All this tumbled into a pile, like a mound of toys – burial places for fake treasures that keep short, one-day memories. Then the fishermen banged pegs into the sand and hung the multicolored mesh nets out to dry while they gathered into a group, smoking and talking quietly.

Initially, they looked askance at me, but soon got used to my presence and stopped paying attention. It was as if I had become ethereal, camouflaged in the colors of the scenery, which accepted me and forgot about my existence. No one struck up a conversation with me however. If they needed to tell me something, they spoke unwillingly, looking off to the side. It was the same in the village: when I ran into someone, they hardly responded to a greeting and quickly turned away, pretending they were preoccupied with their own thoughts. There was no hostility in this: a few times I asked random passersby some innocuous questions, as any visitor would, and then they replied eagerly and in detail, seemingly glad to open their mouths. Yet no one wanted to ask me anything in turn – making it appear like all the natives considered it shameful to show interest in a newcomer. They took pride in their lack of emotion, suppressing the curiosity as if assuming they wouldn't hear anything new, and no unexpected twist would force them to look at things from a different perspective. They also didn't show any notice of the mark on my cheek – and I never once caught a furtive sidelong glance.

The monkey's hand hadn't disappeared, and I knew it would be there forever. Gradually, I got used to it, and then a picture began to take shape before my eyes, accommodating a lot of things which I hadn't wanted to acknowledge yet, hiding behind my so successfully found formulas. I was sliding along the outer boundaries of abstractions, not aiming at the depths. The depths were dangerous, I knew – they contained indisputable answers, those that were still approaching slowly or had already slipped through my fingers. I perceived the deliberateness of the parts meshing together but didn't want to know its rationale. I saw the bitterness and joy in the masks behind the glass but quickly turned away, remaining in quiet ignorance about real faces.

"Yes," I agreed with the persistent whispering of the masks. "The world may notice you if you make a solid effort, if you posture and pull a face or poke about with your cane. It will notice you and maybe even adapt to you for a time. Only its flexibility is deceitful – it doesn't acknowledge novel forms differing from those where its inertia has been immortalized. That's why, if you've been detected and the enormous shadow is approaching from above with its menacing beak, you better search for a proper nook and squeeze into it, keeping your extremities from sticking out. And if you don't find one, they instantly change you according to their rules, reconstruct you to please their fancies, treat you as an average nobody with an unenviable fate…"

And here I was telling myself not to despair yet. Fancies and reconstruction require courage, and courage is what the world doesn't have that much of. Plebian laziness prevails everywhere and no reserves are large enough to waste them on everyone. The world is slow; even its servants admit that; even the servants of servants have gotten used to pretending they're busy with a collective effort and in no rush whatsoever. It doesn't make sense to get distracted by every cipher – consequently, many of the noticed ones are left almost untouched, if, of course, things don't go too far. They simply set us aside for the future, though actually they just wish to forget us. They toss a fleeting, appraising glance at all our funny posturing and hurry to recklessly sort us out to make everything clear. Copies, copies – it's easy to imagine any number of them, leaving out the protruding details, smoothing the corners and grinding down the rough spots.

Let the incomprehensible slip away and hide somewhere inside, in a place where no one usually goes digging. It's not a big deal: from the outside, the essence of what's incomprehensible seems very normal to the servants and the servants of servants – as long as they use a familiar word for it and then confidently proclaim: "Named!"

Oh, the wild power of words, the terrible tenacity of names! It seems to be just a spider's web, but it entangles you like the strongest of nets. The game everyone is playing may not be over, but for you it's too late. They give you a spot in the crowd of commoners and only then inform you of the rules. The main ones are: ignore the obvious that doesn't conceal a riddle anymore, and reduce to the ordinary everything that still does, everything absurd and strange – even if you cut off the corners and overlook its fuzzy essence. That's where the strength is, and "overlook" should be supplanted by "don't let yourself drift into the fuzzy essence," since only then will you land among the winners. And the ones who are resting their hopes on the ambiguity of forms have no chance at all. Only humiliation comes in endless varieties. The servants of servants know this quite well.

That's probably why my mark doesn't arouse any interest, I continued. From a mile away one can see they already calculated the figure and selected the common denominator from the trustworthy list. And it doesn't matter that the total, and hence the label, might be inaccurate, or just dead wrong. They might uncover only the smallest part, simply skimming over the surface at the very beginning of the labyrinth, but the less you complicate things with details, the stronger the verdict. And the label, accurate or inaccurate, is indelible and permanent.

"Thank God it exists," everyone says. "It takes a great weight off our shoulders. Now we can deal with all the others who are still on the loose. Where are they hiding, those 'others' who haven't been figured out yet?"

As for the essence of the unknown that the familiar word has turned into something routine, the world doesn't need it – it doesn't feel at ease with words, not to mention an ability to make out an essence. Moreover, I myself don't really need this now – ha, ha, ha.

When I look at my features under a magnifying glass, I prefer to eschew a precise focus, avoiding answers in the meantime. Who cares who I was and what I became, what changed, and what remained as it was? *The worst is left behind* – the depth of the incomprehensible, the basis for the mark, is safe due to the absence of intruders wishing to probe into it. They look the other way and I don't have to be concerned: the mark is in place – and the depth is secure. I don't need to cherish, sigh, or tremble over it, worrying about stray eyes and curious, voracious fingers…

I reasoned like that throughout the long days, knowing I was going in circles. My mind and my will had been drained; my strength was only enough for fruitless musings gravitating toward insincere sarcasm. Still, I didn't let myself get completely demoralized. And to create at least an impression of an effort, I practiced a number of daily activities, allowing me to believe I hadn't surrendered forever. For instance, I made it a rule to take out the photo of Julian every night and examine it with intent interest, telling myself something like, "That's Julian. He's your enemy and a real asshole. You wanted to kill him. It's a secret." The intentionality of the extinct "wanted" and the artificiality of the insincere "kill" were clear to the point of obvious and pricked me like pins – but the longer I continued, the weaker and weaker it became. There exist other verbs as well, I persuaded myself. The time simply hasn't come to sort through them scrupulously. And this helped – even if my voice showed no desire to strengthen and could hardly have convinced anyone.

Now and then I took a sheet of paper and wrote down the names of my recent companions.

"The Christophers," I scribbled in crooked letters, looked up at the ceiling, and said, "Annoying ignoramuses."

"Gibbs," I penned slowly and added aloud with feeling, "A mercenary educated on the street. Won't end well."

And then I jotted down, "Stella. A petty little soul with a phony spark." Or, "Silvia. A stray cat," – and this last one made me narrow my eyes every time. What I had written and cemented in an ink frame didn't revive either voices or faces, but all the memories emerged obediently like a trail of funny dreams never reaching the final nightmare.

Occasionally, the sight of the paper set my teeth on edge, and the name Julian refused to sound as it should have. Then I lay on my back, closed my eyes, and used the malleable darkness to mold images that had profundity and vibrant colors. Afterward, I put myself inside them and looked at the world from a different angle.

Sometimes, I became a raptorial bird, gliding through the clouds, my eyes sharply following every movement below where the prey promised warm blood. No one could compete with the breadth of my view, yet no detail was too small to slip by my all-seeing eye. I felt the power of ascending currents pushing me upward, into the stratosphere. My throat sensed the emergence of whirlwinds into which I could dive and hurtle forth, swooping down like a ruthless shade. My feathers trembled and I beat my wings with dignity, heading into a perfect arc with one little flap. It's true that flight is nothing new, but there's so much pleasure if one can do it right!

Speed isn't bad either. Besides being a bird, I enjoyed turning into a race car and zipping around hot asphalt. Then I started to gravitate toward more complex devices, imagining myself to be a drill launched into the depths of the earth with a good deal of fuel and ingenious programming. I vibrated together with the steel case, listened to the rhythmical sound of the engine, the tapping of the bearings and the grinding of the cutter digging into the unyielding ground. Awareness of the unavoidability overwhelmed me: the drill couldn't be stopped; no bedrock – neither basalt nor granite – could slow the movement or divert its course even one degree. And no one up above suspected that brutal work was going on somewhere far below their feet. None of them had the slightest idea until the moment terrifying blades suddenly spurted up in fountains of dust, as if confirming that fulfillment is inevitable, whether others agree with it or not.

There were other pictures – a lynx hidden in the thicket; a resting torpedo knowing well how to become merciless, like death advancing on wings; or, for example, a rock face carved out of the mountainside. What could be better than eternal thoughts disturbed only by an earthquake happening once every thousand years? All this calmed me and hardened my soul, and the confusion receded by itself, seemingly repelled by the stability of things and circumstances to which unquestionable meaning had long ago been ascribed. Soon I discovered that the figures and forms, which I learned to penetrate, occupying the very center, gradually altered the direction of my thoughts. Outside irritants shifted into the background; other people and their intentions became insignificant like dull landscapes, and my courage to reason grew day by day.

I wondered about my own content, not considering the exercise useless anymore. I rehashed fragile attributes of personal anatomy this way and that, trying out the various "whats" and "wherefores" that still dominated the "whys." I even became so bold, I began to steal up to the recent clash with the invisible, ruthless force. I was drawn toward it in cautious reminiscences, and at some point acknowledged with certainty that the event, in its entire scope, had really happened to me. No, I wasn't ready to address the details, again reliving the humiliation and pain. I dealt with what had occurred as with an explosive mixture assiduously packed in obscure plastic. The main trick consisted of avoiding quantitative categories – any of which might show up as a reminder that was much too cruel. I had to concentrate on qualities, not quantities, and I succeeded, learning to say "The Black Pelican" to myself and not get nauseous. I began to guess, little by little, what I had actually witnessed – as if finding firm bits in the amorphous matter, clinging to them and selecting the right words. But I was still afraid to formulate all things as they were. I was overly careful and made almost no headway, thoroughly protecting the few safe, well-tested areas. Inside them I felt confident and secure. No visions or mesmerizing cries held sway over this territory that had been won back. I understood: from now on my domains were unchallenged, their nature utterly independent. There wasn't even a need to seek excuses for former blindness, justifying my shameful efforts to sidestep the kernel, dissolve in the dreariness, look for sympathy from others.

All that wasn't me, and now – now I was finally becoming myself. My soul might be broken into many parts, tossed from great heights onto the rock steps, but why not recreate the mosaic anew, gathering up the compatible tiles? There was a base below it, an undeniable fact: something shouted a rebellious "no" at the decisive moment when it seemed it was only possible to give in. That means there is a nut in the nutshell – and that means my secret is alive too, because it comes from the core itself. I just need to think a little more, altering views and looking from all sides. Where are my blank paper sheets? Where are Julian, the Christophers and Gibbs – or, instead, the drill and imperturbable rock face? I now know: one can adjust to anything. Especially if left alone.

CHAPTER 3

The days drifted by quietly, each one similar to the others. Nothing urged me on, and I was in no hurry to leave the village, without any plans for the future. By cautious estimates, the money I gave Maria should have been enough for a long time, although she refused to discuss the subject, becoming unfriendly and rude.

"I'll return whatever's left. I certainly won't keep it for myself," she would grumble whenever this conversation came up. And I backed down, telling myself that, in any case, she wouldn't kick me out all of a sudden. In the meantime, having no concerns, I wandered the area or just stood by the water edge, inhaled the salted air, and counted the waves. When I reached a certain number I'd thought of earlier and no one knew, I glanced back, as if trying to catch my surroundings by surprise. And, with relief, I was reassured the world remained the same, its stability unshakable. No one and nothing was plotting behind my back.

Maria got used to me. In the evenings we would sit together on the porch, silently watching the sun slip behind the Dunes. She invariably smoked a pipe; I, a cigarette, the supply of which was already running out. Sometimes I told her how many fish they'd caught that morning or who had squabbled with whom because of their twisted tackle, and she would nod seriously, showing by the importance of her demeanor she was processing the information. I didn't know what interested her in general and what could move her, break through the strong armor of aloofness. I felt at ease in her presence, probably because she never encroached on my own invisible shell.

After I recovered and life in the house fell into the same day-to-day pattern, guests began to come see us – a couple, the Parkers, who always appeared with their adopted child Charlotte and a trained squirrel in a dainty cage. Charlotte was a skinny young girl of seventeen. She had been an orphan; the Parkers took her from the orphans' asylum two days before she was to be sent to a special institution for the mentally ill. As for the squirrel, it had been caught somewhere in the Cordilleras – or actually it had been picked up in a state close to death and then nursed and trained to do all sorts of amusing things. They never said what took them to the Cordilleras two years ago and seemed to intentionally avoid the subject, but the squirrel, which they called Maggie, was treated with adoration, like a full member of the family.

Charlotte and Maggie weren't overly fond of each other. Maggie displayed a more impatient nature and occasionally snorted in the direction of the girl if she was close. Charlotte just shrugged her shoulders arrogantly and turned away when people showed interest in the squirrel or its tricks, but her eyes betrayed no malice, reflecting only dreaminess and sorrow. The Parkers assured me the girl was completely healthy, complaining about the incompetence of her doctors, although in my opinion anyone would've said Charlotte was hopelessly sick, or at least so abnormal no competence was necessary to determine it. No, she didn't have fits or anything like that; she looked neat and could read and write. Observing her in profile, one could suppose none of her peculiarities were real: the impetuous mimicking was concealed, made less evident, and only her lips moved by themselves, living a separate life. But as soon as she began to speak – and Charlotte couldn't keep quiet for long – all doubts vanished, and your hand reached for the medical book to look up a discomforting diagnosis. Her words, despite their innocence, awakened your consciousness, like an earsplitting alarm, their lack of logic tormenting you or, more likely, their own invisible logic, which your regular mind is unaware of. Moreover, you couldn't chalk up the stormy flow of her phrases to senseless rigmarole. There was power and harmony in her sayings – which she herself was aware of. And no one else could arrange them as subtly, link them together in such a seamless manner, stringing one to another without any difficulty.

When Charlotte wasn't paying attention, the Parkers told me in an undertone, they had repeatedly tried to transfer onto paper the stream of sounds issued from the strange girl, whose care they undertook voluntarily. But nothing came of it – either their hand was not fast enough or what they wrote lost its strangeness when captured, and the magic faded like traces of trick ink. Even recorders had no effect and produced tapes full of gibberish. Maybe the luster of her coal-black pupils was missing, which no machine could catch, or perhaps other odd features of her face or her voice. Whatever the case, they both admired their Charlotte no less than their squirrel Maggie, considering her the healthiest of all the children they knew – just excessively vulnerable and forced to bear too many insults in the past.

On this last point I agreed with them: it was disturbing to imagine how much she had had to endure from other children and self-assured teachers who had witnessed her "illness" and experienced its unusual power, endeavoring, of course, to hurt her in response. Charlotte still looked within and was always ready to recede into her hideout. It wasn't easy with her: everyone had to watch what they said or did – both me and even the Parkers, despite established habit. Only Maria found it effortless to speak her language, and they whispered away for hours on the porch while the rest of us drank tea in the living room to take cover from the mosquitoes. My landlady was mostly silent, of course – it was always difficult to extract an idle word from her. But for that, Charlotte let loose, and we would even hear her tentative, but genuine laughter, which was echoed by Maria's muffled, brusque giggling.

"It's amazing," Mrs. Parker always noted with a perceptible hint of jealousy. "Charlotster almost never laughs at home." To this, her husband gave her a disapproving glance and observed *sotto voce* that Charlotte couldn't bear being called by this vulgar diminutive. Then Mrs. Parker would lapse into a guilty silence, only remarking off to the side, "Well, she doesn't like your 'Charly' much better." And every time I felt awkward, as if they were giving me a glimpse into an unwelcome, intimate detail.

Mr. Parker was a large man going gray, with a fleshy nose and whiskers growing halfway down his cheeks. He was a teacher and made a living by giving ad hoc lessons in the village. I thought they moved here because of Charlotte, but that was just my speculation. It might be different, especially since I couldn't conceive of Parker standing by the blackboard and receiving a teacher's salary his whole life. They – both he and his wife Hanna – appeared satisfied with their lot, though actually I could never say for sure. Their faces, smiles, and the glint in their eyes always tried to slip out of focus like the remains of an unfinished phrase. I only remember they liked to take each other by the hand, especially Hanna. Now and then, she seized his fingers and squeezed them as if she didn't realize what she was doing until Mr. Parker took his hand back for some utilitarian purpose. They were also never rude to each other and didn't evince any mutual irritation – as if long ago memorizing all the possible grudges and reproaches that consequently lost meaning like a word repeated a hundred times in a row.

Hanna Parker did her part to contribute to the family's income by painting clay dishes their neighbor Goran produced with severe determination. He was an ageless man who had roamed about and come here straight from Tibet, according to the rumors. In Maria's kitchen I saw a few of the saucers Hanna had embellished – they weren't worth praising or looking at twice, but obviously this extra work let the Parkers make ends meet. Hanna was talkative, easily amused, and pretty by common standards, despite the absence of thin features. She loved jam and donuts, which could not but affect her figure, whose curves were accentuated by her smallness. Nonetheless, she moved about easily, walked gracefully, and possessed enviable mental quickness, which, along with precise judgment, appeared here and there within her regular womanly chatter.

No matter what, you couldn't deny their vigor. And Hanna Parker, in addition to her handicraft, served as a source of slightly excited enthusiasm whose gentle beams oscillated from her to her husband, adopted child, and trained squirrel. External objects that required her care, whether they were people, animals, or something entirely lifeless, seemed necessary to meet her own inner exigencies – giving meaning to her days and hours by delighting with something in others and bearing the secret echoes of that delight. Sometimes I caught her eye and thought she'd like to nurture me in her own way too, avidly laying her hands on yet another unowned unsettledness. Hanna never tired of extolling Mr. Parker's intelligence and Charlotte's hidden genius and the unique defenselessness of her soul. And this created an invisible halo around the whole family, making you smile now and then, as at an attempt to take on something bigger than the circumstances allowed, but at the same time winning over your heart like any neverending persistence.

Charlotte barely needed this as much as Mr. Parker, who always flourished in Hanna's presence and became confused when she vanished out of eyesight. He also liked to chat, but was fairly reticent and didn't have the habit of questioning others, so our talks were quite neutral. At times, when the conversation died down, Mrs. Parker suggested we play something and wouldn't leave us in peace if we sought laziness as an excuse, trying to get out of it. Indefatigably, she supplied the game pieces – drew charts and prepared crossword puzzles, cut figures out of manila paper, and wrote clever words on cardboard rectangles. Once she even made a real chess board on which Parker and I battled enthusiastically – though at checkers and reversi, not chess. He was much poorer than me at calculating multi-move combinations but played tenaciously and even managed a couple of wins.

Hanna never agreed to participate but watched very slyly – so that I involuntarily suspected her of something and got angry at myself. Once I went as far as to place the paper pieces I prepared the day before in the classic position for the game of *Dzhan* – in its simplest sixty-four field variation – and glanced at both Parkers, quickly pursuing a few attacks and retreats, repeating formations known even to beginners. Mr. Parker didn't react at all, but Hanna, in my opinion, looked at the board a little more closely than was necessary. I intentionally made a wrong move, and the white pieces fanned out to the corners instead of gathering in a formidable, piercing point, yet her face showed no surprise or disappointment. Even then I didn't completely believe her and continued to watch her furtively, hoping to catch some incautious sign. But a placid smile was all that met me until I jumbled the pieces in a pile and left the living room, irritated, though not forgetting to excuse myself politely.

Thus, the Parkers had their mysteries guarded quite meticulously, although maybe the majority of them I imagined out of nothing. And, in any case, I didn't have the courage to get seriously involved and challenge the perfectly proper couple, trying to reveal the truth. Sometimes I came close, or they approached a dangerous border themselves – in the case with the game of *Dzhan*, for example, or when we listened to a violin concert on the radio, afraid to move and frighten off the enchantment of the magical notes. Even the squirrel seemed to quiet down in its cage and Charlotte stopped romping and babbling, while Mr. Parker diverted his red eyes, turning his back to us. When silence ensued, Hanna said with a sigh, "Yes, anyone can understand that music. Too much sorrow – how unfortunate! As if the most desired women left a city, then half the remaining ones, and then all the rest." But Parker coughed crossly and objected that this was all a fantasy and nothing but drivel, old doldrums everyone should have outgrown, and the music wasn't about that at all. It was just about how your cries wouldn't reach anyone – and he muttered something else irritably, while Hanna Parker gazed in his direction with an odd look. But here Maria spoke to Charlotte and began to scold her for something with feigned strictness, so the tension gradually abated, and the incident wound down by itself.

So, yes, I didn't manage to get close to the Parkers, but with them I started to observe that my inner energy was returning and something was beginning to gnaw at my insides, requiring new plans and actions. At least, a certain aggressiveness appeared in me, which Mr. Parker unintentionally provoked with his softness and inability to confront others. Sometimes I wanted to go up and ask, "Listen, Mr. Parker, what's the most important thing about you?" Or, "Do you have your own secret?" – or something else of that ilk. I was annoyed by his unwillingness to break out of whatever chains he'd placed on himself, but what those chains were I could not recognize, and this really frustrated me.

So, not yet solving the riddles, I gradually began to discern their traces, like colored thread in the gray fabric of everyday life that pretends to look overly simplified, only waiting for a chance to laugh behind your back. This was no small step forward, which I couldn't help but notice. And even the mark on my cheek started to look different – at least, I no longer winced when I recalled its origin. Maybe I got used to it and wanted to believe it was the result of my own bold effort. A few times I even contemplated telling the Parkers about Julian, but I didn't risk it, which I praised myself for later. After all, the moment wasn't very propitious: my business with Julian had stalled, and I clearly needed to reassess my former plan. Moreover, how could I trust them, these Parkers? A secret's a secret for a reason – it was enough I had blurted everything out to Stella and she could spread it further, and maybe had already done so. It's frustrating, aggravating – and that's it. I won't make the same dumb mistake again.

Nonetheless, the delicacy of our relations was upset once – it was my fault, of course. This happened a couple weeks after we became acquainted. Mr. Parker and I were standing alone at the edge of the fence, gazing at the stars. He suddenly stopped talking, looked around, and twisted his head, as if freeing himself from unsubstantiated thoughts. Then he spoke about the village, what it had once been like, and told me its whole history, which he knew very well. I learned that old believers had settled here long ago, pioneers from some small sect that had been chased out. They didn't give a hoot for prejudices, and a so-called bad place didn't frighten them in the least. Quickly, they became acclimated and learned to fend for themselves. For a long time no one bothered them – no one even supposed their settlement existed – but later, when the searock became popular, the village was discovered anew. The religious persecution had stopped by that time and commerce came instead, but the hard-core sectarians still departed with their fishing boats. They loaded their houses – disassembled to the last log – onto homemade rafts and headed further south. Then new people started to arrive – from the city and other places.

"We've seen all kinds of strangers here," said Parker reflectively. And at this, annoyed by his slightly patronizing tone, I felt a tingle run up my arm. Suddenly, I pointed to my cheek, asking, "How about this one? Have you seen that or known that before? Does it alarm you or startle you?" Of course, this was a kindergarten stunt, but, at first, I was quite excited: not only was I able to ponder alone in my room – I could also chat with others about utterly forbidden things. Mr. Parker, however, instantly became sad, so I felt awkward and wanted to change the topic to something else or simply part ways.

He then took me by the elbow and said quietly that, of course, he had seen it multiple times, but seeing was one thing and contemplating was something else, and it was pointless to try and shock him. He assured me he didn't get offended, since he didn't think he had the right to pass judgment on it. I made an impatient gesture and he added, as if rushing to finish before I interrupted him, "Yes, yes, but there's no reason for reproach. Especially since it may happen to the brave ones, even to the best. Then there are others, much worse than average, excuse my involuntary snobbism. I've never made an attempt to judge them – and never wanted to. It generally happens to those who believe in nothing – and please note, about you, personally, I'm not making assumptions. But it's clear that people with beliefs and patience – even if their patience is sometimes strained to the limit – don't need such marks. They don't need much at all – they are different and their prayers vary, but they are surely united in something and are hardly inclined to take ill-conceived steps."

"Yeah, they don't need much, including marks. They're already bound, hand and foot, by the beliefs you mentioned, aren't they?" I replied argumentatively, cut to the quick. Mr. Parker just spread his hands and said in a conciliatory tone, "Maybe, or maybe not." And he led me into the house.

His words came back to me, and I reflected on them more than once. Nothing special resulted from these contemplations, except the obvious conclusion that you should only listen to yourself, rather than look around and – I added emotionally – adopt strange children and crippled squirrels. This last bit was unfair – intentionally so. I wanted to be somewhat rude to avoid returning to the subject, sidestepping it by a few miles. Afterward, my talks with the Parkers never went beyond the limits of dull politeness. I even began to feel some condescension toward them – these intelligent and humanistic people, these useless beings incapable of even the most innocuous craziness.

Now there was no way I could tell them about Julian and the black revolver. But I got used to them, and Hanna got used to me, sometimes eyeing me with a smidgen of mature omniscience. With Charlotte, however, I didn't learn to speak without restraint. Her incisive words held something destructive and uncontrollably contradictory – affecting herself, me, the whole world. But she and I still became friends, training ourselves in the art of winking and secret gesticulation, occasionally giving each other signs to make sure our connection was intact. Now and then we sprinkled the conversation with coinciding snickers or chuckled crossly at an identical thought that popped into our heads at the same time.

Late autumn arrived without warning. I had already been in the village for almost two months. The air didn't get much colder; only the ocean harshened, as if pieces of ice were shining in it. And the wind, if it blew from the north, carried the scent of distant snow. All this time the Parkers and my stern landlady formed an exclusive coterie outside of which I knew no one. This didn't bother me – I just took it for a given fact. However, as soon as I happened to meet someone new, the Parkers and Maria shifted into the background, and I was puzzled by what could have appealed to me in those sluggish, identical evenings. Curatives one always forgets quickly, especially when the medicine looks plain and has no smell, like run-of-the-mill anesthesia. But the bitter taste in your mouth sometimes takes a while to go away, and so it was with the Parkers: I suddenly had my fill of them. Although it's true they didn't do anything bad to me.

Anyway, my encounter with Archibald Bely changed everything, and life in the village played to a different tune afterward. It occurred by chance, without any effort on my part, as if to commemorate the new season that came to the seacoast. I saw him for the first time when I was helping the fishermen repair their nets. They were already accustomed to my presence – no longer frowning when I watched them unload the fish or sort the searock and set aside the rare pieces. That morning, crawling through the sand, we thrust in even rows of pointed pegs to stretch old, decrepit tackle beaten up the day before. I was engrossed in the work, proud they entrusted me with such a difficult task. The ocean surged, the surf rumbled wrathfully, and there were no thoughts in my head. I was working silently, concentrated on the faded mesh, when a deafening whistle pierced the air and drowned all the other sounds.

I shivered, dumbstruck, as if torn from a deep sleep, and slowly lifted my eyes. On the cliffs not far away stood a man in a raincoat flapping in the wind. He screamed in an incomprehensible language, looking at the ocean, the waves – or farther, beyond the edge of the sky, beyond the horizon. Screaming once more and waiting, as if listening for an answer, he again whistled, louder than before, and laughed. Then he gazed for a long time at one point, overlapped his raincoat, and wrapped himself in his arms.

I fixed on him, unable to break loose. He didn't resemble anyone and was completely alien to the coast and the fishing boats. At the same time, however, his figure on the crag seemed so natural it blended perfectly into the scenery and splashing water, the gusts of wind and the roar of the waves. It lent refinement and tragedy to the conventional harmony by dignifying it with bold strokes – and when he turned away and began to descend, I deeply regretted the impossibility of re-experiencing the scene that had just pieced itself together from random parts for all of a few seconds.

"Who's that?" I asked an elderly fisherman fiddling with knots next to me. He didn't want to reply, grimaced, and muttered something off to the side. When he saw I hadn't looked away, he said glumly, "That's a crackpot artist," and spit in the sand. I wanted to question him more, but realized he wouldn't tell me anything else. The man in the raincoat, in the meantime, had almost reached the base of the cliff and was about to jump down and out of sight – perhaps forever. I leapt up, quickly brushed off my knees, and ran toward him.

Once he had jumped, he didn't rush to disappear. I went up to him and introduced myself, smiling as affably as possible. Somewhat solemnly he replied, "Archibald Bely. Artist. Local artist, so to say," – stressing the word "local" and looking into my eyes as if searching for the impression he had made.

Archibald was tall, a half-head taller than me, and had long hair that fell onto his shoulders. His narrow, wrinkled face with its pointed chin didn't reveal his age, but I was sure he was significantly older. A black scarf was twisted round his neck; a crudely knit wool sweater with a stringy nap peeked out of his raincoat. The raincoat, sweater, and scarf made it possible to assume the "local artist" was a tramp or someone steadily slipping into poverty, but his fashionable pants and new stylish shoes clearly cost no small sum and demonstrated he was well-off and accustomed to high-quality things.

"Pleased to meet you," I said and choked up, getting stuck as usual on the first phrases that come so easily to others.

"Me too, me too," replied Archibald with a barely perceptible sarcastic smile. "I've heard about you, of course. You're at Maria's, right? She's a charming woman, though she can't stand me, to tell you the truth. But then she's not the only one…"

He made a funny grimace and waved his hand. I murmured

something in response, not knowing how to spark the conversation. Archibald came to the rescue. "They told me you're not from here – I mean, not from the City of M," he began, slightly inclining his head and demonstrating real interest.

"That's right," I took advantage of the convenient subject. "I'm from the capital – just landed here by accident and stuck around. That's how things turned out – and what's your situation? It's probably similar, right?"

"To some extent," Archibald nodded nonchalantly. "It's a long story." He fixed his scarf, waved as if dismissing some thought, and said with a glance at his watch, "You know, I think we do everything dumbly. If we want to get to know each other, then we should do it the right way. What if I invite you to my place this evening – it's the third house from the store, in the direction of the Dunes? I imagine you know where the store is, but if you get confused, don't worry: anyone can tell you where I live. Just be careful with the dogs; there are some very mean dogs in the yards… Any objections?" And without waiting for my agreement, he nodded, put his listless hand in mine, and walked away rapidly, with a slight mince in his step.

The rest of the day I waited impatiently for evening. Some new agitation – or, more likely, an old, temporarily forgotten one – rose up inside me, tugging and not letting me go. I suspected another riddle – not a feeble charade as with the Parkers, but a real skein with many threads. My curiosity, which had been relegated to a dusty corner due to a lack of material, now again asserted its vitality with which little could compete.

There was also something else that made me rub my hands excitedly. I didn't know what to call it: someone's confidence or someone's force, a certain vector directed at an invisible point located further than the ordinary eye might see. I could also peer into far distances, yet all my points had faded and now looked similar to each other. Perhaps someone else's view could noticeably refresh mine? No, I didn't expect direct help, but really, Archibald Bely, the "local artist," with his gaze boring into the horizon as he whistled up his ghosts at a deafening pitch – it was something, wasn't it? It inspired me, no doubt – and what else here, in the village, could provide any inspiration? It suggested reflection – new reflection, quite, quite new!

When I pulled out the photo of Julian and repeated the customary, "That's Julian. He's your enemy and a real asshole," I felt real firmness in my voice and believed for the first time that fall I was a serious threat. I even wanted to go to the Parkers and tell them their life was passing in vain. Yet that was too much, and they might already know that quite well.

As soon as the sun set, I began to get ready. Maria grew suspicious when she saw me in front of the mirror with a razor and a lathery face. She walked back and forth in the corridor, looking glumly through the cracked door each time she passed, and then asked jealously, "Where are you going?" with a curiosity that was uncharacteristic of her.

"To see Archibald," I replied lightheartedly, puffing up my cheek and shaving off the stubble with my dull razorblade that really needed to be changed.

Maria stopped in the opening, staring at the floor as if my response forced her to consider something. "Shame on you," she said, shaking her head disapprovingly. And added in a burst, "His drinking will ruin you both!" But I just waved my hand and grinned at her image in the mirror, feeling a hundred years younger than she and not wishing to hide it.

CHAPTER 4

The artist Archibald Bely lived in a spacious house at the top of a sandy hill. There were hardly any walls inside – most of the space was an open studio that also served as a bedroom. Its layout and accoutrements confirmed unambiguously: pictures were painted here – and I hadn't expected anything else. Yet something stubbornly fouled up the impression, so I looked around stealthily for a few minutes until it dawned on me: there were almost no paintings in the studio. That is, I saw lots of canvases – big and small ones, on tripods and on the floor, in stretchers, frames and simply tacked to wood. But they were all turned to the wall or covered by fabric, so I could only guess what was on the other side, and what in general Archibald Bely was worth in the terms of artistic talent.

Only one painting was visible – a portrait of a woman on an easel in the far corner. It drew my attention like a magnet, but we didn't go up to it, so I couldn't get a good look. Archibald was messing around by the front door where the bar stood. While he mixed me a martini and prepared himself some strange blend of vodka, rum, and green sparkling water, I stood next to him and fretted over my answers to his questions, which were probably just an act of courtesy, but put me in an understandable quandary. Really, what could I say about the reason for my stay in the village? Or about what brought me to M. in the first place? What I fabricated on the spot had a totally implausible storyline, but Archibald was not disconcerted and showed genuine interest, as if truly accepting it as the real thing.

"It's great you decided to come here and to withdraw from life for a while," he said with enthusiasm, shaking his massive head affirmatively to the rhythm of his words. "That always helps; I can guarantee it, even not knowing you well. Something's probably causing an itch in you – something reckless and creative that you can't hide, I noticed it on the coast. Yes, solitude, the ocean... Its power, its eternity... It may be played out, but it's true, isn't it? I have to admit I was very skeptical when I came five years ago. I couldn't get used to the place – was bored, depressed, missed all the usual hustle and bustle. And generally speaking... Oh, here's Maria. Not your Maria, but mine – let me introduce you. She's sort of the landlady, and I'm sort of the tenant."

Archibald gave a short snicker as he nodded at the quiet, forty-five-year-old woman with an unrefined face who had just entered the studio with a tray and was taking clean glasses off it, clearly uncomfortable with the attention she was receiving. I greeted her, and Maria, darting a sharp, slightly frightened look at me, mumbled hello and made haste to leave us alone.

"She's shy, as you noticed," said Archibald, obviously irritated. "However, she's a good woman and cooks fantastically. Her name is Carla, not Maria, but I call her that. I like Maria much better. What's Carla for a name..." He grabbed our drinks, and we went over to a sofa and armchairs in the middle of the room.

"Will you show me your paintings?" I asked, wishing to switch the conversation to another topic.

Archibald wrinkled his brow and gazed in his glass sullenly. "My paintings..." he drawled after a short silence and continued with a slight tone of annoyance, "I'll show you them, why not? Only I have to warn you right away: every picture is different. Often, you know, people just take a look – and they want to criticize it right away. They may disapprove of it only because it has a strange name or has been painted in a provocative manner. This is what they say – 'provocative manner' – although it's obvious they're just revealing their foolishness. And you – are you an *esthete*? That is, do you consider yourself an expert? I don't think you're a professional – meaning arts and stuff."

With these words he finished his aperitif, jumped up, and bounded to the bar. By that time, I had managed to drink just a mouthful, so I recalled Maria's prophecy – *my* Maria, as Archibald would put it. He soon returned with another glass and stared quizzically first at my martini, then at me.

"No, no. I haven't even drunk half of it," I rushed to set him at ease. "And no, I'm no expert, just a regular admirer. Although I play with words sometimes – and with rhymes, that does occur," I added and felt myself redden up to the ears. I cursed my impetuousness inaudibly and said, wishing to get away from the subject, "Actually, I asked because your work isn't hanging on the walls. You might be hiding them, might not want them on display?"

Archibald looked at me with a somewhat bemused expression. "I don't hide them, they're everywhere," he said. "Standing, not hung – but does it matter?" And he cast his eyes over the place.

"But I… I can't see them," I muttered, feeling rather dumb.

"That one – you can see that one all right." He nodded at the portrait in the far corner. "Let's take a closer look at it." And we got up from the sofa and went over to the canvas.

"Every picture is different," Archibald stated again as we crossed the room. "And the viewers, they are thoroughly ungrateful – ungrateful and ungracious. Yet you can't do anything about it – I understood that when I created my first masterpiece. It was a bitter experience, but one can get used to it, one just needs time. A bit of time and a small shred of inner strength."

We went up to the portrait, but before I could consider it, Archibald jumped in front of me and turned the face of the painting to the wall. "It'll have to wait," he said casually. "I still want to tell you about my first masterwork." And he plopped down on the floor, knocking back a good portion of his glass and setting it next to him. I had no other option than to hitch up my pants and follow his example.

"So," Archibald began, gesticulating, with glittering eyes,

"the masterwork and the beastly nature of humankind. It's rather informative, although there's certainly nothing surprising if you look at it from an ordinary perspective, since the painting depicted a parrot with one eye, which annoyed the unprepared public exceedingly. Maybe the title – *Self-Portrait* – also added to it, but the reception was still way too hostile, with no effort – I mean *no* effort – to see it from a broader point of view."

An enshrouding mellowness appeared in Archibald's voice. "Now the piece is in a private collection," he said, not forgetting to take a sip of his pale green mixture. "Some swindler has it – behind a steel door, safe lock, with all the windows armored. Yet back then no one offered a penny for it. Every critic took a dig, and reporters also jumped into the fray. Everyone saw nothing but a crippled bird. And it's ridiculous how much more there was to it!"

"The parrot was probably a symbol for something. One just had to figure it out," I decided to interrupt him to underscore my active interest.

"Yeah, it was a symbol," grumbled Archibald, regarding me mistrustfully. "But no, not a lousy symbol, what are you talking about? It was a condensation – a condensed world, with me in the middle of it. One just needed to look at it carefully!"

"Imagine," he exclaimed, waving his hands. "Imagine, I'm young, everything around me is new. There are so many colors, subjects – it's all so engaging. But, at the same time, I'm wise – yes, young but wise. Some people are wise almost from birth – and I'm not bragging, I'm just being honest. A lot lies within my realm; if I can't change the world, then at least I can seize it and turn it into my own – like a buccaneer, a pirate. So how else should I see myself if not like a brave captain of a prowling pirate ship – with a barrel of rum right there, and a musket, and a black patch over one eye – all the features of the well-known image – even a parrot on my shoulder, probably from Jamaica… That's how it was born – the self-portrait. But if you write everything from beginning to end, it turns out too long and your attention wanes, bogged down by details; you get tired in the middle. Even saying it aloud is too awkward: musket, vat of rum, parrot on your shoulder, pirate with one eye… I realized this right after my first sketches and began to search for how to unravel it more concisely. From the beginning to the end in one fell swoop – omitting unimportant intermediary stages to prevent distraction and get straight to the point. Anyway, it's my world; I created it for myself so I can describe it as I want, right? I felt something serious was brewing – so I worked like hell, spent days at the easel, slept little, and lost weight. And gradually, believe me, the superfluous parts began to evaporate, shrink, and fade away. Symbols remained, as you say, but they aren't entirely symbols, that is, not the surfaces, but the very heart of things. They remained, yes they did, but didn't want to land in their proper places. And then, finally, it came to me, and I knew at once I got it right. In the middle is the one-eyed parrot gazing like a buccaneer – condensing the two figures into one. And all the other attributes are just scattered around – in the corners, hardly visible, ethereal and inconspicuous in general. So inconspicuous no one even noticed them. The audience just saw the bird and made a fuss about it, took a phrase out of context, and was surprised it hung listlessly like a helpless lash. And the tension, the groaning ropes, the very string that connects the beginning and the end despite them ripping away from each other – all this they didn't even try to capture. And how could they have caught it, those half-blind imbeciles?" Archibald shook his head and suddenly began to snicker.

I wondered if he was already drunk and having problems putting his words together, but that wasn't the case. His eyes regained their lucid glare, and he smiled at his next thought, not at wacko reflections distorted by alcohol. "I still suckered them," he informed me, sitting cross-legged and fanning himself a few times with the tail of his scarf. "I tricked them, like a bunch of airheads, and that's what they really are!"

Here Archibald became serious and looked pensively into his empty glass. "Do you know how long it took me to paint the self-portrait with the one-eyed parrot?" he asked provocatively and then answered his own question, "Two months and four days. I might have kept going, but I needed to hurry: the gallery had been rented – the reception, presentation, event… And then – yes, then, in a week, when it became clear I'd have trouble getting my idea across to the public, I painted six pictures, one a day plus Sunday for a break. Please, don't search for comparisons, I don't suffer from megalomania, but still: six paintings, six average-sized canvases. They had difficulty finding a place for them: there wasn't enough wall space because they hadn't reckoned on this earlier, but the organizer saw the threat of a fiasco and tried really hard, grasping – so to say – at straws.

So, six paintings, the gradual striptease of my 'I.' Each of the six unveiled the evanescence of superfluous elements. On the first is a whole group: the pirate is obviously very dashing, a patch over his eye, a parrot and bottle. He sits solemnly on a barrel with gunpowder – a real buccaneer, no doubt about it. Then, in the next one, the musket vanishes from the corner, empty spots appear here and there, the parrot is turned upside down, and the barrel contains rum instead of explosives. And on it went, you get the idea. The original one-eyed parrot crowns everything – like an exclamation point, the seventh circle. And everyone sees clearly: this one must be the last!

As for me, I was a little embarrassed, yet curiosity ate me alive. The organizer expressed all kinds of doubts, but I replied, 'Be a man,' and that was the only thing he could do. And imagine that – the ice was broken. At first they just opened their mouths, but two days later some smartass turned up and offered a concept – I mean, 'what does the artist want to tell us?' With all kinds of nonsense about the transformation of the figure, progressive simplification, and a reduction to one central sphere. Well, maybe not exactly nonsense, but I found it ridiculous, though I also had to agree and say some drivel. And that the six paintings were garbage, no one noticed in the least. They wanted to buy everything together, but I said: no, no way, only the exclamation point is for sale. I knew it was a masterpiece, yet they still didn't pay much, probably dividing it by seven in their minds. The other six, by the way, I burned afterward – that was what they were worth, and I'm not sorry… And you, I see, are not drinking at all – that's not good, even a bit offensive," – and Archibald jumped easily to his feet, with the obvious intention to refill our glasses. I, ashamed, gulped down my martini and got up after him.

"So all pictures are different," he muttered on the way to the bar. I grinned to myself, tripping along after him and asking into his back, "And still – why is it like this here? Why are the canvases turned to the wall?" Without answering, Archibald just briefly looked at me with his clever eyes. And it became clear I'd get no reply until we had perked up with another dose of booze.

"What did you ask?" he said with an innocent look after working the bottles.

"You can only see the backs of the canvases," I repeated patiently. "Why, except for that one? Maybe you want to tell me it means that…"

"Not at all," Archibald broke me off categorically. "Even though I don't know what you have in mind. In any case, you won't be able to figure out my deeply personal reason, nor will you stumble on it in the dark. You could guess it accidentally, but that doesn't count."

He gave me my glass, and we strolled away from the bar. "If you think I'm embarrassed about them," he added, somewhat offended, "then you're wrong – they're quite good. That is, I want to say they're really good. All of them."

He stopped in the middle of the room and began to look around. Then he suggested, "Choose one."

"Huh?" I didn't get it.

"Point to any one," Archibald explained. "Point, and I'll turn it around. If it's bad, it's yours, you can burn it. If it's not finished yet, then we'll switch to the next one."

"Hmm, I don't know…" I drawled, thinking the game wasn't quite fair. I certainly wouldn't take the liberty of condemning someone's work to destruction and would be forced to throw out compliments and try to sound convincing. The prospects were not very inviting, but I couldn't get out of it. The affronted artist, noting my vacillation, repeated insistently, "But please. You choose. Choose."

I shrugged my shoulders and picked randomly – "This one" – a small canvas leaning against the wall right in front of us.

Archibald grabbed it and turned it toward me. On a gray background stretched a crimson line, resignedly and helplessly terminating at the edge. A fragile silhouette hung over it. I immediately recalled my mirages on the coast and the figurine, clambering up out of the straw basket. After a brief hesitation, I was about to go a little closer for a better look, but Archibald said curtly, "It's not finished," and placed the picture back against the wall. "Now for attempt number two."

I glanced around and selected a larger picture hanging nearby, covered by fabric. Archibald whipped off the cover, and I was instantly dazzled. Colors bolted out everywhere, as if intoxicated by freedom after a long imprisonment. There may have been patches of sunlight on water or blossoming fields under bright beams – yet I sensed just a bacchanalia of hues or a triumphant whirl of craziness. "Not finished," Archibald Bely announced cheerfully, returning the covering to its place and plunging the studio back into the penumbrae. "Although it's nearly complete, you almost guessed right. Keep going, keep going."

I looked around again, somewhat distracted. It began to seem like the walls were replete with closed windows to different worlds you shouldn't rush into heedlessly. Wandering through an unfamiliar planet, treading barely discernible paths, leaving traces, and frightening with loud laughter the strange creatures on the tree branches – all this was not quite decent without an invitation from the hosts. Although I'd been pretty much invited. Or maybe not.

"That one," I stuck my finger out at the woman's portrait in the far corner, which had been facing us when we came into the studio. Archibald laughed and shook his head.

"How quickly and easily you surrendered!" he hollered triumphantly. "How quickly indefiniteness wore you down! Not much was necessary to make you head the only familiar way..." He lifted his glass, as if saluting himself, and led me to the portrait.

"Remember, you were surprised the other pictures weren't visible. But if they had been, would it have been easier for you?"

"I don't know. Perhaps," I mumbled, somewhat bewildered.

"You don't know. That's it," Archibald echoed me. "But I *do* know! I know and that's why I always want to spare others. But no – everyone wants to be the leader. Everyone attempts to choose the good from the good, then the best of the best, and finally – just the most outstanding one. Everyone feels sorry for their precious time and their no-less-precious energy, despite that the majority of this preciousness is bullshit. However, they certainly want the very best and immediately – thinking there's nothing else worth looking at. Of course, they may make the right choice: the best is pretty obvious sometimes. Yet how can you help but think that everything else will be dismissed forever right this moment and there will be no returning to it? How can you not get incensed, not grind your teeth? That's the worst part!" he concluded with authority, walked up to the canvas, and turned it and the easel toward me, almost toppling it all to the floor. He's drunk, I thought, drained my martini, and began to examine the painting.

This was really a portrait of a woman, but when I peered up close, I caught myself thinking that without a great effort I could also take it for a landscape full of natural sensuality or a still life of a few objects or simply a picturesque range of colors arranged on the canvas for their own sake. And still it was a woman that embraced many landscapes and played to her heart's content with all the objects one can fancy. Her face was partially turned, attentive and strict, as if she were listening to a companion who had finally reached an important point after a tedious introduction. Her hair was tied up in a heavy headpiece painted in violet with dark contours, stressing its steadiness. Also in violet were her eyebrows and pupils, while the eyes were brown with a funeral-black shimmer. Her cheekbones and firmly compressed lips showed decisiveness and firmness. And – a wide green stripe passed through her whole face, ending at her lips but reappearing unexpectedly on her exposed neck by the collar of her open blouse. It could have been an accidental shadow, invisible in regular light, or a wrinkle of pensiveness she vainly tried to hide. One's gaze involuntarily focused on it, to the surprise of the viewer. And, furthermore, it harmonized oddly with both the oval face and the unusually colorful background that shattered the picture into orange, yellow, and purple fragments.

I looked and couldn't avert my eyes. Never before had I wanted so strongly to turn fantasy into reality and find myself close to this woman – to penetrate at least a part of her secrets, feel her life teeming with passion, hope, and lies. Her world was ready to cry out with all its might, was familiar to anyone and still known to no one, promised strange comfort and hurt in advance with its slightly haughty "no."

"What do you think?" a forgotten Archibald Bely asked. "Do you like it? Or shall I burn it?"

He gazed at me with a mischievous smile, but I caught the tension in his entire pose. And the words voiced jokingly could not deceive me – Archibald was edgy as he waited for my answer, however absurd it was to admit.

"What can I say?" I exclaimed with sincere ardor, really feeling guilty for his agitation. "What is there to say – the picture's amazing, you're aware of it yourself. Yeah, amazing, faultless. I want to ask about a lot of things – who's the woman and what's this and that – but it isn't to detract… Simply that there's so much at once, I can't even choose the right questions. So I'd like to stand here a little longer, if you don't mind. And then I'll ask away."

Archibald nodded with composure and went to the bar. "Maria!" his thunderous shout reverberated off the walls. Instantly the door opened with a screech and he whispered with his landlady. I continued to look at the portrait, hoping to remember the sharp, almost crude strokes, the sparing restraint and the angular features of the unexplainably animated face. A few minutes later I again heard the screech of the door and glanced back. Maria rolled in a small table on casters, cluttered with plates and trays. Then she was gone again, slipping like a mouse back through the slit in the door, and the table appeared in the hands of Archibald, who placed new glasses on it and rolled it toward me, weaving slightly from side to side.

"I suggest finishing with the cocktails and switching over to a serious binge and refreshments," he exclaimed and lifted a bottle with a distinctive label above his head to show me. Soon we were sitting on the floor with glasses of almost straight gin, voraciously helping ourselves to the ham and olives on the plate. And Archibald rhapsodized with a vengeance, managing to speak coherently even with a full mouth.

"Questions!" he declared, "There are always questions. Why ask about what doesn't exist? Who is that woman? I can tell you, but it won't do you any good. Why violet and green? I'd be glad to elaborate, but you won't get it. Or, what else – what's the hidden meaning? Does the play of colors mean a change of mood? Come on – I can talk for an eternity, but you'll be bored in a quarter of an hour, like anyone else, because approximations are helpless and words are futile, as usual. There are none to express it – otherwise, we'd paint with verses instead of oils and brushes."

"But," he raised his glass, "but let's drink! Not everything is so hopeless. I won't exhaust you with explanations, but I'll tell you what's possible to say in words. It may be a story or simply a sketch without a thrilling plot, but that's still something – which is better than nothing. A story has value – even if only in its own right, even without considering the woman in the portrait. It may require explanation no less than any play of colors – here they are equal and don't help each other too much. Yet there is still no better way to explain than by shifting the angle and the direction of the light – two points are better than one, much, much better. Because – and this is very important, so listen carefully – because the story is remembered no less than the picture, and your memory may work on it later, gathering the essentials into one whole, similar to a parrot with a shrewd eye. As for the explanations, which you desperately cling to, they scatter without a trace, like a cloud or mist. They hide in the fog, as smartasses say, and they don't live long, like fog itself. But if you make an honest effort, then the fog just distracts, while you want something that'll last forever!"

"That is why there are pictures in the books." He threatened me with his finger. "Those *writ-t-ters*, they know how to crawl between things. Two points are a lot better than one – it's just too bad there isn't enough space on the reverse side of a canvas to write the appropriate plot. It's only suitable for jotting down petty debts and adding them up in a column. This is a major flaw reflecting an imbalance in the professions. Moreover, there are those who don't even want to listen – write it or not, they don't give a hoot. You're a different case, so for you I'll put something in words. I'll pass it on from mouth to mouth, so to say, as they did in the old days..." – and Archibald suddenly stiffened in obvious tension. It startled me and I wondered if he had choked on an olive pit. But it passed, and his story began after another sip.

"Lorena grew up in a Basque village," Archibald Bely related, looking off to the side. "Where the Bay of Biscay cuts out to the coast, resembling Santander cheese with greenish mold, and provides a deep-blue background for the tree-covered mountains where the settlements and vineyards wave up winding terraces. Her family owned sheep herds, the largest in the area, and could afford all year round to hire shepherds and workers to sheer the skins. But they raised Lorena strictly and instilled in her a permanent love of labor despite prosperity that not many could boast of. Her mother taught her reading and writing, and other things that might be useful in life. When she was fifteen, they chose her fiancé, the son of a beekeeper from the neighboring village, putting the wedding on hold for two years.

Impetuous and almost barbaric in her ways, she loved to run to the mountains and wander down the hardly visible trails, hiding from sheepmen and random travelers, or climbing into fissures, sitting still and watching the broad-winged eagles hunt until twilight closed in and the cold chased her home. She had no friends, but the surrounding landscapes and their colors, unpredictable like the coastal weather, were enough to let her express what had gathered in a heart that didn't yet know passion – and to hear unclear mumbling in response: the murmur of the wind in the pine trees and the splash of the waves far below the bluff, which she could look at until her head spun. And then she lay on her back, eyes wide open, and dissolved into the skies with wads of floating cotton, into the deep blue, always willing to offer refuge to those who really sought it. Up to her twelfth birthday, her parents didn't require anything of her, and it seemed it might continue like that forever, but then they began to gradually involve her in the chores of the large, complicated household, and it was impossible to disobey her mother, who devised all sorts of jobs. Occasionally, at night, she had strange dreams and shivered and trembled. Then, waking up, she cried without tears, as if she longed for her childhood freedom, which had flown off like the scent of a flower. She began to recognize the mercilessness of the world in which they were shaping her path so that one day they could poke her in the back and say: go.

Not long before her marriage in August, her father took her to a French fair to sell wool and hides. And there her life cracked in two, like fragile glass from a thunderclap. In the crowd Lorena saw a young lieutenant of the border patrol. She smiled back at his victorious grin, and that very night they ran off to Marseille, where the lieutenant had been deployed the day before. They ditched Lorena's father, the treated skins and soft wool, mountains with greenish efflorescent fields, mist over the bay, and the inconsolable son of the beekeeper who hadn't had a chance to say a single word to his unfaithful bride. Lorena didn't need much convincing. Something told her this was one of her last chances and there might not be any others. And she liked this swarthy beau more than all the village boys combined, so she wavered only a couple minutes before whispering an emphatic 'Yes' to the lieutenant right at the fair, in front of her fellow countrymen, who watched them closely but didn't realize a thing. That night, she flew like an arrow, young and brimming with energy, on a rangy Corsican mare lent by one of the lieutenant's friends, following the barely visible black silhouette occasionally looking back at her over his shoulder. She was sure she had defeated everyone, slipped out of the cage that had been about to slam shut forever. And this was the peak of her happiness, never to be felt again.

Their runaway was successful and their ensuing life was sufficiently blessed by fortune. They moved repeatedly, wandered about, had troubles and passionate nights, two or three financial windfalls when they got modestly rich and then easily threw the money away, and even one small war after which Lorena's husband developed a strong abhorrence for violence. She gave birth to a son, Pierre, who soon died of pneumonia, and then two daughters – Anna-Maria and Jacqueline, who attended not the most expensive, but a perfectly good boarding school. Overall, Lorena was happy with her fate, and though she sometimes lapsed into unexplainable melancholy, she still loved her black-mustached lieutenant who had already become a colonel in the palace guard and received a spacious government apartment in Paris.

Once, twenty years after the swift nighttime horseback ride that changed her destiny, Lorena and her husband, Colonel Jean-Louis Pinole, arrived in Biarritz for a two-week vacation. Lorena felt low, suffering a migraine, and Jean-Louis, who had lost in cards two days before and still hadn't admitted it to his wife, was also in a lousy mood. As soon as they entered their room, he sprawled out on the sofa, announcing he was planning to rest till evening, while Lorena went for a stroll, happy for the opportunity to be alone. She crossed the square and went to the boardwalk, surprised, as usual, at the colorful tastelessness of the resort stores in comparison to the streets of Paris. As she inhaled the scent of the ocean that cured her throbbing head in a flash, she peered at the dressed-up strollers and quickly looked away if someone tried to make eye contact. Half an hour later, she reached the southern tip of the promenade, stood for a few minutes, leaning over the handrail and gazing with elusive bitterness at the fuzzy contours of Basque country. The lines were barely visible in the haze, and she tried to see the crags the sea carved, the mean mountain peaks, and the herds of sheep with their bells ringing in the air. Then she turned back and went to the hotel, crooning light-mindedly as she walked.

Suddenly she heard something and noticed, surprised, she was understanding foreign words. And then it dawned on her: three young men stood by a cart that formed a small, improvised market and were speaking Basque, which she hadn't heard in many years. Lorena turned pale and bit her lip in agitation. It seemed her childhood was returning – as if in a moment she would again be able to run down the mountain path to the places she alone knew, hide among the trees and rocks, descend to the ocean and catch the salty spray with her tongue. What did it matter that the men were silent now and looking at her in confusion? She was invisible; no one would pick up her trail except birds of prey, but they wouldn't do her any harm – for a long time they had shared the area and not bothered each other. The Parisian house, stone avenues, Jean-Louis in the hotel room – nonsense, drivel, a forgotten tale. It's so congested there – you can't take a step or make a move!

'Would you like to buy something, madam?' one man finally asked, raising his cap.

'No, no, thanks,' Lorena replied distractedly in Basque.

The men exchanged looks of surprise, but she didn't notice any glances. She wanted to remain with them, sell wool and honey to rare buyers, talk in their language similar to a bird, laugh and gnaw on wild nuts without worrying about a thing. Then she felt yet another wish – to go up to any one of them and bury her face in his chest so he would throw her on the cart and vanquish her tyrannically, forcing her to tremble from shame and fear, not from pleasure, as with the gallant Jean-Louis, the only man she had ever known in her life...

Her nostrils swelled and her head spun. She was beckoned, as if for real, by the smells of tangled sheep's wool and treated skin, of a muscular body hot from work, of wood and pitch and grass and rock. And she knew it would never be – no reckless days with shepherd talk in the evening, no embarrassing trembling on the bottom of the cart, no guttural orders and crude caresses. She was an outcast; her guardians wouldn't forgive her, and those men wouldn't forgive either. They were resentful and stubborn, as her father had been in never responding to even one of her penitent letters. As were her beloved crags, resembling Santander cheese, which had now become just an apathetic sketch on the horizon. As her trails, and the ephemeral flowers, growing almost on the bare rock. As the brooks – charming like music. And as everything, everything she couldn't touch anymore – even in her sleep or her dreams.

'Outcast,' she whispered inaudibly, and sobs burst forth from her depths and the migraine returned. Tears welled up in her eyes – bewildered and angry.

'What's with you, madam?' one of the men asked sympathetically in bad French. 'Are you sick? Should we take you home?'

A good guy, thought Lorena. They're all good guys until you get to the main thing, to the supplications and cries of the soul. As soon as you open up and show your weakness, they instantly become indifferent and deaf. The unwritten rules are what's most important. The code of customs is the most reliable foundation... Damn you all, she cried to herself, though aloud she merely replied, 'Thanks, I'm already better,' and walked away, wanting more than anything else to be in Paris that very moment."

"Yes, in Paris," Archibald concluded distractedly. "Paris embraces everyone. That would be the right place for her – to come visit my studio, sit sideways by the window, pose patiently, hour after hour, without changing the inclination of her head. Although in Paris I hardly painted at all." He grabbed a slice of ham and shoved it in his mouth.

"But this woman... The portrait... Is it Lorena?" I asked emotionally, perhaps a little insincerely, and Archibald frowned and waved his arms.

"Forget it," he said angrily. "Don't try to appear dumber than you are – I won't believe it anyway. Lorena, Nina, what's the difference? She could certainly turn out to be Nina. But that's another matter and another story."

At that moment, the door screeched again, cutting him off in midsentence. Something fell and clattered in the entryway, and we heard Maria's frightened sputtering. A high voice asked, "May I join you? And please forgive me, I already broke something."

"Oh," shouted Archibald. "It's Nemo! He can be staggeringly clumsy, but not always, as you might think. Come on, I'll introduce you," and he rushed toward the entryway, whisking me after him. By the doors stood a short, round-headed man of forty in glasses with massive lenses. A shy smile played on his lips. He was unshaven and half-bald, calling to mind a degraded intellectual accustomed to mockery. It even looked like he was now waiting patiently to see what kind of joke the group would make about him, ready not to defend but to laugh at himself together with the others. I was about to decide he was the constant target of Archibald's abuse, but at that moment, from under the thick glasses, sharp pupils flashed – somewhat askew, randomly gauging the area like a lizard's tongue. Clearly, I was wrong – or had at least drawn a hasty conclusion.

Archibald introduced me with deliberate pathos, and the visitor squeezed my hand with his own sweaty one, saying, "A pleasure, a pleasure." I tried to look into his eyes, but the lenses distorted them mercilessly and made them slip away. Not knowing what to focus on, I began to look at his smooth, broad forehead where, it seemed, I could see my reflection as in a mirror. Archibald waited until his new guest was completely confused by his own fervent cordiality and announced with a sigh, "Well, this is Nemo. I'll let you get acquainted," and he went back to the portrait and the table with food. A befuddled Nemo and I milled about and then traipsed after him, following a few unsuccessful attempts to let the other go first.

"So," declaimed Archibald, pouring gin into three glasses. "As the music star said, '…and then there were three.' This is an important development and we should not undervalue it, especially since three is the traditional composition of the enlightened elite in godforsaken places. Do you remember 'in the village, there were three educated people – a doctor, a priest, and a teacher.' That's almost us, because Nemo is actually a doctor. You, Vitus, can decide on your own which of us two is suited for the role of priest. I'm not aspiring to that and won't insist, although in some way it is more flattering – a vicar so to say…" He raised his glass and we solemnly did the same.

Nemo tossed down almost a third in one swig, after which he coughed and began to wipe away tears. "Your gin, Archy, is really damn good, but I can't get used to these strong liquors," he said guiltily. "And with this priest, well, it's certainly not for me to decide, but I just wanted to say you aren't fit to be a teacher – you're too impatient. So I think there's no choice." He took an olive and chewed it slowly.

"Just like that, huh?" Archibald took offence. "Impatient and unfit. Are you fit to be a doctor, Nemo? You must confess, since you've already done so – I remember. Nemo wasn't always a doctor, you know." He turned to me. "He began with fossils and other things. What were they, exactly?"

"The physics and chemistry of minerals, honorary Master's," Nemo presented his qualifications, turning red. "But I did study to become a doctor. So I don't really understand what you're trying to say."

"Oh, nothing at all," Archibald replied, aggravated. "Why are you always such a bore? We weren't talking about you, but about the portrait. This portrait. Take a look."

Nemo obediently stood up, went over to the picture, and examined it for a few minutes. Archibald's averted face exhibited the same pains of anxious expectation. Then Nemo returned to us and said, slightly stuttering, "Yes, yes, the portrait is very fine. I like it a lot, a lot. Only I wanted to ask – if I may, of course, although all questions turn out to be off the mark with you. I'd like to know: who is that woman, where does she come from, and furthermore – what's it all about?"

Archibald gave a drunken laugh and looked at me victoriously. "What else can you want to add?" could be read in his gaze. "That woman!" he said with feeling. "There's a story about her. I just told it before you came. That woman could be called Nina…"

"That's very interesting," Nemo interrupted, visibly agitated. "You know, I had a woman named Nina!"

VADIM BABENKO

"You're comical, Nemo," rumbled Archibald accusatorially. "Who's going to believe in you and your women? Who will take you seriously? Look at yourself. You're an ungainly being who can't attract anyone. Your arms started shaking the moment I mentioned the opposite sex, and everyone knows you live with a nurse who limps and weighs a couple hundred pounds! Listen and don't butt in, otherwise I won't tell you. I'm almost thinking twice about it already."

I thought an argument was going to flare up now and was prepared to reconcile the opposing sides, but Nemo remained completely calm and a satisfied grin nearly played on his lips. "I could get upset, Archy, but I won't," he said tranquilly. "In particular because I really did interrupt you, that's not polite. Moreover, everyone knows, just as well, that you live with Maria – so we're kind of even. But let's hear the story, I'm all attention – we're both all attention, I wanted to say." And he reached for the almost-empty bottle.

"I already forgot the story," said Archibald glumly. "I'm drunk; that happens to me often. With regard to Maria – you're a nasty liar and everyone else is too. She worships me, that's true, but that isn't a reason, and I'm finished with stories for today. Tell Vitus about yourself, entertain our guest. I have to go away for a minute."

Archibald stood up and swayed to the doorway. Nemo sighed and stared at his glass. "No story – no meaning. It's drivel and dull," he babbled angrily, but so that Archibald couldn't hear him. "You don't think so?" He raised his lenses to me. Something powerful glittered in them like blue sparks, and Nemo himself suddenly became larger in the room, as if he had just crawled out of a snail's shell. I sensed an unclear threat through my inebriated fog, which did, however, dissipate as soon as I shook my head slightly.

"In my opinion, the picture is really good," I said dryly, raising my chin like a haughty expert. "It's neither drivel nor dull."

"Of course, of course!" Nemo waved his hands in earnest. "The picture shows talent. Archy's talented – nobody's arguing that. Although if someone decided to discuss it, he'd most probably fail. There won't be any content, just hopeless efforts. All the content is left on the canvas; critics' musings and painters' words are empty, devoid of value."

Nemo took a sip with visible pleasure. He no longer coughed or wiped away tears, but for me, on the contrary, the gin started to taste nasty, so I placed the glass far away and decided not to touch it anymore.

"Archy didn't understand this," Nemo declared peremptorily. "I opened his eyes – I did, nobody else. Because who is he, Archy? Yes, he's an artist. His fate is to doubt and suffer, worry about rejection, stifle the urge to beg for assurance but still solicit assurance time and again. And I could have simply observed his sufferings, chuckling quietly to myself, but I didn't, although he repays me with ingratitude every step of the way. I told him: Archy, find some new content for each canvas, no matter what kind. Think up something baffling that will distract and divert the mob, and you'll see how it'll become easier for you. Make a clay figurine or think up a story with a tricky plot – everyone will search for nonexistent links and bonds. And there will be meaning!" Nemo pounded his fist on his knee. "Yes, there will be meaning and subject matter for discussion. I said to him, Archy, that's how you become famous and burst out of anonymity. He didn't believe me, but take a look – now he always has a story lying in wait, although he considers it to be his own idea. But I know the truth and I never forget to inquire. With every picture, I ask what's at the bottom of it this time. And he always fabricates something – I don't even doubt it anymore. All my questions are only to check and pester him a little – the right of the unrecognized mastermind, so to say."

Nemo looked at me expectantly, and I wanted to humiliate or insult him.. This wasn't right, in particular because he was certainly being sincere with me, and I tried to get myself under control. So I gave Nemo an equally attentive gaze and noted politely, "Yes, but is that content not enough? That which is already on the canvas?"

Nemo flinched like a beagle sniffing the trail. His eyes bore into me. "That's it!" he exclaimed. "That's the main fallacy of every creator! And it's apparent to me because I'm not a creator," he added, blinked comically, and asked with suspicion, "Are you a creator, Vitus?"

"I don't think so," I admitted with a tinge of uncertainty, but Nemo was no longer listening. "My theory of two points accounts for it. And though others may voice reservations, I sense its truth with my whole mind and body," he said quickly, with a slight lisp. "Fossils taught me it – you can't imagine how much wisdom is in fossils. I began to use it here and there, and soon became certain there was nothing truer in the world!"

I obediently nodded, thinking he also deserved pity no less than Archibald, while Nemo calmed down a little, adjusted his position, and continued. "Imagine, you met a woman and made a foolish mistake with her," he said. "Would you then sense the essence of what happened between you two? No, never!" he asserted. "Not until everything repeated itself. Or, place a solitary chapel on an empty plain – and your heart doesn't flinch at the sight of it. But surround it with grey, unattractive homes, a noisy marketplace, and streets full of beggars – and suddenly its beauty, foreign to the mediocrity of the ordinary, jumps out, bringing a tear to your eye. Any wisdom, Vitus, is nothing without a feeble-minded follower who soils the paper with a myriad of justifications. Just as a picture is barren without a story attached to it by an office stapler. And an ingenious piece of music doesn't strike a chord without urban sounds muted by stone walls... Two points, Vitus, two points. They're much, much better than one!" And Nemo, carried away and lisping again, stopped to catch his breath.

"But..." I began and got hung up by his hand, categorically dismissing my next words.

"Don't argue," Nemo advised. "I've argued with objectors lots of times. I know what you're going to say, and I know you'll say the right things. The only problem is that they concern other matters. You're too focused on your own self, Vitus. You apply everything only to yourself – without scrutiny or second thoughts. But is it worth even mentioning those like you and me and our drunk Archibald? Is it worth talking about a handful of people who are so receptive to the harmony or perfection of an idea that they don't need hints and prompts? What's the point in considering them if they, dissolving in the ocean of mankind, can't even change its chemical formula? You're biased and imperceptibly handicapped – that's why you're excluded from the list of worthy opponents. Take Archy: Archy is a creator. He's talented and bold and confident in himself – as much as is possible in his solitary position. But what if you say to him, 'Archy, everyone loves your paintings except the whole human race. Vitus loves them; I, Nemo, esteem them; your old companions have respect if they remember you, as does your worshipping Maria, although she can't understand a damn thing. The rest of mankind, however, doesn't give a crap. They want something simpler and racier on the surface, ground down to porridge, with a lot of female nudity. But what does it matter to you, the true judges are here…' Yes, tell that to Archy, and he'll be offended and may spit in your face. He has good manners, but still – that's really too much. And now, you can see, he prepares a story for every picture, he covers himself with them just in case, although I never said anything like that to him. He senses something or other and I wonder whether it's evidence his pride has been smashed to pieces. And isn't that the best criteria for any theory – outmatch and vanquish the pride of those who consider themselves above others and create what he wants, not wishing to get derailed by theories at all? There's a lot you don't know, Vitus…"

He shook his head and was ready to continue, but at that moment Archibald Bely entered the studio, slamming the door loudly behind him, and Nemo stopped talking, stooping toward the table and pouring the rest of the gin into our glasses. His eyes withdrew, back inside, like a horned snail, and hid behind his glasses.

In the depths of my soul I understood he was right despite being despicable and dodgy. I could tell him about the game of *Dzhan* and brilliant winning combinations starting with a simple trap that would seem so easy to avoid. Isn't this the city noise, the rustling of tires and the roar of police sirens confirming that a brilliant melody is being born somewhere? Isn't this a boring narrative that reveals the authentic depth of a painting on the canvas? Lyubomir Lyubomirov would argue furiously, but who would listen to him, the incurable pragmatic, who perceives the rules of the game just as a means to an end without reflecting on their hidden meanings? And does it make sense to listen to Archibald or others who create – they're pragmatics in their own way, who are occupied entirely with things bringing yawns to simple mortals… I could say a lot to Nemo but sipped my drink instead, looking aside as if I'd been caught thinking dirty thoughts.

"I'm much more sober now," Archibald announced as he came toward us. "So I think nothing keeps us from another bottle." He shoved his hand into the paint drawer and pulled out a new bottle of gin, despite Nemo's plaintive look. We began to drink and get drunk, no longer philosophizing and not recalling any pictures, stories, or homebrewed theories explaining the unexplainable. And if this pertained to the model of two points, then it was in some way too complex to me.

Archibald's jokes became increasingly mean. Time and again, he attacked the quiet doctor, who bore it patiently, obviously used to the character of their sessions.

"Look at Nemo," Archibald sneered, lowering his head and hiding his chin in his scarf. "What do you think – is he a relative of the Nemo we all know? Can you imagine him climbing into a tin can, then descending deep under water and hiding there for years and years? I can see the affinity in their versions of misanthropy, but, even so, our friend is way too weak."

Nemo was silent, shook his head, and just said, "Archy, Archy. That's an old tune. Think up something else." And Archibald narrowed his eyes and chuckled indignantly. "You object, but I'm not listening to objections. You're mute, Nemo," he affirmed, waving his glass like a truncheon. "A retrained physician is speaking for you – you poke about with a scalpel and threateningly aim a stethoscope, but that isn't enough to overcome gravity, to pierce the dense layers and burst through to the stratosphere. Watch: I plug up my ears with my fingers – and I don't hear you, you're isolated, cut off. You don't even have a diving suit with an oxygen mask – how can you fly to the stratosphere, Nemo?"

Nemo drank, winced, grabbed some ham and asked meekly, "Why are you so distressed, Archy? The stratosphere isn't for me – really, I don't need it. If you think you do, then go ahead, by all means."

"Yes!" Archibald screamed. "I need it. And I'm already there. Those who don't believe it must leave the stage. Only the likeminded will remain, putting each other on the throne in succession. The rest are not to be considered and to be chased off entirely. It can only be like that – otherwise you have to explain too much. People are slow – no life is enough to expound it all!"

"Forget it, Archy," Nemo smiled kindly, and I saw the iron luster in the convex lenses. "How can you chase them out? It certainly won't work – and what would you do without them?"

"It won't work?" Archibald hissed. "Everything works for me, even if you look with a prejudice, as you always do. Oh, that eternal vigilant eye! Not that invisible one, but yours, the unseeing one..." – and he sobbed and fell silent, pressing the bottle to his body. Then he jerked up as if waking and again burst into a tirade – irate and excited, incomprehensible and fitful. That's how it continued until well after midnight when we went home, leaving Archibald to sleep right on the floor, consigning him to the care of his ever-patient Maria.

CHAPTER 5

The next morning I lay in bed, tormented by a hangover and the memory of something embarrassing. I tried to reproduce our conversations but achieved little. The significant parts eluded me, leaving just the fluff of exclamations and two or three tacky turns of phrase. It's Nemo's fault, I decided with displeasure and thought that Archibald would also blame the myopic doctor. It's nonsense, of course – Archibald is probably working tirelessly, said someone else inside, despising my laziness as I sprawled in bed. But soon my alter egos made peace with each other and I went out to have a late breakfast in a pretty good frame of mind.

Maria – *my* Maria – was exaggeratedly severe and glanced from time to time with disapproval, but she couldn't make me upset. I merely winked at her and cracked crude jokes. The day was passed strolling idly along the coast – I didn't even want to go see the fishermen, especially since the wind picked up and chilled me to the bone. Close to evening the Parkers arrived, yet I suddenly felt inexplicable irritation and hid in my room – probably surprising them greatly.

I sat there for a while, then pulled out the photo of Julian but quickly shoved it back in my bag. For some reason it seemed foolish to look at it. And indeed, it couldn't bring me anywhere close to my secret and its essence.

Yes, some people do something, paint pictures for example,

while others just vegetate, I thought. How is my useless Colt doing? The gun hadn't been wiped down in so long that I became ashamed, took it out, disassembled it, and began to assiduously clean the dully shining parts. When this was finished and the revolver went back under a thick sweater at the bottom of the bag, I extracted a sheet of paper to begin my customary habit of recording names. Yet I didn't write anything, I just drew a small pyramid and slowly shaded it in, then blurted out, "Silvia," waited a little, and cackled. Afterward I thought some more and decided to start a new life that instant – but instead got up, climbed through the window, and headed to Archibald's.

From then on, I spent almost every evening at his place. There was some friction between us, yet the elusive spirit of the studio, teasing me with the impossible, unveiling the possible where I didn't expect it, beckoned like forbidden fruit. The space held echoes of lives and fragments of the most fantastical fates. The world inside it was becoming unfettered, straightening up, like a spring – it was easy to believe it wasn't all that cramped. Still the next morning I was always drawn to the coast to inhale another kind of vastness – more ordinary than I had dreamed the night before.

Archibald's individuality competed with mine – at least it seemed that way to me. He probably thought I wasn't his rival – indeed, unlike me, he was able to express himself in some form. The whole studio was covered with canvases, even if they still faced the wall. Turn any one for a look – and you're swept into another dimension, a new universe full of harmony. No one else could create it – only he, Archibald Bely, artist and demigod. Here and there he arranged these ingeniously conceived apertures – so that anyone could take a peek at his deepest secrets. His uniqueness was on display – as was his power, which any uniqueness always generates. But still he couldn't chase away the doubt – it sneaked inevitably into every new canvas as if asking: does the magic still exists? And following right behind, there was another poisonous trap you never think of until your energy expires or your fantasies start to repeat themselves. Afterward you may rave in vain, but it's too late. The score has been tallied up, and any of those who marveled, genuinely or not, would say pensively, "Look, that's it. No small amount – indisputably – but that's it. There won't be any more." Any uniqueness is measured by a finite number, even if it's significant sometimes. And once it's reached, the bookkeepers come – come and start counting. Ten pictures, a hundred, three hundred… Five hundred and forty-two – no more? A whole world in each one – yes, yes, we agree. But still, we want to ask: Is that the last one?

Archibald certainly knew this better than me. Anyone would get angry if he's already begun and the count is in progress, while his neighbor only pretends, not offering any quantities for measuring up his ego. Of course, if I'd tell him about the delirium and the poisonous horror, the threatening laughter and the painful falls, with fourteen steps at the end as a brutally formulated outcome, then, I guess, his anger would vanish without a trace. But this was not to be revealed, and, moreover, all the quantities are different. Try as you might to juxtapose and harmonize them – any score will turn out useless when you consider the crudeness of the measurements or the deceitful nature of numbers in general.

However that was, Archibald Bely often got agitated by innocent remarks and tried

to talk me into giving a public demonstration of my own achievements after I'd accidentally mentioned the rhymes flickering in my head. This was childishness on my part, and later I got tired of convincing him the verses weren't serious, though Archibald didn't believe me and stuck out his lips. But there was nothing for me to add. My content and my destiny lay in something else. A name for that something did not come to mind, yet its tenacious essence grew inside and supported me like a talisman. Even the mark on my cheek related to it in a strange way.

In any case, Archibald and I didn't get tired of each other, and I would hang out in his studio until late at night. Doctor Nemo would also come, and it soon became clear they had their own scores to settle – overlaid with a considerable amount of antagonism.

Nemo was Janus-faced. He was harmless and devoid of forthright ambition, but brimming with secret ones and plenty of arrogance as well. Archibald needed him more than me and reacted to him more irritably than to me, seeing in the retrained doctor the despised mob of admirers-dilettantes. They were incapable of creating anything, and perceived the harmony with the wisdom of others. "The public, the public," Archibald sighed, and in this was a lot – the loneliness before the empty canvas, the realization of how futile any effort is, and incomparable satisfaction others cannot understand, when you see your modest landscape or an unpretentious black and white miniature becoming not only an aperture to other worlds, but also an unlocked gate. One can just walk through it, but for the majority, Doctor Nemo included, it doesn't work. They aren't able to figure it out; they take it just for a peephole or a tricky mirror. They stare, step on each other's feet, peering through the clearest of crystals into their own petty souls. And the funniest thing is that these souls interest them much more than all the unlocked gates leading who knows where.

How can the creator of the most precise instrument not get annoyed, and once the annoyance has heightened, how can he not insult patient viewers, not use a poisoned arrow to penetrate their thick armor and hit a random sensitive spot? And in that case even Doctor Nemo, admitting talent and bowing down before it, might be able to get upset and hiss something in response. Or, if not hiss, then conceal a spiteful thought like, "Everyone's aware the world doesn't live on paintings alone, especially the paintings of Archibald Bely. So why is he storming about without looking at the broader picture?"

Therefore they quarreled often. Nemo usually backed off first, although he was no less intelligent and may have even had a sharper tongue. However, the thick glasses and the whole mask of provincial doctor suited his flabby figure and his entire crooked physiognomy. It seemed he didn't want to disturb the completeness of the façade and quickly dove back into his hole, though without hiding the fact it was just a disguise. Sometimes I even thought that precisely this striving for perfection in his image forced him to change professions at some point and settle here in the hinterlands. That meant there was a reason to look closely at Doctor Nemo, who performed so boldly on the canvas of his fate, reaching for excellence visible only to him. I, however, considered it tactless to inquire, and furthermore his masterpiece might not have been finished yet.

As I pondered all this and recalled how and why I had ended up in the same place, I again began to catch myself contemplating what I had experienced at the oceanside. Now the intentions of the universe interested me less than ever. The main thing was to renounce defeat – and I gradually succeeded in this, using the reliable formula that came to my aid just in time. *The worst is behind you*, I tossed away with intentional nonchalance. And I viewed the surroundings as a testing ground for my fresh intentions – if not now, then in the near future.

"Let's consider the trajectory of one drop a little more carefully," I quoted the unknown author, patiently circling within a small, easily intelligible world. Even in its limits there was enough variety in the characters. For instance, take Nemo and Archibald and contrast them with the Parkers and their trained squirrel. Then there's Maria and even the Turk who runs the store. I couldn't say the selection was faultless – a professional ethnographer would just laugh at it – but it was sufficient for me at the moment.

Soon, I started to feel my ego had recuperated considerably. I shuffled through my memories and shifted my gaze, added up my virtues and deducted my weaknesses, which finally didn't make sense to hide. Then, from the pluses and minuses, I again turned to plans broken off in the middle – to my secret, which had been, if not a masterpiece, then at least the only thing I possessed as a goal and a point toward which to direct my efforts. The more time passed, the more I felt ashamed of my idleness. Yet my former focus did not recur, and nothing concrete took its place. I continued my daily review of Julian's photo, although, in truth, I saw the logic of it less and less – even trying to introduce a variety into the routine. I would, for example, sketch the outline of some building on a sheet of paper and then place a cross where Julian would face my revenge. Or I would guess at the interior of a room where this would happen

– mentally arranging the furniture, labeling the bed, desk, and upset chair with different marks. Still, a new strategy failed to materialize. As I got mired in minutiae to arouse my emotions and to again burn with ideas, I ended up irritated instead. There were too many details and behind them the pure line of the basic concept was not visible anymore.

Certainly, Archibald and his one-eyed parrot had influenced me at the wrong time, and I cursed him now and then, yet admitted he was right. Even with the habit of saying, "That's Julian, your archenemy" and other things, I realized it was all too wordy, sacrificing clarity and requiring simplification. I even wanted to throw away my Colt, but thought better of it. That would always be possible, and there was no place for foolishness concerning such issues. It also made sense to keep the photo of Julian for the future, which I did – although it almost never saw the light of day any more. Instead, I would sit at the table and just think freely: now about Archibald and Nemo, now about the mark on my cheek, or I'd simply draw ridiculous tiny monsters, pertly turning up their legs. Then a new activity appeared, which entertained me for a while and at least gave me the semblance of a result. I drew the axis of time marching back into the distant or not-so-distant past and then another axis, perpendicular to the first one. On it I placed theoretical figures – gauging myself and everyone else, merged into one whole. The paper would become covered with the trajectories of rises and falls. From interval to interval, from sector to sector, they formed intricate charts that were here jagged and full of spasmodic jumps, there smooth and calm, as if they knew no doubt. At first, I was afraid to address segments where an unforgettable encounter took place, and all my illusions went into the trashcan along with the other worthless baggage. Yet later I grew bolder and began to include them in my considerations just as much as the others. Only, I had to lower the ranges to correlate amplitudes and not spring beyond the edge of the paper.

Then I extended the game and included Archibald and Nemo as separate capricious curves. Now, after every conversation with them, I could plot our stances higher or lower, depending on my feeling and not necessarily justified by logic. Occasionally I was unscrupulous and elevated the position of my own points – even when there was no basis for it, as if I were pulling myself up by the hair and using the people around me as stairs or a springboard. It was too bad I couldn't show it to Lyubomir Lyubomirov. He certainly would have been ashamed of his mockery then, although he probably would've argued heatedly, not wishing to acknowledge the obvious, as always.

Of course, I was drawn to Archibald's studio independent of charts and temporal axes – to no small extent because he regularly spoiled me and Nemo with masterworks much more evident than our own. The new paintings were always set up in the same corner where the woman's portrait with the green stripe had stood during my first visit. The other canvases, like back then, were turned to the wall or covered with fabric, but I no longer asked unnecessary questions and was satisfied with the picture of the day.

Most frequently they were landscapes. Disheveled, frantic, or deathly flat and oozing with darkness, or completely foreign, with smirches of asymmetrical shadows seeming to divide the image into parts hostile to each other. But he also painted portraits, invariably of women – and each was bound to have its own story. Then the evening would commence with it, but first we would go through the requisite ritual of thoughtful examination and sparingly enthusiastic praise – and I could swear Archibald waited each time for my words with unhealthy impatience. I would offer my approbation – really liking everything – and he immediately became himself, releasing his self-confidence from brief detention and ready to let his unceremonious and majestic self push aside all the other egos around.

The stories, like the portraits, were wildly different. Of course, I sought analogies with my own exercises – for instance, my recent experience with the *Chronicler*. I made comparisons and once even admitted it to Archibald, but he flared up all of a sudden and dismissed the affinity with offensive words. "You don't know what you're talking about!" he grumbled at the end. And protest I did not, especially since I couldn't really grasp what connected his stories or whether there was any order or a logical line of thought that escaped me.

Better than anything else I remembered the "steel canvas," as he proudly called it – a silver stranger on a brown background. And the story was good too, although a little long, so that Archibald was drunk before he reached the end. The woman in the portrait consisted of half-rings, like secret springs with fastened ends. Her immobile arms were folded across her knees, and her face could have been carved out of a brass plate with slits for the mouth and eyes. Something in the lower half of it bore witness to her gentleness and crafty ways. And then, instead of brass, red copper came to mind, while her glittering hair that streamed softly and fluidly hinted at another metal, precious and noble. Yet the general spirit of the picture still remained steel – at least that was suggested by the stable perspective and unflagging confidence in the strokes, even if the colors and shades made you dubious for a moment.

The woman's eyes were set wide apart and drew you in, like massive ancient caves. There was too much cached in them for a random guess, and not everyone would risk immersing himself and exploring their true depths. Her eyebrows, like two black arrows, flew off to the side, rushing away from each other. Her straight nose evinced a pedigree, but her upper lip that covered the lower one with a tepee spoke more of a propensity for quiet sadness than intransigence and pride. She knew a lot – and she could keep a secret. Yet excessive knowledge did not stiffen her soul, which was ready to open itself to someone – someone who would probably never come. The concealed springs accumulated strength, but it had been unclaimed for too long – perhaps for a generation, a century. It was impossible to say with certainty how powerful the mechanism would be if you set it in motion by turning the proper key. And somewhere inside the steel canvas was a living heart – made not of steel. It seemed as if the colors conveyed its pulse – with fitful trembling, agitation and quivering...

"Baroness Paula de Gracia was kidnapped on the first Sunday in October, on the day of her thirty-third birthday," Archibald was saying, sipping his usual green mix. "It rained in the morning, but cleared up toward lunch. The baroness requested her favorite horse and went out for a ride in the deserted park near Ghent. She was already headed back when two figures in raincoats and identical hats appeared at her side and compelled her to stop.

'This is abduction, madam,' one of them said calmly. 'You won't scream, will you? A loud scream goes against proprieties, and, moreover, I have a bomb in my bag, plus a revolver under my coat. There's nothing for me to lose, and I won't leave you alive if you do something stupid.'

The baroness just nodded, clutching her throat in shock. Only afterward, in the cramped car with curtained windows and a fat, black-haired driver, was she able to gain control of herself so much she was not afraid to unglue her disobedient lips. 'Who are you? What do you want?' she asked, ashamed her voice betrayed her fear. Yet she received no answer. The abductors didn't speak until the very end of their trip, and only when the sedan stopped did one of them say to the other, 'Go now. You remember everything?' The latter nodded, opened the door, and disappeared, while the remaining miscreant grabbed the baroness's hand and pulled her out.

Paula de Gracia had never been in these parts. They had probably taken her to a working-class quarter behind the textile factory or to one of the poor settlements on the other side of the river. Right in front of them stood a stone tower. It was the remains of an old fortress, as she found out later, and had been reconstructed forty years before for warehouse purposes, but abandoned again when the whole area slipped into decline. An instant later, the abductor and the baroness were in front of a door that the driver of the car had run ahead to unlock. Then they wound their way up a spiral staircase to the upper half, where the stranger, with grim pleasure and visible physical effort, battened down a massive hatch behind them, cutting off the only way back. The hatch was closed with a greased bolt, and a storage lock was placed in the loop. The villain clicked it shut, slipped the key in his internal chest pocket, then sat right on the floor, leaning against the wall, and laughed. 'Now we're home,' he said cheerfully to the baroness and laughed again, obviously pleased with himself.

'What do you want?' Paula de Gracia asked again, wrapping her arms around herself and trying to quell her nervous shaking. 'My husband is rich; he'll pay a ransom. Only, I beg you to take me back as soon as possible.'

'Oh, yes,' exclaimed her abductor with strange notes in his voice. 'Yes, your husband is rich and you think his riches will secure your freedom. You do not know what freedom is, but you believe it can be bought. You do not know what a dungeon is but instinctively long to leave it. Furthermore, I suspect, you also do not know what passion is...'

'Listen,' said Paula loudly and distinctly, and there was no more fear in her voice. 'I see I'm in your power, but I don't want to hear vulgarities from you!'

'Yes, yes,' the stranger raised his hand. 'You know you're in my power, but you realize already I'm not a maniac and not crazy. I see you have regained a grip so I can finally explain what happened to you. For uncertainty is torture,' he declared. 'And torturing a woman is dishonorable, whether it be a baroness or a maid!'

And he told Paula de Gracia the true meaning of what had taken place on that unhappy day of her thirty-third birthday. She had become part of an unpleasant event, but she had no choice, since the choice had been made earlier by completely different people. That had occurred at a conference of leaders of a radical socialist group in Brussels. Essentially, the leaders had no option – everyone understood the necessity of immediate action. The question was what and who to choose as a target, and finally they decided to make the family de Gracia the victims, selecting Pierre – the abductor bowed – to be the lead executioner. The goal was thoroughly conventional: to free comrades from European jails and change the life sentence of one activist to a retrial with a public hearing. Its suddenness was explained by lower party members' dissatisfaction with the higher ranks deliberating in reaction to the despotism of the governments.

'Here you got unlucky,' Pierre admitted, shaking his head. 'The action had to be blatantly cruel, and, if the demands are not met, I will be forced to kill you. Which, between us, is very likely,' he laughed. 'The elections are soon, and the government will hardly want to look weak. Nonetheless, we won't despair. They've got four days to consider it, and we have roughly half an hour to settle in. Soon it will be bedlam here.'

The place had two rooms. They had come into the large one from the stairs, and the tiny, dark and narrow one, Pierre announced to the horror of the baroness, they would be using as a bathroom. On one side stood bottles of water and baskets with provisions. Blankets lay there as well, and her abductor handed Paula de Gracia two of them with a formal nod, after which he shoved his hands through the straps of a backpack propped against the wall and tossed it on his back. "Dynamite," he winked. 'And that's the fuse,' he pointed at a mottled wick sticking out of the right strap. 'In case they storm us, although that probably won't happen.' Then he kicked the lock on the hatch, harrumphed contentedly, and walked around the room in a circle, looking through the glassless gaps – which were more narrow embrasures than windows.

The baroness could see the tower was an almost ideal hideout. Of course the rescuers would be afraid to storm it: who wanted to take responsibility for the death of Paula de Gracia? And even if they took that chance, Pierre looked like he was completely capable of reaching for the spotted wick. And then, in four days… Fear coursed up from her stomach again, and the baroness sank to the floor, wrapped in her blanket and gazing straight ahead without seeing a thing.

Soon, as Pierre had predicted, the tumult begun. The police arrived, and reporters almost right behind them. Curiosity seekers started to gather, followed by two black cars with some identical-looking people who quickly dissolved into the crowd. Pierre grabbed the megaphone, covered by a heap of rags in the corner, and negotiations commenced. To Paula de Gracia, they were long and thoroughly senseless as she started to count down the last ninety-six hours of her life.

There was, however, nothing to negotiate. The abductors'

demands, as well as their horrifying threats, were meticulously stated in a letter written by Pierre and sent to the police by his comrade. There, he also mentioned the backpack with dynamite and outlined the actions he planned to take in the event of an attack or any other unexpected move. The only hope the police could have was that he lost courage and gave in, but Paula de Gracia was sure nobody actually believed that.

An hour later the mayor with his retinue appeared by the tower, and with them, Baron Ruan de Gracia, who made a foolish and lonely impression amidst the many people in uniform. Pierre called the baroness to the window, and for a few minutes she looked at her husband standing stiffly with enormous binoculars. She even tried to smile at him and nod approvingly, although he only irritated her – because he, a man, was free, and she was confined, with her days numbered; because he seemed depressingly helpless in comparison with energetic officials; and also because it was his title and his money that prompted the conspirators' selection. And *she* had to pay for all the privileges they had enjoyed together without thinking of the cost.

Paula walked away from the window and again sat near the wall. A hoarse Pierre declared through the megaphone that negotiations were over for the day and reminded them again of the dynamite. Then he placed a package of victuals and a pail of water next to her. She had no appetite but broke off some pieces and grudgingly chewed them, washing them down with the warm water tasting of rust. Pierre asked her about something, but she didn't answer. Later she bombarded him with questions and he told her insignificant things with his usual self-confident grin. Gradually, twilight set in; then the room became completely dark, and Pierre announced it was time to sleep, adding that Paula de Gracia would be chained to an iron bar sticking out of the wall. He showed her the small, glittering handcuffs – this enraged her, and she flared up like a fury, but Pierre just shrugged and she again turned indifferent and apathetic. The most difficult thing was forcing herself to use the improvised bathroom, but, like it or not, she had to overcome this barrier too, wondering with a bitter smile what they would write about that in the press.

This was how they spent three days and three nights. They spoke little, but got into furious arguments now and then before quickly gathering the futility of their words. Pierre became increasingly gloomy, and his eyes blazed more and more ruthlessly, while the baroness shrank into herself, supinely registering her feelings were becoming numb. And even the terror of what was inevitably awaiting her became routine and didn't throw her heart into a flutter. At night she hardly slept, listening to the rustling and expecting some happy end every minute. Then, during the daytime, she would glide in and out of sleep as if she were protecting her own mind from realizing what was happening to her.

Everything Paula de Gracia dreamed those days and hours invariably boiled down to one word, *freedom*. This was not limited to dreams about escape, about the sudden disappearance of the narrow room, the moist walls, and the radical socialist Pierre with his backpack of explosives. Paula de Gracia now understood subjugation was everywhere; she could avoid it no more than old age or death. And even if she were saved this time, she would still remain bound hand and foot.

Angrily she pondered what she might never have thought of if she hadn't been forcibly handcuffed at night and tormented in musty captivity as a helpless prisoner not controlling her own fate. She remembered her husband and their dull nine-year marriage, where not one day differed from another. And the code of countless rules and taboos imposed by society, which she despised. And her lovers whom she didn't love… In her fantasies and reveries she tore at the innumerable ropes of the web thrown on her by the insidious and cruel. And in agitation she became convinced these ropes could withstand anything. They might seem to yield at first sight, but unravel them she could not – since nobody recalled how the knots had been tied.

Yet more than anything else, the main trap, the most ingenious pitfall, made her despair. It represented the entire essence of confinement, and the name of it was Paula de Gracia, or more precisely the body of Paula de Gracia, her own body, the fragile vessel, continually showing its possessor the claims and demands of importunate nature, the majority of which you wouldn't even consider in the context of normal comfort. Now she knew whose captive she had been her whole life and whose obedient servant she would have to remain until the very end. All her spirit, all her efforts and hopes didn't mean a thing to the groans of the self-appointed despot whose pleasures have been whisked away and replaced by crude food, smells, dirtiness, and a tenacious fear of death. And she couldn't renounce them, couldn't ignore them and remain her formerly proud self. She sensed her body taking revenge on her and that made her ashamed to no end. And what about the near future? What about the explosives or a pistol awaiting their hour? Her memory might be immortal; her emotions and thoughts might live forever, interweaving with others, blending with traces of distinguished souls preserved over the millennia, but what could be done with this pitiful shell? It would draw her into the abyss – if not now, then later but soon; if not tomorrow, then in some hollow fifty years. Was it what they deserve – she and the others, those who had even the smallest grain of sense? Physical death was for animals, for senseless creatures, having no pride or memories. Why was she being equated with them so unceremoniously?

Pierre had become thinner and grew stubble. 'His body is also taking its revenge on him,' she thought mordantly, hating her abductor with all the power of her soul. 'But he doesn't care, he doesn't notice such things. He's a crude animal himself, possessed by someone else's idea. All men are like that: they need to think they are worth a lot, while only the exceptions are intelligent and have a will of their own, with the rest falling into their net one way or the other... We haven't washed in three days!' she thought, disgusted. 'How horrific! Though he probably doesn't give a damn...'

Under the window during this time, countless authorities of all ranks came and went, trying to persuade Pierre to release his hostage voluntarily. An armed cordon kept watch by the tower around the clock, and at night Paula de Gracia heard whispers and cautious tapping a few times – either below or on the sides. Then Pierre, who slept with a stunning degree of alertness, would scream wildly, 'I'll blow it up! Back off!' And again silence would ensue.

Everything ended toward the evening of the third day – quickly and terribly. Pierre sat on the floor, gnawing his nails and gazing at one point, and the baroness dozed against the wall across from him. Suddenly, a megaphone blared from below, belonging to someone they had not heard before.

'Pierre Ruffo,' the voice thundered. 'We have met your demands. Do you hear us, Pierre Ruffo? We have proof. Your demands have been satisfied!'

Pierre jumped and went up to the embrasure, looked out carefully, and screamed, 'Show me the sign! You must know the sign!'

'Your demands have been satisfied, Pierre Ruffo,' the voice repeated. 'Release your hostage immediately!'

Pierre stood by the window and stared out. 'Show it to me…' he began to scream, but suddenly collapsed and keeled over on his back. His arms flew up lifelessly, and the terrifying wick slipped down on the floor like a spotted snake, not getting a chance to turn the room into a fireball. Only a few seconds later did the dumbstruck Paula de Gracia see the little black hole in Pierre's forehead. She screamed shrilly, deafening herself. She covered her ears and squeezed her eyes shut. But her abductor did not disappear. He lay prostrate on the dirty rock with his chin raised ridiculously.

Releasing the baroness from imprisonment, even after the spectacular assassination of the plotter, was not that easy. A strange apathy overcame her, and nothing could bring her to go to the dead Pierre and take the key to the lock securing the bolt on the hatch. Finally, they broke it open from below. The baroness, wrapped in a blanket, with chattering teeth and a crazed look in her eyes, was accompanied to a car that carried her home in the company of her husband and the chief of the Ghent police.

The men were really excited. After expressing their concern and sympathy with the greatest possible tact, they began competing to tell her about the difficult siege and its happy end. Baron de Gracia tried especially hard – she had never seen him so talkative. He waved his hands about and described in detail his own idea of placing a sniper behind the leaves of the skimpy tree that couldn't hold a man but which – and that was the best part! – could totally hide someone from a not very attentive eye, especially if you added a few camouflage branches. That was done during the night – as it became clear negotiations would lead nowhere and it was time to make a manly decision, even if it came with some risk. It was also he who calculated the degree of that risk and found it thoroughly minor in light of the psychological aspects and other peculiarities of the present moment. Moreover, according to the personal sketch of the baron, they had made a light wooden platform where the sniper could kneel, and everything was prepared so almost nothing was visible from outside the tree...

At this point, Paula de Gracia became hysterical and the baron had to stop talking. Somehow they made it home, and there her hysteria turned into a dangerous fever compounded by delirium. 'Remove my body! Release me from it!' screamed Paula de Gracia and attempted to scratch her own face so they had to tie her hands and leave a nurse in her room for the night. Two days later she got better and they wrote about her rapid recovery in the newspapers. And a day after that, the baron and baroness quickly left for Rome and never returned to Ghent. Besides, an absurd rumor spread that Paula de Gracia succeeded in maiming herself, disfiguring her classical features forever, and that she had tried to jump out a window and seriously crippled her leg. Yet nobody could confirm or refute this gossip, and they soon forgot it, as they forgot the Baron Ruan de Gracia and his unhappy wife."

CHAPTER 6

It was during the day, not night, that Archibald told me the next story, which rooted itself in my memory. He was completely sober, and I heard it on the coast rather than in his studio, on one of the sloping crags masticated by wind and sand. He invited me on a walk after we met by the Turk's store, where I had randomly wandered. Archibald was wearing his raincoat and indispensable scarf, although the air that day was warmer than usual. In his hand, he held an object resembling a small picture wrapped in a piece of fabric.

The object really did end up being a picture, another portrait of a woman, in soft pastel tones. On the cliff, Archibald unveiled the portrait and propped it up with rocks, adjusting it for a while and seeming to ignore my quizzical gaze. Finally, he muttered without turning his head, "What are you looking at? That's Sophia. I brought her out for a walk. And don't start laughing or pretending you see something unnatural."

"No, why would I?" I replied not very confidently. "It only seems to me the ocean air must be bad for the canvas."

"Bad for the canvas..." Archibald mocked me. "Forget about the canvas. The ocean air is good for me, and that's enough. Why should I care about the canvas? I want to think about Sophia – and that is already being considerate enough, is it not? Especially since I created her myself."

He was about to sulk, but loosened up a minute later and said assertively, "Don't chalk me up as a lunatic. You know, it's a lot better than walking alone, especially since I didn't expect to meet you by that lousy store. And to tell you the truth, it's even better – the three of us, I mean – than just two men out for a stroll. I hope you won't take offense – I'm not hinting at anything."

"Of course not. Why would I get offended?" I rejoined, somewhat baffled. "But do you come here often? With this kind of company?"

"No. Not often!" replied Archibald defiantly, and I realized he was still confused. "Not often – actually it's very rare. Since if I do it regularly, everyone will consider me crazy, and that's not good – then I wouldn't even know what to think of myself. So no, not frequently, yet sometimes I do it, and why not? I should have my share of pleasures too. I can't just create and give away, benefiting others – those who are so reluctant to accept the treasures and are usually dissatisfied afterward. And I have more rights – significantly more! I have *every* right, I can do whatever I want: I can destroy it if I want, I can burn it or smash it with a rock. But don't worry, I never go that far; I only take them with me sometimes. I treat them tenderly, with a sweet melancholy – how can I cause them harm? But that's not the point, the point is: if you want to look at it – go ahead. Meanwhile, I've got to climb down there for a minute," – and he carefully crawled along the rock face, leaving me alone with the portrait.

The woman Archibald called Sophia gazed at me directly, without letting my presence agitate her. Bashful grace lived inside the broad face and its round-but-proper features. The portrait was realistic, like a slightly blurry photo, yet a thousand times livelier and warmer. The gentle background created the impression of depth – probably deceptive, like any impression you want to believe in too much. And it seemed there was nothing in this depth except the face, slightly parted lips – thin and pale, but no less sensuous – and the eyes full of stubborn decisiveness, behind which you could see her perpetual readiness to forgive. In fact, there were also objects in the room, and the draperies behind Sophia's back, and a soft velvet chair she sat on the arm of, supported by her elbow resting on the back. But her eyes and lips firmly grasped your attention, and only then was the viewer surprised to notice the whole area was meticulously depicted and the chair did not hang in the air but stood securely, as it should, on a fluffy rug. The dense, metallic-red hair that fell in waves over her shoulders crowned the completeness of her enchantment, which probably not all could perceive. Someone might only see a woman of simple habits and too-obvious wishes, intentionally ignoring the inner strength concealed for the future, like a secret kept by a small clique. I wanted to confess something intimate to her, wanted to share the inspiration of my soul with this woman who did not tolerate insincere words, this defender of those who've been rejected and can't find their place. We stared and understood each other like no one else, not even surprised we had suddenly met in this place we never heard of before. Sooner or later it had to happen, so why not here and now?

"Have you looked long enough?" a voice said behind my back, and I shivered from the unexpectedness of it. Again, as many times before, I had forgotten my surroundings, spellbound by a stream of unreality, although long ago I should've gotten used to the powerful impact of Archibald's canvases. He was sitting behind me, his arms clinging to his knees. The noise of the waves had made me unable to hear him climbing up the rock, and now he whistled inaudibly, puffing out his lips.

"I could look at it for an eternity," I admitted. "This woman is stunning. What did you say her name is? Sophia? Tell me about her – I'm sure you have a story."

"There's no story about Sophia," Archibald grumbled. "Sophia's Sophia – you don't need any fantasy. She was with me in my youth – that is, not with me, but not far. And I was with other women, although, to tell you the truth, I'd rather not have met them – almost all of them. However, I'm not going to speak about either my youth or Sophia. You're too transient in my life, and you won't get a clear picture anyway. There's no sense in it. Senseless, senseless..." – his cheek quivered and he again began whistling thoughtlessly.

"You know, when I go for a walk with her alone – just me and her portrait – I really want to engage her in conversation but I hold back," – he suddenly turned to me again. "Because, you know, talking with a portrait is too much, and I have to admit: I'm a slave to the opinions of others. At the notion that others consider me an eccentric or, even worse, deranged – I'm all in a sweat. Nemo probably told you about that already. Between us, he's a chatterer and an unreliable jerk!"

Archibald pulled his scarf a little tighter and stopped talking. Then, after a quarter of an hour, he sighed, turned his head, looked around, and stretched with feeling. I watched him stealthily, thinking I could now put down many new dots on my charts. And my own trajectories would curve upward, no doubt – it won't even be necessary to pretend.

"All that is too gloomy," Archibald blurted out and stared at the portrait. "However, I'll tell you a story after all – I see you want it. It's not about Sophia though, it's about something entirely different. Although, with some effort... If you use some observation... But no, never mind. That will take us too far." He stood up, straightened his wrinkled raincoat, sat down again, and started to talk, occasionally looking at the canvas.

"A Russian woman Nastasia Vladimirovna Dulse was constantly haunted by visions," his resonant baritone carried over the cliffs and ocean sand. "She didn't say a word about it to her sixty-year-old aunt, her friends in the card club, or even the head clerk at the stationary store, the Pole Wojtek Malkovsky, who visited her twice a week and whose nondescript features concealed impressive amorous stamina. Usually, she experienced them in the quiet hours before noon, sitting by the window in her living room or in the comfortable chair in her study. Later, as the whole house slept, she tried to bring back what she had seen and dissolve into it again, lying in the dark with her eyes open. Sometimes she succeeded, but more often than not her persistence turned out to be fruitless, and a vapid, depressing dream came instead of that colorful life.

Nastasia Vladimirovna had been living in Hanover for three years after moving from Greece in the wake of her jeweler husband's death. Its suddenness thoroughly complicated the inheritance, which a lot more people contested than Nastasia Vladimirovna thought reasonable. Moreover, soon various indiscretions of the deceased surfaced she would normally have pretended not to notice, but she was now forced to carry out a protracted fight with vulgar seamstresses and stripers that weren't worth even a third of those little stones the passionate jeweler bequeathed to them. Everything ended quite well, but it seriously frayed her nerves, and Nastasia Vladimirovna was glad to accept an invitation from her forgotten aunt to live far from the hot and dirty country where no small number of her enemies remained. She liked Hanover and purchased her own house close to the central square. Then she rented the lower floor to an enterprising German and thus secured herself a fairly comfortable life.

Her visions however did not let her comfort gain a complete foothold. From time to time they left Nastasia Vladimirovna in distress and brought an angry expression to her face. But sometimes, on the contrary, her cheeks became all flushed and her eyes sparkled. Her aunt had gotten used to these metamorphoses, and her thin-nosed Pole probably didn't notice them, being totally fixated on energetic lovemaking. Nastasia Vladimirovna tried to speak with her doctor, a chipper old man with a double chin, but after listening a little, he pointedly asked whether she was planning to get married, whether she had a lover, and whether he was good – which made Nastasia Vladimirovna flare up and lose all interest in the conversation.

The visions were mostly harmless. Only once did her dead husband appear, without an arm for some reason – it floated separately near him and moved its fingers in reproach or despair. And in the rest, silent creatures prevailed: birds of various bright colors, wooden statues of animals, or gigantic dandelions with fluffy heads. By themselves, they didn't arouse any intrigue or mystery, yet in them, behind them, below them or somewhere else, in other dimensions that cannot be described in words, some dense substance trembled and pulsated. Entire universes were created and crumbled, without a glance or sensation being able to find their way to them. Nastasia Vladimirovna recognized all the emptiness and banality of regular life in comparison to that extraordinary world. Her body and soul were drawn towards those messengers from the extraterrestrial sphere that emerged unhurriedly in front of pale lilac curtains. But it seemed the strongest of walls rose between them and her. She could push with her hand or bang with her fist, yet there wasn't the smallest chance of getting inside.

That's how it continued until the March day when Nastasia Vladimirovna saw the Pink Ball. This happened at an odd hour, right before twilight. The pointy-nosed clerk had just left her; she was languishing in the chair, half-dressed and sipping on cold lemonade. Her head was empty; her gaze slipped lazily from object to object, but then her entire body tensed like a violin string as it received a fierce signal from the neurons in her brain. Her fingers spasmodically clenched up the skirt of her negligee, and her eyes, like two projectors, flared with the rose light reflecting in them. Right outside the window hung a flawless ball with a pure, unblemished hue that did not resemble anything and did not mask itself in well-known forms or images. It didn't move and didn't produce any sounds, but it was there, and that was enough to understand: everything had changed and can never be the same. The ball hung as if to confirm: 'You see – the time has come; I'm not hiding anymore. I'm the real thing – maybe I'm strange and peculiar to others, but I'm perfect, and that excuses everything. Is it clear to you now?'

Yes, Nastasia Vladimirovna nodded. Yes, now it is clear. She sat, afraid to whisper, afraid to lower her eyelashes and frighten off the long-awaited moment. The ball did not move a single inch, and the whole world froze in a cataleptic fit. An entire eternity passed like this, but all of a sudden her heart leapt anxiously. Then it happened again, and again. There could be no doubt: the ball moved and began to slowly recede from the window.

Nastasia Vladimirovna jumped out of her chair and rushed about the room in a panic. Every second confirmed her terrible suspicion: the ball was there, outside the window, but it was floating farther and farther away, as if teasing her – it had promised everything in the world and instantly forgot its promise, hurrying to the others, the new sufferers and new gullible ones. 'No, no!' Nastasia Vladimirovna screamed, raced downstairs, through the foyer, tossed a coat over her negligee, and ran away from the house as she was, bareheaded, in slippers, hoping for who knows what, almost certain the pink ball, like every unfaithful sign, had left her and disappeared forever.

But the ball was there. It hung, slightly quivering, in front of the windows of her bedroom on the second floor, right where she had seen it the first time. And it was retreating, more and more quickly, leading and enticing her.

Nobody seemed to notice it. People on the street were staring into the shop windows, walking idly or striding purposefully to deal with their affairs. Had they, the others, gotten so accustomed to it, they didn't even lift their heads to check for its presence? In any case, Nastasia Vladimirovna was completely disinterested in fellow humans. She slowly wandered down the sidewalk, occasionally raising her eyes to verify the ball was there, above her, and also moving to the south, toward the old city gates. Then she lowered her head, seemingly to avoid the gazes, and took light steps, ignoring her disorderly appearance or the fact that many passersby turned to look and clearly thought something wasn't right about her.

But everything was alright. It was even more than that. Everything was better than before – more perfect, mysterious, complete. A cat ran out of a gateway, recoiled, and darted off to the side. Nastasia Vladimirovna thought it was probably able to fly or add numbers, although the cat was very ordinary and of a thoroughly dubious breed. A gas lamp, just lit and hissing plaintively because of its defective torch, seemed to be a magical lantern specially hung to illuminate the way. The showcase windows of shops and stores were entrances to fantastical caves loaded with valuable treasures; the paved road under her feet – an old trail from fairytales or the continuation of the Milky Way. And even the people, regular residents, dreadfully morose and dull, each possessed their own secrets which would probably be a great pleasure to discover.

Then the ball floated more swiftly, and Nastasia Vladimirovna quickened her step, sometimes switching to a jog that made her pant and avidly suck in air. They had already reached the city limits. Almost nobody passed them, and those who did cross their path scurried out of the way, looking at her in fright. Nastasia Vladimirovna was hot. She opened her coat, not thinking about her lace negligee. With the last of her energy, she put her feet to the ground, even failing to notice the city was behind her and the ball was floating over a vast empty field lit only by stars and the moon. Soon they reached the edge of a forest, and there the ball disappeared abruptly, vanishing without a trace. Nastasia was carried a few more yards by her own momentum, then spun around helplessly in circles and stopped.

It was dark and gloomy, yet not far away she glimpsed the flicker of a fire and walked toward it, stepping carefully over the uneven soil in her evening slippers, which now felt uncomfortable. Her soul was uplifted and sang; strength came back to her in abundance; she wanted to love someone and strive for something, although she couldn't say who or what. The disappearance of the ball didn't upset her. From the very beginning she had known it would not be with her for long. It was enough to have had it at her side, to see it in all its glory, to wander after it for miles. An unprecedented success, good luck that comes to exceptionally few, if anyone at all!

The darkness around her seemed charged with electricity, as after a thunderstorm. The air smelled sweet; blood ran through her veins quickly and easily, as in her early youth. For some reason, Nastasia Vladimirovna knew this moment would not be repeated and the flawless pink ball would never again appear in the vicinity. Yet she went through the event over and over again and sensed with inexpressible confidence that she could live in the memory of it for countless years, to the very end – even if it turned out life was forever and no end would ever come.

Before long she reached a campfire, where a few people were sitting on logs. Nastasia Vladimirovna took a seat without saying a word, not even thinking they might do her harm. A half-smile played on her face; she was completely engrossed in herself. And nothing, not noise, not a scream, not even pain seemed to be able to pull her out of this voluntary trance.

Her appearance forced the whole group to stop talking. They peered for a long time at the evening slippers, the negligee sticking out of her coat, and her uncovered, disheveled hair. Then they began to heckle Nastasia Vladimirovna and shower her with scorn. They told dirty jokes and shouted rough words. Some of them jumped to their feet and made faces right in front of her eyes, laughing and hooting. A girl with sores on her gaunt cheeks even ornamented her face with ashes, but Nastasia Vladimirovna only smiled at everyone, without moving or replying to their rudeness. Then they decided she was just an escaped lunatic from an asylum, and they all walked into the darkness, leaving Nastasia Vladimirovna totally alone.

Policemen found her early in the morning – shivering from cold, but perfectly calm, and not displaying any signs of mental disorder. She admitted to having lost her sense of reason for a brief spell, but that had already passed. She was tired and really wanted to sleep.

They were relieved to hand Nastasia Vladimirovna over to her aunt, who, just in case, called a psychiatrist recommended by the neighbors. He examined her and was compelled to admit his patient was not sick at all. She was actually very healthy and so stable psychologically he could only envy her. Nevertheless, the doctor added, he wanted to observe her over a period of time – more out of scientific interest than medical necessity. And he began to visit her every two or three days – and then every morning, especially since some irregularities did appear in Nastasia Vladimirovna's behavior.

First of all, she got rid of the ratlike Pole and did it in a thoroughly spirited way, by simply flinging a coffeepot at him as he stepped across the threshold of the living room. Poor Wojtek barely managed to dodge it, and then had to turn tail, chased out by her screams and rage, not understanding anything and only grumbling to the dumbstruck housekeeper the lady had clearly gone off her rocker – whatever the doctor claimed. Second, Nastasia Vladimirovna began more and more frequently to shut herself in silence and, not much later, stopped talking altogether – just occasionally nodding to a conversation partner or shaking her head in the negative, but most of the time only looking in the other's face with her own attentive, bright gray eyes. It was then the famous doctor made his visits more frequent. To his credit, he firmly announced every time it came up that Nastasia Vladimirovna was not sick at all and there was no need for his attention. But afterward he really shocked society by giving up his practice and moving into her place in the most private way, which obviously subjected him to collective censure.

People nattered about them for some time; then the chitchat began to die down and would have flamed out if there hadn't been a tragedy that shook all of Hanover and even made it into the Berlin newspapers. One morning the city was awakened by an explosion that caused the glass to burst in many buildings. It was nothing other than the home of Nastasia Vladimirovna that exploded together with her, the former doctor, and the elderly aunt. Of course, the officials quickly established the reason for the disaster, writing it off as a fault in the gas pipes, but people were disinclined to believe such a prosaic explanation. Everyone wanted to voice doubts and shrug their shoulders meaningfully. However the destroyed house buried all the secrets, and ultimately even the most vigorous gossipers realized there was nothing more to discuss. The cruel society concluded Nastasia Vladimirovna and the doctor met with a horrendous, but justified end. Only the aunt, a dumb crone, though a completely respectable woman, suffered for nothing at all, as is often the case."

Archibald Bely finished the story, turned from the ocean, and looked at me, raising his chin victoriously. I averted my eyes in some confusion, and an envious thought flickered through my mind: he sure can do it, you can't argue. How can you not believe in a pink ball or in anything else in the world – especially if you have a portrait right in front of you? The fabricated is no worse than the real if it has a soul, and the soul breathes.

"Well, yes," I said thoughtfully, regarded the portrait of Sophia again, and asked, "Confess, Archibald, do you think up these stories yourself?"

He narrowed his eyes and inquired rather aggressively, "What's it to you whether I do or not? You want to dispute something? Go right ahead!"

"No, no, it's only out of curiosity," I replied peacefully, pondering where today's story would end up in the scope of my graphic exercises. "Personally I can't come up with such long ones, so I'm interested in how it is with you. There's no more to it, and nothing to argue about."

"How is there nothing to argue about?" asked Archibald acrimoniously. "Are you such a pushover you can't challenge an idea? Or do you think there's no idea there? In general, Vitus..." he said reflectively, then tilted his head and continued, "In general, I've noticed you're quietly laughing at me, you and Nemo. You're hand in glove with him – and what else was I to expect? But that's okay, I don't get offended easily," he added, seeing my gestures of protest. "And, of course, I won't seek revenge."

Archibald raised the portrait of Sophia and began to wrap it carefully in the soft cloth, mumbling some hardly audible lines that rhymed. "I pass through close-knit groups /nothing to share with them /they're reckless proud old brutes /with laughter that's inhuman..." I heard through the din of the ocean. "How cumbersome!" he added, straightening up. "As for the stories, think as you like. I'll tell you one thing: however strange they may seem to you, it's not my fault. I after all..." He stopped talking and froze, looking directly at me. "I, after all, cannot concoct a falsehood; that's the whole point. I can only listen in and pass on later what I've heard. Adding something is out of the question, and deliberate distortion is even less possible."

He slipped the picture under his arm, and we began to go down, trying not to fall on the slippery rocks. "By the way," Archibald turned to me again when we reached the sand. "By the way, I won't have time for new stories now. For a few evenings I'll be up to my ears in work. Come to my place in three days, on Thursday – I have an annual meeting, and it's pretty amusing. I already told Nemo; he's waiting impatiently. Make sure you're there – no excuses. You see, I'm inviting you well in advance!"

"Okay, okay," I hastened to calm him. "But this annual thing, you said. Who exactly are you meeting with?"

"Oh, yeah," Archibald stumbled with a wry grin. "It's a long-lasting friend of mine. His name is Arnold, Arnold Ostraker, a typical, frizzy-haired Jew. We studied together and were thick as thieves. Everyone said: two As, Archibald and Arnold. And now we meet from time to time. You'll see." He stamped, glanced sideways, and clearly wanted to part.

"Good. Sounds great," I said somewhat distractedly. "Former student friend, two As – I envy you. You know, I'd rather like to walk over to the fishermen. Do you want to come with me?"

"No, no. I'm going home, home," said Archibald rapid-fire and suddenly froze, staring at me. "Listen, Vitus," he said feelingly. "I have a request: write me a poem."

"What poem?" I didn't understand and even looked at the artist with some sense of dread, so Archibald became confused and winced in disappointment. "Any poem. Any one at all," he began to explain hastily. "It's more for you – I'm just, like, supporting you... And God knows what you've cooked up," he added reproachfully. "Your suspicions are groundless, and I'm not that at all. I firmly and exclusively focus on women – although I don't know whether it's for the better or not."

I grinned, as if to excuse myself. "Well, okay, alright. But a poem is required," Archibald concluded with unexpected firmness. "And write it down so you won't forget it."

"Again!" I thought, yet nodded in agreement. We separated and headed in different directions although a few steps later I heard him cry, "Vitus!"

I turned around. "Remember. You promised!" Archibald screamed with childish ardor and threatened me with his finger. Involuntarily, I laughed. His figure looked both ridiculous and insidious in the dark raincoat with wind-whipped hair against the backdrop of the indifferent cliffs, silent like someone who had once chased after a pink ball. I waved to him in response and went on, wondering whether I would find anyone by the boats. Or had they already returned to the village, leaving only their wet nets behind on the coast?

CHAPTER 7

Arnold Ostraker, despite his Nordic name, really looked like a typical Jew. He had fuzzy, charcoal-black hair that showed the first traces of gray, a prominent nose, and eyes in the depths of which flickered the reflection of either painstakingly concealed passion or ordinary contempt for humanity. Seeming younger than Archibald and also stronger and more confident in himself, he came across as an emissary of a new generation who had arrived to lead lost souls and shake up a decaying routine. Only something, a minor intangible, revealed an inclination more for contemplation than action. With an attentive look it became clear he would hardly aspire to be the leader, but if Archibald, in all his arrogance and wittiness, didn't learn how to hide his vulnerability, then his first-letter twin, the second A of their alliance, would proudly display his thick armor. It was like a warning: I'm not an easy target! So attackers, especially not too mettlesome ones, had a reason to think hard before making any aggressive moves.

When we met, he immediately looked at my mark and a barely perceptible smile crossed his well-groomed face, almost provoking me to say something rude in response. My revenge was to stare at him in a ponderous reverie, as if assessing what he was actually good for. But Arnold was not to be confused by such nonsense, so I soon got tired of my entertainment. He was thoroughly polite to me, as he was to Nemo, and quite indifferent to us both. It was obvious he was only interested in Archibald, and the rest of us just made up a fairly irrelevant background.

In the morning of that very day I had run into Doctor Nemo on the coast and, unable to restrain myself, began asking him about Ostraker and the annual meetings of these two As, one of whom we would soon behold. Nemo, as always in the early hours, was much more awkward in conversation than during our evening gatherings in Archibald's studio. However, the subject of Arnold Ostraker quickly made him eloquent. The whites of his eyes flashing red, he informed me in a long-winded monologue the man was a real villain, a bloodsucker and hardhearted werewolf, and if it were up to him, Nemo, he would put him behind bars and never let him out. I insisted on an explanation, stunned by the ardor of his view. Gradually Nemo cooled down and took back almost all his epithets, remaining adamant, even if not as graphically, that Ostraker was indeed a villain and an evil genius, the root of our Archibald's suffering and probably that of many other unknown victims – although certainly they were both, Archibald and Arnold, as harmless as insects if you didn't take their trifles seriously. Nonetheless, he insisted, Ostraker was like a wounded conscience, an importunate vision one couldn't exorcise. And Archibald, as vulnerable as he was, suffered regularly and for a while every time his boyhood pal sent him a line or, like today, showed up to palaver.

"What's amusing is that they still can't live without each other," Nemo said, livening up again and gesticulating with his chubby arms. "I know, I know – many people say without any particular reason that opposites attract. But, in the first place, these two aren't really opposites and, second, the rule itself is too nebulous, you can't prove or, for instance, patent it. I would also consider it an obvious demonstration of my two-point theory – or more precisely, its concretization in the theory of two mirrors, so to speak." And Nemo regarded me askance with a somewhat wary look.

I diligently nodded, and he went on, becoming more and more animated, "Imagine one mirror reflecting in another, then the second one reflecting in the first, and so on, endlessly. You have to agree this is more than simply two points. Take a picture and the story for it – the loop there immediately closes by itself. Yet here it isn't that easy – you bounce back and forth like a ping-pong ball, sometimes not knowing how to stop. And, really, you can push it pretty far. A beam of light fades by itself, though not instantly as we know – but when a fire rages inside you, then it may reflect and reflect, infinitely, endlessly. You may get exhausted all over and lose track in the process. I can confirm it as a doctor: it's dangerous, yes, yet it draws you in and you can't, just can't break away!" Nemo made an energetic negative gesture with his hand.

"Okay," I said, also waving my hand as if that would help me catch the elusive meaning. "Okay, but those mirrors, as you call them, must be scattered all over the place. You and I, for example. Or Maria, perhaps. Why just these two? It's too artificial."

"No!" Nemo yelled in despair. "No, you didn't understand anything. You need more than one or two reflections – you need the fire! I already explained it, didn't I? The bouncing ball; the same essence on both sides, from every point of view. You and Archy don't have any common essence. And I'm lazy and a wimp – everyone knows that." And Nemo grinned badly.

"Something very important has to match," he continued, taking my elbow and drawing me along the coast. "It's their youth or the identical craziness in their eyes, as you'll see. Otherwise it'd fade out; there'd be no reflection – like being in the desert. The wheels on both sides may spin only after they've meshed, their teeth interlocking. And then the mirrors appear out of nowhere, and strange images reflect in them – one after another. Amusing things can come out of it – if, of course, one doesn't abuse this paradigm too much," he added enigmatically and winked.

Now, in Archibald's studio, I peered at both like a spectator at a magic show. But as hard as I tried, I couldn't discern either the exchange of secret reflections or the spark of craziness in Arnold Ostraker's eye. His pampered features expressed slightly haughty cordiality, which was artificial, no doubt. And we all were too ceremonious, having nice clothes on and suddenly remembering our refined manners. Even Maria, who waited on us with her customary timid formality, put on a new apron, and Nemo flaunted a double-breasted jacket the color of wet sand. It also seemed odd there was no alcohol on the table, and this surprised not just me. Nemo, too, regarded the bottle of mineral water by the salads with displeasure, and Archibald fidgeted impatiently in his chair, as if waiting for something.

The conversation didn't gel, and no one showed any willingness to liven it up. Nemo sat with the look of a humble provincial, tucked his napkin under his chin, and carefully broke off tiny pieces of a biscuit. With restraint, Ostraker munched on the dried flounder and just as restrainedly agreed with Archibald, who was discussing some completely uninteresting subjects.

Before that, he introduced us, "Meet my friends, Arnold. This is Nemo, our doctor – oh, yes, I forgot, you're already acquainted. And this is someone new, a poet from the capital, so to say," and then he enjoyed watching how I, all sweaty, plunged into the chaos of clumsy denials. Now he was speaking about Nile alligators and their ages, maintaining that the strongest of them live for a hundred and twenty years, but only in captivity, being kept in a zoo. In natural conditions they don't even reach ninety, which is quite strange indeed. Nemo mentioned a couple of times Archibald's information was out of date, but Arnold Ostraker confirmed the numbers by referring to the annual scientific almanac. Then he expanded the topic with a tedious explanation of the difference between an alligator and the more well-known Nile crocodile. All three of them were being exceedingly dull, and I wanted to pull off some stunt – throw a fork in the wall, tease Arnold with a sharp question, or tell a dirty joke. But at that moment Maria wheeled a table full of bottles with cool classical labels into the studio, and Archibald, his face lighting up, clapped his hands together.

"Hurray!" he screamed. "Here's the long-awaited surprise! I beg your forgiveness: by no means did I intend to torture you with a delay. They were late delivering it, but it was worth the wait. That's eighteen-year-old Macallan, the best scotch money can buy in these places," and he grabbed one of the bottles and began to examine the label fondly.

Of course I experienced an immediate feeling of déjà vu, recalling Gibbs and the last evening in the house on the coast. As back then, the liquor came at just the right time. No one turned it down, including Arnold Ostraker, who poured himself a half-glass and consumed it in one giant gulp, so I gave him a look of respect. Apparently, both As had trained well in their adolescence. The rest of us didn't waste time either, giving the Macallan its deserved credit. And the atmosphere changed instantly.

Archibald remained firmly in control. "I'll tell you about Arnold," he turned to me and Nemo. "Arnold's an *artist* in the true sense of the word. But before speaking of him, we need to ask ourselves directly: what is *art*? And I'll give you if not an answer, then an illustration at least, to outline the limits." He took a sip from his glass, and Nemo instantly took advantage of the pause.

"I can also express an opinion on art," he blurted out. "From the point of view of my theory of two points…"

"Nemo!" roared Archibald. "I beg you not to interrupt your elders. Even though we were born in the same year, I'm centuries your senior in art. So, let me continue…"

Archibald spoke, and I quietly observed Arnold Ostraker, in whom a noticeable change had taken place. He now was clearly on the alert and even slightly tensed his muscles. In his eyes I noticed traces akin to Archibald's agitation every time the latter led me to a new canvas of his.

"If you stubbornly follow the naked truth, then you really risk being ridiculed," declared Archibald in the meantime, waving his glass. "So I'll be flexible in interpretation – simply to not incur unwanted sneers. Hence, art; let's talk about art, yes, but we have to discuss another concept first: the eternal concept of time. Time dominates any conversation; it's always the main motive for one, and the engine, and, forgive my vulgarity, the fuel. We pour whiskey in glasses – and that is the subject of time. We are bored – and time slips away. We speak about whatever – about horse races, weather, women – and time is on our heels. It reminds us of itself in every phrase. You can't hide from it, you can't drop out of it to return later. And the main thing is: you can't force it to stop. Oh, of course, a lot of people have lamented this before me. There are a myriad of theories – even our Nemo here probably tried hard. And a whole storm of others, better and worse than Nemo; and me too – I'm among them, and don't judge me harshly!"

Archibald regarded Nemo rather meanly and repeated, "Don't judge. I'm like anyone else. All the theorists are anxious about the same practical issue: capturing, grasping, slowing down the merciless flow, so that they – we! – could stay in it as long as possible. They – we! – all want the trip to last longer, imagining whatever one likes most: mountains of oysters and liters of cognac, women for anyone's taste, or – on the other hand – glory, honor, immortality. The right words haven't been found yet, but the core isn't in words. Try as you might, time just slips through your fingers. The theorists struggle, making an agonizing effort, and at the end – it just falls through your fingers, not even leaving a trace. It's upsetting, it kills all hope – and I was about to lose all hope, but then inspiration came: I thought up the System!"

Archibald stopped talking, gazed at his empty glass, splashed some scotch into it, and said resentfully, "But, of course, if it isn't interesting, I don't have to go on…"

"No, no, Archy, please continue," Nemo replied with enthusiasm, and Arnold Ostraker nodded energetically in approval, while I just tossed a skeptical look, recalling my own efforts with temporal axes and fleetingly wondering whether he was deriding me along with the rest. I even chuckled contemptuously, yet apologized with a gesture that said: continue, Archibald, that wasn't meant for you. He re-examined us, his splayed pupils resting on me, sighed, and began to speak again.

"So, the System," he pronounced. "It's obviously destined to seize time or constrain it in motion. Any philosopher would laugh in my face – but let's put pride aside and forgive them all. Let's be patient – and with patience, we can continue and see. It isn't visible to an inattentive eye, yet its structure has been developed for thousands of years – those few thousand years during which intelligent mankind, even if acting unintelligently on the whole, produced, with surprising consistency, individuals who, despite all logic, created things useless for life. You understand, of course: things that aren't relevant to daily life, but embellish the world – at the sight of them, at the smell, touch of them, at the apprehension of their taste or sound, or by means of their letters and signs. They make the human mind reflective, the mind is stunned or at least pays homage – and even that is enough. Here the invisible link connecting individuals emerges stronger than any other. And this moment is a fixed moment; time is caught for a tiny second. The cruel inanity of its relentless run is erased by the awareness of harmony found by someone, because the thread extending from one thought to another – not by light, not by beams, not by the most responsive neuron – lies outside of hours, days, years. From ancient Greek statues to nineteenth century symphonies – in a flash! From papyrus to contemporary volumes – in an instant! Where's time? Show it to me. It's nowhere; it's powerless. Stands in place. Isn't that magical?"

Archibald's cheeks were red, his hands shook, the scotch slopped about. "The System, it's growing!" he continued, his irises glittering. "Its structure is becoming more solid. There still aren't many joints in the net, so the years seep through easily – but just wait. Nothing vanishes for naught. A picture is a new joint. An ingenious motive, even if it's grossly sentimental, can be taken as well, why not. A manuscript or a statue – that also works. Everything goes! Everything forces you to pause and mull it over. The system grows, and it becomes more and more difficult for time – at some point, it will stop flowing as freely. It'll trickle through drop by drop, and then stop entirely – The End! The spirit will have prevailed over time, woven its web with trillions of cells. I don't know where we'll end up in all this, yet that's not the point. The point is that these cells are not identical, no. And the joints also differ; time slides through some of them almost without slowing down, while others hold it up so that whirlpools and waves are created. And here…" he paused.

"Here, I'll shift to my Arnold and his artistry. And if he loses his temper, then hold him down so he doesn't get in the way!"

I looked at Ostraker. A spasm of displeasure ran across his face, yet he sat in a calm, almost casual pose. Nemo also moved his gaze from one A to the other and wiggled slightly in his chair. Archibald held the light pause, cast his feverish eyes over us and, all of a sudden, laughed – defenselessly and amiably.

"But what's he got to be worried about? He knows: I just praise him," he confessed with laughter and reached for the bottle. "Because: not being envious, I admit the facts. And I'm not the only one!" Archibald summed up with surprising gloom, topped off his whiskey, and smelled it meditatively.

"Let's examine the nature of a joint in the System's net from the perspective of its familiarity for the mind or the ear or at least for the eye," he began again, adopting a pedantic professor tone. "Take, for instance, a landscape with cliffs: it's nice and ordinary – should you stand in front of it for an hour, you can keep your thoughts fixed on it entirely and not get sidetracked by something else. But it's trivial and lame, so you won't stay there long. A portrait is more complicated – your insides start to tingle and doubts appear from nowhere, doubts and confusion. A picture with some strange yellow birds against an impossible red, for example, is even trickier, yet still visually simple in a way. And then suddenly there's a painting by Arnold Ostraker and others of his kind, but we'll speak just about him for now. Nothing ordinary and nothing familiar –just imagine: one line that divides two stripes on a bizarre background – first it's dark green, and then even darker and greener. Or flashes on white – so that it seems to be careless blotches of color. And more in this vein – with countless variations. Our Arnold is an abstra-a-actionist," Archibald drawled with tenderness and made an indefinite gesture with his fingers. "A great honor and source of endless arguments: Is it real? Is there something to it, or is it only fake?"

He paused, raised his glass slowly to his lips, drank a little scotch, and said importantly, "In the System, the characteristics of any joint of an abstract type immeasurably exceed the characteristics of a joint produced by something concrete. That's my belief, Archibald Bely's, a man who experiments with anything concrete but never delves into pure abstraction. Because I'm scared and not trying to hide it, and there's another reason too. I won't say it however; I'll just tell you this: go up to a painting of Arnold Ostraker, go up and listen carefully. You'll hear: in the flow of time, the whirlpools whir, the rapids gurgle, and the froth fumes. Abstract pictures are at such heights, so detached and elevated to the skies that they reach the most distant horizons, they connect to everything – and if they don't, then his art is a lie, a falsification, pitiful scrawling. That's how it is; there's no other way. It's either in the skies, above all, or a pathetic sham. Everyone either envies it tremendously or mercilessly curses and damns it. That's a real joint and real courage! However I'm going in circles. Let me sum it up: Ostraker is an artist among great artists, *despite* the fact he's an abstractionist and nothing else!" Archibald finished, made a joking gesture with his glass in the direction of Arnold and drained it in one gulp.

Everyone was silent for some time, and I looked at the floor, feeling awkward. Finally, Nemo clicked his tongue and asked, "But why? Why approbation and approbation and then 'despite?' You, Archy, did nothing less than grossly contradicted yourself. Froth, whirlpools, and this afterward. It's really strange."

"That's it!" Archibald cried, poking his finger into Nemo's chest. "I knew it all along! Use a bit of imagination, jump once or twice from one logical point to another, and they don't understand you, just don't. But have you, Nemo, have you ever seen any of Arnold Ostraker's pictures?"

"Enough," Arnold interrupted. "Settle down, Archibald. This is already becoming a little too personal."

"It's nothing personal," Archibald persisted like a child. "Nothing personal, and you know that perfectly well. What, your pals aren't plagued by the same thing, those reticent inveterate drunks? Yes, abstraction. The road to the top where there's only ice and snow. No smog, no exhaust, not even a cloud. But admit it, Arnold, those who view your paintings, are they able to fly out there too? And if the answer is yes, then where do they grow their wings? That's it; you realize it well. They swarm around at the bottom, as always. They take your picture, stick their heads in it, study every centimeter with magnifying lenses, and what? They may enjoy the colors – like the peel of an orange. They may like the irregularity of the forms – a twisted cone or a rhombus with wrong angles. Something perplexing touches their soul, but it slips away a moment later. Their thoughts aren't suddenly sparked, and they don't veer off the well-trodden path... This, of course, is not about the System; the System is for others. This is about something else – and this something is of much more importance for you, Arnold. So now," Archibald pointed his frightening finger to Ostraker, "talking about this other thing. Let's note in parenthesis: when you indulge that pitiful audience of yours, aren't you adding a little extra here and there – a shade of color that looks nice, a line or shape that feels familiar? The temptation is great, especially since nobody will blame you." Archibald snickered slightly, but dropped it.

"Moreover," he said seriously, "I didn't mention – on purpose – another aspect that reveals a lot, putting almost everything in place. It's one thing to paint for days and weeks, dabble with color or pencil, add one detail after another, layering on stroke after stroke, clarifying forms. Yet it's another to walk away and say: that's it, finished! You always have to stop somewhere – stop and acknowledge: finished, won't get any better or any fuller. Oh, it's not easy to finish and no longer touch it – never, never, not even a smudge. It's frightening to tear it away from yourself – especially if you aren't so exhausted already that even looking at it makes you sick. A bit later you will, of course, dive back in – correct and adjust something. Yet it's too late, it's impenetrable, inaccessible; it lives its own life and you're superfluous. But as long as it hasn't separated from you – how do you find courage to call the new masterpiece done?"

"Yeah, generally it's tough," he continued, frowning. "But when something recognizable is on the canvas – again a landscape or a portrait – it's easier: you can judge by the parts, and on the whole it's clearer as well. Sometimes you add something and then erase it right away – as an *obvious* unnecessary extra. Then it's soon behind you; time comes for it, calls, and knocks on the door. But in your lines and patterns, Arnold, when you add or remove a curve or a stain – will it make anything obvious? You yourself will admit it if you're honest: not a damn thing is obvious!"

"But…" said Arnold uneasily. "But not to such degree. You're onto something there, yes, though just to a point."

"Forget it," Archibald grimaced. "Don't try to wiggle out of it, you're among friends. I know you can go up to any of your canvases and add a detail or two. Nobody, including you, can say for sure whether it'll be better or worse, further from the finish or closer, more precise or just slightly more crafty. And so, how do you notice the difference?" he exclaimed, clutching his head. "What is a masterpiece if you can draw a line across and it'll remain faultless all the same? You, Arnold, rise up, toward the icy peaks; you make a surgical cut, but your hand shakes and the uneven edge of the flat plane trembles. Yet you hold it up as perfection. Does that mean such a joint in the System is not genuine?" Archibald asked ruefully and looked at Arnold, tilting his head. "How can it be like that?"

"Perfection," Arnold frowned, shifting in the chair. "Perfection is a trite word. Slander and envy hide behind it, while cowards run from it as fast as they can. The joint is not genuine? Well, excuse me then!"

"Yup, I excuse you," Archibald agreed easily. "Why wouldn't I excuse you when you repent? And please, don't toss me those aggressive looks – I'm joking, of course. Perfection *is* a trite word, but everybody's afraid of it, that's true."

"In general," he addressed all of us, "I'm not speaking about Arnold, don't get me wrong. It's just an illustration; I'm not even pointing fingers. And, in any case, Arnold is not one of the easily intimidated – he's a real fighter for the purity of the ranks. I took him just as an ex-am-ple," he said distinctly and authoritatively. "And, as for the same example, who has the guts to declare me wrong? Who can say I play tricks? Maybe only Arnold, my second A, my dear friend? He's always ready to accuse me; I got used to it long ago.

But others? Vitus?" Archibald looked at me challengingly. "Or you, Nemo, my unhappy wimp women don't like. What do you have to say?"

"Okay, Archibald, that's enough clowning around," a reanimated and imposing Ostraker broke in. "You're making an awkward impression and look ridiculous – like a ridiculous A. And you've got to admit it's not very hospitable. I know all your insinuations; you aren't saying anything new. And by the way, why did we get stuck on painting in the first place?" he asked, casting a weighty gaze over us all. "There are countless other subjects. Not that long ago, for instance, I was contemplating the interpretation of dreams as a means of defending against inner emptiness. Why shouldn't we talk about the interpretation of dreams? Or if it has to be about art, there are other forms too – literature or sculpture or, let's say, dance. I think dance is the most convenient way to express yourself – suitable both for creation and for consumption. Even music involves more mediation, but dance – dance is as immediate as breathing, smelling, tasting food. But there, too, you can rise to the very peak by your precise metaphor, Archibald. You can climb and then reach as far as you want. Only dance doesn't have much of a lifespan, being transient and subtle like a sigh. That's its tragedy of atonement – a true and profound tragedy. Don't we want to talk about dance – or music, at least? Or horses, or peculiarities in the ocean currents – about anything we can discuss in peace?"

"Come on," Archibald replied sullenly. "Now you want peace. You get me started and all excited, and then abruptly retreat, fall back. For all I care, you can talk about dance or dreams, but first I'm going to finish my thought, which is simple. Yes, I'm a realist. I'm a re-creator of reality, even if my interpretation doesn't always make it easy to recognize. Yes, I'm afraid of pure abstraction and run from it like the sturdiest of retrogrades, but you can't accuse me of indulgence in the taste of a crowd. No, you cannot!" He looked us over slowly and severely. "And you – when you move from the concrete to your abstract universe, you might just as well try to make the crowd happy. The dumbbells will be pleased, and others won't even notice. So, look at yourself before making accusations – or even thinking about them!" Archibald again poked his finger in Arnold's direction, who grimaced in annoyance and stood up.

"I'm going out to get some fresh air for a moment," he informed us grouchily. "Let him keep speechifying – he goes in circles anyway. I've already heard it many times," – and he headed out of the studio, while Archibald fell resentfully silent and followed him with his eyes.

"That's how it always is," he told us when the door shut behind Ostraker. "He slips away, like an oiled wrestler." And he didn't utter another word, only groaning from time to time, stooping, turning the glass in his hands, and gazing attentively at its content.

Arnold soon returned, noticeably happier. He cheerfully grabbed something from the table and turned to Archibald, who was still silent and gloomy.

"I'll give you an answer," said Arnold Ostraker. "But I won't reply to the reproaches that don't deserve a word. You want to discuss the main thing, straight up? Okay, let's talk about the main thing. Let's wrinkle our brow and look intently, and agree right away that time is not a subject for jokes and doesn't take pity on anyone. It's dumb to argue about this – however, listen, how is it related to this System of yours? Excuse me, but it is naïve and reeks of nonsense. You can't stop anything, no matter how well your joints are tied. And if they begin to cluster – that's an illusion: each one will be as far from the others as they are from the planets or stars. An abyss yawns between them, and that abyss will always remain; the best proof of that is you and me. There's nothing in common – each soul soars by itself, and your time is yours and mine is mine!"

Arnold smoked a thin cigar and exhaled the smoke toward the ceiling. Nemo and I didn't speak, only occasionally glancing at each other. Archibald Bely continued to spin his glass and was pensive and remote, obviously not planning to agree or disagree.

"Every soul is alone," Arnold repeated confidently. "I paint pictures for myself. For me and my own pleasure I go further and further, discarding and collecting bit by bit; observing, simplifying, generalizing, transferring everything to the canvas. The more abstract, the purer – yes, you're right. The purer, the easier it is to see and the more you can read into it. But why should it matter to me what others will fantasize and read into it? I'll expire anyway, and others – others won't help me. So the only joy is in pleasing yourself – creating, stepping aside, and looking as a spectator, with admiration and despair. Even with tears sometimes," he added, shaking his head sadly. "The more abstract it is, the shorter the road. Details frequently stimulate your senses no less than the whole, yet those details must be sacrificed for the benefit of your own insatiable idol, harping on just one thing: move, move, move! Move forward, he says – because time doesn't wait. We'll soon be getting old, Archibald. We'll be growing decrepit and losing strength. And then – you know what'll happen then. If you prefer to pointlessly console yourself, go ahead, hide in the sticks, invent your System and produce the joints so they hold down the years – portrait after portrait. Who cares what you're gratifying – your own deliriums or the mood of the crowd? The one and the other are of exactly the same faultiness. You're angry at me because I don't see the importance of your reclusion. You impose its significance on me, officiously, like a mediocre comedian, but I won't buy it. I have my own principles – they weren't easy to discover. And it was even harder to come to terms with myself, so I'm not going to get distracted by someone else's theories and excuses…"

He probably would have continued for a long time, but Nemo suddenly interrupted him. "I don't believe you!" our doctor shouted, and we all stared at him in incredulity. Nemo immediately began blinking and blushed like a girl, yet he stubbornly repeated it, although more quietly, "I don't believe what you say. It's spinning in loops, and it's useless. We are not as gullible as you think, my friend!"

Arnold puffed his cheeks and Archibald contorted his face, but Nemo went on, "I'm not trying to shut you up, Arnold, but we don't know you very well. And as for Archy, we're friends with him, at least I am for sure, and his orating lies close to my heart. I may be full of nonsense, I mean, the two points – I haven't had a chance to tell you yet – but you, Arnold, you come and make such wide-ranging statements! With so much certitude... I hate certitude!" Nemo concluded crossly and began to pick at his cuff, not looking at anyone.

"The voice of the infant!" Archibald exclaimed, splashed some whiskey in his glass, and spilled half of it on the tablecloth. "The great mute has spoken. Who else is going to stand up for the wretched? It's your turn, Vitus."

"No!" yelled Arnold. "Let me reply. I've been accused, that's clear, but do the accusers understand one iota of this? Do you, excuse me – Nemo? Have I got your name right? Do you understand one iota?"

"I do understand an iota," said Nemo firmly, still fiddling with his cuff.

"Very well," agreed Arnold. "Then you should note if I'm not right, you, too, have nothing to boast of. You spread rumors about each other, you play with the same well-known words, while everything around rumbles on without noticing you. What are you waiting for, anyway? Life's rolling on – you need to hurry and bend things your way. It's all screwed up, yes, but you can move it in your direction – or at least turn it toward yourself. You just need to grab onto the handrail and pull everything after you, rather than look sadly over your shoulder, your arms crossed, as if in a hospital bed. I've been criticized for certitude, but how can you afford not being certain? Although you probably won't get my point – I see, you're all envious, spiteful people!" he added in an unexpected burst and stopped talking.

"Grab the railing yourself," muttered Archibald in the silence. "You always look smart and bold while others are in a funk."

"I already hold it," Arnold responded hostilely. "I hold on tight. You should worry about yourself."

"But of course you do," said Archibald incisively. "You grab the butts of models and hold on. Do you think I don't remember how you smeared them with color, and then – butts on the canvas? A new method, a new method... It's not all that new. It's already been invented – one of your brilliant drunks, a true pioneer and genius, used it before you came along. But you naturally grab on to the railing now. And you can grab on to something else, too!"

"The method is just a method, and I employ any one I want," replied Arnold hastily. "Worry about your own fancy ways. You talk about perfection – and certitude and other such issues – but remember how you used to shape a figure from clay, then timidly put it on the canvas, in some still life, in a far corner, and then make a new figure, looking at the one in the painting. You do this – I know and others know too. So, do you really think if you discard the superfluous not like me, in one fell swoop, but gradually, stripe by stripe, then a desirable compromise will be achieved? And the rabble will understand and love you, and the wolves and the sheep will come together? It certainly hasn't been achieved yet – and I don't see clay figurines in your work anymore," and Arnold shut up again and sulked.

"Forget about the figures," Archibald waved his hand. "As if it has to do with figures… But our discussion is turning out excellently," he added in a glum tone and swiveled to me. "Well, Vitus, let's have you take part. Say something at last, it's your turn – don't just sit there like a mummy."

I lifted my head and looked them all over. Strange thoughts thrashed about, one outstripping another. Why do all the images in the world sometimes appear so unexpectedly alike? It was like seeing myself again – as I beat off the phantoms and brandished my useless weapon, muttered curses and slipped from step to step, frenetically guessing whether the end had come, whether it was all over forever, with my own will never returning to me. The memory, which I was terrified of, rolled forth in a powerful wave. And I didn't oppose it, didn't push it away or stash it in a corner. I relived the most terrible event of my past and didn't shudder, feeling control over it, as over my own ominous force, whose appellation is only known to those who won't let the uninitiated worm it out of them.

The uninitiated… Alcoholic vapors steamed through my mind. The scotch took its course, and maybe this was the reason odd things happened with reality. Arnold, rising in the air like a balloon, abruptly sank back down to the floor, sputtering and deflating in an instant. Archibald turned into an old gnome with a quivering head, while quiet Doctor Nemo rapidly ascended over both of them like a magical giant, his chest puffing out and his shoulders expanding. It all looked very comical, and I wanted to laugh. But that would've been impolite and no one would've understood me anyway. Yet I didn't want to sharpen my sight and sober up. I was more sober and free than all of them, feeling capable of ruling them, even if only like dots on a chart, recalling at first just the past month, but then continuing the graph into future years – and the dotted line would hardly veer that far from the actual path. And it seemed I could gaze from the heights of Arnold's abstractions, looking at the microscopic figures below, reconciling them to some dimensionless canvas not even Archibald would be capable of producing, correlating the short trajectories of their sallies and passions with the line of the ocean coast and the fissures of the sharp cliffs.

"It's my turn?" I asked back. "Oh, of course. Just a sec." I touched my monkey's hand and wondered at myself, my stupidity and blindness. How could I have failed to see it before? Here they are – Archibald and Arnold, the best examples, the clearest of all. Two As, doubles, irreconcilable opposites. These aren't the Parkers, phlegmatic like artificial flowers – and I wouldn't even nibble at the Parkers' bait. Two As rush to different sides and end up in the same furrow. They contradict each other but realize unexpectedly they are almost singing the same tune. Then they try to agree on something and get whisked off into separate universes, baffling and angering each other impotently. All because they have different eyes, and in their eyes is a different madness. Not at all the same – here Nemo messed it up. Everyone is mad in their own way, or, maybe, rational in their own way – however you name it. That's why you can't simplify; everything's accepted, down to the last sign. Any generalization just reveals new details you never thought about. And if the differences are timidly ignored, then delusion gains the upper hand right away, and you can only wallow in its captivity, squeezing in all the new facts that don't fit the form…

"Yes. One sec," I repeated and pulled a crumpled sheet of paper from my back pocket. It was the poem Archibald had asked me to write – I'd decided to keep my word and wrote it down despite my rules. Now it turned out to be just the thing to have – what else could I offer these three? Invisible walls divided us, yet a poem couldn't care less. I don't know how it is with time, whether you can stop it or not, but I know about walls for sure – you won't one-up me in that area. And I can create something that easily penetrates them – these lines, for instance, which came out ridiculously short, or a story, be it about Vera or Gretchen, or – even – Lyubomir Lyubomirov, or anyone else I've outgrown.

I remembered my searches for the connection between Archibald's stories, pictograms of essentials I had picked out – protest-captivity-craziness or insult-escape-death. Those were futile efforts: the essentials didn't have great breadth. That's like a map, useless in the Dunes, only in a different way: picture-story-picture. It seems you're delving into the depths, yet it turns out far too slow, everything around changes, and not just once. But we don't give in. We paint, imagine, paint what we've imagined, use what we've painted to imagine again…

And Arnold's getting at the same thing. Figure-picture-figure… We crawl deeper, but place marks in the labyrinth so we don't lose our way and always have a road back. Picture-figure-story… Sooner or later, it becomes obvious: the contours are there, but the life's been lost. That's why we hide in a forgotten corner – so no one can upset us with premature judgments. But do timely judgments ever occur? No, there are no judges – everyone lies. It's too bad for Archibald – yes, too bad!

I spread the paper and cleared my throat, but the door slammed and we saw Maria – *my* Maria – standing on the threshold to the studio and looking directly at me. "Someone's come to see you," she said loudly. "Let's go. He's waiting."

"Who came? Who's waiting?" I asked. But she only repeated,

"Someone's come to see you," and continued to stand there, her arms crossed over her stomach.

"Let him wait, I'm busy," I said, annoyed, thinking about Parker because I had no one else to expect, although Parker would certainly be considered more of Maria's guest than mine. "Go home, Maria, thanks. I'll be there a little later." But she didn't move from her spot and her eyes continued to bore into me.

I became uncomfortable, even shivered a bit, and Archibald, watching the scene in silence, suddenly said, "Go, Vitus. You better take a look."

Then it occurred to me my Maria wouldn't enter his studio without the utmost necessity and would be even less inclined to insist on a request like that. It made total sense to take her words seriously.

"Come. He's waiting," she repeated again.

I got up, thinking I would probably never meet Arnold Ostraker again, though I didn't regret it in the least. I was only sorry to leave the scotch and the smoky comfort for the nighttime darkness, but there was nothing to be done and I traipsed after Maria, occasionally stumbling and cursing under my breath. A few times dogs barked at us, but we made it home without any adventures and I immediately poked my head into the living room, which was empty.

I gave Maria a puzzled look. "Go on," she said gloomily, pointing toward my bedroom. Shrugging my shoulders, I flung open the door, walked in and froze, instantly sobering up: on the bed sat Gibbs. It was as if the room had expanded, freeing the space for the two of us. I stood and looked at him silently, yet in my mind, for some incomprehensible reason, there rang the lines I hadn't been able to read in the studio, though they were out of place, and Archibald himself probably wouldn't have liked them all that much. But now it had become my favorite poem, only the piece of paper it was written on seemed completely redundant. I crumpled it in my pocket, like the last suspicious piece of evidence. Again I liberated myself from something – invisibly to everyone, as if I had finally learned to hide and be hidden.

CHAPTER 8

"You look good – I can see you're comfortable and even drunk," Gibbs declared after we'd examined each other for a fairly long time: he with calm confidence, I with astonishment and narrowed, alert eyes.

"Listen," I said quietly. "What do you want? I'm not as angry at you as I was before and won't get into a fight, but I've got nothing to talk about with you. Say why you've come and go away."

"Yes, it's pointless for you to get in a fight," Gibbs agreed. "And I'm leaving in a moment; don't get all worked up. Sit down – we'll finish our business and part."

"Business? No way!" I blurted, but Gibbs raised his hand, shielding himself from my indignation.

"Don't act like an idiot," he said coldly. "I brought you money, your share, down to the last cent." And without wasting another word, he pulled some cash from the pockets of his loose raincoat and laid it on the bed. I looked on in baffled silence as Gibbs finished counting, gathered the bills in an orderly packet, and extended it to me. I continued to stand without moving, and he, shrugging his shoulders, placed the packet on the bed and covered it with a pillow.

"Better to keep it hidden," he explained. "There's quite a bit in there. Although not *that* much. Depends on your appetite."

"But," I began afresh and stopped. Share or no share, I didn't care, especially since money is always good.

"Don't worry. They don't smell," Gibbs grinned. "And there aren't any stains on them. And since we're talking about stains, I apologize for what happened – well, in general, for using force. There was no other option." He stood up.

I realized he was about to leave, and I suddenly wanted to ask him about a lot but only said, "Yes, I understand."

"It's easy to deal with people who understand," Gibbs muttered and took a step toward the door, but stopped and looked at me sharply. "What's that on your cheek?" he asked in an impartial voice. "Is that some kind of mark?"

Inexplicable rancor made my head roar. Something must have shown on the outside too, because Gibbs became serious and braced himself.

"What's that with your face?" I inquired insinuatingly, clenching my fists. "Looks like a reminder of something or someone's joke?"

He returned my threatening stare and we stood there, gazing directly at each other, eye to eye. But then Gibbs chuckled and began to laugh with restraint, hooting like an owl. To my surprise, I also laughed nervously. And when our laughter abated, the hostility disappeared as well, and my thoughts swirled with all kinds of idiocy – for example, whether or not I should go with him if he asked me.

"I have a question for you," I said. "Why did you give me so much? We didn't have an agreement, and if we'd had one, then I still wouldn't have been able to demand it. I could never have found you in the first place."

"You earned it," Gibbs replied dryly. "And one has to pay people what they've earned. Furthermore, you didn't complain. And that means a lot."

"Didn't complain?" I repeated in surprise. "When did I not complain?"

"Who cares?" Gibbs dismissed it. "Anyway, do you want some grass tea?"

A minute later we were sitting next to each other on the bed, sipping an acerbic drink from a canvas army flask. "It may seem a little strong," Gibbs warned before I took a gulp. "But there's nothing disgusting in it, don't be scared." And my ears really did begin ringing, with every trace of my recent intoxication receding in an instant. In the bedroom, it was quiet, only an insect buzzed in the corner, while Gibbs concentrated on the wall in front of him.

"Tell me about the life here," he turned to me abruptly. "How are the girls? How's high society?"

"Girls? What girls?" I replied distractedly. "There are only oldies. I'm probably going to leave soon, anyway. And high society consists of artists and a local doctor. I just came from there – we were talking about art, as always."

"It must be interesting to discuss art – if you comprehend it, of course," said Gibbs, mocking me slightly. "I heard about someone here. He walks around in a scarf all the time. And it's unclear what's under his scarf… Although you can guess, of course. And you can err too," he drawled with a crackle.

"That's one of them," I confirmed with unanticipated vehemence. "He always has a scarf on. His name is Archibald, and he has a friend – also an A, Arnold. And there's Doctor Nemo, but he doesn't count. He's afraid of everything, although he doesn't wrap a scarf around his neck. We were speaking about abstract art today, but it probably doesn't interest you, Gibbs – dots scattered on a canvas, lines that don't connect, all sorts of clumsy shapes. Yet there's a lot in it – enough to conceal yourself, and that's what they do, one more, another less, or perhaps the other way round, it's hard to tell. Only Nemo knows it for sure, but he keeps his mouth shut. And I don't understand one thing about this Archibald: who makes him hide in this village, as if he's on the run, and turn all his canvases to the wall?"

Gibbs frowned and said, "Okay, but you should calm down – you're probably exaggerating a little. The one in the scarf is a weakling, and the others are too, if they measure themselves against him. They certainly aren't fighters, are they? Well, of course they're sissies!" He chewed his lips and added, "I'm joking. Don't glower."

We stopped talking for a little, passing the flask back and forth.

"Actually," Gibbs said, "almost everyone becomes a weakling when they don't know what's ahead of them. You acted bravely, didn't shit in your pants, though you were warned – but others, they would've been more cautious. They would've imagined something behind every bush, because they close their eyes and their noggins are just loaded with fantasies or abstractions – as with your pals. You, I guess, also envisioned a lot, but you didn't complain – thanks for that. And now, for you, there's nothing to be afraid of – nothing! Let others be afraid, even if they don't know the danger. They stick their heads in the sand – and think it's their fortress. They flounder in the flock – and feel dusty but cozy. It's overcrowded, of course, but better than outside and alone. So they crawl through their burrows and get bored from boredom. Yet you – you wander well above. It's not boring there, only sad – and you yearn from yearning. However, that's no great misfortune. One can survive it."

Gibbs fell silent and squinted strangely on the normal side of his face. A web stretched from his eye to his temple, and his mouth became slightly crooked, like a satyr that has some treachery up his sleeve. "By the way, if you feel like it, you can take your revenge on them – those fools with their closed eyes. I'm past it already; I took mine back, but somebody else may still have the desire," he said significantly, looking askance at me. "It's a hopeless thing of course, but the blood quickens – and the yearning may fade a bit."

"Drop it, Gibbs. I'm not a warrior," I dismissed it, waving my hand. But in my head a thought flashed – what's he getting at? Could he be recalling the revolver? Maybe he even figured out the Julian part? He could, the sly dog.

"Hah, who's saying you're a warrior?" Gibbs grinned. "I'm just referring to a fact we shouldn't conceal from ourselves: they marked us – yes, they did! But once they did it, they instantly forgot us – filed us away, thinking we weren't dangerous anymore. And they amble about freely, without fear, without hiding – flocks and flocks of them. And there are marks on them as well – no, not just marks but obvious stamps: 'blind' or 'deaf' or, more frequently – 'moron.' As for me, I'm not bitter, but for those who are bitter, it's a big, big advantage

– and nobody even suspects it… The main thing is not to stick out," he added, looking at me with the same strange expression. "You can even wrap a scarf around your neck to feel safer, because for those who do stick out – for them, things get much tougher. Although I don't know for certain about the scarf. That just came to mind."

"I also don't know about the scarf," I said thoughtfully, not understanding what he was driving at. "I don't know yet, although it's interesting, of course. And I'm not bitter, either. But in general… You know, what you're talking about, I've thought about it – for days and days. And I agree with a lot of it – almost everything, in fact. It was as if some veil fell from my eyes…"

"A veil?" Gibbs asked, breaking me off in midsentence. "Don't start inventing things. Nothing fell – the veil never falls, and if it suddenly does, then there's no longer any reason to live. You're still young." He became silent and, somehow bored, again stared at the opposite wall.

"What about you?" I inquired. "Do you also have a veil or something else?"

Gibbs slowly turned and looked me in the eye with a ponderous, steady gaze. "One doesn't ask such questions," he said distinctly. "What, was it unclear everyone has their own scores to settle? Or did you not completely understand something? There won't be a second explanation. That's how it is: either you admit it or you flock from corner to corner with the crowd. It's not as terrifying with the crowd, and you have no time to think."

All his friendliness disappeared. A threatening wisp infiltrated his voice, and I felt he was right and there was no point in being stubborn. "I'm sorry," I said quietly. "I admit it was a stupid thing to ask."

Something in his words caught me and didn't want to let go. Again I recalled how horrible it was when only disdain and mockery cascaded down from all sides and the ground was traitorously slipping out from under my feet. But even then, there was someone inside who didn't want to impotently give in and sign off…

"And yes, I agree with you," I added with a nod. "I simply

named it something else. We should have settled the terminology at the start."

"Let's say we've settled," Gibbs grumbled. "Which means we don't have anything more to talk about." He screwed on the top of the half-empty flask and landed on his feet in one movement.

"Wait, wait," I blurted out. "I wanted to ask you something else. Are you… Are you, what, against everyone?"

"Me? Of course not. I'm for myself," Gibbs replied lazily. "What do I care about everyone else? What can you demand from everyone anyway?" And he turned to the door, declared, "It's late already – time to go," and added, glancing over his shoulder, "If you're in the city, I recommend staying at the Arcada. Ask for Jeremy, he's the manager. Tell him I sent you – he'll help you with anything if you pay him."

"Gibbs, take me with you," I said. "I won't meddle in your affairs, and I'll get along with the Christophers, you'll see."

"Don't be silly," Gibbs snapped. "We're not a poorhouse. You can earn a buck in another place. What do we need you for? What are you good for?" He stood a little, contemplating something, then grinned and added, "Remember – don't pry! That's it."

I also smirked in response – not really expecting anything else. Gibbs nodded to me and headed toward the door, but at the threshold he stopped and said, "You have your own work to do – that's why you didn't complain. Take it up now – it's the right time. The worst is behind you." And he vanished without saying goodbye.

He's right, I thought. Everyone has their own scores to settle. It makes sense – but why do I always happen to agree with him?

I didn't have an answer to that question, yet I sat there for a while and looked at the same wall as Gibbs had, pondering I don't know what.

The next morning I woke up with the feeling I couldn't remain in the village any longer. I recounted the money I'd been given the night before, which turned out to be no small sum. Then I discussed the bill with Maria and learned from the Turk that the truck from the city was expected the next day. Maria received the news of my departure with complete indifference, but clearly blabbed about it to someone, because in the early afternoon the Parkers appeared for a last tea party, which I stoically endured, trying not to get irritated at their questions about my future plans. Hanna Parker tactfully switched the conversation to another subject after suggesting a very nice explanation for my leaving so suddenly. Mr. Parker himself was listless and looked really dejected, so he didn't annoy me with excessive attention, although I could've done without any inquiries or parting words. Only Charlotte was moved, calling me aside with impatient gestures and thrusting a present into my hand – a shell worn down by the waves and resembling a small ship. I instantly recalled Stella and my heart shriveled, but Charlotte beamed with a totally different smile. The memory rapidly faded; I cheered up and kissed the fragile girl's hand like an adult, and she burst out laughing and raced to Maria in the kitchen.

Then the Parkers left, and I went to pass the hours on the coast, languishing from the endlessness of the day. When dusk set in, I asked Maria to clean some clothes and headed out one last time to see Archibald Bely, guessing what kind of mood he would be in after yesterday's session.

Sitting on the porch, in a sweater, scarf, and ugly indoor slippers, Archibald whittled a dry branch and whistled through his teeth. He was downcast and unshaven, with bags under his eyes.

"I was expecting you," he informed me. "I've already heard. So you're leaving us? Running, rushing – toward something or just away?"

"I have things to do," I replied dryly, thinking I shouldn't have come.

"Things to do – do, do..." said Archibald distractedly and we went into the studio, which was in perfect order, without the smallest trace of yesterday's gathering. "Maria managed well, didn't she?" he grumbled, gazing about the room. "We clowned around for a while after you left. That woman's a piece of gold – priceless, really priceless. Only she's painfully modest."

Archibald went up to the bar and returned with two bottles of mineral water. "I've stopped drinking," he announced in response to my surprised look. "Not forever, of course, but for the moment. And I won't offer you anything, otherwise I'll be jealous and unbearable. So what were we talking about?"

"Nothing," I shrugged my shoulders.

"Oh, yeah," Archibald agreed. "Then come here, I want to show you something, as always."

In the corner, as I expected, hung the next portrait of a woman, this time in charcoal on cardboard. Her pretty and mournful face seemed to ooze out of photo paper that had been under a developer generously poured in the center but used very sparsely on the sides. Her thick eyelashes curved up playfully, but in the creases around her mouth you could infer the resoluteness of her "Don't touch me." Her nose was straight and elegant; her lips proportionately full; her eyebrows arched in thin lines that lent her whole face a surprised expression, making it sharply contrast with the direct and stubborn gaze of her almond eyes. It was impossible to talk with this woman if you weren't introduced properly; you couldn't be vulgar with her without despising yourself. But still something was lacking, disallowing her from being included among the ranks of true aristocrats. Some imperfection hid behind her sleek features, some excessive love of life. It even seemed the artist mercifully reduced the number of details to not reveal the defect too clearly. After examining it, I winked at the portrait, but that was too much. It was as if the woman slightly frowned at such frivolity, so I turned away, afraid I would begin to blush.

"How do you like it?" asked Archibald. I looked at him, recalling yesterday evening and the arguments that led them all to dead ends. I imagined him to be a Lilliputian wandering among titans – the canvases, looming haughtily, even if some of them had clay legs and uneven shoulders. He speaks to them – they don't answer. He tries to remind them of himself – they don't wish to know him. Really, he's minor in comparison to what he's created – minor and uninteresting.

Viewers wouldn't like him, even those inflamed with passion for any of his myriad paintings...

Archibald was still waiting for my reply, and I told him, "Yes, it's excellent as always, and I haven't lied once. Do you believe me about that? And how is it with the stories? Or is there no story when there's no color, just black and white?"

"Who cares whether there's color or not? And there's a story – why shouldn't there be one?" Archibald bristled. "You draw charts, Nemo blabbed about it, but I don't have anything to plot. I just fantasize as best I can, that's all." As usual, he plopped down on the floor and stared fixedly into the neck of the half-empty water bottle, holding it at a tilt like a microscope. Then he suddenly came back to life and said, "So, the story. This time they relate, the story and the portrait, because the portrait is of Nicole Truax, in the vernacular, Coco. A woman who never told a falsehood in her life."

Archibald made himself more comfortable and started to talk in a monotone. "Essentially, there's no plot, no beginning, no end," he said, distorting his face as if he had a headache. "Just some parts and pieces related to the main subject. Coco really couldn't lie, and, as you can imagine, this caused her quite a bit of difficulty, but the real problems began when she grew up. At twenty-three she finished acting school and was invited to join one of the professional Parisian theaters, although she was a thoroughly mediocre actress – she lacked fine features and a real stage voice. She was, however, truly in love with art, and her commitment showed. For that, she was appreciated, but the theater was only half the problem. Worst of all was that Nicole became a married woman at the same time, and that combination – marriage and the stage – made for a highly flammable mixture that caught fire not just once, never causing a real explosion, but frequently letting off somewhat unpleasant sparks."

He studied the neck of the bottle again, and I took a sip of my disgusting warm water and quietly set it off to the side. "You're grimacing, yes you are," Archibald grinned. "But you can't sin all the time. You've got to pay for it too! By the way, it's good for your liver.

I'm saying this to myself, not you. You're just a living illustration of the concept," he clarified and, sighing, gulped down some more.

"So, Coco's marriage was obviously a precipitous step," Archibald continued, livening up somewhat. "Conflict is clear: game and life, principles and flaws, hypocrisy and inborn veracity. True, we should have some compassion for the poor girl: when she worked on a new role, she became a heroine for real, with everything that ensues. Love meant true love, intrigue – true intrigue. Imagine: Coco comes home way after midnight, drunk and disheveled, like a hooker. She looks like a fallen angel, not entirely snapping out of a trance. Her husband is really interested in where she was, and Coco honestly replies – in the bar. Ah, thinks her husband and asks who she drank with there, at the bar. And Coco, not concealing anything, names a couple of actresses from her troupe and a few of their friends. Her husband, of course, likes it less and less. He inhales deeply to calm his quickened pulse and very cautiously inquires, as if beside the point: there, in the bar, with all those disreputable people – was everything there irreproachable and morally acceptable? That is, were there no subtle passes or hints? And did she, Coco, not do anything reprehensible without considering it in her drunken state? Now Coco is no longer Coco, but Nicole Truax. Her nostrils flare; she almost becomes sober. What nonsense, she declares in outrage and goes into the bathroom, still swaying a little, yet already embodying the customary aura of virtue – and her husband's embarrassed and particularly affectionate to Nicole that night. Soon, she falls asleep, exhausted by the wine and her difficult day. However, he lies awake in bed for a long time, and in the morning there are whispers behind his back and sinister allusions: it seems the whole city considers him a cuckold… And that's how it continues – the perfectly faithful marriage and the complete abandonment to her occupation. People tell him about the police scandals at the nightclubs in Montmartre and the blatant debauchery in the cheapest of them. He learns about a certain romantic episode of Coco's with a retired general from the government. It is full of old-fashioned affection and platonic passion, but did not prevent the general's envious wife from making

VADIM BABENKO

an ugly scene in the theater. He gave up being jealous long ago –
especially since Nicole sincerely takes offense. She doesn't lie to him,
after all, she can't lie. Here's her boudoir – she doesn't throw away
even one note. Here are her bills, he can check everything down to
the last franc. Here's her planner, her underwear, her perfume…
Okay, and what's in the theater program, he wonders as if by
chance, moved not by jealousy, but curiosity. Can he look at the list
of her roles? At least he needs to know what to expect, he justifies
himself, reading the schedule of plays and heroines that would be
tangling his Nicole in the turbid jungles of passions that suddenly
become so real. Alas, there's nothing to console him. Coco, probably
because of her average talent, is exclusively assigned character roles:
demimondes, seasoned intriguers, wicked maids, and gossipers
who never miss a chance to give a reason for gossip themselves.
Nothing pure, her husband thinks angrily. No morality. My God,
what does our playwriting teach us? What taste it creates, and how
does it turn out that Nicole – such a great woman, simply a find,
created to bring happiness – belongs to this theatre, to this crap, this
deception? Sincere to the depths of her soul, yet totally immersed in
simulation… Oh, how he resented it and suffered – the husband of
Nicole, I mean!"

Archibald shook his head, turned to the portrait, and considered
it for a minute or two.

"And what happened next?" I encouraged him. "Did he continue
to live with her or lose patience and leave her? Or perhaps some
terrifying role – as Desdemona, for example?"

"Nothing else happened," muttered Archibald with
dissatisfaction. "I warned you, no plot and no denouement.
Ultimately they separated, of course. But ending up like Desdemona
– no. You're going too far there. Such things don't happen."

"Everyone said," he admitted after a short silence. "Everyone
unanimously agreed that Nicole Truax should not become the wife
of Archibald Bely. Should not. End of subject. And they were right!"
He raised his finger didactically. "Although they didn't even know
her this much," – Archibald measured out a miniscule part of the

361

nail on his raised finger. "And if they had known the entire truth, they wouldn't have had enough brains to say anything intelligent anyway," he concluded crossly. Then he jumped to his feet and, with the words, "We've looked at it long enough," began to drape gray fabric over the portrait.

A strange thought occurred to me. "Archibald," I asked quietly, "tell me, why do you always have a scarf on?"

Archibald winced at the unexpected question and regarded me with suspicion. "What of it?" he gruffly rejoined and coughed as he cleared his throat.

"Nothing," I said. "But who knows, maybe there's something to it. Really, Archibald, what do you have under the scarf?"

I took a step in his direction, and Archibald moved back. Fright flickered in his eyes, and I closed in, surprising myself at this exertion of force, yet not wanting to stop. Archibald slowly receded, and I carefully went closer to him, not lifting my eye from the rumpled, twisted scarf.

"You know it's very unusual to feel like a victim with you, Vitus." Archibald Bely tried to grin but didn't pull it off too well. "You've changed all of a sudden, and I don't understand what you actually want."

"Well, really, Archibald," I said in a low voice. "You make yourself out to be an imposing creator. You force feed me pictures and stories that you've chosen and require sincerity in return, while you yourself conceal something – what's fair about that? Let's play honestly – question for question, answer for answer. You can't always measure out candidness in pharmacy vials. Otherwise I'll start to feel like an experimental animal that's being manipulated for some purpose. Either you don't say a word or you say everything..." – I droned on and on, as if hypnotizing him and pressing him against the wall. And finally he ended up at the wall, leaning against it and looking at the ground beneath my feet.

"Take off the scarf, Archibald," I instructed harshly, but he didn't move or raise his eyes. And then I stretched out my hand, grabbed one of the hanging ends and began to unwrap it coil by coil. Archibald didn't resist. A wry grin was plastered on his lips, his face immobile, like a mask made from colorless clay.

The scarf fell to the floor, baring his pale neck, which sharply contrasted with his sun-tanned cheeks and forehead. There was nothing on it – just a prominent Adam's apple covered with stubble and bouncing up and down when Archibald swallowed nervously. Then he raised his head, stared me in the eye, and asked hostilely, "Well, are you satisfied?"

"Completely," I replied, picked up his scarf, and shook off the dust. "Here, now we're even. You can put it back on if you want. I won't even ask why, and believe me, I won't tell anyone."

Archibald slowly wound the scarf around his neck and defiantly inquired, "Did that help you somehow?"

"I don't know," I shrugged my shoulders. "Rather yes than no. I'm going. Goodbye."

He narrowed his eyes and gave me his hand. "Tell me," I asked after a limp handshake. "Why have you settled in this hole? You have talent; there could be exhibitions and more. But here no one sees anything."

"There's nobody to show it to," Archibald replied with just a hint of irritation. "You won't believe me, but it's a fact, a confession. Nobody – so it's better to be away from them all. Arnold comes here once a year or, as you see, chance foists someone like you on me... There are no in-di-vi-du-als in the mob," he murmured, leaning toward my ear. "Not one human being who could give me a reason to move to a place with people and tolerate the rest. And if someone emerges, then they have their own concerns and misfortunes. Anyway, I'm used to it," he admitted, grinning. "Go. Take care; we already said goodbye!" And I walked away, nodding to him at the door and waving to *his* Maria, who ran into me in the foyer, got frightened as usual, and quickly dove into a closet nearby.

When I returned home, I collected all my papers with diagrams and charts, entertaining me for the whole month, all the pages with lists of useless names piled in the drawer, and threw them away without any regret after assiduously ripping them up into tiny pieces.

Afterward, I sent some other stuff in the same direction – snippets of my thoughts on the most diverse topics written here and there in a careless manner. I wasn't the least bit sorry to lose them; they evoked nothing but a yawn in me now. Then I jumped in bed and sank into a serene sleep. And the next day I left the village – without anyone seeing me off.

The truck driver was a huge man with a doughy face. He looked me over briefly, asked where I was headed, phlegmatically nodded at the name of the hotel Gibbs had told me about, and informed me I could simply call him Ben. He was sullen and slovenly, and the cabin of his truck reeked of sweat, gasoline, and cheap tobacco. No sooner had he laid his enormous clumsy hands on the wheel and turned onto the road than Ben lost all interest in it and began to engage me in conversation, which was apparently included in the cost of the trip.

"Who are you?" he asked right after learning my name.

"What do you mean?" I didn't get it.

"Well, how do you make a living?" Ben explained, spinning his hand in the air. "How do you pay for your grub and everything else?"

"Oh, I see. I'm an artist," I lied. Lied again, as in the hotel with Piolin, for some incomprehensible reason, and instantly regretted it. But it was too late: I couldn't take it back and say it was just a dumb joke. What a ridiculous way to boast, I lamented to myself, yet Ben was not surprised at what he'd heard. "An artist," he drawled. "That's as great an honor as can be, and a smart way to earn money!"

"Depends on how you look at it…" I was about to gainsay him, but Ben was not interested in my opinion. "And I, bro, am just a simple truck driver," he finished his thought, shaking his head dejectedly, and without delay began to relate the detailed chronology of his thirty-five-year life.

He didn't go far: in a few minutes I felt I was really fed up with stories – others' stories and others' fates. So I interrupted him with something unrelated and then closed my eyes, pretending to fall asleep. The driver got silent and we didn't speak again for two hours or so. By then we had travelled fairly far from the village and were darting through hills that didn't resemble either the Dunes or the wetlands through which our small group had once traipsed with Gibbs in the lead. It was overcast, and the stunted trees seemed immersed in a gooey dirty-gray mist.

"You're a painter," Ben said suddenly, with some apparent slyness in his voice. "So, what do you paint, in general?"

I cursed myself once again and replied reluctantly, "I paint different things – people, landscapes…" Then I added, "I'm actually closer to abstractionists," hoping the unfamiliar word would repulse Ben's desire to talk, but it wasn't that easy to dissuade him.

"People!" he grasped the weak link. "People are a good topic, although the majority of them are crap, to put it bluntly. Especially the bitches!" He was beginning to sniffle, clearly distracted by the thought, but then returned to the main subject, "Do you paint the bitches as well?"

"Hmm, in general, rarely," I replied cautiously, not knowing what he was getting at, and Ben livened up.

"Good!" he exclaimed. "They're just nonsense and kerfuffle, and are simply a straight-up danger to a normal individual, especially an unlucky one. You better choose something else instead. I tell you what: why don't you paint my portrait?" he blurted out to my utter confusion and stared in my face, expecting a reaction and completely forgetting the road. "Paint it and give it to me as a present – and I won't charge you anything for the trip!"

I instantly recalled the Christophers and their self-confident bravado. Another one of those, I reflected with hostility, then gave a haughty look and said lazily, "No pal, I doubt it. My pictures cost thousands. You and your trip are not even close."

Ben, not at all discouraged, continued to stare at me. "Thousands or not, can't we work something out?" he rumbled with self-assurance.

"Watch the road," I replied, not interested in landing in a ditch. Ben sulked and faced forward. "Don't be a wuss, you're not in danger," he muttered gloomily and shifted his powerful shoulders, as if confirming his superiority. "I've seen artists – and driven them more than once. Nobody's ever complained."

The conversation came to a halt, and the rest of the way we sat, gazing in front of us, dissatisfied with each other. The driver, who could not keep silent for long, occasionally mumbled to himself, but without any hope of fellowship. "Costs thousands…" I heard. "Suckers pay thousands, and if they don't, then the bitches get the money. All bad things are from them bitches. They get at you like dogs and yelp endlessly, or maybe not like dogs, but hyenas – yelp and mock… Every creature was given a tree – why did hyenas receive the baobab? Nothing but idiocy comes from them – they planted it upside down and have been laughing ever since. And baobab, it lives for a thousand years…"

I gradually drifted off into slumber. Ben's babbling and my own musings got muddled up. A swamp has sucked me in, I thought to myself and suddenly felt I couldn't wait to arrive, to get immersed in the commotion and urban noise. Any city, even the provincial City of M., seemed to be able to save me from something that had nearly snatched me with its tentacles. Yet I knew I had already overcome that something, I duped it, almost without lying – just sacrificing a small part of me I no longer remembered. I envisioned the streets and entryways, the dark facades and the streams of rushing cars, instantly feeling pricks of momentary melancholy for my own Alpha Romeo which was waiting for me with the patience of a forsaken pet. I recalled the sounds and lights, the coziness of bars and cafes – and my imagination, as if awakening from its winter sleep, tossed anxiously in the secret corner where I had chased it into long exile. The alternation of light and dark stones on the streets, the cracks in the asphalt and the wriggles of the narrow alleys again rose before my eyes, joining in combinations of either poetic lines or moves on one hundred and forty-four fields, turning into groups of clumsy figures, or even vaguely hinting at dashes of black ink on the horizon.

My fingers touched the imprint on my cheek. Stone walls arose somewhere in the depths of my memory, but, as two days before, they didn't frighten or confuse me. "The worst is behind you," I whispered to myself, yet I didn't continue with the second part of the formula. A weakness lay there, even if it was so well hidden no one but me could have recognized it. As for the memory itself, it now contained a resilient power. I felt it, knew it, wouldn't have needed Gibbs to confirm my conjecture: if you keep your eyes open, then you can recoup a lot. For what and at whose expense? It makes no real difference; there's no point in calling names. When you sort through them all, you can spread your thoughts too thin – while actually any name will do. I, moreover, have an identifiable enemy, I do. Julian, Julian… Why have I been vegetating in the sticks and losing so much time? Do I always have to be hurried by someone?

The road became flatter, the jolting stopped, the truck rumbled along rhythmically, and I dozed, my chin dangling over my chest. Half-asleep, I followed my secret's resurrection from the ruins, its rebirth, and the new life flowing into it. Yes, that was so naïve – the destruction, the shots and blood, the romanticized murder, like romanticized love derived from cheap books. And the attempt to glorify myself by destroying someone else, eliminating his memory and thoughts, was ridiculous indeed. There was no depth in that, just pitiful plagiarism. That "someone else," devoid of his mind, is indifferent to all meaning, he's deaf and blind. That's the greatest scorn awaiting you, the dimwitted avenger: the very cause of your revenge will turn its face to you and say, ha-ha-ha, I don't see you, I don't heed you and I don't want to know you. And you can't, you'd add, but that would be little consolation, powerless in the face of the missed chance, the effort thrown away for nothing. No, the idea should be about something other than annihilation and burning bridges. It should be a creative act – even if only a few will consider it a masterpiece!

Everything's in my hands, I suddenly understood, and nothing would be superfluous – neither the revolver, the walk through the Dunes, the Parkers, nor Archibald's portraits, even if some of the pieces don't find their place immediately. A lot can happen, and much will certainly happen the way I'd like it…

Then before my eyes the lined board again arose. Black and white pieces moved across it. For ages I hadn't battled anyone, intentionally leaving the limelight for the shadows, abandoning once and for all what I could do better than anything else. Where are you, my competitors, nourishing your own bloodthirstiness? I cannot detach myself from you – what you can do better than others will not let you go, even after years and years. And where else but in the eternal game of *Dzhan* is your weakness so plainly able to turn into the strength of a sudden dash if you don't get distracted and see it through to the end?

Hi, I said to Lyubomir Lyubomirov, who poked his nose out of a far corner and made a face, the detestable bully and only person who could understand me. I wanted to add something else or simply give him one of the usual signs from the code we had worked out to not betray our thoughts or intentions, but at that moment the truck stopped abruptly and my head almost banged into the windshield. "We've arrived," Ben's hoarse voice said. "Let's have the money, Mr. Artist." I stretched, nodded, and dug out my wallet full of bills that, according to Gibbs, were stainless and smelled of nothing.

CHAPTER 9

The Arcada Hotel turned out to be quite decent. Its neon facade glittered and gleamed enigmatically, so I even imagined the inside to be teeming with amusing objects, but the lobby looked very ordinary, as did the dull clerk at the black glass desk with a crack cutting diagonally across it. More than anything else, it resembled a guesthouse for middle-class retirees, and I felt momentarily disappointed, yet my room ended up being spacious, the metal fixtures and mirrors in the bathroom glistened invitingly, while the TV in the corner looked ritzier than the establishment itself and the City of M. in general. Mentally thanking Gibbs for the good advice, I undressed and went to shower.

When I returned to the room with a towel around my waist, a chambermaid was working away there. I told her I'd arrived a few minutes ago and the room was clean, but she just greeted me curtly, without turning her head, and again began to flaunt her rag, wiping off surface after surface. I lay down on the made bed and gazed at the ceiling, somewhat annoyed at the unwelcome intrusion. The chambermaid was petite and skinny, somewhere around twenty-three, with an expression of woeful stubbornness pasted on her face; she didn't arouse my interest at all.

When she finished cleaning and was walking toward the door, still without raising her eyes, I called to her a second time, politely asking whether she knew Jeremy, the manager of the place. The girl stopped in the threshold and looked at me suspiciously. "Everybody knows him," she replied and reached for the doorknob. She clearly wanted to leave, but I said to her, adjusting my towel, "Wait up, don't run away. I won't bite and I'd like to talk with this Jeremy of yours – could you get him for me?"

"Get him yourself," retorted the chambermaid. "I'm not your secretary or something." But at that instant I showed her a small bill, pulled from the pocket of my pants. She flashed a greedy glance at it and changed her tone. "Well, if that's how it is, then why shouldn't I get him?" she drawled, taking a step toward the bed, me, and the money. "Do you want him now or later?"

"Now," I nodded, extending the cash toward her and feeling uncomfortable under her gaze in just a towel. "Here, take it. Thanks."

The chambermaid took the bill, smiled awkwardly, and hid it in her clothing with a quick movement. "Thank you," she said, continuing to look at me as if assessing something. Then she put her hands on her hips and declared with the same insincere smile, "I have a sister by the way."

"So?" I didn't understand.

"Nothing actually." She faltered and lowered her eyes. "You know about these sort of things, I'm sure. I'm only telling you I have a sister who's taller and a little larger here and here. As for me, I'm a modest girl, and I have a fiancée…"

"What's it to me?" I snapped back, thinking she wanted more money. "If you have a fiancée, then go get married."

"But my sister?" The chambermaid didn't give in. "She doesn't have a fiancée. And she's quite nice and all that. Likes to flirt with men and all that… Especially if the man is interesting," she added coquettishly, lowering her voice and almost winking. "How about my sister?"

"Nothing, no, forget it." I cringed and waved my hand, finally understanding what she was implying. "I need Jeremy, not your sister. Go already!"

"Well, it's up to you," the chambermaid uttered with

disappointment and left, swinging her thin hips. I dressed hastily, as I imagined her enterprising sister with distinct hostility.

Jeremy didn't make me wait long and appeared in a quarter of an hour. He wasn't tall but rather round, like a ball, and even moved as if bouncing on his short, fat legs. It seemed you could throw him against the wall and he would spring off it and fly back, rolling over his head a few times and landing on his feet again, grinning just as civilly. The room instantly smelled of cheap grease, which his impeccably parted hair was loaded with, while my eyes rippled with the fake sheen of studs and a tie clip.

"In what capacity may I be of service?" he asked ingratiatingly – and I thought I'd heard that silky baritone somewhere else, but couldn't remember where or when. Despite his mushy figure, Jeremy gave the impression of being a thoroughly street-tough guy. His small eyes watched sharply and tenaciously, so I came to the conclusion it was a good recommendation and he should be capable of fulfilling my request.

"A man by the name of Gibbs advised me to see you," I said in an even, measured voice. "I have a matter to take care of in the city, and I need assistance. For the assistance, of course, I will pay."

Jeremy inclined his head slightly at the mention of Gibbs and pulled a small notebook with a stub of pencil from his pectoral pocket. "I'm listening," he said, showing respectful attention. I rummaged in my bag, dug out the photo of Julian, and laid it on the table. Jeremy came over, stood next to me politely, and looked at it without saying a word.

"I need to find this man," I said, already tired of his affectation. "His name is Julian – at least that's what he used to be called. He arrived from the capital a few months ago. He's living... I don't know where he's living."

I fell silent, realizing I had nothing else to add, and the request seemed utterly impossible. Bring me something I don't know what, flew through my head. This Jeremy will be right if he leaves me straight away, laughing afterward behind the door.

The manager, however, did not look daunted. "I need a few more details," he said, opening his notebook and sitting down at the table. "Where, by the way, did you get to know this man named Gibbs?"

"We met in the Dunes," I muttered in irritation. "I'm not searching for Gibbs, but this man, Julian. Apparently you misunderstood me."

"Oh, no, I understood, understood," rejoined Jeremy rapidly. "Julian, that's what I'm going to take down." He wrote "Julian" at the top of the blank page, delighted in the heading, and said with a slight sigh, "Well, let's begin with his habits…"

Over the course of the next hour, Jeremy, like an experienced investigator, extracted from me everything I remembered about my target, deftly sifting and organizing the scant and somewhat unrelated data. "Cards, drinking?" he mumbled, peering into my face. "Have you seen him drunk? Does he cry, brag, or get in fights? Further – cigarettes: kind, how does he hold them, how does he ash? The cigarette butt, too, is very important. Does he smoke down to the filter or does he leave some behind? Does he stub out the end or flick it?"

Initially it all seemed like a children's game to me, but I soon acknowledged the seriousness of the questions and assiduously strained my memory. Jeremy was calm and didn't rush or pressure me, even when I descended from facts into dubious assumptions. "Now, if it's okay, we'll move on to something else," he would simply say when one of his queries brought us to a standstill. Then he would tap his pencil on the edge of the table, ponder for a second, and ask something completely different.

"What does he like to read?" he inquired in his velvety baritone. "Newspapers, magazines, or does he even buy books sometimes? And also pictures with, you know, naked girls – does he look at them often or not?"

I wrinkled my brow and honestly tried to answer everything. With astonishment I noticed that Julian kept showing me new sides of himself. My old enemy, whom I seemed to know so well, turned into an enigmatic artifact of an unpredictable sort.

Everyone is blind, everyone, I thought crossly, angry at myself. I should have prepared better for my hunt and turned my brain to practical things instead of delving into self-observing, if not self-taunting, without any obvious benefit.

"Now to clothing," Jeremy continued in a monotone. "People have autumnal habits, and then there are habits in general. Let's talk about autumnal ones…"

I envisioned Julian the first time I saw him, rosy-cheeked and beaming with health, though wrapped in a coat too warm for the middle of September. "He likes jackets and raincoats," I replied confidently. "A sporty style, no ostentatious stiffness." Then doubt overcame me; I added something about fashionable shirts and blazers and recalled other details, confusing myself and the manager. Something wasn't right, as if some fine points contradicted each other. Even the questions that arranged the past in nice rows could not clear up the aberrations and false discoveries.

This didn't bother Jeremy in the least. He had methods he believed in, as if showing the skeptics, like me, that even useless parts could be gathered into a fairly decent whole, as with a building kit where half the pieces are missing. You just needed to equip yourself with the right system and stick to your guns – the blanks will get filled in by themselves or they'll stop flying in your face. Moreover, the system will reject what's superfluous: for example, he didn't ask me about Julian's moods and feelings, secret thoughts, doubts, and fears – about everything that makes up his true character and differentiates him from others, even those who are very similar on the outside. I could fantasize about that to my heart's content and even think up a story no worse than Archibald's, but obviously it would serve a quite different purpose.

"Okay, okay," Jeremy said, nodding and scribbling with his pencil. "Now let's talk about women a little. Is he impertinent and insolent with them or does he seek to gain their favor? Does he like waitresses? Secretaries? Librarians?"

Here I could tell him a thing or two, but it was impossible to confide to a stranger how it turned out for Julian and Vera, especially without mentioning my own self, the indispensable apex of the steadfast triangle. And Jeremy kept going, giving me no respite,

"Now let's go through the food. Be patient, there's only a little left; we're almost finished," – and I saw that, yes, almost everything had already been grouped together. Julian appeared before me, and the new content attenuated my vision and distracted my thoughts. It diverted me from the simplicity I had once accepted like a brief annotation card that supplants a thick manuscript – though generally I'm not given to simplifications.

"Okay, that's fantastic," said a satisfied Jeremy, reviewing the two pages of minute handwriting. "We have something to work with here. Your Julian for me now is a man like all others, and it's not difficult to find a man and do whatever you want with him. But you'll take care of the *doing* yourself, right?"

I didn't like that last phrase, reeking of familiarity, which the manager of the Arcada had no right to. "Your task is to find him – don't worry about the rest," I replied coldly. "And one more thing: ask someone to get my car. It's parked at the hotel where I was staying before." I took a piece of paper from the table and wrote the model and the license plate number of my Alfa Romeo.

"Will do," Jeremy agreed and yawned. "Which hotel did you say?"

Here it occurred to me that the name of the place where I'd met Gibbs had flown out of my mind. I could only remember its location visually, but didn't have the exact address. "The hotel…" I stumbled. "A three-story building not far from the market… To tell you the truth, I've forgotten. There are glass doors – and what else? Some guy named Piolin is in charge. He's acquainted with Gibbs – maybe you know him?"

Jeremy suddenly jumped up, placed his hands behind him and walked-rolled toward the opposite wall, where he turned and trundled back again, looking at me quite harshly. A wrinkle appeared on his perfectly round face, passing from his part to his chin, and one eye narrowed into a slit. "You guessed wrong," he said, beaming with a smile and threatening with his wrinkle. "Of course I don't know any Piolin, and nobody here has ever heard of him." He shrugged his shoulders, as if marveling at a minor misunderstanding, paced back and forth afresh, and added, "I'm even sure that others – that man named Gibbs, for example, whom you accidentally mentioned, couldn't possibly know Piolin – and if they, by chance, do, then it's certainly not the person you mean. Moreover," Jeremy tilted his head to the side and assumed a sly look, as if he were preparing to surprise me. "Moreover, I realize it was a joke: you, I assume, don't know any Piolin either. If someone were to come up to you and ask directly, then you, both annoyed and indignant, would chew out this impudent fellow, since why should you know some Piolin? For no reason, I assure you, no reason at all – and I'm assuring you in case someone actually comes up and asks."

He nodded to himself, and, obviously considering the subject exhausted, took his notebook from the table and slipped it back in his breast pocket. I sighed and cursed to myself – there are always problems with this Piolin. It was he who introduced himself to me – I didn't seek him out and didn't pry into his secrets, yet now it keeps turning out I'm prying. But you can't explain that to everyone, of course.

"Does that mean you won't be able to find my car?" I asked Jeremy with an intentionally forlorn look.

"But why?" He waved his hands. "We'll bring you your car, don't worry. We'll find it, and the hotel by the market. When do you need it? Soon? We could take care of it today – right away."

He folded his arms over his stomach and looked at me with the same cunning smile. The wrinkle disappeared from his face and I felt relieved, as if the most difficult part was over.

"Would you prefer to pay in advance or afterward?" Jeremy inquired cautiously, shifting from one foot to the other.

"In advance, definitely," I said to calm him. "How much should I give you?"

"However much you can spare," he said with the expression of a modest aristocrat and licked his lips.

I nodded, grabbed my wallet, and took three large bills from it. Then thought a little and added another, wondering casually, "Is that enough?"

Jeremy took the money, slipped it into the pocket of his pants and said a little insolently, "Definitely, why not? It'll take about three days. I'll inform you when we're done. And you'll have the car today, in tip-top shape." He cast one more glance around the room, bowed respectfully, and retreated toward the door, but here I clapped myself on the forehead and dove into my bag.

"The keys to the car," I exclaimed in response to his curious look. "I almost forgot," – and I tossed him the heavy bunch.

"The keys?" Jeremy repeated somewhat distractedly. "You have the keys? Then it'll be easier, much easier…" He stood, thinking, and said uncertainly, "Yes, then it'll be easier and run you less. Perhaps you need something else too? A girl, for example, I have lots of them. It'll take three days or so, and it's boring to wait. Or we could organize something more elaborate – whatever you like."

"No, thanks," I replied, somewhat confused. "However, I'll think about it."

"Yes, think about it." Jeremy assumed a deferential expression for the last time and disappeared behind the door, shutting it without a sound.

Then I simply wallowed in bed, waiting for my Alfa Romeo and contemplating a little of everything. Julian kept climbing into my head, but I chased him away. He was unnecessary now – things were going smoothly without his involvement, if, of course, he hadn't left the City of M. before my new course of action had even started. Then Jeremy's guys would return from their searches empty-handed and the entire operation would be destroyed, I thought lazily. Yet there was no bitterness in this thought, not even a substantial shred of pity, as if someone invisible was whispering that another opening would unfold in due time.

Soon, someone knocked at the door. A pimply youngster, sniffling, delivered the keys to my car and informed me nasally it was in the courtyard, twenty meters from the entryway. "A sign is hanging from the rearview mirror. It means 'don't touch,'" he explained unclearly. "Take the sign down, and when you return, hang it back up. Then everything will be alright. Everything's alright in general here

– always," he assured me, received a couple coins, and disappeared. I quickly dressed and headed out for a drive around the city.

The City of M. was the same and also quite different. I recognized and didn't recognize it, maybe expecting more than I should have. The buildings seemed to have decayed during the weeks I had spent at the ocean; the streets were dirtier; I saw only potholes and patches, clear traces of squalor, instead of the enigmatic drawings and fragile webs of cracks I had recently dreamed of. It was the same with the people – their faces faded and their shoulders sunk in despondency. Each of them sped along, hiding behind the spectral shadows of their collars, and it was impossible to make out one from another. Individuality vanished, turning into elements of the crowd – an amorphous substance abolishing distinctions and names, living as a united organism guided by the most primitive instincts.

I darted from one alley to another, swerved randomly, getting stuck in clogged archways and again returning to the avenues. One and the same thing was everywhere, yet many fine points distinguished one spot from the next: street from street, square from adjacent square, one intersection from another with a blinking traffic light. It was as if the city was presenting dashes of heterogeneity as opposed to the formless mass of people.

It took only one shy step, but that should also be enough, I thought gloomily. Morsels of diversity – that's significant for those who aren't able to toss the veil from their eyes and look beyond the neighbor's balcony. A few drops of novelty are enough to add spice to their dull life and give them a reason to bustle about every day, so there's no space for any extra thought…

Look, look, I said to myself, this is the habitat of those who marked and filed you away – identified and thus no danger. They sustain themselves on dusty grass and watch the world through stifling smog. They're proud of their customs, not one of which differentiates them from four-legged creatures, and they despise strangers, not having the slightest interest in the nature of foreignness. They know how to stick together and thoroughly rebuff others. They have no mark on their cheek or anything worse, although, as Gibbs affirms, a label is glued to each of them if you look hard enough. At one time I wanted to be with them, camouflaging myself like an inept chameleon; I was upset with my own ineptitude – how many centuries ago? Probably no one can count them now...

Please, let Julian still be in the city, I thought and felt a sharp pang of hunger, recalling I'd hardly eaten all day.

It took me a while to stumble upon a decent restaurant: I had lost my way in the outskirts and drifted through the identical gray buildings lit by lanterns here and there. Only half an hour later, when it was totally dark, did I manage to drive onto the central square, full of people. With some difficulty, I parked the car in front of the post office and headed into the first café with a bright sign. The inside had the usual: smoke and warmth. Apathetic eyes slid over me, instantly shifting away and forgetting. The waiter didn't come for a long time, being occupied with a large group at the neighboring table. At least no one paid attention to the monkey's hand, and, I think, if I hadn't had a face and looked out from the back of my neck, it'd hardly have made an impression on them. Filed away, filed away, I repeated silently, grinning to myself, and relaxed. My conjectures were right, and that played into my hands.

Dinner, when they finally brought it, was quite acceptable – and, completing it with coffee and cognac, I left in a very good mood. The thought flickered through my mind that maybe I should try to meet a woman, which would be thoroughly fitting after my voluntary confinement in the village by the ocean. I began to look around with a certain kind of curiosity, but didn't see anyone attractive enough. I meandered on, stopped at my car, smoked and waited, wondering whether I should buy a flower as an enticement, or rely solely on my charm, or maybe forget it entirely and head back to the hotel without any extra trouble. Still, the lure of adventure overpowered me and I continued to stand with a careless look, playing with my cigarette and glancing around until a pretty girl with a dangling lock of hair and tightly pursed lips surfaced from the crowd and passed right in front of me.

My heart skipped a beat; I took a short step forward and said, smiling cordially, "What a surprise! You vanished, you're very bad – not a call, not a visit…" It's an old trick, but it works on many – and it was working now. The girl was taken aback and glued her eyes on me instead of walking by.

"Do I know you?" she asked in bewilderment, looking at me intently. I noticed she was quite young and certainly not very smart, but it was too late to contemplate – success must be secured without delay.

"Of course!" I informed her confidently, adding gentle huskiness to my voice. "We've known each other for some time already. I'm Vitus," – and I was prepared to take her by the elbow to guide our relations in the right direction, but at that moment I heard a loud crack and the tingling of broken glass behind my back. I turned, as if stung, sensing, before I saw it, that something bad had happened to my car, so dear to me after our long separation.

And that's what it was. Right in front of me a bulky Chrysler was blocking the street. It had apparently been trying to park next to me and, as a result, had demolished the back light on the right side of my Alfa Romeo. Now its muffler was puffing dully as it stood diagonally and didn't let others pass. Hurrying denizens stopped, avidly swiveling their heads, while I, forgetting about the girl, ran into the middle of the street in complete despair.

Both front doors of the Chrysler swung open and two people jumped out at the same time: the driver, a middle-aged man with disheveled hair and a large face pitted with hollows, and his fidgety girlfriend, a pointy-nosed blonde in a bright-blue jeans suit. No sooner had she alighted onto the road than the blonde screamed for the whole neighborhood to hear, "Joe, Joe, the bumper… Look at what you've done!"

Chubby-faced Joe hushed her and she shut up instantaneously, only waving her arms and swishing her long ponytail. Then he turned to me, his head tilting threateningly.

"You moron," he began. "Do you realize how badly you've parked?" But here he stopped, meeting my gaze. Probably a serious blast of hate poured out of me. At least, my insides were boiling over – not so much from the smashed light as from the "moron" and the self-confident manner of these two. And I was ready to pummel him first, although he looked down on me, being taller and having broader shoulders.

"Are you wondering who's at fault? It's you who's at fault. Blame your own stupidity and say you're sorry for calling me a moron right away, you asshole!" I said in a voice hoarse with fury. Then I took a step toward him and added, hastily clearing my throat, "Yeah, and open your fucking eyes. You need to watch where you're driving."

The blonde screeched something indignantly, but Joe didn't heed her. He stood opposite me, clearly assessing what I was capable of and whether he could overcome me in a fight. He was unlucky: at that moment I was capable of a lot – and it was good I'd left my revolver in the hotel room. Visceral anger I'd never known raged inside, thwarting my breathing and causing my heart to pound violently, as if I was about to jump into a precipice. My normal ego, foreign to aggression, flipped over, asking in disbelief: What happened, why this craziness? Are you really that upset about the car? And in response came whispers telling it fiercely to quiet down – perhaps forever. Something new settled within me and showed its teeth, not possessing one bit of patience, something ready to spring on the surrounding world as soon as the world asked for trouble. And yes, I was sorry about my defenseless sedan, all its glittering parts exposed to clumsy, awkward strangers, to a soulless, destructive force. I myself was invulnerable to them – and I knew that now, seeing the decisiveness rapidly fade in Joe's squint. I didn't need anyone to look after me, but it, my Alfa Romeo, without an indelible mark – who except me could take care of it?

"Joe!" the blonde shrieked again. "Why are you standing there? Do something!"

"Give him a good whack, Joe," someone screamed from the crowd and cackled stupidly, but Joe stepped back and said to no one in particular, "To hell with him – he's drunk, can't you see? Let's go, Micky."

He was beginning to head toward his Chrysler when he

suddenly turned and kicked the shards on the road – the remains of the smashed light – so they flew onto the sidewalk, on me and the recoiling gapers. I could no longer hold back my fury. I wanted to throw myself on the self-satisfied jerk who was escaping my retaliation so faintheartedly – wanted to rip him to shreds and dig my teeth into him. I wasn't scared at all – only disgust prevented me from causing an ugly melee. Something inside me objected to contact with a foreign body, as with infectious, unclean matter. I looked around, strode off to the side, and grabbed a garbage can that was fortunately empty. Someone in the crowd yelled "Ooh," Micky screamed, and I swung my arms, lifting the heavy weapon over my head and flinging it onto the hood of the Chrysler with all my anger going into the throw. The can landed with a deafening crash; a dent appeared in the hood, and something sprung off the side. Joe dashed to stunned Micky, who was silently opening and closing her mouth, jammed her into the car with a shove, and jumped behind the wheel, hollering into the air, "Drunk! Drunk! The idiot!" The tires of the Chrysler screeched and it zipped away, grazing another innocent vehicle on the way, while I stood on the road, looking around angrily, as if searching for my next target.

Someone touched my arm. The girl with the dangling lock looked at me with inquiring shyness. Her lips spread slightly, losing their inaccessibility; her lashes twittered and her eyes seemed about to tear up.

"Are you okay?" she asked sympathetically. "I'm Irma. Who are you? Do I know you or not?"

A chill ran through me. The depressing inanity of what was happening gushed over me from top to bottom. I wrapped my arms around my shoulders and shook my head. The girl didn't shift her eyes, and I was sorry for her.

"No, Irma, you don't know me," I replied with a sigh. "I took you for somebody else, excuse me."

The veil swished back over her puppet face, her eyes dulled and her lips contracted into a line again. "You're prettier than the one I was thinking of," I said to her, not finding anything better for consolation. Then I shrugged and climbed behind the wheel of my car, not regarding Irma or the others still standing around.

The motor rumbled soothingly, the city noise remained outside, behind the closed windows, no longer invading my territory. I slowly drove to the Arcada, yielding to everyone who wanted to cut in, without reacting to the cacophony of irritating horns that filled the evening streets. The recent brush with Joe and his hysterical girlfriend felt like an episode from the long-lost past, where the details had grown fainter, leaving only a general senselessness.

So, I thought, we'll proceed as we learned: note and forget. Or, better yet, we'll add to the general collection, and then lay it all out and sort the elements properly. The main thing is not to vary the criteria too much – I should stay focused and not pile on unnecessary pieces…

I imagined the snow-white title page with the heading *My Secret* calligraphed in black, and began to contemplate it calmly and somewhat lazily, realizing I would never succeed in surprising anyone, and if it did occur, then it still wouldn't make much sense. That's why there's no need for extremes like deafening explosions or poisonous arrows. Let's not try too hard, I thought phlegmatically, braking in front of a Volkswagen that shot out from the side. The world isn't worth that. Besides, everything that's possible has already been conjured up more than once. The strength of a story is in the details, nowhere else. The plot may have been used often, which will make the tale even better – otherwise no one will figure out what's what and who's who. All observers will get lost and confused – so, let's not rack our brains in vain. Let's take the obvious, which is on the tip of the tongue… And, as if encouraged by the support, my consciousness obediently switched to the particulars of my new plan that instantly began to take shape. After half an hour of winding through the alleys, I managed to think out nearly every aspect and entered the hotel fully confident about what I should do and how I could do it. The picture stood before my eyes. Just a few last strokes were needed to complete it, and I was sure they'd soon come to mind.

After nodding to the doorman, I went up to my room, lay down on the bed without getting undressed, and felt completely satisfied with myself. The private shell of the hotel room, my next temporary refuge, already seemed to be a comfortable citadel, so pleasant to return to from the hostile world outside. Something, though, was lacking in my reconciliation with life; some desire wouldn't leave me alone, pushing me toward the phone on the table by the bed. I struggled with it for some time and then gave in, picked up the receiver, and asked the porter whether he could find the manager right away.

"Will do," came back through the line calmly and soon Jeremy was at my door. "The car?" he began, having barely entered. "I saw it, I saw it. You want it repaired?"

"Oh, yeah, the car," I recalled. "If it's possible, please repair it, I'll pay. Here are the keys. And, Jeremy, you asked… That is, you said, and I rejected…"

"A girl?" he came to my rescue. "We'll send one up right away. What kind do you prefer?"

I muttered something unclear, yet Jeremy nodded in confirmation and disappeared. Half an hour later someone knocked on the door. Her melodic voice spoke the questioning "Hello?" and Mia appeared in my room.

CHAPTER 10

When I saw her, I was somewhat stunned: she seemed to be the tallest woman I had ever met. Only after she had tossed off her shoes and velvet beret, and her fair hair swished over her shoulders, did the image lose some of its mysteriousness – I no longer imagined an Amazon or local basketball star had turned up in front of me. And then I got used to her and stopped wondering whether to consider it a flaw that she was almost a head taller than me, especially since her body excited me even from afar.

Mia, noticing I was silent, just staring at her, didn't become at all flustered. She tossed off her backpack made from multicolored patches, looked around, and nodded to me affably, telling me her name and asking me mine, which she repeated out loud to herself a few times, as if testing it on her tongue and lips and adapting a few appropriate intonations to it. Then a walk around the unfamiliar place began: Mia moved from object to object, conducting a mute dialogue with me and them – making funny contortions and waving her arms. Some things she just glanced at from all sides; with others she leaned closer or touched them to get their feel. She turned off the lamp in the corner, dousing the room in darkness, and immediately switched it back on, curving her eyebrows in feigned fright, peered in the bathroom and nodded approvingly, stuck her head out the half-opened window and shrugged her shoulders in puzzlement.

I gradually came to know her. Her gait and gestures told me

more than words – while she ruffled her hair, opened her eyes wide, and wrinkled her elegant nose, as if adapting to an invisible partner or guessing the required tone. A few minutes later it was like we were quite good friends – with a subtext of something spicier than regular empathy. That something teased and aroused my desire, which hadn't needed any stimulus. So the next time Mia came near the bed, I tried to hug her and pull her to me, but she nimbly slipped away and hid in the bathroom.

The wait seemed endless, although it was, really, quite short. She emerged completely naked a few minutes later, turned around a few times so I could give her a good look, and then entwined me in her arms. We embarked on a lengthy session of lovemaking, at the end of which the whole bed was turned upside down, as if a powerful typhoon had passed over it. Rising from the tempestuous waves to the surface, I found myself lying on my back, flaccid and limp. My head was resting on the attentively fluffed pillow. Right across from me sparkled the eyes of an unfamiliar being from another planet. Adjusting the focus, I again recognized my indefatigable partner, who was observing me with tenderness and slight curiosity.

"Now we know each other a little better," she declared. "Maybe we should introduce ourselves again. My name is Mia," – and she gave me a smooth kiss on the forehead, which reminded me of Gretchen's childhood caresses. I still didn't want to talk and silently studied her face, then propped myself up on my elbows and began to examine all of her. She stretched and laughed, rubbed against me and wiggled playfully. Her long body wound like an interminable river. Perhaps there was something lacking in the flow of its lines, but everything matched alright, as in a well-made toy. "Mia, Mia," I said in a strange hoarse voice, and she chuckled, cuddled with me a little more, and then stood up from the bed and grabbed her multicolored backpack.

"Let's review the contents," she said, glanced askance at me, and arched her eyebrows. "You probably think it's too small for a big girl like me, but you shouldn't, because when it's closed, you don't know what's inside. You can easily make a mistake – it may be much more capacious than you realize. Making mistakes is a bad habit – you need to avoid it..." She rummaged through the backpack, pulled out a small fabric bag, and extracted an old, worn thermos. "We can drink tea," she suggested. "This is very good tea – I brewed it myself with spikes of wild mint. And then it'll be as if we've known each other for ages, maybe even lived together somewhere and are reuniting after a separation. Or I have this," – a bottle of gin appeared. "And I even have tonic, so we can drink alcohol, like two strangers who just met and still can't get used to each other. Take your pick." Mia neatly turned on one leg, two-stepped, and directed a questioning look at me, tilting her head like a large bird. "Just remember: with alcohol, I never drink much," she added and nodded at me with a serious expression.

I was amused at how she pronounced "alco-ohol" – slightly stumbling on the middle *o*, as if being excessively careful. That's how it was with a few more words – they froze at the peak of the flip for just a split second, trying to complete the pirouette, and then, after momentary stabilization, tumbled, gliding gently onward and downward, with some relief.

"Where are you from?" I asked her, choosing tea over "alco-ohol," and guessing some small southern country.

"From a village in Norway," Mia readily replied, giving me a steaming glass. "I'm sure you never heard its name."

I regarded her in profile. The proper features, healthy flush of the cheeks, lips maybe a little plump... Yes, you can never be sure with a guess – I was wrong by a whole continent. Norwegians had luck with their women, however.

"Do you miss home?" I wondered, making myself more comfortable.

"Not at all," Mia shook her head emphatically. "I don't miss it and I'm not planning to. I don't recall the place anymore," she added as if justifying herself. "It was all long ago – six or seven years back. It's like looking at a picture and noting: that bridge and pond and worn-out fence – you've seen them somewhere, only you don't know where. If I were there, I wouldn't have any idea how to act...

And if one of them saw me here," Mia's eyes grew large, "if someone actually saw me here, they'd walk by, pretending they hadn't noticed me. Because what I do isn't proper," she explained didactically. "But to me it is proper because I like it."

She became talkative after sex and tea, and we chatted for a long time, touching each other under the blanket. I felt really relaxed with her; she filled the emptiness and healed the wounds. Along with her scent and warmth, she emanated a confident acceptance of reality, sharing this confidence with me without any grudge. I certainly knew other things could be hiding under the surface, but at the moment it didn't bother me. There was no reason for us to deceive each other, to catch a lie or bring to light what remained behind the curtains. We were free, like random companions on a night trip, capable of amazing with candidness or bestowing unselfish caresses and not thinking about the future that wouldn't come – for better or worse.

I closed my eyes and constructed my own refuge out of her whispering and touching. Hastily built, it didn't impress with a beauty of form. Yet I didn't have any doubt about its soundness – the walls were high enough, the wooden beams under its roof didn't creak and hadn't sunk over time. Mia was young – I suddenly sensed she was much younger than me, and this was a new sensation I'd never felt before. I didn't like it, but that made it seem even more comfortable inside the illusory edifice, where the numbers worked out according to their own laws and other people's opinions didn't have any influence. I wanted to stay there for a long time and close all the doors – even though I knew I'd have to leave at some point. I wanted to soothe my soul and wander aimlessly from floor to floor – even remembering that my own intentions, which I couldn't elude, were impatiently lying in wait somewhere outside.

Gradually, I was drifting off to slumber and Mia quieted down too. I noticed her eyelashes were darker than her ash-blonde hair, and this touched me as a sign of defenselessness I had detected inadvertently. I put my arm around her shoulder. Mia opened her eyes and smiled broadly.

"Do you want to sleep?" she inquired and answered her own

question, "Of course you do. Wait, I'll be quick," – and she scooted out from under the blanket and went to the bathroom. I sat on the bed and smoked a cigarette, guessing at what kind of agreement she had reached with Jeremy, and when she would have to leave me. I didn't want her to go but was unsure how these things worked. Better to ask her directly, I concluded with a frown and decided to do it as soon as she came out, although the crudeness of the question already made me feel awkward.

"Mia," I said when she appeared in the doorway.

"What, my dear?" she replied lightly, crooning *sotto voce.*

"Tell me, sweetie pie..." I began somewhat insolently, then became embarrassed and changed my tone. "Mia, are you staying or already going? That is, what's your plan? That is, what did you agree to?" The questions sounded dumb, and I, dissatisfied with myself, sulked and shut up.

"Where should I be going?" Mia drawled in surprise. "I don't have to go anywhere." She shook her hair, walked up to the mirror above the desk, and started to examine something on her face. Then she turned to me and scolded me reproachfully for my absurd suspicion.

No, said Mia, faking offence, she wasn't one of those girls who promised to stay three days and accepted payment for three days and then tried to weasel out of it by thinking up some lame story. She also had her pride, and she couldn't stand telling a fib for no reason. She wouldn't concoct some tale about a sick child or an elderly mother, who was worried and couldn't sleep, even if she didn't like it with me, but she did like it, even quite a bit. And she didn't have any children, didn't have a soft spot for children in general, and her mother was far away in Norway. She only had a friend, and her friend, yes, would be baffled about her whereabouts. Usually if she had to disappear, she warned her Vivian, who then looked after her apartment and watered the flowers. Today, everything had happened so unexpectedly, and Jeremy had been so insistent... But he would handle it – she had asked him to call her friend so that Vivi wouldn't worry too much. She could call her from my room phone, of course, however it wasn't her habit to incur extra expenses for others, even if they were minimal. So let Jeremy do it, she could trust him with those things, and no, she wasn't planning to go – unless, of course, I wanted to kick her out. But I surely didn't want to, she knew that, because if I'd wanted to, then I would've just done it.

"Mia," I admitted to her, "you are extraordinarily nice. Just don't forget that I sleep badly when I have company – I'm not used to it and sleeping isn't my strong point anyway."

Mia nodded her head and assured me she understood the matter well. It might occur when not alone: tossing and turning the whole night and having bad dreams. But there was no need to worry – she could help me fall back asleep when some incubus of nonsense came to haunt me. I just had to wake her up – everything would be corrected instantly. I didn't believe her, but she wrapped herself around me, entwining me with her whole body, like fragrant ivy. She whispered something, tickled me with her breath, and I slept the whole night through, without any nightmares or agitated thoughts.

For the next three days we didn't leave the room. The City of M., where I'd wanted to return to so much, suddenly lost all its appeal. Its aura of mysteriousness disappeared without a trace, as if no mystery had ever been hidden there and all its legends had been thought up by those who wanted to profit from them. Certainly, I was being dishonest and intentionally straightening twisted lines, but superficial judgments and right angles completely suited me at that moment. The main riddle was no longer a riddle, of which any mirror could always remind me, and the rest didn't make much sense. I was busy – Julian and my new plan were more important than the mysteries of others. Tender Mia was more attractive than the diversity outdoors – I felt I was fed up with diversities for now.

My temporary girlfriend entertained me thoughtfully and diligently. She patronized me like a skilled doctor ignoring the complaints of the patient he heals. Most of the time we spent in bed. Mia generously offered all of herself, time and again reviving my interest in the bends and curves of her pliant body which she did not, as opposed to many women, use to protect herself like a shield and did not flaunt like a fashionable dress. Her movements and gestures, her embraces and fervent words were inseparable from some essence inside her. Her whole self seemed to be the embodiment of completeness. Probably even if she were feigning, she would put everything into it so no one would be able to distinguish the pretense from the truth. Any regular pleasure gained new life with her each time – especially since Mia knew no embarrassment and thoroughly embraced variety. A random spectator might have been flabbergasted if he glimpsed our activities between the sheets – but there were no spectators to be had, and it all seemed completely natural to us.

After we exhausted ourselves, Mia would switch over to concern for my comfort. She gave me tea and gin, washed me in the tub, firmly rejecting all my efforts to help her, sang me songs in a low voice, propping her elbow on the pillow and gazing seriously into my eyes. In three days it seemed I had lived half a life with her, soaking up more than I had with others in a few years – and this was solely her achievement, my own role remained passive. At first I didn't even know how to behave with her – the commercial nature of our relations, mixed with their enviable ardor, confused me and made me uptight. Everything was not as it should have been, that is, as I would have imagined it: inviting a pretty girl into my room and agreeing with her on the price; flirting a bit just out of habit but knowing very well I'm buying her body – and putting the illusions aside. Some of the things are never easy to buy – you can't even mention them in your business offer, foreseeing the cold astonishment. But Mia was a stranger to all coldness and offered a peek into her most secret compartments without any affectation. It seemed she knew I could fully appreciate what was being concealed until the best times arrived, or she became momentarily convinced the best times were now, already there, and the riches could be pulled out of the dark. Sometimes, tormented by absurd jealousy, I tried to guess what she was like with others and what they, those unworthy ones, would get out of her. Perhaps she's quite different with them, I assured myself. She's probably reserved and professional and impersonal – otherwise her strengths would end soon and her soul would wear thin for nothing. But some itching doubt stole up on me: what if her resources were actually limitless, so that in a few days anyone can obtain as much as they need for years and she'd still have more than enough for the rest?

Then, for simplicity, I agreed with myself on the undeniable fact of the pecuniary component which, however you twist it, should be accepted as the main basis. And the other part, whether an illusion or not, I had to regard as good luck and enjoy while I had the chance. It's no one's fault that Mia's conscientiousness couldn't be rarer and she fulfills her obligations without searching for an easy way out. An unpleasant aftertaste remained from the word "obligation," although I'd only said it to myself. I winced at the false note, understanding, however, there was nothing dumber than inventing a mendacious depth which would promptly lead to problems. I didn't need problems, and I had to admit: let Mia be my reward, which came at just the right moment. I didn't know why they gave it to me, but I sensed I deserved it.

Mia didn't ask me about the past, perhaps due to her professional ethics, but did talk willingly about herself and wasn't at all bothered by my persistent questions. I really wanted to know more about her – as if to store it for closing the inevitable future gaps and feed them piece by piece to my voracious memory. That's why I often interrupted her with requests for elaboration, and Mia patiently ushered up partially forgotten events and faces, shook off the dust and refreshed the details, ready to return to them again and again. And sometimes I left her in peace and simply listened to her melodic speech with its assiduously pronounced vowels, imagining where she had been and lived, and following her with a curious eye.

Mia grew up in a small town in northern Norway. Most of the population consisted of her close and distant relatives, who owned the land and buildings, as well as farmhands and servants who helped manage the household. A few other families lived there, too, and earned a living by fishing, but they were looked down upon since their small boats and pitiful shanties were clearly inferior to the massive property of her clan. Mia was allowed to play with the fishermen's children, but it was frequently emphasized they were not equal to her. And the fishers themselves she saw only on Sundays in the local church, which all the townspeople duly attended.

The main thing in their life was increasing the family's wealth, which was no easy matter because of the brutal temperatures, repeatedly bad weather, and other northern nastiness. The winter nights were cruel: the sun shined for just a few hours and the rest of the time it was completely dark, and there were blizzards and snowstorms in late autumn, which cut the place off from the rest of the world – it was impossible to cross the sea or to travel along the mountain roads. Every form of life froze in the rocky fiords; only the waves crashed and the wind whistled, and it seemed the land had been dead for thousands of years and their hamlet was the last to remain. This was hard to take; that's why the locals didn't complain about trifles – they knew what was permitted to think and say and what had to be avoided and driven out like a dangerous whim. Commercial concerns were the most reliable soil for the unity of opinion, and the family business had firmly established itself as the main criterion of human value.

Everyone had to work efficiently and endlessly. Everyone could do everything – from her childhood, Mia was also taught various trades, and her sincerity and devotion to diligence had been soaked up with her mother's milk. She was especially good at handling the domestic livestock, which were respected no less than the laboring hands, and they even called her when it was necessary to calm a mischievous cow or horse, with whom she would find a common language. With people, Mia had a harder time, and many didn't like her. They considered her an upstart and a hotshot, although she wasn't presumptuous – and didn't see any reason for it, sincerely believing she was no different from the others. Still, many whispered behind her back, and when Mia grew up, the gossip became even meaner and more frank. They suspected her of a wide range of sins and proclivities, some of which she had never even heard of in her naïvety back then. Finally, someone came right out and called her a witch. Word spread through the village, and her father set Mia in a sleigh and took her to the nearest city, placing her in a private college that was quite expensive but seemed to be less of an evil than the future losses from unrest with the simpleminded locals.

"He regarded them as morons," she said, grinning craftily. "Yet to tell you the truth, many of them knew what they were doing. But he didn't want to think about it – he declared me a schismatic because I caused a schism, and there was nothing worse than a schism. And my task was quite clear: to learn different things, and then he would think about how to use me to return what had been spent. With that he rode away and I remained – certainly afraid, but not that much…"

Mia liked it in the city, and best of all she liked the college, where she instantly found friends who adored her. They taught her to curl her hair and choose clothing, and she entertained everyone from evening to evening with stories of her life in the coastal fiords, concocting lots of tales and mixing reality with characters from children's books she had inherited from her older brothers and sisters. She was always willing to have heart-to-heart talks with roommates if one of them had intimate secrets on her mind – and no one suspected her of perverse peculiarities anymore, so soon Mia blossomed and let her soul run free. She didn't really like studying, but, accustomed to doing everything properly, she wanted to succeed there too, making it with some difficulty to the second year, when they discovered her aptitude for foreign languages, after which everything went quite well.

Her relatives wrote to her more and more rarely, and she, although at first missing the northern countryside where she had spent her childhood, soon got so acclimated to the new place that she forgot to think about the gloomy customs and dull people of her village. As for the future, she didn't bother to make any plans, assuming, as her friends did, that it would work out on its own. And that's what happened, although it ended up somewhat differently than anyone would have suggested.

A bump emerged in the smooth flow of events and afterward, an abrupt turn. It started when Mia completed her third year of school

– the second-to-last of the mandatory four. Officials from Oslo arrived in their city along with a rainy spring. They were searching the depths of Norway for girls to compete for the title of the most attractive Norwegian – not to be confused with the vulgar display of half-naked pretties with painted faces. No, those competitors weren't supposed to flaunt their bodies in bikinis in public, exhibiting themselves for show. On the contrary, true modesty was thoroughly welcomed, while enchantment and liveliness were also valued, as well as housekeeping skills and a general spirit of national distinctiveness. Two of her best friends dragged Mia along to a tryout, and they, filled with envy, kicked themselves afterward. Unexpectedly, she became a local star, outshining all the other participants in both the preliminary and the main qualifying rounds, which was mentioned in an excerpt with a bad photo in the daily local newspaper. Her success surprised Mia, but the experts from the capital were fascinated – undoubtedly, she conveyed the aforementioned Norwegian distinctiveness in its most exemplary form. Of course, her domestic proficiency played its role, but this alone would hardly surprise the judges. The city was full of well-proportioned, cherubic girls able to do everything necessary in a household. Mia possessed something greater: she just had to say a word, smile, or simply walk across the stage, and no one doubted her sterling victory.

Soon Mia was taken to Oslo to prepare for the decisive contest – and there things didn't go that smoothly, although she definitely liked and even later found handy the choreography classes they had every day. Then the sessions ended and the crucial day approached, but it never came. Disorder broke out in the organization of the pageant; the press raised a ruckus; and some slicksters, promising riches and plush jobs around the world, began to swirl around the attractive Norwegians, taking advantage of the pause.

Mia was the first to agree to an offer – the whirling winds of change intoxicated her like music or wine, and she didn't want to stop halfway. She landed in another country with an Italian producer who took her virginity, which didn't really impress her much. He showed her a few expensive hotels with luxury that astonished her only at first, and tried to fix her up with one of the talent agencies or get her cast in elaborate shows, but fortune did not smile on them. Gradually, the Italian became impatient, got irritated over nothing, and reproached Mia for her inability to present herself, and then informed her future attempts were useless. Her ankles were too thick, he said, and were impossible to alter, as breast or hips would be, so she could dump any thought of the podium or the stage. She took it coolly – the winds of change were dying down and no longer made her head spin. They still remained together for a while and then separated, tired of each other. A new producer engaged Mia, but he had no more success, and then she decided she was sick of men offering help and a firm shoulder, and began to rely on herself.

Mia didn't want to return home – she had gotten used to the warmer climate, and the thought of polar nights horrified her. She made a living with random jobs, mainly dancing in clubs and bars until an elderly regular at one of them made her a blatant offer. The quick cash was to her liking – especially, Mia stressed, for such an insignificant thing, which may even be pleasant – and since then it had been easy for her to make ends meet. The following two years she changed countries and places a few times and finally settled here, in the City of M., which was more comfortable than the capitals where life was tough and reckless and everyone wanted more from each other than they were capable of giving. Furthermore, there was the ocean – she often went to the coast and wandered along it for hours. It was gloomy and strong and gentle and similar to the immense northern seas. And the prices were lower, Mia added, and there were heaps of tourists. She was very popular and even wondered whether or not she should find a permanent boyfriend among the locals. Jeremy, for example, was very, very nice – but she still hadn't decided and, really, there was no reason to rush: she had enough time, and it was a serious step. She knew men, so it was better not to hurry and save as much money as possible first.

With that she abruptly broke off her story. The thought again flashed through my mind: is everything so simple in our seclusion, and is she not fancying some invisible nets, with Jeremy dragged in only to divert me? But Mia gazed tranquilly, you could hardly suspect her of duplicity. So I calmed down and used the subsequent silence as a reason to kiss her, which Mia, as always, responded to with eager willingness.

The whole time the surrounding world showed no more interest in us than we did in it – that is, none at all. Almost no one disturbed us. Only once did the same sniffling youngster come in, freezing in the doorway and trying not to look at Mia, and wheeze nasally that my car had been repaired and the sign hung in it again, as before; that it would be better to pay now, and I should decide for myself how much the repairs cost. I turned to the wardrobe where my bag was hidden, while Mia, just wearing a carelessly closed robe, went up to the messenger and asked in a strict tone why I had to pay now and how he could not know the exact price. He looked up, shrank back against the wall, and stiffened, so I told her to leave the boy alone, seriously afraid a nervous shock would overwhelm him. I then gave him some money and thanked him politely, but he, without even glancing at the bills, just licked his lips feverishly and slipped out of the room. Mia laughed for a long time, mocking his fretting face.

Besides the stripling, only an elderly waiter came and brought food and removed empty plates. Mia didn't, by any means, suffer from a lack of appetite and selected all the dishes for us both, elaborately explaining on the phone how they should be prepared. Then she examined what they gave us, not letting the waiter go until she had completed her review.

"I eat a lot of fruit," she told me when we, starving, enthusiastically worked our forks and knives. "Fruit is healthy; it improves your skin. But you men need meat and sometimes fish, but not any fish. There are fish that are not very good for men," – and she presented an entire lecture on fish dishes and their various qualities. "Cod helps your eyesight, but it can make your head ache, while fresh tuna is very beneficial to your stomach. Salmon is good for everyone, but you get tired of it quickly and then you need to eat some trout – it drives off the memory of salmon. And you should never eat lobsters. They are only for gluttons and make your belly grow and your brain lazy," Mia said categorically and I nodded, observing with distracted interest how she licked jam from her fingers or sunk her teeth into a firm green apple.

"Look at this orange!" she exclaimed, summoning me as a witness before the waiter, who lingered obediently. "It has the right form and is very beautiful. It has a thick rind to preserve all the juice, but I bet there isn't enough juice in it to start with, while the flesh is probably hard from sitting around too long. Take it away, please," Mia requested kindly but firmly, "and bring us another, a better one. And if they're all like this, just good for deceiving people, then it would be better to bring us bananas and a piece of melon." And the waiter departed, shuffling his swollen legs, and returned with a replacement, again patiently awaiting her verdict.

"A chicken leg is very good!" Mia informed me when we were finally alone and dug into our food. "My grandma said in our childhood if girls eat a lot of chicken, they'll grow feathers. That's because I always asked for it, but they crammed me full of cheaper things. And I was and remain indifferent to pork chops, although they were considered the greatest delicacy in our household and were served on holidays with raspberries and whortleberries and juniper liquor. Speaking of liquor – pour me some gin. I want to be a little drunk and lewd after lunch. Do you like the food, my dear?"

At some point on the second day I lost track of time. It seemed we had been locked in the room for ages, unable to remove the spell on the walls and get out. However we had a goal that gave us confidence, and our state of limbo did not appear senseless. We were waiting for Jeremy, each in our own way, knowing his appearance would break the magic.

The day would begin, turn pale, and vanish. We ate, napped, had sex, and talked about all sorts of odds and ends. I would recount hassles in the capital and dull days in the office, a boring routine full of nonsense. I would tell her about Lyubomir Lyubomirov and his scornful melancholy, which couldn't be hidden in either a dim light or in cigarette smoke. Then I would go on about rhymes and lines that entered my head at the right or wrong time, disturbing me with something unexplored, which an invisible being would whisper about, and which I never properly heeded. In turn Mia entertained me with descriptions of glaciers and rock slopes that glittered like mica and were sharp like razor blades. She would relate accounts of fishers' tricks and the brutality of those struggling against the cruelty of nature that didn't pardon human weakness. Sometimes we battled in cards, and I usually lost. Here, too, Mia demonstrated a rare determination I was too lazy to contend with. For every loss, though, she rewarded me with caresses and took sympathetic interest as to whether or not I was angry and maybe even secretly cursing myself. And only when she was convinced everything was okay with me did she start the next game, her steely skill catching every blunder I made.

Once Mia spoke about me and said she liked me a lot, which happened quite rarely, and that I was a good lover, which occurred more often, but by no means all the time. "I could even have fallen in love with you," she reasoned seriously, "if, of course, we had met differently. But now – now it can't be, and that's unfortunate, although I probably shouldn't get upset about it. There's a catch to all good luck and to every pursuit as well, no matter how much you try, and long ago I learned all of mine. It's you who might become sorry – and maybe you already are. Of course, if I was to fall for you, then you couldn't help but do the same. Don't laugh – I'm telling the truth: a girl can get whatever she wants if she knows the right words. It's certainly a pity they're different for everyone, but for you I would have found the right ones easily – and not many of them would've been needed. I'm a different story – I would have required a whole book. And even so, I would've searched for the hidden meaning between the lines anyway, double-checking and weighing it this way and that and swinging each one to and fro. All because I stand firmly on my two feet, and you – you tiptoe and are chasing something you can't even see. But then you're big, and I'm – well – small, although of course I'm tall, and you're not…"

I listened attentively, picking through her hair. Mia recited everything she could have loved me for if we had met randomly or there had been no catch to her pursuits – my even teeth, dense hair, the ironic crease in my mouth. "And you walk with a slight spring in your step," she added with a chuckle and stopped talking to think about something.

I regarded her and admitted to myself I'd never had a woman like her and probably never would again. I had dreamed of her many times and hadn't wanted the dream to turn into reality. For three days Mia had been sent to me, like a fantasy which is way too brief and will never become real.

"I wonder," I asked casually, "could you think up something other than my walk and ironic wrinkle? I mean, some oddity of all oddities, which no one else has – or are the exceptions discarded and only the rules count?"

"No one else has…" Mia repeated gently and touched my monkey's hand. "What can it possibly be?"

She lay down on her back and threw her arms over her head. Something tapped at the window. It was raining, and the room became even more inaccessible to any enemy from outside, like a fortress, the firmness of which had been well-tested.

"Exceptions…" said Mia. "Exceptions are good, but they don't last long. Can you fall in love with what doesn't last long?"

"I don't know," I replied, stroking her like a large kitten. "I don't know about exceptions, forget about them. But what about a secret, what if we call it that? Otherwise it's worthless – then everything is just accidents and a little common sense… However, don't listen to me. I'm not good at falling in love. Now I'm trying to like, at least, myself, and even that doesn't always work."

Mia closed her eyes, almost purred, then smiled and swung her head from side to side. "No," she drawled, "a secret won't help here. In love, no advantage comes from it. While it's in you and you don't let it out, then it isn't noticeable – it's unripe and doesn't want to be told. If someone drags it out, then he regrets it, and you yourself regret it even more. That's why you keep silent – and only when silence becomes unbearable do you give everything away to someone, like me, for example. Then the secret stops being a secret, and your life goes the same way it did before – the exceptions don't last long, I warned you – until something new germinates inside. Many people never experience that, or do once and never again. And others – they can't live without that, some candle is always burning. They can't love – the candle distracts them – and it's also frightening to love these people. That almost happened to me once, and it probably would've been better if it hadn't, although I didn't forget it and want more. But that doesn't have to do with exceptions, that's a rule, only you have to apply it cleverly and not waste the effort on whatever comes your way. The candle's a rule, but you can't make rules from secrets. They are just for your own use – to walk around with a bored expression or look down on others. But I also don't really want to judge that. I don't have anything like it, although I can perceive – both the one and the other and those who don't have it at all…"

Then evening and night swooped in. Mia fell asleep quickly, and I lay gazing into the darkness and thought about Julian, imagining how any secret stops being a secret, losing its halo and turning into a momentary life. Finally, I dozed off and in the morning, at breakfast, I surprised even myself by suddenly starting to talk about Jeremy and my job for him. Then I switched to Julian and didn't desist until I had babbled out everything down to the last details of my new plan, ruefully recalling how I had once told it all to Stella, and how no good had come of that. "Everything," however, was not quite everything this time. I was more cautious and didn't utter a word about the revolver or Vera or even my past career intrigues, and certainly didn't make Julian the epitome of the world's imperfection. No point in explaining why I needed him and no one else; no point in painting abstract pictures in the air. Just the tip of the iceberg suffices, and the rest is an exception that doesn't last long, which is why silence rules here, as in my luckily found formula.

So no, not everything, moreover Mia was not Stella, I reminded myself, chasing away my doubts. She's not a common woman with her own skein of concerns against which she tries you out, voluntarily or not. She is an illusion, a dream which will dissolve and no longer belong to me. Any future was possible to imagine with her because there wouldn't actually be any. I can place her right next to me, there where all the rest couldn't last long because for them it was uncomfortable and entirely pointless. I can even decide the barriers don't exist anymore; someone understood me at the very first hint, following me into the labyrinth, not getting bored in the dead ends, and not complaining when the tricky paths lead back to the starting point. It still wouldn't happen – not this way or another – but, look, she's sitting in front of me, the unselfish priestess of prepaid intimacy, and I'm not scared of sharing anything with her because she is like the one I always wanted, who I thought up and now need.

"I was going to destroy him," I told her sullenly, "but that was a really bad idea. It's good I had time to think it over, otherwise I would have been ashamed afterward. Furthermore I realized: it wouldn't resolve anything, wouldn't tip the scales in my favor, because no one would take a close look. That plan was just a childish plot, and I began to think over a different one, but everything I chose turned out to be nothing. Then I stopped thinking and simply started to toss off all the parts, one after the other, erasing and no longer returning until just one remained. That's how I decided – and there was nothing else to decide…"

I spoke extensively and indistinctly, but Mia didn't rush me. When I finished, she asked me to tell it all over again and confirmed my new plan was good and could no longer be a secret. We chit-chatted for a few hours, discussing details that even gave Mia a role, which excited her so much she even danced for me a little – something she had never done before. The dance switched over to ardent caresses, and we didn't get out of bed until dusk, and then simply lay in the dimness, talking quietly, like old accomplices, and waiting for Jeremy. The last of the days he required for the searches was inexorably approaching its close.

CHAPTER 11

Jeremy appeared around six o'clock. He knocked and waited at the door while I rushed to pull on my pants and ushered Mia into the bathroom with a pile of clothes in her hands. Then he came in and sat down at the table, darting his sly eyes at the bed that had been turned on its head.

"Well?" I asked. "How'd it go? Did you find anything out?"

"No need to worry," he replied civilly, but with some coldness in his voice. "We found everything – we wouldn't have accepted the job if we couldn't. We also, you know, value our time, and when a client is dissatisfied, then time is thrown away."

Jeremy chewed his lips, pulled a folded piece of paper out of his pocket, and spread it on the table. I was beginning to extend my hand but was met with a preemptive gesture. "One moment," said Jeremy. "First of all, if you'll allow me, I'll give you a brief overview. The file here," he pointed at the paper, "the file contains all the data you need, but it doesn't hurt to hear the details, too. So please be patient." He covered the sheet with his hand, leaned against the back of the stool, and began to tell the story in his baritone voice.

"Your friend, in truth, is not being particularly careful. Nor is he very original, I might add. We found him in The Yellow Arrow – a famous place for visitors who want to enjoy a drink after work. He sat by himself the whole time there, a modest guy – sat and nursed his cheap beer. He didn't play pool or cards with the fellows, didn't even wink at the girls. My detectives soon got bored. Very uninteresting man, they said, a scarecrow on a pole would be more entertaining to look at. I silenced them, of course, to keep everything in order, but I have to admit: the guy's pretty colorless. No life in him – although, he looks quite composed and is probably contemplating something in his head. But no one knows what that might be – he certainly offers no hints, only chats with the neighbors sometimes about nonsense and quiets down again, like the smoothness of a lake. Try and guess what kind of devils hide there, in the lake... And I don't understand how a woman could live with him."

He nodded pensively, then coughed and with the words, "Alright, let's get serious," switched to recounting the bare facts. Julian, according to his watchers, frequents the aforementioned cafe every day – from six to nine. At nine he leaves punctually and heads straight home – "The address is here," Jeremy clapped the sheet. A person of the female gender waits for him there – the detectives did not "escort" her because nobody asked them to do that, but they caught a glimpse of her a few times and took down a short wordy note: brunette, not tall or short, nice face, but not outrageously attractive, has a haughty look, probably not a local.

I narrowed my eyes. The description could easily match Vera, and this added a new twist. My mind instantly became alert and even sent a momentary signal with the long-forgotten question mark at the end, but nothing came in response and I calmed down. No memory stirred in my soul. Something had gone away without leaving a replacement, and that alarmed me for a moment, but I decided I'd figure it out later.

"He leaves for work early," Jeremy continued, "but he doesn't put his heart into it. He may be absent for up to a half-day, and nobody cares. He works, by the way, in FF – the security is tight, so we didn't manage to find out a whole lot. We know one girl there, in the offices, but she's a real dumbbell, and we didn't get much from her. She only said he hadn't been there long, had been brought in on a temporary basis – like a consultant or something of that sort. Otherwise, she just made eyes and giggled – ha-ha-ha – as if someone were tickling her, the idiot. So we didn't get too far with work, though we've studied everything with regard to his lunch habits. We can name the restaurants, and what he likes to order – including the whole menu on any specific day..."

Jeremy expanded on his report for a quarter of an hour, thoroughly describing what Julian was wearing and furnishing me with his recent picture. Julian sat at a table, listlessly looking off to the side and pouting a bit. I was surprised to see he had begun to grow a goatee, which did not fit him at all. But the rest of his appearance had not undergone any noticeable change. Only a slightly apparent shabbiness had emerged in his features, yet that was probably a consequence of a laidback provincial life.

"So," Jeremy said when he had finished his monologue. "We did what we could. And here's the paperwork – with dry, soulless material."

He handed over the "material" somewhat solemnly, and I thanked him somewhat solemnly, inquiring, as if it were beside the point, whether or not I should add a bonus for the detectives. "A bonus isn't necessary, it'll spoil them," replied Jeremy with a snicker. "Let's calculate it all again. There was a search, then a car we repaired for you... And a girl. By the way, did you like the girl?"

I nodded dryly and gave him a sullen look from under my brow, feeling a needle suddenly prick me. "Okay, okay," said Jeremy, eyeing me searchingly for a response, then raised his eyes to the ceiling, chewed his lips, and summed it up, "Yes, I think, everything works out – if, of course, you don't have any objections."

I understood I had paid him too much, but it would be dumb to negotiate now, and it wasn't worth regretting money that had come my way by chance. "No, no objections," I said curtly. Jeremy again tossed a brief, almost derisive glance at me, yet instantly put on his regular mask, and we said goodbye, shaking hands. The scent of grease wafted through the room, like an intrusive messenger ousting the aura of comfort accumulated there over the last three days. Instead came a sense of administrative formalness, as if someone were paging through a dull document. I opened the window, letting the cold and sounds of the street into the cozy den. Then I sat a little longer on the bed, mumbling jumbled phrases, put the sheet I'd received from Jeremy at the bottom of my bag, and went to the bathroom for Mia.

She was splashing and singing in soapy water – carefree and gorgeous, like a model stepping out of a TV commercial. "Oh," she exclaimed on seeing me, "the men have finished their business and returned to their abandoned girlfriends. Do you want to jump in?"

I shook my head, but Mia extended her arm and tried to drag me to her. Realizing she wouldn't succeed, she heaved a sigh and said with feigned sadness, "That's how you get pushed away when you offer yourself to a man…" And she added, laughing in response to my sour face, "Okay, okay, don't frown. I'm joking!"

"Forget the jokes," I demanded, winking and trying to look a little more cheerful. "The real work begins now. We need to finish bathing and move into the ready position. Any questions?"

"No, boss!" Mia retorted gallantly and gave me a salute. Then with a surprised "Oops," she pinched her nose and plunged her head under the water.

"At ease," I muttered gloomily and traipsed back into the bedroom, closing the door behind me.

Mia returned completely dressed and began to collect the remains of her things. Her hair was braided, her eyes and lips were carefully penciled. Everything about her seemed older and more removed than just an hour ago. I told her in a nutshell about The Yellow Arrow and Julian's habits, adding it would be possible to catch him that very evening if she hurried up. "Chasing me out, chasing me away…" Mia grumbled into the air, but I knew she was just teasing me and didn't listen. "And your photo?" she asked, and I angrily slammed my hand on the table, cursing my short memory. Then I had to call downstairs, search for Jeremy and explain the situation. Fortunately, he understood my sense of urgency and rushed up in a quarter of an hour with an old Polaroid. An appropriate photo was instantly produced. Jeremy departed with another handshake and a look in the eye. Mia and I were alone again and knew it was time to part.

"Well," she began briskly but got confused. "No, I wanted to put it differently – just a sec."

I cheered her up with a buffoonish nod.

Mia rubbed her temples, raised her head, smiled, and straightened. "Attempt number two," she informed an invisible audience on the side. "Well, please, think of me occasionally…"

We looked at each other as if on command, burst out in caustic laughter, and Mia threw herself around my neck. I hugged her as hard as I could. We stood like that for a minute or two, then she let go carefully, pecked me on the cheek, let her fingers slide down it, as she'd once done with the monkey's hand, and slipped out of the room, leaving the scent of sensual perfume and the empty bottle of gin.

I never saw her again. The depressing city swallowed Mia up, turned her into a stashed-away story only I knew, as in an endless universe, all the parts of which quickly fly apart. I was smarting from the wound, but there was no sense in denying it.

If you place a bet on one card, then you don't long for the rest of the deck, I said to myself dryly, looking around to see whether my thoughts, brimming with regrets, were intending a mutiny. If you bet on what's inside you, then you don't wait for the outer world to extend a helping hand. And if extended, don't take it: every helping hand offers a heap of unwanted concerns. You don't need them; otherwise, your prospects fade, the focus becomes fuzzy, and the goal slips away inexorably. What's inside you won't forgive imprecision.

Everything was fair, everything was painful and difficult. I cursed quietly, dug out the paper covered with Jeremy's scribbled handwriting, and began to memorize the addresses and figures, phone numbers and names of places, as if recalling what was supposed to be more important than anything else. These completely useless exercises distracted me from sad thoughts, especially since the thread uniting me and Mia had not yet been broken completely. The hands of the clock were approaching nine – if her mission unfolded successfully, the phone would ring soon. I brought it closer to the head of the bed, lay on my back and closed my eyes.

Mia called in an hour. "Everything's arranged, my dear," she assured me. "I'm sorry to have kept you waiting. I overdid it slightly and couldn't get away." I heard a brief chuckle at the other end, which told me she wasn't completely sober. "Make yourself comfortable; I'm going to report it all in order…"

According to our plan, Mia had to initiate the action – prod Julian into taking the first step. I wanted him to seek a meeting with me, not vice versa, and I didn't doubt Mia would achieve her end. I knew her determination wasn't easy to resist, even if you suspected some hidden danger. Julian could hardly have grounds for suspicion, especially since, in general, contemplation wasn't really one of his habits. That's how it turned out – as in a written-out scenario, with some improvisation that always comes in handy.

"I recognized him right away," Mia was saying swiftly. "He sat in the corner and looked exactly as he did in the photo – the little beard and everything else. He sipped his beer, glancing around dully, and I went up to the adjacent table and asked for a lighter from two twerps who started staring at my legs and exchanging glances. Disgusting guys – I got great pleasure out of hurling their Ronson back and informing them it didn't work and was probably a knockoff, so their faces became long and they opened their mouths. You know, one of them even had a gold tooth," she added and snickered.

"So," Mia continued, again turning serious and efficient, "we squabbled a little until everyone around us began to look in our direction. Then I spun around to face your Julian and grimaced innocently, and said to him in the sweetest of voices, 'You wouldn't by chance have something to light the cigarette of a solitary girl?' Any man would loosen up and give me whatever I needed, not just the lighter that I handled so gracefully and thanked him for so profusely. He was all eyes, though I didn't say anything else – just gave him a modest smile and started to walk away. But then I got clumsy with my little backpack. I swung it carelessly on the walk and – bang! – hit his bottle, made it fall, and sent beer spilling onto the floor. Your friend sprung up with enviable nimbleness so the drink wouldn't fall on his pants, and I jumped to the side in fright and accidentally bumped right into him – an extra measure, just in case, to increase the effect. Of course, there were oohs and aahs, my apologies and his concern for whether I had hurt myself, and all that sort of stuff. When everything calmed down a little, I said modestly, toning down my gaze, 'Wouldn't you like to come to the bar with me until they wipe off your spot here? I'd like to treat you to something strong instead of that crummy beer that's dripping on the floor and completely unsuitable for use.' And, of course, he wanted to come with me and he wanted to treat me – so we strolled away, and those two with their Ronson followed us, gaping and burning with fierce jealousy. It served them right. Not everyone gets lucky, as they say."

The rest unfolded exactly as we planned it. Mia had just made herself comfortable on a barstool beside Julian when she began to ask him the what and how: where he came from, how he earned a living and so on, untying his tongue with shameless, crude flattery. "He says quite humbly, I'm from the capital," she told me, mimicking Julian's voice very well. "And I exclaim – from the ca-pi-tal? Oh! And point out to him that the capital is quite different, of course, and the people there are different, and that I'd been there once and know that men from the capital – they are... Oh! Not just these awkward locals. And I roll my eyes – some emotional coloring, if it isn't excessive, never does any harm – so he, the poor guy, even turned a little red and got completely confused. Then I took the next step: 'Do you know,' I asked seriously, 'that you have a very expressive face?' No, he replies, he didn't, and starts to look somewhat agitated – probably guessing I'm a dork or some wacko. So I assure him with the most open smile: I'm no wacko, just a specialist – a photographer, a retoucher. I make stories out of reality and the stories become truly real. And then I enlightened him a little on the subject, adding on details that made his head spin..."

Mia knew no small amount about retouching photographs – although only in theory, having heard a lot on it from one of her longstanding clients. The old guy liked to chat for hours and told her how his profession was improving the world, using a lot of technical jargon in the process. Meticulous Mia always demanded explanations and ultimately picked up enough terminology to show off to laymen if need be. The old photographer honestly considered himself and his colleagues to be the only people who had discovered the recipe for rejuvenation, even if illusory, achieving the miracle by upgrading the raw material while maintaining the visual similarity. He believed that illusory youth, although it did in some way lack the quality of the real thing, was a fairly good alternative, especially in the absence of a choice. And, in some aspects, he insisted, it even had solid advantages. Not quite solid, Mia noted, recalling that the optimistic retoucher had passed away a year ago due to a rare heart disease. However, she did still have respect for retouching photographs and loved to put her knowledge on display when given the chance.

"Julian believed me immediately," she reported, very satisfied with herself. "Believed me and asked questions too – in other words, showed interest. Generally speaking, he seemed fairly nice," she giggled again, and I coughed dryly, telling her not to get distracted.

"Alright, alright. Don't get jealous," Mia murmured. "You're better than all the others, no matter what. Your Julian may be amiable, I don't deny it, but he has slippery eyes and is pompous in some sense. In this 'some sense' he's blown up like a balloon – I don't like that type. So, he was sold on the retouching – nodded enthusiastically and all that. And I was all modesty – didn't even let him touch my hand. Just complete inaccessibility, no flirting or other nonsense, and then I saw the right moment had come. It was time to make the decisive move – and I was about to do just that when he himself, without letting me say a word, crawled into the mousetrap and the door closed behind him.

Could you, miss, he asks me – we were still speaking formally, not taking liberties – could you take a professional shot of my wife – with the subsequent, obligatory retouching? I reply to him seriously that I probably could, why not? And then I casually wonder outloud, with a hint of compassion, is she that much older than him? Here he began to squirm, became even more agitated, and sputtered that no, she isn't older at all, she isn't even his wife, to be truthful.

They just live together, that's how it turned out – but when people live together, then nothing is simple. And she doesn't have a good photograph, what a pity, while he wants, he said, to carry her photo around in his wallet, occasionally glance at it and admire her. So the better it is, the more frequently he'll want to pull it out to enjoy.

'And show others to give them pleasure,' I added in the same tone. 'Yes, yes, and others too,' Julian agreed. 'Very good,' I said, 'this is exactly what I do well. Tell me your phone number, pleeaase. I'll call you and we'll arrange everything.' And here, without delay, I switched over to the main feature of the program. I dug into my spectacular backpack and pulled out my little notebook with various pieces of paper sticking out of it. Yes, I'm an artist of sorts, I've got a creative character, and I'm inclined to be a bit disorderly. And here I did something awkward, the book opened, the papers fell on the table with your picture on the very top – right in front of him.

The backpack also fell – on the floor, very unhygienic. I gasped, slid off the stool, took the backpack, and blew it off on all sides. When I sat up again and raised my eyes, your friend was already caught: he was staring right at the photo, looking and not shifting his gaze. Done, I thought – and carefully turned his attention back to me.

'You see,' I told him, 'everything slips out of my hand. Alright, give me your number; I'm ready to write it down.'

'Yes, yes,' he replies, 'please, please, and by the way, who is this? Did you touch him up too?'

'That?' I ask. 'No, that's something else.' And I made a thoughtful face and turned away, as if protecting something – either a secret or my sensitive soul…"

Mia sighed and said gloomily, "Yes, that was the sad part. Let me smoke."

"Are you tired?" I asked. "This is quite a story you're telling me…"

"Not at all," she cut in. "Just listen; the most interesting part is coming. So I turned away…"

Mia recounted the further course of events in the same detail, not hiding the pride she took in her overall success. Julian confessed he knew the man in the photo from the ancient past. "What a coincidence!" she exclaimed, then lowered her voice and informed him under an oath of the utmost secrecy that she and I were not at all connected on a professional level but had been involved in a romantic episode that had unfortunately ended not long ago, yet left such a noticeable trace in her heart she still lacked the courage to remove the photograph from her wallet and shove it into some distant corner. In accordance with our plan, Mia portrayed herself as the victim of male callousness, unjustly forgotten for the benefit of incomprehensible "business," which for men, alas, so frequently turns out to be more important than impulses of spirit. She also referred to some "serious connections" I had, at some point, mentioned in passing, and, not dithering with epithets, she hinted at the great prospects I was supposed to have in front of me – if they hadn't already been realized.

"He listened quite attentively," Mia said. "He listened and his eyes became sharper and sharper. I was trying to guess whether I had gone far enough or not, whether I should let up – and I finally decided that's sufficient or I'll overplay it. And I stopped talking and lowered my eyelashes, as if emotionally overwhelmed. I sat, silent, sipping my cocktail, detached and thinking to myself: what if he suddenly pays and leaves – then all my efforts are in vain. But no, your Jules coughed, wheezed uneasily, and declared: the coincidence is pretty damn amusing. Then he leant a little closer to me and asked quietly, almost whispering – is he, that is you, still in the city or not? Excuse me, he adds, for the indiscreet question.

Yes, he's in the city, I replied sadly, but for poor me it doesn't matter. I see, I see, he said, and then he got really interested. Do I not know, he asked, where he could find his old friend? To chat, schmooze – about the past, about this and that.

I don't know, I said, shrugging with a proud, detached look. He used to be staying at the Arcada, I added. He's probably still there. If you want, honey – we were speaking informally now – you can call and ask. Only please, I grab him by the sleeve, pl-ea-se, don't mention me whatever you do. Promise me here and now. Otherwise I'm not letting you go!

So we agreed. I instantly switched the topic to something else, but that was it – Jules got bored and began to look at his watch. And for me it was also time to go – you, I thought, are already waiting, worried. I wrote down his phone number – you have it on that piece of paper by the way – and I wondered to myself, just out of curiosity, is he going to make a pass at me or what?

'So,' I said, innocently tilting my head, 'well then, see you later. Thanks for the pleasant company.'

'Later, later,' he replied distractedly, but his eyes didn't even glitter. 'I'm pleased to have met you,' he said. 'Call if you decide to take up that order for retouching.'

Phew, I thought, what a chicken – although I need him like one-day-old snow. And that's all – I flew out of there and ran to a phone to call you, my dear, to report I had done everything in my power…"

She broke off her phrase in the middle, and it hung, swinging helplessly, like a trapeze in the circus. The thread's been broken, I thought. It may have been way too thin, but it's still sad – its frailty is scary, like a hint at mortality. One way or the other, the act was over, the flying shadows descended from the cupola to the arena and lined up by the barrier, expecting applause.

"Don't get upset, Mia, your attractiveness is indisputable," I said to her gloomily. "Julian is just shy about tall women. We aren't alike in that respect, as in all others, by the way… So," I pondered for an instant, "so, you're a heroic figure. I thank you. I send you a kiss."

"Oh, stop it," Mia became confused, then suddenly got quiet, and silence hovered on the line. Only the electric static crackled, and our breaths rose and fell irregularly. Both of us understood we had nothing else to talk about. This was forever – the universe was expanding, the distances were growing every second, and in a few days would be translated into thousands of miles. Even memory would give in, misinterpreting details, and a familiar face in a crowd would seem strange and foreign behind the veil of concerns unknown to you.

"Goodbye, Mia," I said hoarsely and laid the receiver on the hook with a jerk. Ultimately, it's better to be abrupt, and that's it. Break it off immediately rather than inch to the end. It was intolerable to think I had been meanly deceived: the world had arranged a dirty trick and showed its real face – by pampering me, teasing me, and instantly taking it all away. But it had to be endured, and I knew I would get used to it, as I did to all other thoughts.

"Julian, Julian," I muttered my usual incantation aloud, rushing to feel the ground beneath my feet – the only foundation, fixed and lasting. Now it didn't help me much – no formula is all-powerful. But it was better than nothing, and I soon calmed down, making peace with myself. I thought about Mia, who had been with me just a few hours ago, with the customary sadness of a voyager who knows the price of loss, not letting my heart seize up in anguish. Then my mind tired and I fell asleep, rejecting the dreams that were ready with their gentle fans, like cunning servants who you always suspect of lying.

CHAPTER 12

Julian called the next day, shortly after noon. I knew it was him before I heard his voice – sensing the enemy by invisible magnetism, my hair tingling and a powerful dose of adrenaline bursting into my blood. All morning, wallowing in bed, I had been tuning myself to the right tone, occasionally drifting to recollections of Mia or something else – attractive and unrelated to the matter. Caught on that, my guilty thoughts lined up hurriedly to march in file over the well-trodden training grounds. But a minute later they would all disperse again – until the next stern command.

For some reason I was sure the call would come without delay. As soon as the ringer began to shake the phone, a hot wave coursed through my body. Before answering, I stopped for a second in the middle of the room and imagined myself to be a large tiger, directing an unblinking eye at its frozen victim. I tasted the saltiness in my mouth and even recognized the exultant tickling of the animalistic roar rising from my abdomen. "Hello," I said indifferently and was satisfied with myself: the situation was under control, my secret had moved out of the shadows with the light step of a predator accustomed to victories.

Julian, not suspecting anything, was all cordiality and openness. "Did you recognize my voice?" he asked straight off, looking forward to an unanticipated surprise. And with that he jabbered assertively, "Yes, yes, the world is small – any new city just reaffirms that. I admit I was startled when I heard you were here. And I decided to call right away, thinking I'd let an old friend be startled too… Where did I hear it? Well, I can't tell you everything off the bat. Everyone has their channels, you know. I don't just sit on my ass – that's not my way. Someone mentioned you by chance, dropped your name. I can't say, but believe me, some serious people talk about you. That's understandable – we are capital guys, rare birds in this hole…"

He prattled on in this vein, bringing in some nonsense about old times and somewhat officiously emphasizing a dubious *we*. His geniality didn't ebb, flavoring every phrase, and only my experienced ear could catch the hardly discernible automation of routine, the absence of real involvement, like metallic laughter. "Yes, that's him alright," I satisfied myself and calmed down completely, as at the end of a difficult trip when a familiar sight appears around the bend and you realize you've almost arrived and won't get lost now.

I replied without being too zealous and not evincing any particular surprise. Yes, it's always nice to hear a voice from the past – and here, far from the blessings of the enlightenment, when an old pal calls, it can only be a pleasure. Yes, I've been in M. for a few months, and about him, no, I hadn't known, had been busy, and there was no time to ask. But still, if it wasn't a secret, how had he found me? Though if it was a secret, then we'd drop it, forget it. It was just that I dealt with different people, and would like to know where our spheres crossed. Okay, okay, if you don't want to, don't answer. Then tell me – are you here for long?

And so on in that key, as if gradually losing interest in the talk, despite the effusive influence of Julian's sentimentality, whose reserves were also limited and soon exhausted themselves. I even let myself yawn slightly, demonstrating I had had enough of the prelude and expected further developments. Of course, there was the danger he would simply close out the conversation and say goodbye, after which I would have to think up an excuse and call him myself, adopting a weak position. But the confidence of an unblinking predator didn't leave me. It was as if I knew he knew I had something hidden, and it was really so, and gained strength every second. It seemed I was moving in circles, winding coil after coil – from my secret plan to my animate interlocutor, from him back to my plan – each time intensifying the feeling of the one and the other, steadily finding more confirmation of their pertinence to something important, massive, menacing. In the middle of this something I settled down – indeed like a predator waiting for the right moment. I didn't even have to be too friendly – Julian wouldn't want to slip away. The invisible magnetism acted on both sides – its field lines streamed in both directions and became entangled in a web of dangling curiosity whose tenacity is so difficult to overcome.

"Well," he said with a low laugh, "reveal it, tell me – how'd you end up here? They couldn't have sent you from us – I saw all the lists, and anyway I know that you jumped ship, so to speak, gave notice and disappeared without saying a word. I confess, I immediately thought: something isn't right, our Vitus has got a plan, he's a mysterious guy – but we heard nothing and even partially forgot you. Yet now I realize it wasn't all that simple; I was right back then. Admit it, I was right, wasn't I?"

"Right or not – the categories are relative," I replied with slight irony, pausing, as if weighing my words on an imaginary scale. "Everything depends on your own attitude toward them. I can say just one thing: yes, I have a lot in mind, I can assure you of that. In mind and almost in my hands – maybe even more in my hands. And with regard to being a mysterious guy – that's nonsense. That's probably from reading too many books, Julian. The key here is my new skin that grew in the favorable local air, not a mystery or fairy tale. You get it?"

"You bet," Julian played along with me.

No, you don't, I thought with satisfaction. You don't understand now and you never will.

"Yes," he said again, then coughed and asked cheerfully as if I hadn't said a thing, "So why are you here? I gather the firm didn't send you. So you came on your own?"

"Exactly," I responded calmly. "Why should I need the firm? It just gets in the way."

Julian chuckled as if he had solved a difficult riddle and blurted straight out, "If our firm gets in the way, that means some of the locals have paved the way for you. Tell me, is there something interesting? Lucrative? With prospects?"

I can tell you, I said to myself, but I don't think you'll find it interesting. Although there are prospects... I'll lay the bait for you – you asked for it yourself – but later, later, not yet.

Everything I needed had been ready for a while, yet I wasn't planning to pour it all out in our first phone call. And in general I didn't want to do it on the phone. I had to at least look at Julian and correlate my intentions with those aspects and vibrations which were flowing between us at that instant. And persuasion, if necessary, is all the more convenient eye to eye rather than through the pulsation of a cold, mechanical membrane. Moreover, long ago I had outlined the sequence of events, and point one, "call," was followed by number two, none other than "meet." Only then, but under no circumstances before, came the critical "deceive," and I didn't want to deviate from my plan, even if one always needs to allow for some flexibility.

"There are interesting things everywhere, Julian," I said, recalling Archibald and his raised index finger. "Only they aren't visible to everyone all the time."

"That's for sure," Julian agreed with a trace of a satisfaction. "I was always saying so. That means you've already dug something up – you even abandoned the capital. Shrewd, shrewd..."

We laughed and then I asked in the same tone, "And if I've dug up something, what then? Why do you think I'm going to share it with you?"

"What do you mean why?" Julian was surprised. "I'm assuming I'm the first to ask – of your old friends, I mean. The first to ask gets an answer – it has to be that way. And what's more, you know me pretty well," he rushed. "I've never had a loose tongue, and am more cautious than anyone else you know. And, I'm sure, it'll do you good – I'm also not just here for the heck of it and can help you if needed. As you should recall, I grasp things quickly!"

He's prying, I thought. No one's even asked him, but he's already clicked in. It reminds me of someone in the past, guess who.

I sighed and sort of drawled, as if giving in a little, "Well… As for your help, I don't need any, but still, there's one picture I could show you. And I'd share the story – a picture, you know, often comes with a story. But it's fairly long and certainly not for the phone."

"Definitely not for the phone!" Julian exclaimed. "Even leaving your picture aside. We haven't seen each other for almost six months, and you have new skin now – or are in a new hide… I was about to say we absolutely have to meet. Meet and talk – at our leisure and, I assume, without wives. I forgot to ask, by the way, how are family affairs looking?"

That was really too much, but I replied calmly, ignoring the last question, "Yes, let's meet and talk. Let me take a look: tomorrow's okay, after that two evenings are free in a week, then… What's your schedule?"

"On the whole not bad, I don't even know…" Julian began to dither. "I'm not particularly busy. Let's meet tomorrow then, or what?"

I quickly agreed, recommending somewhat insistently the restaurant in the Arcada, only to make sure the last decision would be made by me, and said goodbye in a businesslike manner, not reminiscing about our joint past and not even hiding I was in somewhat of a rush.

After putting down the receiver, I caught my breath and grinned at the silent phone. Everything was unfolding quite well. The predator was shifting into position for the crucial jump, focusing his yellow eyes on the carefree victim. Just don't make any abrupt moves, I reminded myself. It's easy to frighten him, and then you won't even catch his shadow. The abrupt movements, I had to admit, were my weak spot. Maybe the weakest of all, but it wasn't worth lamenting weaknesses at this point.

Now I had to take the next important step. I already had the necessary elements: the above-mentioned picture and a story, plus arrogance, bullshit and deceit, false friendliness and phony brass substituting for real gold. The whole set from that world in which the victim belonged, a pile of invented factors, guiding the object right into the trammel, limiting its freedom of movement and, ideally, excluding any possibility of escape. There was quite a bit to create, but the result would justify the means.

Tomorrow, tomorrow, I said to myself, inhaling and exhaling somewhat deeply. The adrenaline still didn't abate. My face was burning and my mind required action. It would be a good time for a game or two of *Dzhan*, I thought sorrowfully, although I knew it was impossible – there were no partners, not even an appropriate board. I tried playing out a simple setup in my head, but soon lost the thread and hounded myself into a completely absurd formation that was senseless to develop. Then, for distraction, I recalled Mia and her multicolored backpack, and afterward switched over to Jeremy and imagined the two of them married, admitting against my will that the picture was not lacking harmony. From somewhere or other I also took Arnold Ostraker, and Doctor Nemo seemed to appear nearby, occasionally blurting something in a weak descant. I was powerless to break free of them all, and that's how the rest of the day went – in wearisome inertia and interwoven fantasies that disturbed me without leaving a trace.

In the morning I went to a kiosk close by and hauled up a whole stack of fresh papers with the banal goal of filling the hours. They quickly set my teeth on edge. All the phrases were similar to each other, and the exaggerated cheerfulness of the words made me laugh like someone's idiocy put awkwardly on display. Moreover, my thoughts were soaring somewhere else. I was now news to myself, an amusing story – and what was happening with everyone else didn't concern me much. But I had to kill the time that remained until evening, and I distractedly examined the summaries of incidents, tiresome political discussions, and weather prognoses for the forthcoming season, which were hardly glittering with optimism. All told, the City of M. should not hope for a better climate and, consequently, for the status of an authentic resort town, which many of the reporters complained of, stubbornly glossing over the fact that hordes of tourists attracted by completely different things flocked here anyway. It was funny and intersected in some sense with the deceit I'd prepared, but the newspapers viewed the problem from a polar perspective. No sooner had I laughed at the journalistic tendency to close their eyes to the main issues, intransigently regurgitating minor subjects, that something unexpectedly riveted me, like a bright flash, and I delved into a short article, avidly reading and returning to some paragraphs a few times.

Some intellectual was musing on the phenomenon of Little Blue Birds, and I couldn't miss that, although I almost did at first, only catching it by chance. Certainly, such an article was not something special from a local perspective but could be taken for bad manners. "The myth about the Little Blue Birds, which occupies a special place in the legends of M., is, for some reason, recalled by the locals reluctantly," the author wrote, immediately setting the grouchy tone, and that grouchiness made me want to slam him in response, which I might have done if I'd run into him on the street. "But what do you want from our denizens?" the next phrase inquired, and I couldn't help but agree with it before he continued with a simplified version of the tale that everyone knew, even if the interpretations differed vastly.

It might be bad manners for someone else, but for me it was a real pleasure. I felt I was reliving the recent past when my comrades had seemed capable of a great deal, and, in our imaginations, all of us fostered some special future fate. The Little Blue Birds, together with other symbols we invented or read about, served as evidence of the romantic essence of the world – in contrast to the dryness of the pragmatic, which our immature minds and especially our souls tried hard to reject. Admittedly, the evidence was quite fragile, but youth preferred to close its eyes to the flaws of logic for the benefit of grand goals. And we assiduously avoided the tedious, meticulous questions of the rationalists, who, one after the other, raised more and more doubts until they completely denied the existence of the phenomenon as a whole.

This was like a loyalty test. Those who didn't believe weren't allowed into the ephemeral circle – a circle of the reckless and fearless of which not one remains. The insiders knew the price of things, which was incomprehensible to others and would arouse the vague hope that the world was not as dull as the rightful ones wanted to see it. Of course, afterward, many of us became detractors of the former naïvety, pointing out the weaknesses in the delusions of the past. There were more than enough of them, but was that the point? No, the point was that almost everyone soon crossed over to the rightful side and the remaining few were bamboozled, their heads spinning in awe, feeling the air around them become so thin, they couldn't hear each other. The point was that it happened in the blink of an eye, and each individual fate turned into a record in a massive volume you didn't want to page through – since you won't find anything new there. And also the point was that all this filled up our souls with deep sadness, but – "silence still rules," and here Julian would answer for everything, although he might not clearly understand his guilt.

At any rate, it's inspiring to get a sign, a reference to my distant youth, right before my critical act, I thought to myself, grinning and peering at the article as if trying to discern familiar faces in it. If someone is still thinking about the Birds, then you can't just wave them off, and it's more difficult to keep your eyes closed. This alone is positive enough, even if it doesn't help all that much...

The peevish intellectual's version almost coincided word for word with what I too had once heard – living in the capital and not yet contemplating any secrets. According to it, roughly two centuries ago, a marsh fever of a formerly unknown sort swept through the unremarkable City of M., vegetating in poverty and exposed to the threatening ocean winds. The first manifestations of illness came to the poorest outskirts. They were mostly ignored – like the usual tales of dangers awaiting any worthy local in the wasteland outside the city limits and even in those districts that abutted them. The epidemic, however, spread quickly, and soon physicians rang the alarm, running their feet off and becoming embittered from their powerlessness. Consequently, society too picked up the rumor of the approaching catastrophe, readily succumbing to panic, which government slogans and admonitions vainly tried to curb.

The people didn't believe the government, and they were fully justified in this. It was obvious authorities had no better control of the situation than any average citizen. Everyone knew the mayor made an ugly scene in front of the most respected doctors, stamping and stammering in fear, and that one or two of his relatives at home were sick. Then the policemen vanished from the streets and lists of official decrees, pasted on the walls every Wednesday, appeared with increasing delays. Then the new ones completely stopped being posted, and those that were already hung up soon became covered with vulgar graffiti and dirty verses.

Finally, the city realized a serious disaster was headed their way. They hoisted a black flag on the gate to warn incautious travelers, and people tried not to leave their houses, receding into themselves and gloomily waiting for the terrible symptoms. Prayers were said now and then in church, but the initial enthusiasm perceptibly waned there too with the absence of any alteration for the better. One pharmacist made a grand announcement he had found the magic mixture that would beat back the attack, and everyone from the poor to respected authorities stormed the drugstore. Yet two days after, rumors swirled on all sides, discrediting the fraudulent medicine, and a little later a resentful crowd smashed the store to pieces. Its owner, who had managed to escape through the back door, was discovered in his relatives' home and they dragged him out and trampled him to death right in front of the porch.

The unusualness of the symptoms also did its part to contribute to the state of general perplexity. Shivering and gastric spasms was observed in the ill – this was familiar and didn't surprise anyone. The sick lurched from hot to cold, were drowned in a feverish sweat one minute and covered with an icy vapor the next – at this the doctors nodded in agreement, as did the elderly nurses, who had seen no small number of fevers in their time. But along with the regular indications, something incongruous occurred – as if the minds of the sick were being infected during the recurring attacks. Their eyes flit madly about the faces of their relatives and friends, not recognizing them and getting startled by any voice. They didn't understand human speech and couldn't put two words together, just indistinctly babbling something about the color blue, which they thought was in objects and people and smells and sounds. Blue lips, they cried in horror and despair, blue walls, blue air – remove it, repaint it, cover it… People were baffled and frightened of each other. The healthy ones started to have strange visions too, and it was difficult to figure out who had fallen into the clutches of the incomprehensible illness and who was still awaiting their hour. It looked like the whole city was gradually going crazy. The locked buildings seemed ready to dissolve, the dogs howled plaintively in the streets, and something unexplainably malicious appeared in every sign. The torment of the sick did not subside, but rather grew stronger with every passing day. Yet the fever didn't carry off that many lives, another manifestation of spooky oddness. Only the old and weak passed away, although the number of infected people rose inexorably, and more and more frequently voices were heard saying the outbreak would never end and not even death was capable of overcoming it.

Soon everyone completely lost their grip. On the streets and from the open windows came the cries of the unfortunate victims cursing the hated color. A spontaneous revolt took place in the outskirts, aimed at either the doctors, suspected of spreading the virus, or the local government, powerless to deal with the event. Everyone understood the riot would soon repeat itself with more violence, turning into real chaos. All the terror the locals felt over this invisible something that had chosen M. for its monstrous attack would pour into it. And then, at that shaky and tragic moment, Little Blue Birds appeared in the city.

At first it seemed low clouds were moving in from the east, but then it became clear it was an enormous flock of feathery animals of an unknown sort. They glittered in the air like quick smudges of an ultramarine brush. They flew into the city from all directions, circled over the central square and open area in front of city hall. There were thousands of them; they outnumbered the residents, who scratched their heads and muttered curses. Toward evening, the streets quieted down in the clutches of a new fear – as if an angel of blue death had arrived for each and every person, and it made no sense to run or protest. People didn't say a word, even the sick shut up and silently shook under their sweaty blankets, and only the unexpected messengers chirped sweetly as they sat on their shrubs and trees. No one hoped to live until the morning, let alone through the next long day – yet night passed without bringing even one death, and when the sun rose, the whole winged army flapped out of the hospitable branches, circled the city a few times, and headed toward the ocean.

No one ever saw them again. The epidemic receded, the terrible blue color no longer appeared in horrendous nightmares, and the denizens slowly returned to themselves, though preferring in every way to avoid mention of the events as one does a secret disgrace left behind. The myth, however, was whispered from generation to generation – sometimes provoking quite loud outbursts. Once masked men burned down the studio of an artist who had painted something similar to blue birds in oil, and, more than once, fellows with loose tongues were beat up in bars when they made ambiguous hints at the past subject. Gradually, the story assumed contradictory details, becoming more and more innocuous until it finally emerged in the form of a funny tale, not presenting any threat to social mores. Then it got serialized as a legend and began to be considered sufficiently decent, and afterward was even distinguished in a special article, intended to catapult the innocent feathered beings – actually the story about them – into the ranks of one of the city's symbols. This led to the appearance of an unsightly monument at the entrance to the city, though the enthusiasm soon dwindled to nothing and later relinquished its spot to the former circumspection. So, nowadays, the locals are reluctant to speak about the Little Blue Birds, especially in public places.

Why? – the writer asked and descended into rambling sophistication, which I forced myself to read, suppressing a yawn. It's true that margin notes are almost always superfluous and often ridiculous and pitiful, like a left-behind passenger trying to jump on a train that's already left the station. I even wanted to share my resentment with someone – with Lyubomir Lyubomirov, for example, who would certainly have torn the smart aleck to shreds. Yet he was far away, along with everyone else. Only Jeremy was at hand, but I was afraid I couldn't have a worthwhile conversation with him.

"Our social sphere latently rejects the historical memory of interference from the outside, even if the intentions were good. We also suspect the motives and the means of interference were not recognized properly. Attempts to reinterpret them do not succeed for some reason," the author waxed on, obviously spellbound by his own eloquence. Incapable of holding back my irritation, I snorted loudly and chucked the paper into the corner. Really, idiots are the nastiest of plagues, worse than marsh fever. And no one will arrive to liberate you from them – efforts to liberate "do not succeed for some reason," as was said above. But I love Little Blue Birds with all my heart, and what's the difference whether or not they actually existed and who's afraid of mentioning them and why…

Nodding to myself, I heaved a sigh, gazed with contempt at the newspapers in the corner, and shuffled to the shower to refresh my blazing head and concentrate on my meeting with Julian, which was not all that far off.

CHAPTER 13

I arrived at Arcada restaurant five minutes after the agreed time and saw Julian already sitting at a table by the central pillar. His goatee made him appear a bit strange, but it was impossible not to recognize him – the photo Jeremy had provided was totally needless. Julian looked at me with some confusion – probably all my recent wanderings had left a trace, or my minor fashion stunt achieved its end. Shortly before our meeting, an idea dawned on me: I rushed to the men's apparel store and bought a fancy suit of thin English wool that fit me quite well. He had probably never seen me in anything other than casual pants and shirts, and the change clearly made an impression on him. I grinned to myself and called over the maître d', rebuking him a little as I insisted that I'd reserved a table by the window in a nook of the hall, where they finally led us, apologizing for the misunderstanding.

"Well," said Julian, regarding me pensively and shaking his head. Then he added cheerfully, "You haven't changed at all," obviously not wishing to admit the opposite.

"You see," I replied, "time is passing, and we aren't aging. Although, to be honest, you look different somehow. Maybe it's the beard… Or am I imaging things?"

In fact, I didn't see anything changed in him. The same aspect, teeming with pedantic impudence, the same ordinary features with somewhat chubby cheeks and a pronounced chin that certainly attracted women, the same eternal smile that had made me want to be truculent without any reason. Only his wrinkles dug a little deeper and the corners of his lips curved down slightly, but that could be written off as fatigue or lack of sleep.

We examined each other tranquilly, exchanging irrelevant pleasantries. Then we discussed the meager menu and sent the waiter to the kitchen for exact details. Finally, all the preliminary commotion ended and an awkward silence hung over the table. It was time to change to something more substantive, but both of us stalled, granting the other the right to start.

It was Julian who began, and he did it in an unexpected way. "So," he said with a short sigh, "I don't know what sort of gossip has reached you, but we probably need to address this issue straightaway. Yes, we *are* living together, and I'm here with her too, though I have to admit it isn't easy. She can't find a job and is terribly bored." He crossed his arms over his chest and regarded me with an important look, as if being ready to show firmness and poise no matter what effect the news had on me.

"With what her?" I asked distractedly, as if thinking of another subject, despite, of course, instantly realizing he was talking about Vera. I was even about to burst out laughing, surprised at my complete indifference to the resuscitated phantom that had just recently seemed so threatening.

"What do you mean, 'what her,'" Julian drawled, somewhat discouraged. "Vera Guttenberger, who else. You couldn't possibly have forgotten."

"Oh, Guttenberger..." I puffed out my lips and gazed off into the foggy distance with an expression of gloomy contemplation, partially expecting that something would really stir inside me and burn me like a whistling whip. Nothing happened. Not even one picture flickered before my eyes, and I concluded phlegmatically, disappointed no less than him, "Yes, now I remember. I had an emotional period with her. Emotional, but that was long ago." Here they brought us the wine, at just the right moment. We tasted it, and when the waiter left, I asked Julian, "So, she's with you now? How funny! And where's her husband?"

Julian, eyeing me doubtfully, began to talk about him and Vera, while I just sat there with a cheerful look, genuinely amusing myself with the situation. If only she were here too, in person, Frau Guttenberger, who had apparently become a Fraulein again; that would be a complete set of material for a short story or even a novel. The trio from the love triangle – polygon would be more accurate – meet in exile and recall days past. However, she would certainly draw attention to herself, destroying the fragile balance, and everything would end with an ordinary argument. How dull. But Julian's good – he's tackling it as if it were serious. Or is he pretending?

"Yes, it was difficult – for her and, I admit, for me," Julian explained. "But her husband disappeared, that is, she left him because he – let's keep this to ourselves – turned out to be a total asshole. Of course, you can understand him: who would like that kind of situation? First, she told him about you – an unanticipated explosion, an outburst of passion and so on, you probably remember it well. He tolerated it for a while, but then the new story began even before the end of the first one…" Julian chuckled. "Please, don't take offense – the past is past, as you put it. You, of course, shouldn't feel insulted. But her husband, he was hurt, all right – and suddenly lost his patience and fought back. He made scenes in the evenings, called her names and all sorts of things, summoned her from time to time for a serious conversation, to determine the future. He was very – I mean, *very* annoying. And our Vera…"

"Your Vera," I corrected him. "She's yours, not ours."

"Well, yes," Julian agreed reluctantly. "Excuse my sloppiness." He sipped the wine and turned the glass in his hands as if pondering whether to continue. I encouraged him with a nod, and he began again, assiduously avoiding the possessive pronoun.

"So, Vera, as you know, isn't made of iron. One day they had a heart-to-heart talk and he explained everything to her: who she was, and what he had made her – introduced her to society, bought her dresses, taught her to appreciate real things, and so on. And he pointed out whose money enabled her to live in style, exploding with sudden fervor time and again. He was right in some sense, of course," Julian grimaced. "But nobody wants to hear that, so she lashed out like a skittish pony and came to my place for the night, all in tears. That's it, she says, I can't go back there. It's unbelievable what he thinks he can get away with. Who is he, a pitiful scribbler of children's books? What can he understand about other people's lives and emotions? Yes, I agreed, nothing, but I also felt my own freedom was coming to an end. Still, I didn't have the courage to force her to go back to him – it would have been rather mean, wouldn't it? So, along these lines, everything was decided – the next day she moved in her belongings and we began to live together, by mutual consent, although I can't figure out when I was asked about it. Frankly, I waited for her husband to come to his senses and request her return so that things could resume in the old way, but he didn't call, didn't write – probably suffered too much and couldn't recover. And then this business trip started swirling – with this experience, new positions may be open to me. Of course, more people than necessary applied, so I had to make the rounds, keep my eyes peeled, and with all that I had no energy left for personal matters. Okay, I thought, let it just keep going like this – so, it ended up that I went on the trip and hauled Vera along. She clutched at me so firmly I couldn't tear her off, and now she's climbing the walls in boredom because there's nothing to do. But it's no problem – in a few months we're headed back. And we'll figure out the future there... But don't think I regretted it," he exclaimed with sudden alarm. "I don't regret it at all. Vera – you know what she is? A beauty and on the whole... You should remember; I don't have to tell you."

"I remember, I remember," I concurred generously. At least I didn't feel any jealousy now, and I had to admit the drama ended in a positive way. It's good, I thought, and it's always nice to know the outcome – although for a full picture, I'd have to look at Frau-Fraulein Guttenberger with my contemporary eyes. Too bad that isn't in my plan.

As if he were reading my mind, Julian asked crossly, "Do you want to see her? Chat with her a little?"

I merely shook my head, gazing at him without a smile.

"Okay," he nodded understandingly and, as if dejected by his own monologue, puckered his brow and began gobbling up the hors d'oeuvres. I followed his example, and we didn't speak for some time, each contemplating his own thoughts. Julian nonetheless returned directly to himself and asked about my private life with the insistency of a childhood friend, which he wasn't. To close the subject, I informed him casually that I've certainly been seeing an attractive girl – for a long time already – but I didn't enter into any details, so he had to retreat.

Soon we had eaten everything and leaned against the backs of our stools. It was getting dark outside, our profiles reflected in the windowpane lit up by dull electric lamps. The room began to stink of burnt food from the kitchen, and an elderly woman at the adjacent table sniffed indignantly, looking around in search of a waiter. Our eyes met and we shared sympathetic disgust.

"What's with your career?" I inquired, again turning to Julian. "Have you had, as always, luck and promising prospects?"

He grinned with fake modesty and began a detailed account of his business adventures, though I soon lost the thread and didn't even try to penetrate its viscous web. Someone had suggested schemes, gathering gullible supporters, while others formed a trenchant opposition, arguing and conspiring. Sometimes a certain "call" rang out in the upper echelons, which Julian said with respectful importance, lowering his voice, and afterward everything got confused again. The schemes were called off, the supporters scattered in despair, ready to join the next endeavor, and new trends and plans arose, on the back of which the subsequent temporary heroes advanced. Sometimes a big event similar to the shift of a glacial layer took place. Someone rose higher while some others were forced into a dead end everyone knew led no further. Such metamorphoses again roiled the submerged kingdom, recomposing invisible lists and shaking up the forms – so that everyone sneezed from the dust and froze listening to the rustling pages. But after wiping their tearstained eyes, they peered at the familiar landscape and everything began again...

I certainly remembered how this action looked from the inside, but Julian's view was much more purposeful and consequently narrow and imprecise, so his interpretation of career machinations seemed to be a bad paraphrase of a poorly written play. He, however, found content hidden from my weakened eye, and occasionally reached an odd conclusion that was striking for being unobvious, like a dramatic pause at an inappropriate moment. Without a doubt, he knew better – and informed me with pride that one after another of his combinations led to minor interim success. And somewhere ahead, real triumph was looming. For its sake, all the internal skirmishes flared up, and the trip to the City of M. – a big secret, by the way, which the average employee, like me for example, didn't know about – was also supposed to become a part of the forthcoming picture.

At some point, my attention began to wane and I no longer helped keep up the conversation, so Julian gradually tailed off and lost most of his courage. He still put on airs, hemmed and hawed and showed with all his might that he had something to be proud of, secretly or visibly. But behind the outer bravado hovered other thoughts his mind would get sidetracked on, like it or not. One time he even stumbled on some phrase and skipped irrelevantly from one subject to another, looking at me with dissatisfaction, as if I had confused him, though I hadn't, and he had no basis to accuse me of that.

Then they finally brought us the main course – spicy Hungarian goulash prepared quite unimaginatively – and Julian subsided, as if he sensed my disdain for a far-removed life, which I'd left behind without regret after finding something else to replace it. I knew sooner or later he'd show interest in this "something else" – which was why he'd come – and wouldn't depart until he'd obtained all the information he could.

After we finished our meal and washed it down with the wine to cool our burning mouths, we smoked and again stared at each other. I saw Julian struggling with his curiosity, doing everything to conceal his impatience. "You know…" I said, simply with the wish to annoy him a little, and leaned forward, as if underscoring the importance of the forthcoming admission. "You know, my girlfriend would have sent this dish back to the kitchen after the first forkful. She's a Slav; she knows how to deal with meat. It's staggering how sloppily they cooked it, don't you think?"

"Yeah, yeah," Julian replied, obviously expecting to hear something more worthwhile. He turned in disappointment and began to pluck at his teeth with a toothpick, his palm covering the lower half of his face. I noticed his beard was cut unevenly on one side. In the past, that wouldn't have happened: he always paid excessive attention to his appearance. Either the provincial city or living permanently with Vera Guttenberger is having an effect, I thought but didn't guess any further.

"So, this is how things are," said Julian dully and yawned. "We're working, growing, so to say, and tolerate some privations – like this dreary town. As you correctly observed, they can't even cook properly here, and the rest – the rest is even worse!" He fidgeted in his chair, took another toothpick, and began to complain about the City of M. with unconcealed bitterness, noting how inconvenient everything was there and how happy he would be to leave at the first occasion.

"But tell me," he asked, his eyes gleaming maliciously. "Tell me why all of them think so highly of themselves? They should sit still and be quiet – they live in a hole, a real hole. But no, they aren't quiet – and even when silent, they swagger around with their inflated egos. It's imperceptible, on the sly, an inaudible whisper – yet they mock you, grumble, censure you behind your back. But why? What's so great about this place? I just don't get it."

Julian lit a cigarette and looked at me, probably expecting agreement. However I wasn't going to play along, especially since such an attitude didn't suit my plan and even contradicted it in a way. I grinned ambiguously and asked half-jokingly, "What's upset you? Did they call you names or something?"

"No," Julian frowned. "If they called me names, I'd reply appropriately. On the contrary, everyone is polite and treats me with respect – and really, I'm a specialist, not just your average Joe," – he unconsciously thrust out his chest. "But I feel that everyone is calculating… I can't mix with them, can't approach them – although, you know, I'm always good at approaching people. Why does every effort here amount to nothing? I don't get it… I don't get it!" he repeated, pouting his lips stubbornly and staring into space.

I continued to look at his face with a partial grin. His forgotten cigarette smoldered in the ashtray; smoke rose to the ceiling, dividing us in two like a weightless curtain. "Everyone in the capital drove me crazy with their tales," Julian went on, again not receiving any sympathy from me. "Some seemed even jealous – ooh, magic, ahh, legends. Well, I found the books, read about the legends. It was interesting, yes, although idiocy in my opinion. Where's the magic? I haven't noticed it – they probably thought it all up. And then, oh, the Dunes, the Dunes… I haven't even seen these Dunes, I have no time, and what's there, what can be so great about the Dunes that it can't be described intelligibly? It can't be much," – he nodded, noticing how I shrugged my shoulders. "And everyone pumps themselves up, as if there really was something. But ask anyone – openly, honestly – and they won't tell you a thing, just regard you like a moron and smile to themselves. And you can't figure it out… Or take even this, the Blue Birds. There's a statue in their honor – why? Does anybody know? I don't think anybody does. I inquired a few times, and people simply turned away from me as if I'd done something indecent. They're like savages, aren't they? I didn't do anything, merely asked. Are they unable to answer?"

Julian kept on droning resentfully until the waiter inquired about dessert. It's time to act, I decided. My victim has exposed himself and shown his weakness, although no one provoked him. Again I imagined myself to be a ruthless tiger and touched the mark on my cheek to prepare the right tone.

"Listen," I said firmly, and he pricked up his ears. "You're grumbling and complaining, but there's nothing to it, just a sentiment. Things aren't that bad here. You're just too sensitive and not persistent enough."

"I'm sensitive? I'm not persistent?" Julian was bewildered, and I regarded his bemused face with pleasure, realizing how unusual it was for him to hear that from me. "Really…" He shook his head, but I calmly confirmed, "Definitely," and began to speak with insistence and passion, as if my turn had come to share revelations begging to be voiced.

"The City of M. isn't as small as it might seem," I repeated what I'd once heard from Piolin. "You shouldn't size it up so easily, and you won't understand it that quickly. Sometimes a pause is necessary – to contemplate peacefully, with no one urging you on. Otherwise, believe me, you won't discover a lot, you'll miss the substance because it will slip away. Even if you just study a map – and I have very good maps – it's impossible not to notice one or two really strange places. And there are other oddities, not depicted on the maps. It isn't easy to get to them – you have to meet the right people, who may not want to talk to you at first…"

Julian regarded me skeptically, but I stuck to my line. "I know you're not drawn to peculiarities like a trusting child," I emphasized, articulating each word carefully. "But don't rush to draw conclusions, Julian, even about those, as you put it, Blue Birds. You say the people here are savages, yet all savages have their pagan gold, which one shouldn't ignore if it's possible to grasp it!"

I gazed at silent Julian with reproach and said, somewhat offended, "And your talk about the Dunes is miles wide of the mark. If you haven't been there, you shouldn't spout such drivel. The Dunes are a special story – you think you don't need it, and maybe you don't if you succeed in something else, but you, I see, haven't achieved much yet. Yes, not much, don't grimace. It's so very boring – the capital, career… Do you know what's going on now with the searock here? No, you don't, yet there are people who know for certain and use it for their own good. And there are others who divide the notorious

Dunes into equal portions, delineate squares with a black pencil, and move from one to the other, and glue pieces of adhesive paper onto the map. You think it's senseless? Oh no, every quarter is worth something – maybe a lot, a real lot. There are also northern women with astonishing beauty, who longed for warm countries all through their youth and now don't wish to leave this place for anything in the world. They aren't like Vera Guttenberger, who doesn't know how to occupy herself. And finally…" I took a short pause and filled my chest with air, again touching my monkey's hand. "And finally this whole area will soon be a part of a very promising picture – and the name of the picture is Strategic Highway, it alone may be worth the rest. But everything has its own turn; we'll get to that without rushing."

The main words had been spoken. Now I just had to give them time to take effect. I called the waiter and politely said, "Bring us another bottle, please, and some fresh fruit." Then I drummed my fingers on the armrests, broke off a piece of the breadstick, popped it in my mouth, and gave Julian an open smile.

He was still on the alert and pinched his beard from time to time. But his eyes gleamed and his pose showed undeniable interest. I poured us more wine, winked at Julian, and raised my glass.

"Another toast to our meeting," I took a gulp, then dug into the inside pocket of my new suit, pulled out a piece of paper folded in four, and spread it out on the table. Julian fixed his gaze on it, narrowing his eyes sharply. "Here's the picture," I informed him solemnly. "It has everything that's necessary for any future understanding. Certainly, you won't get it right away, but the picture isn't the only thing. A story comes with it too, as with all meaningful things, particularly with everything painted or shaped from nature. This isn't from nature, although you can recognize a thing or two – even if only schematically, as in a draft. But a naked scheme often helps a matter immensely since it can be enough to just fasten your wandering eye on the subject. And to fasten your wandering mind with wandering thoughts in its wake, since there's nothing more dangerous for any business than letting your thoughts stray and end up in the wrong place. Look…" And I began to move my finger across the sheet, explaining to a somewhat dumbfounded Julian how the entire area was represented on it: the City of M. as an uneven spot, the coast as a wavy line, between them – a loose medley of small dots that designated the Dunes, and above the dots a wide road, concrete and steel, the pride of my fantasies fearlessly let loose.

"That's it, the highway," I said, sounding rather enraptured. "The road of strategic importance and commensurate cost, and I'm its strategist and maybe even its tactician – but that's getting ahead. For now, we'll operate with preliminary assumptions: here are the Dunes and the coast, here's the city with its surrounding swamps, here's the even stripe connecting the two points. And from them, we'll continue – with the story that I promised on the phone. The story and the picture – they are like two points, two separate focuses, and they send different beams in the intersections of which sit those who are capable of understanding the situation for all it's worth. I, for example," – I modestly dropped my eyes and thought fleetingly that Doctor Nemo might be annoyed at the obvious plagiarism. "But I'm not the only one, not alone, and I want to share it with you too, having something profitable in mind. But first we'll drink," – and I again grabbed my glass, sipped quickly, and, looking directly at Julian, began to present the prepared story which had become so familiar to me and looked so unmistakably real, I already believed it myself.

"Imagine being a wanderer who's travelled to the City of M. without having any plans or clear goals," I said, pattering my fingers to the rhythm of the words. "He's homeless, jobless, his bridges burned and ties all severed. What happened? We won't delve into the insignificant. We'll just say he wanted to become someone else and there was no one to stop him, so – a rupture, turmoil, flight. That's how he ends up in this city, which he knows only by hearsay and where he doesn't have one single friend. He begins to get used to life there, not knowing what the city needs him for and what he wants from it. The start is thoroughly depressing – back alleys and pennilessness loom ahead, with no hope whatsoever. Everything hints at an inglorious return and a new round of failure. But suddenly fate smiles on the wanderer – bestows on him the same unwitting smile that everyone awaits day and night…"

"Imagine: evening, crowded cafe," I continued with a pensive nod. "I'm sitting and sipping gin, enjoying the solitude, which is already getting boring. Everything around me is calm and peaceful, provincial and tedious, but suddenly – bang, an unprecedented scene. Out of nowhere appear a gang of thugs in black coats – three or four, I couldn't even tell. There are cries, curses, and blood. Everything spins; I land right in the thick of it – and I see: one of the black coats pulls an iron chain out of his pocket and, in front of him, with his back turned, is one of the guys who are actually being attacked. Here something tosses me up like a spring – I guess, it looked spectacular: I jump up, grab my stool, fling it at the attacker, scream something… Well, I was kicked in the side immediately, then the light went out, and darkness covered the rest. And the end was very prosaic: the police appeared, they took the thugs away, and the assaulted men almost forcibly sat me down at their table to express their gratitude and drink away the chaos. That's how it all started."

I paused and searched for the cigarettes. My hands shook slightly – as if I were seeing the fight in Piolin's restaurant on fast forward, down to the last shot. Julian extended an open pack to me with some haste, which was a good sign. I smoked and repeated, shaking my head, "Yes, it all started with that."

"One of them turned out to be the king of the local architects and we found some common ground," I elaborated, watching his impatience grow. "I had to fake it, of course, change my profile somewhat, but it all went down smoothly and didn't arouse any suspicion. I didn't even understand who attacked them and why – I think it was all because of his companion, who was also no simple guy, although in a different department. But that's not important, the main thing is that the next morning I paid the architect a visit. On his table – some sketches, models and, naturally, he asked my opinion, which I gave, very apropos. They took me seriously and suggested I participate in something, in a leisurely manner, while I was relaxing from work in the capital. My new friend also had a daughter – a very interesting damsel, I have to say. She played her role too – she liked me, I won't deny it – so, all in all, I quickly found myself making the rounds to the offices of the local bigwigs to explain what was what. It was like a game – and I played it as an amusing game…"

I fell silent and then admitted confidentially, "I, Julian, just like you said before, am a real specialist. I have a very well-trained eye!"

Julian confirmed authoritatively that yes, I was a specialist all right, and suggested we drink to it, that is, to me, that very minute. We did exactly that, clinking cheap glasses after which he instantly filled them, with me receiving more than he poured for himself. Does he want to make me tipsy, the thought flickered. And why not? Why shouldn't I look a bit drunk for a better semblance of authenticity?

"Then suddenly things changed," I said and nodded to myself in affirmation. "The path led me by itself to the highest local personages – more precisely, to one and only once, yet that was enough because I firmly intended not to let the opportunity pass me by. I told myself, it's a game no longer, you can't screw this up. And I prepared assiduously, dressed appropriately, forged a recommendation letter just in case and concocted one fantasy, one strange-random project that hit the nail right on the head, banging it into the sore spot – for I was very aware of the local sore spots at that time."

Julian listened, not averting his eyes. "The high honcho met me one on one," I continued, taking another gulp and slightly slurring my speech. "At first the conversation didn't go smoothly, but then I got animated, and then he stated, somewhat casually, that my project was good, yes, but minor, not worth much, and to put it bluntly, he wanted to use me in an entirely different matter. And he announced, lowering his voice, that a huge venture was afoot with work that was right in my line. I already knew about it, but I faked astonishment, of course, and thrust my own ideas about the matter at him. The head honcho, however, just chewed his lips and said – it's not bad, yes, but it's still not quite right. It isn't proper; it needs to make everyone lick their lips and blink in stupefaction. And I could already tell: he looked at me in doubt – but right then it dawned on me, at the most important moment.

I know, I cried out, I understand – know exactly what to do: we need to *name* it something else and then it'll *look* different! And it happened: I outlined my Strategic Highway. It was born right there, I drew it on the paper, thinking on the fly – and his face immediately livened up, and we entered into a serious talk, which continued the next day and then began to pick up steam. Certainly, other 'experts' had their own ideas. Everyone wanted to jump on the bandwagon, and, in particular, the king of architects turned out to be a real ass. And his daughter messed around in it as well, but gradually everything settled down and from the whole pie I received in advance a large slice – the local fat cats gave me a good-sized bundle of the new shares. That's what I was looking for – because just a salary wouldn't interest me enough. I've already worked for salary, thank you very much, but the share package was really something – and may even become really stunning, but you can't talk about that ahead of time. You can just cross your fingers and wait, wait, wait."

I diligently crossed my fingers in front of Julian's nose. He regarded me with a tenacious gaze and rapidly filled up my glass. Then he excused himself and went to the restroom, and I reclined in my chair, relaxing and blowing smoke toward the ceiling. For some reason I bandied about thoughts of Archibald Bely and Doctor Nemo, idly contemplating whether they would've believed me if I'd told them something similar.

"Yes, they might have believed me, but would they have listened in the first place?" I asked myself next. However Julian's voice brought me back from contemplation.

"The lavatories are thoroughly unpleasant here," he complained while making himself comfortable. "Shall we drink?" We drank and poured some more. The approaching waiter whirled around us and disappeared, as if he felt extraneous. I had to continue the act without wasting time, so I said sternly, "Okay, now, to the point," and forged ahead, propping my elbows on the table.

"Imagine," I explained to Julian as he fiddled with his beard.

"Imagine those who sit on a gold vein and cannot dig even a meter because their hands are tied. Or those who have the carrot dangling in front of their nose but can't move at all – they're stuck fast in a quagmire. What prevents the City of M. from becoming a second Acapulco, the local elite ask, whose mouths have been gaping at the tourist money for ages. And they answer their own question: nothing, but it doesn't happen, try as they might. A unique place, but the majority of it remains useless if not forgotten. That the climate here isn't good is fudge – the climate's great, they include it as a reason just out of despair. That the ocean is restless – it's restless everywhere, that's why people like it, otherwise they would splash about in a pond, swimming pool, or puddle – and know no distress. And the sand at the coast is top quality, first-class, the kind of sand you search for but can hardly find anywhere. What's the problem then, any one of the tycoons could ask, and the answer is obvious. The City of M. together with its ocean, long summers, fishing villages, etc. can be anything you want, but not a fashionable resort because its essence is different. There's no cheerful festiveness in M.; it's opaque; even when the sun shines, a haze is visible somewhere in the distance – either the marsh vapor or mist from who knows where. And instead of pleasant thoughts, lots of nonsense enters your head so any joyful mood risks being ruined every minute. Bring whole families of rosy-cheeked idiots; build hundred-story hotels for them, restaurants and clubs, dance halls and casinos; then offer them the local atmosphere as an invitation to have a great time – and it'll instantly go up in flames and make you look like a fool. Only oddballs who are sold on the enigmatic and unusual come here, those who travel for secrets and secret meanings – but you don't make money on secrets. That can't be compared to the pilgrimage of the rosy-cheeks and heavy-asses you can observe some two hundred miles north, where the water is colder and the sand quality much, much worse…"

Words and phrases came easily, my inspiration propelled me onward like wings. It seemed I could really see everything I was talking about, was painting it from nature, and was consequently not afraid to lie awkwardly or make a mistake in the details. "A paradox?" I asked Julian and answered myself, "No, it's not a paradox. The hazy essence and opaque shell, through which you don't poke your finger, scares you away like rotten eggs since they bear the power of detachment, tease with incomprehensibility, and prevent the organization of the masses into a solid crowd of tourists. It's, like, nerve-wracking here – nerve-wracking and unclear, uncertain and depressing. So rosy-cheeked men and women soon become uncomfortable and nervous. They endeavor to escape – they and their credit cards. And the industry, as opposed to the more successful places, doesn't grow, like a mushroom or a blister, no matter how much you sprinkle the magic potion, whisper, and jiggle amulets."

"Yeah, totally," Julian broke in with a serious, concentrated look. "I noticed something like that, too, but couldn't pin it down. You're totally right! And, you know," he admitted confusedly, "as for me, I haven't been to the ocean once."

"If you haven't been, go. It's no problem," I dismissed it. Julian obediently fell silent. I took another sip and said emphatically, "Now let's get back to the fat cats…"

Over the course of the following half-hour I told him in detail how the idea grew in fierce contention, how competitors set up traps and tried to discredit me with whatever came to mind, how I had to dodge and lie where telling the truth seemed obligatory at first because it was impossible to let my sponsors get bored and the truth looked duller than lies. I gathered everything I knew about the art of navigation among jagged reefs in those waters where big money changed hands. I imagined myself as one of the shark family and clicked my pointed teeth not just once or twice, and Julian agreed with me and believed me. I could have easily put him on guard by falling out of tune and cracking into a falsetto under the stress, but I didn't fall or crack and didn't strain myself too much.

He nodded and nodded, and it became steadily freer and easier for me. At some point I again returned to my picture, proposing he envision the intricate construction with his own two eyes, mentally paint the truncated sinusoid of bridges and the parabolas of protective ropes on both sides, hear the noise of the tires in all eight lanes, and even make out the boom of the surf, meeting and accompanying the speeding cars, which seem like toys from the heights of a bird. Without blinking an eye, I fantasized about the topographical layout of almost all the lengths of the road, about the nearly finished paperwork and the impatient contractors with their excavators ready. I compared the future concrete strip with a mechanical hand extended from city hall, grabbing the ocean by its curl, with a gigantic muscle tying together the city and the elements, the conquered rock and distant horizon. From the vague and diffuse, the world turned out visible and delineated by a thick line, like a border, outside which was no place for any folly. The highway, whatever you say, had a fixed length, and the city firmly stood in its place, and the coast represented the most solid invariant, a point that would not be shifted barring a cosmic catastrophe. So, only a finite part of the area was relegated to legends and myths, and, moreover, you could observe this part at your leisure from the window of a slowly moving car, transforming the once-ominous forces into profitable tourist attractions. "It's a picture for people who want to think big and make a real buck!" I exclaimed rhetorically, assuming Julian knew nothing about past attempts to subjugate the Dunes and failures to build even regular roads through them. "This is a frisky stallion that you can ride to where they hand out goodies!"

Julian looked at me now with unconcealed envy, sipping from his glass and glancing sideways at mine, which was empty. "Should we order more wine?" he asked. "Or some cognac for a change?"

"Let's get cognac," I waved my hand, intentionally indicating I wasn't that sober. "It's easy to drink in enjoyable company."

Julian signaled to the waiter, ordered the drinks, and told me with a quite sour look that, yes, the picture is convincing indeed. He can only be happy for me – someone else's success can be pleasant, although not always. I regarded him guardedly and rested my heavy head on my hand.

"Thanks for being happy," I said in a tipsy voice. "But is it enough for you – just to praise someone's success?" And I noted with satisfaction that Julian got serious again and tensed up all over.

"Is there an offer?" he asked quietly, nursing his drink.

"There's an offer!" I confirmed, faltering a bit. "Do you think I've been pontificating simply for the hell of it, to brag? No, my friend, it's not all that simple. That is, although everything's good, not everything's good enough, and although everything has already been decided, there are things that need to be fine-tuned."

Julian turned into one big ear, and I again leaned toward the table and lowered my voice to a near whisper. "I can do everything alone, but then I'll have to be extremely lucky," I muttered, puckering my brow and staring constantly in Julian's eyes. "Otherwise, whether you're right or wrong, mistaken or not, they'll still eat you up at some point. I've been lucky so far, yet the amount of good luck one has in reserve cannot be determined in advance. That's why I prowl around – who else is there to team up with and pull all the lucky stars in a collective heap? I prowl and can't find anyone, and the options aren't great, to put it bluntly. Some are quick to the punch, but really dumb and stupid, while others possess too much provincial cunningness – so you can't predict when they'll choose to jump ship and join the other side. A man was in sight, but he valued the pure abstract idea too much. He refused money, didn't know what was in his interest – yet an idea is a flimsy thing, you can't trust such a lunatic. The others were worthless and unsuitable, and they wanted too much for too little – which means you can't trust them either. So, utter extremes, no golden middle – that's why when you called, the thought instantly occurred to me: this couldn't have been planned better. You're famous for your luck and you always focus on rewards for yourself, not to mention you have the skills – we've worked together, I know you well. So, I admit, I immediately thought of luring you in, if only you weren't already up to your neck in some other big venture, and something's telling me you aren't. Am I right?"

"Well, that's fairly correct," stumbled Julian. "I'm busy but not up to my neck. And, of course, it depends on the details... Have you already thought about the details?"

"Yes!" I nodded brusquely. "And I've come up with something. I can tell you if you want, but first please excuse me. I have to leave you for a second."

I headed to the restroom, observing with some surprise that I was actually swaying a little. When I returned, I caught Julian conversing with the morose waiter. "We're closing soon," he muttered upon seeing me. "Everyone's already left. We need to clean up."

I gave him a haughty look, pulled out my wallet and a decent bill from it, casually waved it around for him to see, and tossed it on the table. The waiter immediately changed his pose and demonstrated irreproachable attention. "Do you want a tip?" I asked imposingly. "Don't mumble, I know you do. So, explain to your colleagues that my companion and I are having a talk here –they'll understand. And bring us some coffee right away."

The waiter disappeared and I took my seat, shifting my gaze to Julian. He was serious, energetic, and waited, anticipating the promised details. "So," I said, brushing invisible dust off my jacket. "We met at just the right time – at this point, it's easy for an independent person to butt in. I can't be everywhere at once, like some Figaro or two-faced Janus, and there's one hindrance, of a purely technical nature, which almost no one knows about yet, but they definitely will. There's no getting around it, it's only possible to resolve head on – go to the place and get it done, which really doesn't look that complicated. But imagine, there's no one to send for even that little thing. Everyone is either superstitiously scared or not worth anything, no matter how much you train them. But you aren't superstitious, for one, and you're a spe-cia-list like me – precisely in the area of shifting substances."

I stopped talking, swiveled my head as if in irritation, lit a cigarette, and said emotionally, "Why does every highway have two ends? It can't hang in the air no matter what – and both ends need to sit on something. Here, in the city, we've already selected the square – solid, wide, right in the thick of things. And we also chose the places for the intermediary supports – not all the points, just the first few, but at least that. Yet with the end by the ocean, the matter is going badly – that is, not badly, but rather not going at all: no samples, no structural profiles, nothing. We've had no chance to deal with it, and the archives are empty – as if they've never built anything there. And maybe they haven't – the place is wild, uncivilized, shrouded in ancient rumors like a deadly wasteland or, say, national park. But there's nothing deadly there, and it isn't a reserve either – I checked that out immediately, otherwise they wouldn't issue permits to build anything, out of concern for the wonders of nature. So everything's okay with the licenses, but without samples, you can't make much of an argument. If I were in the place of the enviers, the first thing I'd do is poke into this, and they already did, no doubt, but I'm still withstanding the siege. I'm telling some guys from the central office will be arriving soon and measuring it properly – some serious guys, old connections of mine. And, you see, you'll look exactly like that – an old connection, yes, and from the central office!"

Julian regarded me steadily, listening to every word. "It's not a big deal – just mark and measure the usual elements: density, humidity, stuff like that. But not the whole chart – we only need a few samples for the initial tests," I mumbled. "There's no one else to send – just one moron after another, and I can't do it myself, it'll take at least three days. I can't be away that long, and it would look strange, people would wonder why I did everything on my own. It would be better if it's an independent expert – then we'd have two voices singing in duet. Now there are only photos from a helicopter, but when you bring the samples we'll put everything together and it'll look perfect! But, of course, if you don't want to or aren't certain, then you should say so right away so we don't lose time. Think it over – for a couple days, if you have to – and call, don't drag it out. I can't have any delays, they don't benefit me – or us, I should say…"

An hour later we finished our coffee and had discussed everything that was possible to discuss. Essentially, Julian only asked two questions – about his compensation and the location of the measurements – and he received two ambiguous answers that had also been prepared in advance.

"We'll give you all the formal papers, no problem," I promised him as we were heading to the door. "And afterward, when you return, I'll acquaint you with the old-timers here. You'll sign a contract and so on – if, of course, they like you." At that, Julian lifted an alarmed look my way, but I winked reassuringly – don't take it seriously, it's a joke – and slapped him on the back like an old friend with whom any kind of familiarity is acceptable.

One way or the other, I did everything I could and felt that the last drop had been squeezed out of me – it had been a long time since I'd worked my tongue for so many hours. Julian was cheerful but meditative – I hoped that meant something – and on the restaurant porch he shook my hand at length before jumping into a patiently waiting taxi. "See you soon," I tossed in at the end and went past a frozen doorman, who regarded my suit and victorious gaze with due respect.

After reaching my room, I stretched out on the bed and closed my eyes, fully dressed. My head roared. I still had the taste of bad coffee in my mouth, while sadness and filth lay on my soul. All the nonsense I had said to Julian now seemed to be a dubious fantasy or entirely obvious drivel. Certainly, serious matters aren't handled like that, and he probably knew it. But it was also possible to believe anything if you want, if the likelihood of personal benefit blinded your eyes and your interlocutor pressed relentlessly. I was betting on that and couldn't propose anything else anyway. The only hope was that my effort had been eloquent enough, had filled all the logical voids or at least the majority of them. And Julian hungered for money, real money and success, so the dread of forfeiting a serious jackpot might prevail over intelligent arguments.

Still, if he refuses and wants to see one of the "fat cats" ahead of time, there's no cover for me, I thought absentmindedly. The whole plan will go up in smoke, and I don't have another. Well, it's not worth thinking about now. That's enough of Julian for today.

I slowly undressed, went to the bathroom, and stood under a cold shower, then switched it to hot so that I barely had the strength to bear it, and then back to cold – until I shivered and had goosebumps. After drying off with a towel and ensconcing myself in a bathrobe, I felt much fresher. It was late, but I didn't want to sleep. Wandering about the room, I stopped before the pile of newspapers, gazed at them reflectively, then sat down at the table and grabbed a piece of paper with the hotel insignia at the top, saying, "Now, now I'll show you…" Everything got mixed up in my mind: the detestable aftertaste of my own lying and indignation at other people's self-satisfaction, memories and legends, nighttime reality and distant sins. I wrote boldly in the middle of the page, "On the question of Little Blue Birds, human idiocy, and the blindness of souls," then turned it over and began to scribble furiously, scratching the innocent paper, pouring out all the irritation that had accumulated inside me.

"My cries may not be able to reach you," I penned, nibbling my lip. "You may hear me, but you don't want to hear, as poor Parker complained, although Parker is essentially no different than you. Yet that doesn't mean you'll be left in peace and avoid getting stuck, nose first, in the muck of your most embarrassing moments. I know you won't be ashamed, only slightly surprised at first, but it doesn't matter – your nose will be stuck, stuck fast, and maybe it will eventually shake you up. Yes, every attempt is like the clattering of broken glass or even a crystal vase; yes, the most fervent impulses have insufficient strength to produce the slightest of shifts, but you should know: your stubbornness also has its limits, and something uninvited occasionally pierces through the clanging armor which is the pride of anyone who grew up and joined the ranks in your way. Joined the ranks: a line is formed and the song is reckless, but there's still fear in the depths. Fear makes you flounder in a pile and cling together, incapable of taking a step to the side; fear forces all of you to look at the same spot, without letting you turn your head or even glance sideways. Lead us, you appeal to the next leader that's popped up, only his nimbleness distinguishing him from the others. And he leads, he's obedient – but you continue to crowd together on the narrow patch, as if there were no roads heading far, wide, away…"

"But that is not what I'm talking about," I continued on the next sheet. "There is no point in juggling words, defining and redefining what has been named before me. I'm talking about fervent impulses and the indifference of glaciers, about flecks of harmony and rusty dungeon bars, about a despairing cry and a spiteful laughter. Yes, you know how to repulse with anger what's been given from a pure heart; you know how to ignore the invaluable gifts that have been presented for judgment to your false pastors; and you also love to deprive the givers of the last thing they press to their chest in silent prayer. Those who create for you are despised because they are not like you; those who rob you gain your utmost respect, since your secret ideal is in them. By placing hypocrisy on the throne, you cry duplicitous tears when it's too late and nothing can be given back, and you make yourself content with the crumbs instead of great treasures, becoming lazy and bored, scared of doubts and dependent on the opinions of fools. I know, the crumbs are better than nothing – but when I look at how you wander the dusty paths, your soles treading on what's been attained by the great effort of some creative stranger, I want to take you by the collar and – stick, stick your nose in the muck, so you'll feel awkward, although I know it won't happen."

I grabbed the next sheet and continued, more calmly now, "It won't happen. Ever. But, again, I don't care that much. Why do I keep thinking about you although you aren't worth a written word – that's a good question, yet here there's no room for it. I just want to ask: have you even occasionally directed your look, which has grown foggy from cheap glitz, at those who have zealous souls and the impulses of bighearted passion, whether you have pondered the likes of strangers who have been cast away and have neither pastors nor flocks? What forces them to choose roads that are teeming with thorns, enduring mockeries and restless agonies, re-creating patiently, in miniscule fragments, lines, and forms close to perfection? What does perfection mean to them, and what does the rest mean to them? You would be horrified by the questions alone if you let them truly permeate you – and as for the answers, you'll never get them, don't worry. Just remember: the ones on the thorny roads, they are a hundred times happier than you, however much you want to believe otherwise. And they're stronger, each with their own strength, stronger than all your mediocre power combined in a joint vector. They live in a vast expanse while you became accustomed to suffocating tightness. They deal with quiet eternity while you hear a ruthless clock counting your seconds all the time, and the further you get, the quicker and quicker it moves. You can never understand them; you never reach them with your hand or thought. You won't change, even if someone finally sticks your nose into your own shame, which, I repeat, will never happen, as this someone is nowhere to be found. Yes, you are unlucky: you interest no one – not even each other. One can only consider you a collective abstract phenomenon, lacking particulars and distinctions – an aggregate of existences, uniform substance, molecular protoplasm. Creators and strangers can look at it attentively – if something flares up briefly, becomes tense like a string, or rumbles, swells, breaks. They'll examine it and create an image that absorbs a lot, and they'll present it to you as a generous gift. And you'll drop it in the dust as usual, then maybe notice it by chance, shake it off, look, and gape – your hair standing on end. That's how it'll be, your own shame, not someone else's. Yet, even so, you got used to it long ago. You'll just shake your head and keep going – the line is formed, the song is reckless. And I keep going too, like a detested traitor, carelessly marked by your guards, disturbed, restless, and totally baffled. This is what worries me and doesn't allow me to sleep, what makes me anxious and twitchy, torments me and doesn't let me go: why were you given the ability to think at all? And furthermore: were you actually given it, or is that another delusion I believe so naively?"

I placed that fat question mark and leaned against the back of the stool. You joker, Vitus, you joker and entertainer... The written sheets lay there, pleasing my eyes; my soul was at peace. Flush them down the toilet, I thought lazily, knowing the message I'd formulated did not and could not have a reader. It had its benefits however – I now felt tired and empty, and the Little Blue Birds got their revenge. No one was asking for any more.

I went up to the window, opened it, and looked outside. The city was still sleeping, but somewhere locks were already opening and truck motors were humming. The nighttime cold invigorated me. I inhaled it and whispered a hardly audible greeting – I'm here, if anyone needs me. I stood a little, shivering from the cold and imbued with the sentiment of a fulfilled obligation, then slammed the shutters and slowly walked to the bed that had been waiting for ages.

CHAPTER 14

The morning began badly. Everything was gray outside the window, and gusts of wind pounded the double frame. I had a hangover, and a terrible dream rattled me not long before dawn. I saw Gibbs dead, although he tried to appear alive. Everyone around him pretended nothing had happened, but I realized there was no more life in him. I knew all the others were gloating to themselves, happy he would no longer become his former self. I knew it and couldn't do anything because I didn't understand the essence of the ominous masquerade and that last scheme of his. "He could have told me," I thought crossly, quivering in fear. "I certainly deserve it, that minor courtesy." But that didn't concern him – maybe he didn't notice me at all, being occupied with something else. Dissipating in the air, but still retaining his usual silhouette, almost non-transparent, at least for all the rest. And only I observed objects beginning to show through him.

The dream left a gnawing emptiness inside me, and I kept thinking about it. The world filled up with unfamiliar disquietude. Even my secret now seemed an undertaking of dubious importance, which it probably was. The big fuss to entice Julian to the coast, decking myself out in an English suit, and acting the successful businessman, all were recalled with uneasiness and discomfort. I went to the table, looked at yesterday's scribbled sheets, reread them unhurriedly, ripped them up, and tossed the pieces into the trashcan.

Something wasn't right throughout the universe, something had lost its permanence, shifted, changed. I convinced myself as best as I could it was all a result of superfluous sensitivity, but, no matter what, the world didn't want to congeal. With great difficulty I overcame the temptation to call Jeremy and ask him to find Mia at once. She'd be able to help me, but that'd mean I was giving in to my own weakness, and I couldn't do that – no matter what nightmares I had.

Sometime after lunch I left the hotel and wandered about, not recognizing the streets, peering into the show windows with astonishment and probably making the occasional passersby nervous. The wind blew in my face; litter swirled and dead leaves rose into the air. I didn't complain, receding into myself and shutting down my organs of feeling. Helpless Gibbs in a death mask still didn't disappear from the back of my eye, arising as an ethereal shade here on the sidewalk to the left, there at the intersection ahead, hiding behind the lamp post, or crossing the street in front of cars incapable of hurting him. He turned to me silently and then again rushed away with a slight spring in his step. I knew it was hopeless to chase after him, but I trailed along anyway, following him stealthily, without admitting it, until he finally vanished, losing me in the middle of a noisy avenue two steps from the side street leading to the hotel.

I returned to my room and just lay on the bed, staring at the ceiling. The cracks in it didn't lead anywhere. It was clear all the labyrinths were artificial, and moving through them, straying off course and going in circles, would soon become a senseless act. My head was empty and hollow, like a bottomless well. Only close to evening did I gradually come back to myself, lazily picking at my dinner plate and forcing my jaded mind to return to pressing matters, the main one being the wait – and what I was waiting for could not be rushed.

My morning despair receded a bit, and my depression lifted slightly. Yet my plan still seemed like worldly drivel, not holding any substantive content. I strolled around the room, looking now out the window, now at the old newspapers in the corner. Then I searched out and reread the recent article, trying to get excited, out of retribution if nothing else would help. But these were all half-measures not useful even for self-deception. I still didn't see myself as an avenger, nor did I forget my strange dream.

I looked at the ceiling and again searched it for clues, but none were offered, and it was pointless to count on them. I didn't even manage to doze off – and finally I flared up at myself for real. Afterward, my lost decisiveness seemed to come back; I drove away all the clamorous what-fors and whys, beckoned with my finger to the shy hows, planted it in its honorable spot, and stuck a marshal's baton in its hand. "Enough of this seeking content in what has not yet been done," I told myself. "Events follow each other, and each comes at its right moment – both the action and the meaning. This is the generosity of time, the only generosity it has. The rest just consists of malevolent tricks – so why are you whining instead of appreciating it?"

This simple concept turned out to be truly helpful, and I grabbed hold of it as firmly as I could. Let's forget about transiency and celebrate the progressive nature of Chronos. "It's all because of that dream," I whispered. "Because of that dream and Gibbs…" Recalling Gibbs, I caught my indistinct desire to tell him everything I had rethought and, hopefully, would implement, work over, complete. How would he view my actions – would he dismiss them, like trifles, laughing contemptuously, or appreciate and praise them? Or maybe he'd even be envious? I mused quickly: Gibbs is certainly difficult to locate, but with the proper effort I could still find him. Jeremy, for instance, must know where to look. In all likelihood he wouldn't be happy to see me, but I'm not asking for his friendship, I just want to share my thoughts. I'll find him and tell him – frankly and in detail. It seems intrusive and shameful at first thought, but it's actually not shameful at all. In some way it's bold and the only right thing to do!

My former courage gradually returned. Just recently I had felt so disgusting and had lost almost all my energy, but now I couldn't sit still. I even jumped up from the bed and paced back and forth across the room. Then I said aloud, "Julian, Julian," and listened to my voice carefully. How does it sound – is there enough boldness? Can the brutal roar be heard? Is no note of indifference trailing behind?

The next day, just after noon, the phone rang and Julian said he would accept the offer and take part in "the highway project," as he put it. He was noticeably proud of himself, proud and delighted, as if sensing the significance of his decision and expecting a commensurate reaction from me. I reacted affably and smoothly. Julian, still huffing and puffing with importance, added that he had taken a week's vacation, as of the day after tomorrow, and was ready to get down to work immediately rather than dawdle and procrastinate. His mentioning procrastination made me chuckle – and he probably became a bit bewildered. But I gained control over myself and switched to a businesslike tone, agreeing there was no time to lose.

We quickly went over the particulars of the trip again, especially the part where Julian would have to travel alone. That was not an easy moment, and I wracked my brain to present it so he would be ready for a real hardship, still not becoming frightened too much right away. Then we addressed the professional routine: what and where to measure, and how and with what. That was a complete waste of time, but Julian, not suspecting anything, eagerly inquired into the details. Fortunately, not much equipment was required and there wouldn't be any difficulty getting it at the company he was assigned to. Then I read him an exact list of other necessary articles, including a sleeping bag and an all-weather raincoat. We discussed some minor points, even argued about some of them until I quickly broke off, demonstrating ample authority, which Julian accepted as he should, surely harboring the idea that his hour would come in due time. "Don't forget canned food and crackers and water for a couple days," I insisted, and he assiduously scratched with his pencil, deducing a picture from these minutiae and not suspecting its irrelevance to reality, which he valued so dearly.

"We'll be in touch," I wrapped it up. "And don't worry about the paperwork, I'll handle that."

"So when are we leaving?" Julian asked somewhat anxiously. "You haven't said, and I need to know."

"Your vacation starts the day after tomorrow?" I asked. "So we'll go the day after tomorrow. See you soon!" And I hung up the receiver.

Now I had to finish the last preparations, for which I again needed Jeremy. I called the portiere, and soon the manager stood in my room, gazing tenaciously, although with his usual respectfulness.

"Jeremy," I grumbled, feeling inexplicable hostility toward him, "I need to prepare a few papers on impressive stationary. Here are the layouts and text. Take a look, please – is that doable?"

He turned my prepared drafts in his hands, saying with disappointment, "Oh, they're just letters..." Then he regarded me and asked, "Or do you need real signatures?"

"No, not at all," I waved my hands. "No signatures, just so they look nice. Can you get that together for me?"

"Why not?" Jeremy muttered, having completely lost interest. "I'll bring them to you tomorrow morning, in an unmarked envelope." He grinned and winked familiarly.

"Great," I rejoined and glanced to the side. The sight of him had become unbearable. "And one more thing. Can you tell me the name of the road to the village by the ocean? You know, the one to the south, where the Dunes end, where they've traded the searock and fished for ages. I don't know its name, but it's probably the only one. I arrived from there in a truck."

The question again sounded dumb, yet not dumber than the previous ones, so I didn't even get confused. Jeremy chewed his lips and said doubtfully, "You came in a truck? And now you want to go back? Hmm..." Then he frowned and added, "Maybe it's better for you to take the truck back? Your toy car may get stuck in the mud."

"That's okay, we'll dig it out," I replied, sighing. "The truck doesn't suit me, it doesn't make the trip often enough."

"Doesn't suit you..." Jeremy repeated. "I see." He walked across the room, looked out the window, and said, turning to me again, "Then, whether it suits you or not, you've got to hire a guide."

"Why a guide?" I asked warily. "I don't need a guide. You sketch me the road, and we're done."

"I can't," Jeremy shrugged his shoulders. "We don't do that here. Moreover, whether I sketch it or not, you'll still get lost."

"Let someone who knows do it!" I was becoming angry; the manager already irritated me too much. "Do you, if you don't know it, know someone who does know?"

Barely perceptibly, Jeremy smiled at the twisted formulation, and that infuriated me even more. "And you don't need to snow job me with what you don't do," I added roughly. "These aren't the Dunes, this is different territory. You can certainly get everything for it – the diagrams, the maps, whatever."

Jeremy regarded me silently with a repulsive grin. "We don't do that here," he repeated, smiling to his heart's content. "Ask anybody. So, are you taking a guide or are you going to try your luck on your own?"

I weighed my chances. One day remained until our departure; driving without knowing the road seemed to be a huge risk, and I doubt I would've found another local to help me. "Alright, I'll take a guide," I nodded, caving in. "If, of course, he's reliable and knows the way well. Are you certain we're talking about the same village?"

"We aren't talking about a village," Jeremy evaded the question. "We're talking about the road, the road and the guide. You'll discuss that with him – the village. But don't worry," he added wearily, seeing my agitation was again percolating. "He'll take you to the village, why not? It's the one close to the outpost, correct?"

"That's the one," I confirmed, calming down and not even wanting to think there might be other outposts and other villages near them. "We're leaving the day after tomorrow. Does that work for him?"

"It works, it works," Jeremy assured me with a snicker. "I employ him to handle such tasks, so he does what I tell him. Only I ask you to pay in advance. You, I presume, are leaving us?"

I wasn't planning to leave the Arcada, but now I knew I didn't want to return and see Jeremy ever again. Ultimately, he wasn't the only person who could hunt down Gibbs, I decided, affirming with a nod that I was indeed leaving the hotel, and asked, "How much?"

"Not much," the manager grinned and named the amount, which made my eyes dim. It consisted of almost half my remaining money, and I hadn't expected the price to be that insane. "Are you... Are you joking?" I inquired cautiously. "It seems like a lot."

Jeremy shrugged with complete indifference, though I saw hostile fires burning in his eyes. "It costs what it costs," he said lazily. "Maybe you'll get a better offer somewhere else? Go there, if this is a lot. But without a guide you'll get lost – so it's better not to fool around." He turned his back to me and headed toward the door.

"Wait up," I said to his back. "Okay, alright. Here, count it."

Jeremy took the bills and said with his former respectfulness, which now resembled something more like a sneer, "The day after tomorrow he'll be waiting for you from sunup. When you're ready, call downstairs – he'll help you with your things should that be necessary." Then he bowed curtly and added, "Have a nice trip."

"Thank you," I muttered, and Jeremy, like a ball, rolled toward the door, but before he slipped out, he turned with a crooked grimace and asked quietly, "Have you really been to the Dunes or were you just joking? If you have, you shouldn't be surprised at the price," – and he disappeared before I could answer. Instantly, the phone rang. It was Julian with a heap of questions about the weather, the clothes he should wear, and other details related to the trip. As soon as I had finished with him, some fellow entered to show me samples of the official stationary for my forged letters, and, it seemed, the whole next day the bustle of activity around me would not subside – as if my plan had really come to life and was unfolding by itself, with me being only one of its parts, entangled in its movement together with the others.

Finally, the morning of our departure arrived. I ate a hearty breakfast, poured a thermos of hot coffee, and asked for a few sandwiches with cheese and boiled veal in a paper bag. Then I quickly packed my belongings and smoked a cigarette, sitting on the bed and thoughtlessly looking out the open window. After finishing it, I winked at my reflection in the wall mirror and descended the stairs, as usual driving out sad thoughts about yet another home I'd never return to, and feeling the slight customary itch of anticipation over new events and new places. And new faces, I wanted to add, but the faces were the same – on the couch in the corner of the lobby sat Julian, serious and even glum, and the familiar pimpled youngster sniffled by the counter, obviously assigned to me as a guide. I frowned, but there was nothing to be done – probably Jeremy's army of helpers was not that huge. Soon we headed out to my car, the teen named Louis lurched back and forth with Julian's big backpack, at the top of which a down sleeping bag was tied. A few minutes later, after we'd loaded the things and taken our seats, we gave the Arcada a last look: I with regret, and my fellow travelers probably without any emotion at all.

"Drive to the avenue and make a right, then just go straight," Louis's nasal voice said and added, "When we get out of the city, it'll go faster." I silently steered down the narrow street, trying not to graze the double-parked cars. The weather had turned for the worse; it was drizzling, and the windshield wipers screeched awfully against the glass. Julian wasn't lucky, I thought distractedly and checked myself in my customary way – no compassion, just the yellow eyes of a predator and a cold gaze.

A little while later we really did come out on a broad avenue. I'd never been on it and looked with curiosity at the new nine-story buildings that had been constructed on both sides. The City of M. seemed cleaner and tidier here despite the lead-gray clouds. It didn't have a face, however, as if it'd been fenced off without pity from all the secrets and eccentricities. There were not many cars, but I didn't rush or accelerate – everything seemed under control, and I wanted to prolong this feeling. Julian, who had fallen into the net and was practically tied hand and foot, was calm, silent, and looked straight ahead. The guide kept sniffling his eternally runny nose in the backseat, and my trustworthy Alfa Romeo hummed along as if being happy to have a full tank and thoroughly good asphalt.

Then the avenue ended, and we rode into the surrounding suburbs with their crooked streets and decaying low homes. Louis livened up and began to babble, explaining when and where I should go. I glared at him disapprovingly, but he, apparently misconstruing my look, chattered even more, trying to inform us of something about almost every side street along the way. Soon it became intolerable, and I had to silence him harshly, so Julian even looked at me and raised his eyebrows. The stripling piped down in fright and almost missed the next turn.

Tourist, I thought about Julian, giving him a reassuring nod at the same time. Regarding the teenager there was nothing to even think – he was too young and dumb. What terrible company I've got here… And the unwelcome memories started flowing: how only a couple of months ago I had been jolting along in a heavy Land Rover toward the same Dunes, only to the north, not the south. I recalled the streets with mansions – and the Christophers, Silvia who resembled a gypsy, the cold beauty of Stella. And, of course, Gibbs… Again the thought of my recent dream flashed , but I soon felt re-energized, focusing on the critical talk, which awaited me and him and was still ahead. I will settle my current affairs and then – yes, I'll find him; he won't be able to spurn me and not listen. How funny though: why did I want to become friends with those scoundrels, while these two were completely foreign to me, like extraneous biological species?

I blinked angrily a few times, as if expelling unneeded sentimentality. Extraneous, not extraneous, there was no choice anyway.

"There, by the sign – make a left onto the byway; in a half mile we'll pop out on a track," gurgled Louis from the back and sneezed. The rain lashed down harder, and, after the turn, the car started to jolt from side to side on the dirt. I decelerated and concentrated on the slippery rut. Fortunately, we soon landed on something resembling a paved road – crumbling and requiring repair but still retaining the remains of a hard surface.

I felt encouraged, and the spirits of my fellow travelers also seemed to pick up. The teen had begun to whistle an off-key tune, but halted in a flash after I gave him another strict look, and Julian squirmed in his seat, lit a cigarette, and, obviously tired of silence, engaged me in a tedious conversation. I replied, not very willingly, yet still demonstrating a certain friendliness. It wasn't worth becoming antisocial and leaving him alone with his own thoughts, which might not lead to good conclusions. The presence of a stranger didn't allow us to talk about business, which I immediately hinted at, and, as a result, the talk wound down to Julian's monologue on the bad weather, the road, and the ordinary scenes flying by. On the whole, he was complacent and relaxed, probably consumed with anticipation of real masculine fulfillment. I glanced at him, the young, strong, confident man, and felt just as confident, young, and strong, but all the fulfillments waiting ahead agitated my blood much less, including the one we were rushing toward now, spraying mud onto the roadside. I even envied his ignorance, but my envy was quickly banished as unworthy of me, the leader of a small battalion that had to obey my will. In ignorance, you can't lead, I reproached myself and made a wisecrack in response to the inevitable question from Julian, "Are those the Dunes already?"

No, those weren't the Dunes but regular mounds of clay extending to the left and right as far as the eye could see, and even Louis giggled at such an absurdity. In the meantime, the rain had become more furious. Everything around us appeared desolate and depressing. Julian fell silent for a few minutes, then sighed, narrowed his gaze at the mirror where the teen slumped in the back, and said to me in a low voice, "By the way, I didn't mention you to Vee. She was upset anyway – that I was disappearing somewhere, even if not for long. It's brutal to leave her there alone, she complained, and moreover, it's unclear where I was actually going… She probably suspects I'm going to see girls," he admitted. "Although I'm nu-not!"

"You were right to keep your mouth shut," I encouraged him. "Otherwise you know what would've happened – questions, lots of questions. You'll be better off to simply let her know in the future: you have a partner. Just a partner, that is."

"That's true," Julian agreed sluggishly. "But why did she get so upset? She was strongly opposed to the whole venture – although I didn't go into details, just outlined it in vague terms. But that was enough for her – she became distressed and whined all day long. All that, she said, is incomprehensible and strange, sketchy and too unexpected. Yeah, it's surprising, certainly, I told her, but why not – chance is always hanging around. But she doesn't like chance, chance just frightens her. A little slower would be better, she said, slower and so that there's no room for chance. Let's finish this business trip, let's return to the boutiques, opera, and theater, and everything will be normal again, she insisted. And they'll promote you, we haven't suffered for nothing, so why, she rebuked, are you suddenly going to chase some birds in the sky? I made a joke – well, I said, like the Blue ones, what the monument is for. But she didn't get it, was all upset and even cried. A down-to-earth girl, like all of them."

Julian got serious and abruptly admitted, "You know, sometimes I'm afraid of her. She knows everything in advance – imagine dealing with that."

I almost told him he should be afraid of me now, not Vera, but that probably wouldn't have been a good joke. So I merely agreed with him, sounding compassionate, again sensing a remote signal of solidarity springing up between us despite my belligerent disposition. The rain didn't abate and the road was getting worse; the firm surface yielded to pasty, soaked dirt on which my Alfa Romeo was rather shaky. Ahead of us appeared a fork in the road, but our guide was silent, had even stopped sniffling. "Louis!" I hollered, and he started, swiveled this way and that, and said, "Left."

I asked him again, hoping it was an error. A nearly undrivable track headed off to the left, full of potholes and huge puddles. "Left, left," the stripling confirmed. "We're pretty close now." I cursed, turned grudgingly, and we bumbled from hole to hole, trying to keep our teeth from chattering. Sometimes the car skidded, and I tried to be as careful as possible, but still got distracted once by a silhouette, seeming to shimmer on the roadside, and yanked the steering wheel the wrong way, driving the front wheels into thick mud. Instantly we were stuck, turning almost sideways, only a miracle saving us from crashing into the ditch along the edge.

I had to give my companions their due – no one murmured or complained, despite the fact it was them, not me, the one at fault for the event, who had to climb out of the warmth into the rain and push a disobedient car that didn't want to move an inch. Ultimately, I shared their lot, handing the wheel over to Louis, who was the lightest of us, and strictly instructing him to be careful with the clutch. Only then did the car give in, and soon we were again rolling on, coated in dirt from head to toe, laughing at ourselves and cursing the wretched weather.

Julian, as if invigorated by the fresh air, forgot about Vera and cheered up again. Besides, the rain finally stopped and sandy hills rose up to our left, very similar to the real Dunes, which I told him cautiously, afraid that Louis might correct me. But the guide was silent, staring out the window, while Julian squinted victoriously, feeling like a daring pioneer. I didn't tell him that driving in a car on a road around the place wasn't the same as when you walked. It could well be he'd soon know this better than me. Personally, as I gazed at the slopes overgrown with shrubs, I didn't feel anything – neither animation nor bitterness. I just briefly recalled my unsuccessful nighttime escape that had happened ages ago.

We drove a few more miles without any adventures. Then I looked at the clock and ordered a break, especially since Louis had been squirming in the back seat for a while and was noticeably uncomfortable.

"Do we still have far to go?" I asked him, carefully steering us onto the shoulder and making sure the ground beneath the tires was firm enough.

"No, we're almost there," – he waved his hand casually and trotted off to the closest hill. Julian and I followed his example, and, upon returning, took out the thermoses and food, but Louis didn't come back. After waiting half an hour, we got worried and went out to search, which, as could be anticipated, was futile. For some incomprehensible reason our guide had disappeared without a trace.

This was a deviation in the plan, an unforeseen and extremely unpleasant one. I suddenly sensed all the severity of the landscape, where we were unwelcome strangers, and recalled my earlier experiences, which now rang vain warnings. The world around me became much gloomier, and the car shrunk and seemed ready to crumble like a tin can under foot.

Julian sensed my uncertainty and asked hoarsely, "Well? Lost, huh? If we wait, maybe he'll return?"

Inaudible malice rose within me – at him, at Louis, at the Dunes to our left and the mud-covered road, at the hateful rain that was misting again, and at myself, ready to become limp as soon as something didn't go my way.

"No, we're not waiting," I replied coldly, trying not to let my voice betray me. "There's no time to wait. The hell with him, it's his problem. I'll pick him up on the way back."

With these words I grabbed both thermoses and walked to the car as though I didn't want to discuss the obvious anymore. Julian silently sat down in the passenger's seat, and we rolled on, peering into the gray drizzle and probably contemplating the same thing.

Yes, was spinning in my head, I should have expected this or something of the sort. When you deal with such people as Jeremy... And this Louis is the same – even though he's still a boy and probably a dimwit. He undoubtedly thought up something from the beginning – so the road led someplace he needed to go, which means the village could be somewhere completely different. Should we turn around? Turn around now or keep going a little?

Julian coughed and again asked, "Do you know where to go? Perhaps we should drive back?"

Ditherer, I thought furiously. No more signals were travelling between us; the hint of solidarity that had arisen after the conversation about Vera and pushing the car had completely disappeared. I assessed him with a hateful look and growled through my teeth, "Don't worry, I've driven here more than once. We'll be there in half an hour." He turned away with a morose expression, in all likelihood not believing me, but I didn't care.

They decided to frighten us, I raged to myself. It's a trifle, cheap. And look at him here – look how he's twitching... No problem, let him twitch. He's got nowhere to go: he won't get out of here on foot – so he'll ride with me, my passenger with no rights. I have two-thirds of a tank and a canister in the trunk. We'll roll along while we have gas – take this road to the end and then go back to the fork and head down the other. How was it with Gibbs in his original plan – moving progressively from quarter to quarter and gluing pieces of adhesive paper over each one? Ingenious, I have to confess. He's really a joker, that Gibbs!

At this thought, we drove up the next hill and Julian said in astonishment, "Look, there's the sea," – pointing ahead. I narrowed my eyes and made out, through the veil of rain, a gray strip almost indistinguishable from the sky weighted down by clouds. He's quicksighted, I noted to myself and replied indifferently, "What sea, Julian? An ocean isn't a sea, it's on an entirely different level. But you'll get it later." The road, in the meantime, was clearly bringing us closer to the coast, and soon, to my great surprise, the first houses appeared on our right. A few minutes later we landed at the store, where the road ended at a small square with a puddle in the middle of it.

"We're there," I said. "Get ready." He glanced from side to side, and I, after cautiously halting at the curb, went to arrange the parking spot with the Turk. Less than anything else did I want to meet one of my acquaintances inside – especially Mr. Parker or Archibald – but, luckily, the store was empty. Just the owner, even fatter than before, sat still on his stool in the corner. For some reason, he pretended to be annoyed with me and angry, and didn't even take the cigarette I extended him, but I had no time to figure out his moods. Pulling out money and asking him to watch the car till tomorrow, I received an affirmative nod, laid a few small bills on the counter, and hurried out.

Soon we were striding north. Behind the fences, dogs barked as if testifying that life hadn't left the place in the week during my absence, yet not one person crossed our path. Before long Maria's house appeared – the last of them all, rickety and standing apart. My heart flinched involuntarily; I wanted to knock and hear the voice of the grumpy owner with the kindest of souls, but I only pointed at the locked gate and told Julian, "You can stay there. Just in case…" – and knew I had now eased his future lot as much as I could. Maybe even too much.

Then we walked along the coast, over the hard sand by the water, occasionally turning away from particularly rambunctious waves. The rain had stopped; the wind had become crisper and picked up, but blew from the side, from the shore, and didn't slow us. It was difficult to talk, we were mostly silent, just infrequently exchanging a few brief words and filling our chests with the fresh ocean air.

Various feelings gripped me. I believed and didn't believe that the whole plan would come to an end soon, wishing the denouement would take place, and at the same time driving off any thought of it. Occasionally, fervent impatience swept over me, but then my head would cool down again. I looked around, examined the area, and watched Julian with some abstract curiosity. His enormous backpack did not encumber him yet. He walked nimbly, obviously sensing that the dusty office and Vera, languishing in boredom, remained behind him and no more chains held him back and fettered his movement. I liked this version of him, however pathetic it was to admit that, and I again thought that every scheme always runs into contradictions capable of bringing a lot to nothing. But that doesn't hurt the initial courage – that's the beauty of being short-sighted with any plan.

The outpost appeared in front of us. "The police point," I told Julian, indicating it with a nod. "Representatives of the government, so to speak, but who knows what they're here for. Remember them, but don't reveal too much if something happens. That is, don't reveal anything, just wave the papers in their face."

"Got it," Julian grinned, excited like a puppy. "But where are the papers? I don't have any."

"They're here," I said firmly, showing him my breast pocket. "When we've cleared the post, I'll hand them over." And I strode on, not going into unnecessary explanations.

Walking up to the fence, I yanked the locked gate and yelled, "Hey, is anybody here?" Julian stood a little off to the side, observing the event with polite interest. No one was there, not even a dog, and this didn't particularly please me. If no one comes, we'll climb over it and that's it, I thought discontently, but at that instant the disheveled and somewhat swollen Fantik emerged from the cabin.

"What do you want?" he asked in an irritated falsetto, trying to sound strict and threatening.

"Don't you recognize me?" I inquired. "Here, open up. Where's Caspar?"

Fantik stuffed his hands in his pockets and, shuffling his heels, walked up to the gate from the inside, looking at me with an unfriendly grin. "Whether I recognize you or not..." he muttered. "Who can tell? You all look the same. There are a lot of you and only one of me!" He sighed and scratched his nose. "I'm alone here; Caspar's in the city. The boss called him in."

I saw he was annoyed and frightened and not inclined to welcome strangers. "If Caspar's in the city, all right then," I said indifferently. "When he comes back, tell him I said hello. Open up already, we need to keep going."

"Show me your documents," said Fantik with visible spite, baring his teeth as he grinned hostilely. "No documents – no entrance."

I shrugged my shoulders, pulled the prepared letters out of my pocket, and thrust them at the policeman, adding coldly, "Study 'em to your heart's content, but watch your greasy fingers. We still need 'em."

Fantik twirled the letters in his hands, exhaled, started to read one of them, then shifted his eyes to Julian and examined his backpack with suspicion. Julian returned the look without confusion and even somewhat challengingly. That he can do well, I thought with strange satisfaction, as if taking pride in some achievement of mine.

"Well, I don't know," Fantik drawled. "Go if you want – what's it to me? I'm alone," he repeated nastily, opening the gate and gazing to the side as we pushed by him and waited at the opposite fence, which was also locked. "Take care," I tossed back at him, but he didn't say anything in response.

The going became more difficult. The coast curved toward the west, and the wind now almost blew in our faces. Julian turned wary and looked around him more and more frequently. Fantik's anxiety seemed to have passed on to him. His liveliness vanished, yielding to gloomy pensiveness.

"I see you've been here before," he either asked or noted without looking at me. "Why haven't you taken the measurements yourself? Or is it still far?"

His voice sounded unsteady and even a little grumpy. "It's not that far," I replied, turning away. "You'll make it by dark."

All my emotion disappeared; only irritation rose within me – at Fantik, at Julian, at all mankind. Why can't you get away from the wishes and doubts of others when it's not easy to cope even with your own? Whatever you plan, some strangers are always slowing you down. They have the right; they know that alone you won't accomplish much, so accept them, persuade them, convince, force, support…

Let it all end soon, I thought angrily. I have no more patience, and the story has almost been exhausted. Should I leave him right here?

"If it's close, then why are you going with me?" Julian didn't let up. "And, again, why didn't you measure everything before, when you were here? Something doesn't make sense."

"I didn't have time, so I didn't measure," I grumbled in response. "And I'm going with you so I don't return immediately. The policeman would be puzzled by that."

I looked at Julian and saw he was really frightened. He's sensed something, I thought. He's about to become obstinate and refuse to go on.

"Can we stop and have a bite to eat?" Julian asked with hope in his voice, as if confirming my reflections. I replied calmly, "You can eat afterward," and wanted to add something encouraging, but suddenly noticed two strange dots over the water in the distance, which didn't resemble ordinary seagulls. It seemed they were approaching us, but a moment later they vanished from sight. My throat dried up and all my words disappeared. I halted, trying to collect my thoughts, adjusted the unfastened bag on my shoulder so I could easily slip my hand in if necessary, and turned around, toward the outpost, which was already hidden far behind the hills. Julian stood a little further off and threw his backpack on the sand.

"So, we are going to eat something? Or are we just taking a break to smoke?" he inquired, glancing around.

"Look," I responded, "we'll smoke, and then you keep going. It's time for me to head back." He nodded uncertainly and we lit cigarettes, quickly pulling on them and avoiding each other's eyes.

With all my skin I felt the tension thickening in the air. The space between us filled rapidly with charged particles; spirals twirled and microscopic bolts of lightning flashed, outlining the traces of what had been left unsaid, deliberate, poorly hidden. All the deficiencies of the hasty lie, all the weak points were visible to me with astonishing clarity, and I knew Julian clearly perceived them as if they were under a magnifying glass.

"Well," I said, flicking the butt into the sand. "It's time for me to leave you. In about three hours you'll see a concrete pedestal right by the water. They tossed it down from a helicopter – that's the place. Call me when you get back to the city. I'll make arrangements with the track for you in the village now."

Julian raised his eyes to me and sneered. I knew I shouldn't look at him, wouldn't hold out and would give myself away, yet I couldn't resist: for a few seconds our eyes bore into each other and we didn't say a word. It suddenly became clear that nothing can be concealed, nothing and never. Impatience engulfed me – and he saw my impatience. I was indifferent to his fate – and he saw my indifference as clear as day, and he also saw that I wanted to avoid his gaze – avoid and take cover. At first a question flickered in his eyes, then disbelief and offense, then there was a strange blaze, which I couldn't figure out at all.

Surprisingly, my confidence didn't leave me. I knew he wouldn't get it that quickly, even in a sudden revelation, couldn't assimilate, guess, or find a true defense for what I'd nurtured for many months. My plan wasn't ideal, far from it, but so much energy and contemplation had gone into the whole thing that it couldn't be flung aside instantaneously.

"Go, Julian," I said firmly. "Go, it's already getting late."

"Yeah, it's getting late…" he muttered, gazing with the same odd glare, then roused himself, took his backpack, and easily tossed it onto his shoulder. "How long did you say I need to get to the right place?" he asked distractedly, as if uninterested in the answer.

"Three hours or so – there's a pedestal there, you'll see it," I repeated, laying my right hand on the unfastened bag. The revolver lay at the top, just under my clothing. I had already decided not to shoot at Julian, but I was very ready to fire in the air as a warning.

Julian was about to take an irresolute step, then again turned around and stared at me point-blank. "Is this all really true – about the highway, the measurements, everything?" he asked, the tension rising in his voice, which also held both hope and fear, and the abrupt realization it was impossible to back down now.

"It's all really true," I replied cruelly. "Why are you twitching? Are you afraid?"

No, he wasn't afraid – at least not afraid of me. I understood him very well at that moment – better than anyone else. I knew now there was no need to shoot – on his own he had chased himself into a corner from which there was no exit. You can't fight your own delusions; you protect your blindness down to the last drop. Invisible voices may scream inside you, warning and making you listen; uncertainty confuses you and your thoughts; but in a gathering of chimeras, especially lacking the habit, you won't find sensible ground for indecisiveness and doubt. Of course, if *my* Stella appeared at his side, then everything might turn out differently, but Stella wasn't there, only Vera was, left far beyond the parentheses and not taken into account. There was no reason to refuse; there was not enough naïve vigor to withdraw decisively, although as he peered at me, he probably imagined a lot. He might become muddled with foreboding – but you don't expose yourself to laughter because of what you read in someone's eyes.

"Go, Julian," I said once again.

"Okay," he simply replied, nodded at me with a forced smile, and walked away without looking back.

I watched him until he disappeared behind the next bend of the coast – watched and saw my enemy leave. He was walking toward something invisible, incomprehensible, and promising more than he was capable of grasping. I envied him fiercely, was ready to change places with him that very second, feeling a century older and wiser, more powerless and restless, more drained and cruder. In the distance the same strange dots suddenly appeared. Now their number had increased, and they moved more quickly. I tossed one glance in their direction and dropped to the sand, burying my hands and face in it.

That's a victory, I thought, and there's no more secret – it has outlived itself. The wind threw fistfuls of sand at my hair. I pulled my jacket over my head and forced my thoughts to disappear, imagining myself to be a formless clot of emptiness with a rough soft cover. "Go, Julian," someone whispered inside me, and then I didn't hear anything at all, even the crashing waves or the howling wind. Only the sand rustled against the waterproof fabric, like a fantasy set free, to return no more.

CHAPTER 15

When I stood up, brushing myself off and looking around, the day was already winding down. All trace of Julian had vanished, with no black dots or ominous signs left in my field of vision. Nothing disturbed the desolate coast. The waves rolled in rhythmically, the wind whistled, rippling the water in the distance, toward the horizon. It was cold, and I felt it. Trying to warm up, I walked quickly along the wet sand, sometimes switching over to a jog.

Fragments of thoughts glittered and spun chaotically, like shreds of ripped-up letters. I was not happy and not proud. I knew I had achieved my goal, but I understood it didn't change anything – in me or around me. Only in Julian could there be changes, and there would be, oh yes, but what did it matter, what did I care? It wouldn't benefit me, I wouldn't even be able to watch the after-effects – neither watch it nor ask anyone about it later. What had I been reckoning on in general?

Instantly, invisible voices whispered, encouraging me: everything's still ahead. Isn't it pointless? – I asked them, but got no reply. I felt not a grain of anger in my soul; there was only tiredness and some new vulnerability – and also a sense of incompleteness, as it is when you try to place the period too soon. Why's that? – I wondered and winced, unable to find an answer. I turned to the ocean, grabbed my useless revolver, and flung it far into the waves, as if trying to raise one more barrier between myself and my former secret. Yet that didn't help either. I instantly missed my Colt, and the feeling of the period placed too early chafed at my mind, like an undeserved offense.

When I got back to the village it was already dark. Everything went smoothly at the outpost: Fantik didn't have much interest in me.

"Alone?" he asked, peering into my face and out the back of me, as if trying to discern some vanishing shadows. Then he just twisted his mouth and opened both gates, waving, "Alright, go on."

"Of course," I grumbled as a warning. "Don't pretend to be the boss. Where's the dog?"

"It ran away," Fantik shrugged his shoulders. "When Casper left, it took off. But where can you run to here? So they abandoned me without even a dog. I'm alone..." he began with his former tediousness, and I hurried away, unconcerned about his gripes.

Maria's house loomed darkly as an angular silhouette, with light shining through the blinds in the kitchen. I vacillated next to it in doubt, but admitted driving along the Dunes at night, on a barely visible road, didn't appeal to me in the least. I knocked – once and again. Maria didn't open up quickly and was not at all happy when she did. "You're here," she stated with dissatisfaction and stepped aside, letting me in. "Comes so late in the evening and knocks as if I should be waiting for him. Departs, arrives. There's no peace."

"Don't complain, Maria," I entreated her. "I'm only staying until tomorrow morning. And I'll pay, of course. I just hope you don't have visitors..."

The thought of any human company was really intolerable to me. Almost any – this didn't apply to Maria, with her it was always easy, especially since she soon loosened up and gave me some eggs with potatoes and bacon, saying while I ate that the Parkers were either sick or angry at her about something and had stopped coming. Yet Archibald, whom she called "your hopeless drunk," had wandered over twice and inquired about me, though he was strictly informed he was asking at the wrong place.

I listened and nodded, occasionally chuckling in response, but, in truth, the village news didn't resonate with me. I thought about the strange dots on the background of leaden clouds and about my former enemy, noticing he was getting increasingly indistinct in my memory, like a figurine slithering from canvas to canvas until it becomes impossible to recognize.

"Wake me up early, Maria. I have to leave at dawn," I said, thanking her for the eggs, and she took me to the same room I had lived in during those memorable weeks. I threw myself on the bed and fell asleep instantly. In the morning I wolfed down a pile of hot pancakes and departed from the village without meeting anyone – to my great relief. Maria flatly refused to accept money from me, but I managed to slip a bill under the old candleholder in the living room.

The road to the city was easy – I confidently turned at the forks, thinking I could sketch out a detailed map of the locality for anyone who wanted it. There weren't a whole lot who would, however. Only Jeremy might be interested, I thought to myself vengefully and instantly forgot about him. The greedy manager remained in the past, like a random ancillary instrument – and I didn't want to stir up the past, didn't care about the wasted money or the guide who had vanished inexplicably. I just regretted in passing that I'd no longer want to stay in the Arcada where, whatever you might say, I'd been totally comfortable.

The thought of the Arcada returned me to Julian and our last dinner, and then to other details of the recently completed plan – right up to the separation from my beloved revolver. I felt even more poignantly than yesterday that I had not pursued my idea to the very end, and no amount of persuasion helped me ensure the opposite. I sought liberation within myself and didn't find it, knowing that one more step was still necessary, some further action was needed to crown it all. These contemplations did not let me rest, and then a bright flash bolted through my head: of course – Gibbs! How could I have forgotten? I'll tell him and comprehend it better, share it and remove the burden from my shoulders, I repeated to myself, not able to explain why it had to be like that, but not doubting it, understanding my secret should stop being a secret, and then things would clear up in some, maybe even illogical, way.

That calmed my soul. My thoughts, tired of eternally running in circles, stumbled and froze in place. This probably wouldn't last long, but what of it? Hardly anything lasts long, even a mark on your cheek may sooner or later turn into a forgery. Evaluate – and err. Err – and embarrass yourself. Now I know that anyone can embarrass himself easily – some even do it with overwhelming willingness. I know and am ready to not close my eyes, although I feel I need peace and want to dump it all and do something different, perhaps leave this city right now, like a tiresome place you've been fed up with for ages. But I won't surrender to this sally and will keep listening and looking deeper into the impenetrable darkness – what's there, who's there, what are you talking about? How did Piolin put it – instead of X, you discover Y, and only then do you understand that you need Z? And he also said, you think you're searching for Julian, but you find someone named Gibbs. And now, that's how it's turning out, and, moreover, it seems I am that Z, no one else. I definitely have enough strength for that – let me be Z, and I could also be ZZ, it sounds still better. I might even become ZZZ, which looks really solid, and by the way, if we're on the subject of Piolin, why not roll into his hotel and search for Gibbs there? It works out nicely – the restaurant, the beginning, the end. Piolin is certainly the villain of all villains, but why should I be afraid of him? No reason at all, and I'm not.

Playing with this thought a little longer, I still postponed the decision until later, despite the fact the fringe of the city was already flickering by outside the window. The serious matters would have to wait: first I wanted to satisfy one unwitting caprice, a funny charade that had occurred to me yesterday on the empty ocean shore. Maybe it wasn't that funny, but when something is itching inside you, then it's easier to surrender without contemplating – rather than sort through intelligent reasons not to pursue it.

I headed right for the central square, spoke to a bored policeman at the intersection, and soon steered toward an inconspicuous street in the eastern half of the city. Julian's building was no different from the other multistory houses in the densely settled community. I parked close to a modest café, went inside, and asked for permission to make a call. No one answered for a while, but then I heard a click, and a woman's voice, out of breath, said the touchingly recognizable "Hello."

Yes, it was dumb and even risky – to call Vera, surfacing from an entirely new realm to intrude on her new life – but this risk was more inviting than anything else. She probably felt the same, not hiding her slight irritation, mixed with surprise and inevitable curiosity, upon which I'd placed my bet. Ultimately it won, and Vera agreed to come down to the café, warning me she needed a while to get ready – she'd been lying in bed all morning, and my call had dragged her out of the bathtub.

She took no small amount of time – I managed to drive down to a gas station, return, have a bite to eat, and get pretty bored. The thought even flashed through my head that I should disappear now, when the first, most exciting part was behind me and the continuation could well turn out to be a big disappointment. But then Vera materialized in the doorway, impulsive as before, a little haughty, but still elusively different, as if her armor had become more solid and shed its transparency while her movements did not have their former extravagant lavishness. "Hi," she said gently and sat down at my table, without taking off her coat. "I'd like coffee without milk and some toast, please."

I, clicking on the mask of courteous ladies' man, peered at her closely. She hadn't lost her beauty, even the opposite, but it was as if an ultrafine web had been thrown over her pretty, classical features, emphasizing what would be better to hide. Perhaps I was too judgmental and somewhat unjust, yet however it was – neither her makeup nor her graceful look disguised that patina of wrinkles in which you could see mistrust and stubbornness, and traces of deep-concealed anger. I looked at her furtively, noted it to myself, and dismissed it all – it was pointless.

Neither former feelings nor memories stirred my soul – just as my monkey's hand didn't make any impression on Vera. "What's that on you? You need to put some make-up on it," she only said in passing. I was about to fool around and descend into confusing explanations, but she waved her hand in annoyance, "Oh, stop," and switched to something else.

For some time, we struggled to keep the conversation going, although Vera chattered quite glibly. "I don't know why I'm doing this – that is, meeting you here," she announced. "What happened is in the past, you probably realize that. As for me, I realize it very well and convince Jules of it when he suddenly starts to say all sorts of neurotic things. You men aren't very intelligent in these areas, although I have to admit he hardly talks about it anymore. How do I look? – Oh, thanks, thanks, you flatter me. I've lost my looks far away from society, can't even find a decent hairdresser. This place is terrible – I mean, really! Once I even told Jules: if one of my old friends saw me, Vit for example, he would be struck by the change and chide the satrap who held me in a dungeon here like a white-winged swan. He didn't like it though – not because of the dungeon, but, I think, because of Vit. That's a small compliment for you."

I didn't like it either – and also because of Vit. The idiotic, long-forgotten nickname grated against my ear. "My name is Vitus, Vera, not Vit but Vitus," I said rather coldly, dispensing with courtesy since it was no longer needed.

She froze with the cup in her hand and drawled in surprise, "A-ah, if that's how you like it..." Yes, like that, I wanted to say and still wanted to add she could call me ZZZ if she liked that more or if the regular Vitus did not suit her for some reason. But I didn't, since I couldn't count on her understanding and it would have been too tedious to explain.

This episode clearly confounded her. She couldn't decide what tone to adopt with me and kept squeezing her long, pretty fingers whose playfulness I remembered well. She began sentences and instantly aborted them, asking something and distractedly waving off the answer, frowning and grinning without reason. Finally she shut up, lit a cigarette, pondered something, turning to the side, and then asked demandingly and seriously, "Well, why did you invite me here?"

I feigned astonishment. "What do you mean?"

"I mean, what do you want?" she specified. "We've made small talk long enough. Something in your innocent sentimentality isn't believable. And your eyes are strange, and you have some filthy thing on your cheek. In general, you've changed, Vitus," she added with an intentional stress on the last word.

"We all change," I mumbled back to her in the same tone. And I didn't want anything from her – even if in the forgotten past I'd been preparing to shoot Julian, concerning his woman I hadn't had any plans, irrespective of whether that woman had once belonged to me. Now she was clearly not mine – one look was enough to know. Let him deal with her if he wants, I thought, I've had enough. Especially since my curiosity has been satisfied – everything repeated all over again: "Vit, Vit" and tenacious, painted nails. The habits of a panther, but can she be a predator? That's the question. She's still somewhat cowardly – although what's there for her to be afraid of?

"Believe it or not, sentimentality is there," I admitted. "Precisely the most innocent kind – I just wanted to see you. Taking advantage, in a manner of speaking, of the chance and the concatenation of circumstances. That's the only reason – don't judge me too harshly."

Vera tossed her head and was about to purse her lips in offense, but then smiled at me with some affected naturalness. "Taking advantage of the chance..." she repeated after me. "What chance?"

"That Julian's number landed in my hands," I replied casually. "It was a random coincidence, don't take it seriously. So I decided to check," – and I made a slightly depressed face.

"So? How did your check go?" Vera asked mockingly. "Don't lie. You knew everything, why would you have to check now? And don't play the fool either."

She pulled out a mirror and began to fix her hair, then requested with the same elusive affectation, "Order me another coffee, please. With cognac."

I raised my eyebrows. "Isn't it a little early for cognac?"

"I don't care," Vera slipped her mirror in her bag, snapping it angrily shut. "Decorum doesn't matter here. Everything's permitted – as long as it helps you not to die of boredom."

I gestured to the waiter and thought with some irritation she was clearly not planning on leaving. Vera drank the cognac instantly, which brought color to her cheeks and made her look even more attractive. "I don't do it often," she informed me. "This sort of thing – cognac in the morning or a little grass. But sometimes I do, and I'm not ashamed. And what of it?" She looked at me challengingly. "I'm an individual, I need freedom. And I have a right to occasional indulgences – I'm young, don't forget!"

"Yes, certainly," I assented, feeling like I was losing time for nothing and thinking of a way to escape. But Vera suddenly leaned over the table and took my hand in hers.

"I need freedom," she repeated quietly. "I need emotions, passions. I want to sail, want to fly – you know how terrible it is when it seems your wings have been clipped forever. For some reason…" she gazed in my eyes. "For some reason I've recalled you frequently in the last month. What happened is in the past, I know, but even the old can occasionally be viewed in new colors. And now – so unexpectedly… Tell me, are you in the city for long?"

"No, not long," I said, somewhat dumbfounded, and lapsed into silence. Vera nodded encouragingly and smoothed my hand. This was all too much, was becoming absurd, grotesque. I had been ready for anything except hints at banal intrigue. Yes, Julian, your Vera wants to sleep with others out of ennui, and she's even ready to return to her castoff lover – you lucky guy, what else can I say? Is the whole world actually worth mere contempt?

A sharp feeling of anger pierced me. Why do even amusing puzzles require just the most primitive of answers? Defilement everywhere, I thought sadly. Everything is only worth a few cents.

"No, not long," I said again and squeezed her hand in response, feeling my lips twist into an unkind smile and something tickle in my throat. Really, Vera was always able to upset my equilibrium. Calm down, I shouted at myself, leave your emotions and hide your grin. This is just a funny exhibit in a museum of parodies – and you bought the ticket yourself for a penny. Why not joke around in response? This is as absurd as it can get – and you are also good with the absurd…

I relaxed my facial muscles and tried to change my smile to a seductive one. Then I gathered air in my chest and again squeezed her fingers. They were pliant and quivered like sharp sensors. For some time we silently looked at each other, then I said – a little awkwardly, but intensely and passionately, "I can't stay here for long, I'm leaving soon, but that isn't an obstacle, quite the opposite, in fact. You're right a thousand times over – you can repaint the old again and again. This is what I came here to say: drop everything and come with me, that's the most honest thing you can do. Decide – you're still young, still effervescent and capable of craziness!"

Vera froze in astonishment. Her hand strained in mine and seemed to turn lifeless, while her eyelashes and eyebrows shot up like frightened dragonflies.

"It's easier than easy if you thrust aside unneeded doubts. Only at first is it dreadful to imagine," I muttered, not letting her speak. "I've reconsidered a lot and recalled you often – in fact, I never forgot you at all. I admit I'm only here to free you, to release you from your prison and take you away."

It was too bookish and I was dissatisfied with myself, but it made an impression on Vera, despite the artificiality of the style. "But…" she said indecisively and blinked a few times.

"Wait, wait," I exclaimed, interrupting her. "I know what you're going to say, yet believe me – I'm not the same as I was. I've changed – yes, changed dramatically, realized the price of many things. I even learned to earn money – what else is required of a man? Now I know what you need, maybe better than you. Think about it, you're ruining yourself, wilting and losing years. You'll find love with me and you'll find passion. I'll care for you and keep watch over your sleep. I'm ready to indulge your whims, I'll be stronger than everyone when you want to be weak. I'll transform into a giant, a titan, strong like a rock, as immovable as a mountain…"

Vera looked at me without turning away, slightly narrowing her eyes. She was clearly befuddled. It seemed I heard the clicking of calculators in her pretty head – they were working at full steam: recombining, matching, trying to guess the odds. Their power was well known. The head-tart I had been given was dwindling rapidly and exposure loomed somewhere close by.

"I'll be beside you when you're beside yourself," I hurried on, lowering my voice and adding a slight hoarseness. "I'll wait for you if you decide to disappear – wait for a long time, even my whole life. I won't upset you with even one complaint – I'll always be kind and tender, no matter what nags at your soul. Like a stone wall, I'll protect you from all attacks and all offense. I'll be…"

My voice shook traitorously. I coughed, and Vera immediately withdrew her hand, straightened her back, and arrogantly raised her chin. Something changed in her face; the calculating had probably culminated and produced an answer.

"We'll always be…" I began again, but stuttered and desisted, as if I'd instantly lost all my words.

"Enough!" Vera screeched. "Who do you pretend to be? Who believes you? You've remained as you were: a babbler. You're only good for mocking others!"

She opened her bag, shoved her cigarettes in it, and snapped it shut. "Pay for my coffee, please, I have to go. And remember…" Her voice became even colder, and something resembling a threat appeared in it. "Remember, entertain yourself however you can but don't touch serious things, which one can't talk about in vain. Sooner or later you'll pay the price."

Yes, I thought. Your advice is just what I need. All-knowing Cassandra…

Don't trouble yourself, I'm not from your hen-house, I almost said aloud, but bit my tongue in time. It didn't make sense to get dragged into an altercation, as in old times. And I was already exceedingly angry at myself – for performing an amateurish show, and in front of whom? It's just buffoonery; buffoonery and a farce.

It'd be better to leave immediately, but I sat as if glued to the chair. Something forced me to snap in response, leaving the last word for me. I was sad about my memories – cheerful and irksome, abrupt and threatening like a typhoon. I was also sad about the former Vera, who made my soul tremble in anxiety, returning to me in random women and unfamiliar places. And I greatly missed what would never come back: the attic by the stadium, the large bumblebees flying around in May, all my youth that had disappeared forever. Nothing ever returns – and now the past had been ruined by new poison for which there is no antidote.

"We'll always be together," I said coldly, looking her in the eye. "Together, not doubting each other and not conceiving of disloyalty. It was dreary for us with others: we sought variety and, finding it, suffered ourselves. But now it's over – attaining dignity and rejecting the lie, we'll cleanse our souls and drop our hesitations. Unsuitable companions interfered with us, but we disposed of all companions – look, for your sake I enticed the last of them into a trap. He disappeared for three days, but three days can turn into an eternity. There's no barrier for your desires – the circumstances give in to them!"

I wanted to add something else, but Vera's pupils suddenly became very wide, and she again strained, thinking something rashly. "Trap… For three days…" she repeated after me. "So it was you who did that!" I was silent, and she continued quietly, "I knew it, I sensed it right away. I said – don't go, we don't need it. How could I have allowed it?"

"Forget it. I'm not the problem," I began, but Vera didn't look at me and didn't hear my words, entirely preoccupied with her own feverish thoughts. I shrugged my shoulders and turned away from her, trying to catch the eye of the waiter circling nearby. My dissatisfaction with myself became unbearable. Everything had turned out wrong, distorted and crooked, and there was nothing to do about it.

The waiter finally nodded and slowly made his way toward us. I laid the money on the edge of the table, lifted my eyes, and stumbled on an icy, hateful gaze.

"Do you understand that you always ruin everything?" Vera asked with unconcealed spite. "Have you even once noticed that the moment you touch something, you contaminate it – at first a little, almost imperceptibly, then more and more? You're simply sick, don't you think? Sick and maybe contagious – for those idiots who are ready to stare and heed all sorts of nonsense. And Jules – how could he manage to be such a fool? He's always been normal, there's no comparing you two."

She spoke to me but clearly without recognizing my existence. Her face swiftly aged, the light web turned into fabric with a rough knit, and her fingers entwined in a tense, merciless knot. As for me, I felt apathetic, just waiting for the outcome – either dull and boring or spectacularly theatrical. Only refuse and debris remained on my conscience while my secret and the ocean coast seemed to totally evaporate.

"I lived peacefully for almost a whole year," Vera rambled as she peered angrily into space. "Back then you also confused me – and ruined my marriage by the way – but, fortunately, Jules came at just the right time and you disappeared, good riddance. Okay, I thought, I'll relax now – and I relaxed and calmed down and completely believed I had finally found it... Even if not entirely, not as I had dreamed, but life is life, you can't patch up the holes with childhood romanticism. And it worked out – we just had to endure a few months more here, and everything would end up right. He would marry me, wouldn't have any other option, and would be promoted; it's already his turn. And we'd buy an apartment, and furniture, and stuff... Yes, it's awfully boring here, I find it so tedious I sometimes want to scream – but it's not a reason for him to rush stupidly who knows where. And I felt it, felt it right away. As soon as he hinted at it, I realized – something was wrong. I sensed it through every pore – and now, hello Mr. Vitus, the hero-loner appears. And it's clear as day – the thing won't end well. With you, everything always gets screwed up!"

Vera focused her sharp, contracted irises on me again. "You know," she hissed, "Jules is mine. I'm not giving him up, no matter who lures or flummoxes him. I don't know where you took him, even if to some girl, but he'll return, he won't vanish forever. He'll return and take care of me – for real, not like you pretended to. All his belongings are here, and his clothes... Thanks for the coffee!"

She jumped up impulsively, her burning beams piercing me one last time. As she turned to leave she bent over and said threateningly, showing her moist teeth, "And I'll get pregnant, I'll have a baby. He'll care for my baby!" And she strode away, confident and inaccessible, with a proudly raised head, attracting everyone's eye.

The waiter brought the change. I thanked him and sat for a few more minutes, grinning thoughtfully. Yes, Julian doesn't have much luck, but he'll throw her out, I guess. I'm not wishing her harm, yet he'll definitely do it – it can't be any other way. Though how should I know? And who's going to sweep the garbage and debris out of my conscience now?

It seemed I'd be in a bad mood for a while, but shortly after I noticed that both the irritation and anger at myself had dissipated, replaced by some playful recklessness, like after a difficult and dangerous affair that finally lies behind you. The present Vera faded from my mind, as if she hadn't been sitting in front of me just a couple minutes ago – I probably couldn't have described her face, gestures, or movements anymore. I only retained a feeling of something tenacious and stifling, concentrated and intransigent, which rustled a meter away, but fortunately didn't graze me and was now safely moving off. I realized my life could be different – temporarily or forever. I realized that, became belatedly horrified, and stopped thinking about it, like random danger that missed me on its own.

A large group poured into the café; it became uncomfortable and noisy. It was time to go in search of Gibbs – everything else was in the past. Evening enshrouded in the window; the City of M., no longer agitating, oppressed me. No problem, a little remains, I calmed myself, rubbed my monkey's hand, and walked to my car, nodding to the barman who looked at me stealthily with professional interest.

Finding Piolin's hotel didn't turn out to be easy, but ultimately

I managed to locate it. The same elderly clerk stood behind the counter, the lobby was empty and dim. He didn't recognize me or pretended not to, and this made an unpleasant impression.

"Hotels, unfamiliar houses, rooms in which no one is waiting," I whispered as I rode up in the elevator. I wanted to grumble to myself but didn't wish to talk with anyone else, especially Piolin. I'll take a rest, I decided, going into the room – so I tossed my coat and bag in the corner, flicked the remote control, and plopped down in the only chair.

The screen blinked, then lit up with a steady light, and an action movie flashed on it. The hero, glamorous and courageous, made the daughter of a gangster fall in love and unraveled a series of insidious plans. Lucky him, I thought, the script is written by someone clever, and all the traps are marked in advance with crosses. No need to worry, the conclusion is foretold anyway. They'll put someone in jail, others will get married, and it'll all be over. No, let's flip the station, here's another film – an old one, black and white, perhaps I'll return later. And here's something from the life of big cats – reminds me of the driver Ben…

I switched absentmindedly from channel to channel until I came to the local news. The anchor was talking with some important man in a three-piece suit that was soon replaced by a policeman with a chronicle of the events of the past few days. I listened halfheartedly – a car chase, a drunken fight, a fire in an outlying warehouse. They flashed photos of some slums where terrible things probably happened every day. Life, whatever you say, can be a thoroughly risky matter. You should remember that, I thought, stretching and enjoying the sense of my own security here, behind the solid hotel walls. I even turned my head and examined each of them separately, resting with a haughty grimace on the window, with its closed curtains, which no curious gaze could penetrate.

"…the operation, conducted today… a group of dealers were seized… brief shooting… the ringleader of the criminals was most probably killed…" the monotonous voice mumbled. I again turned to the television and froze. The whole screen was covered by a large photo of Gibbs. This was a blow I didn't expect and couldn't duck; the air filled with millions of sharp needles, something snapped inside me, fell onto the concrete stones and smashed into a thousand pieces.

"...long sought in connection with... under the pseudonyms... two policemen seriously wounded..." – the voice did not subside. They scrolled through a few different shots, then Gibbs appeared again, and the commentator declared with the same neutral tone, "...according to eyewitnesses he was killed outright... no official confirmation yet... the body has not been found..."

I didn't want to believe my eyes, but it was impossible to confuse the face with someone else's. Half of it still grinned contemptuously, not aware how fleeting that grin would be. Then they removed the photo and the broadcaster switched to another topic, yet I, not moving from my spot, continued to see that dead mien, which, if you hadn't known it, could have seemed alive. But I felt I knew – knew and couldn't deceive myself, gathering every second that something irreparable had happened, something you can't compare with anything else, can't fling aside or distance yourself from. It was really frightening, and a recent predator, which was now pushed beyond the limits of the mind, probably howled in horror, its hair bristling and its four paws pounding the ground. But its cry couldn't be heard here, behind the impervious walls, bringing joy with their solidity just a minute ago and now surrounding me on all sides, bearing down, as if in a prison cell from which I wouldn't escape no matter how hard I banged my fists on the door.

Chapter 16

Minutes passed, maybe even hours. I sat staring at the dirty gray screen and tried to grasp what had happened – gather the scattered bits and choke off the incoherent cries. The photo of Gibbs was long gone and the policeman yielded to a cheerful girl, twittering something about an approaching cyclone. Tears were running down my cheeks and I couldn't lift my hand to wipe them away. I was crushed, as if all my achievements had finally been recalled and struck off – and the judges put me in the spotlight to convince themselves they were right. And, when satisfied, they pasted the last stamp on me, the label that cannot be erased even if it isn't correct.

Something disjointed quivered in my head – like live pictures in quicksand. Gibbs and the Christophers, two malicious buffoons, Gibbs and the crazy owner of the motel, Gibbs in my room at Maria's house… The images didn't come one by one. It was as if they all rolled in at once – in turbid waves, flopping over each other and getting all mixed up. I couldn't make out the outlines or colors – and then they retreated, grew pale, leaving nothing but emptiness – a blind vacuum where no light, no sound, and no thought was able to penetrate. Nothing was able to penetrate, to confirm even a weak trace of someone's presence – if not me, then at least my barely visible reflection. Purple slime again swamped my inwardly directed eye, reviving the flickering of ethereal silhouettes, each one vanishing into another. Gibbs returned, arrogant and glum, derisive and tough like a taut spring – I saw and didn't see; knew he was there, in front of my eyes, but remembered every moment it was all nonsense – you can't see the nonexistent and hang on to what has ceased to live.

I could admit to myself now that only he could become my friend – if he wanted to, although he probably wouldn't. I could confess to myself that he had the right to judge me and my efforts – but what's the point of confessions, even when they are set free forever? The angular shadow of Death towered between us – you couldn't shock it with a face split in half, you couldn't lie to it with a pathetic mark, couldn't confuse it with stories, or hasty concoctions of fuzzy words that try so hard to break beyond the bounds of the ordinary but give up long before approaching the main secret. There's no one to complain to, and it isn't even worth regretting. Regret is for fools; you only freeze up from despair and obediently wait until it ebbs – and it will ebb, don't doubt it, since it isn't long, just as everything else isn't long, doomed to an end, like all the rest.

> There's no crossing fortune's hand
> the same fate's marching on for all
> along the narrow wasteland path
> creaking on a wooden crutch.
>
> Her midnight cloak lies black as soot
> the same will surely come for all
> without respect for wealth or rank
> be you bursars, torturers, or bards...

I spoke to who knows who, mumbling to myself, crying out inaudibly to the pretty girl on television since no one else was around. The name for those lines was powerlessness and couldn't be otherwise – I felt powerless now, like the most insignificant creature. But even an insignificant creature wants to share its thoughts with someone, especially in despair, as if despair can be blurted out in hoarse rapid-fire lines, and I quickly composed incantations, rhyming roughly and – whispering, whispering, whispering.

> Don't you rage at fate in vain
> this one song will not last long
> let's just sing it one more time –
> here's the poem's concluding chime.
>
> Jesting clown, take your ease
> don't conceal your wily face
> have your fun, your merry joy
> hasten on – escape forever!

Here I again recalled Gibbs, looking from the indifferent screen, and I groaned quietly from the self-pity that was creeping up inside me. I was alone now, and how naïve all my former loneliness appeared, whose price had been the smattering of illusions that accentuated the true darkness like an iridescent soap bubble. A gust blows it off, blows it off and bursts it; a mark on your cheek is the remainder, but that algebra also brings no relief. What else remains, what can I grab hold of, what will support me?

I got up awkwardly and began to traipse from one end of the cramped room to the other, from wall to wall. My lips were moving – at first silently, then muttering curses and damnations, then gruffly flustering chaotic lines, dozens and dozens of them coming to mind and instantly disappearing into the unknown – not remembered, not healing the suffering and not leaving any trace. Not one or any, as it seemed initially, but this too was not quite true – something still gathered in the area. I caught the imprints of elusive words, even if only for a split second. They created their material, ephemeral and imperceptible, enduring, everlasting, stretching to where the uninitiated not only didn't reach by sight, but also by thought, even if they would venture into such thought. The world changed by not actually changing at all. Its outlines were robed in a chain of signs, in rhymes and rhythms. I imagined them, created by me. They became substantial and real, and I knew it all existed somewhere, even if it couldn't exist for a typical ignorant eye. Harmony and beauty reappeared in faultless forms – and someone landing there could touch them with his soul, as if sensing eternity. Figures danced intricately on the one hundred and forty-four squares, attesting to unthinkable combinations that still have to be guessed at by those who would discover them at some point. The dashes of black ink over the ocean surf found their beginning there, as well as the patches of moonlight on the quicksand – and everything else that fits and materializes in the newly built reality which you have enough energy to reach, recognize and believe…

Despite you who don't accept complications, I said to the auditorium of outsiders, their miserable spirit alien to me, and to whom I myself was irreconcilably strange. In spite of you or simply not noticing you, not taking you into account, because in the formulas of my calculations exist things impossible to touch by hand, on which, to put it differently, it is impossible to lay your greedy hands – they'll slip through your fingers, dissolve like a mirage or a phantom. "What's that? Did something happen?" someone would ask, and the surrounding crowd would just shrug their shoulders in disbelief, feeling though not wanting to admit: it was and is. "What do you call it?" the meticulous ones, a few of them, wouldn't let up – and then they would fiddle with appellations, one worse than the next, stubbornly matching them with their yardsticks, but this too would be in vain.

Ask those who question day and night without you, I continued irritably. Ask Archibald Bely if you don't believe me – and he'll just laugh in your face. In order to access the mystery, you have to be worthy of it, and you, lazybones, will be rejected at the first door. But the mystery doesn't wane due to this, it doesn't need you – that's the main truth, which is so easy to realize if you are in the habit of occasional contemplation. It's you who need this mystery more than anything else, more strongly than satiation and pleasures, which is all you can concentrate on. Residing in the small part, it's not easy to peep over the border. It's only possible for a few – those to whom you are so merciless. But the borders do not fall away as a result of this, not at all. And what is behind them – behind and far beyond – remains as it was, whether you see it or not. It exists, more comprehensively than you can imagine; and the lie exists with which you calm yourself to keep from trembling in horror every hour, recalling the inevitability of death; and Gibbs exists somewhere: they didn't find his body – you hear, disbelievers? – he's more alive than any of you. They probably had a boat – and Stella said something about a boat! There's the key, he took it and ran – letting those who didn't understand shake their heads. Forget sadness, even if only in my world. If you get even one hint, then you can take an iron hold on it – take it and unravel the whole ball to the last thread!

I froze in the middle of the room and flapped my arms – I'm so dumb, I'm losing time! That's enough senseless whispering; I need to turn up my sleeves and do what I want to. You have a plan – see it through! If something needs to be changed along the way – no problem, we'll change it, restructure it, correct it.

I raced over to the table, grabbed an envelope, and wrote in big letters: "For Piolin for Gibbs. From Vitus. Please pass on." No problem, no problem, we'll see. Killed outright… Bullshit! Official confirmation had not come, they admitted it themselves. He had a boat. It's clear to anyone who understands…

I dug all the paper out of the drawer and wrote at the top of the first sheet, "Dear Gibbs!" Then I moved down a little and penned the first sentence, "To this day I remember the long road to the City of M." At this, I thought for a minute and began to scribble, not raising my head, covering the snow-white surface with even lines, describing everything that I did and did not want to tell him, that I could and could not, was able and unable to confess. "This one is not going to the trashcan," I mumbled. "I'm not ripping this up. I have the addressee and I'm sending it to my addressee; I'll pass it on, even if it has to wait an eternity. It will last – I believe, it will last and reach him, and those who do not believe – well, to hell with them!"

Rushing and stumbling from one thing to the next, I outlined the chronology of my secret, not embellishing anything and not trying to seem more far-sighted than I was, although now, in retrospect, much of it looked ridiculously naïve. I was only silent about Vera. The rest – my career, the sunny morning, the sudden decision, and the black Colt that I had parted with so disgracefully – all that found its time and place. I mentioned the game of *Dzhan,* and Lyubomir Lyubomirov stuck his nose out of the corner, and then, when the story again switched to the City of M., reaching our hike to the shore, I even heard once more the rustling of lizards and the terrible cry of the ocean owl. I imagined the Dunes at night and the endless gloomy coast. Events rolled in and formed tight-knit rows; patterns and images, colors and sounds were under my control now – I ruled over them with my powerful hand, as if looking down from above with nothing in my way.

Finally, the time came to recall the most important event, if not to say the strangest or the scariest of all. And here I stalled for a minute or two with my pen frozen in the air, then merely wrote, "…and you, Gibbs, know what I'm talking about." For some reason, I firmly understood that not only the name, but even a bashful euphemism would be inappropriate here. He really knew, and I knew; neither he nor I cared about the opinions of others, and it wasn't worth discussing at length, although I did add one unnecessary phrase in my delirious attempt to explain the unexplainable.

"I now know there is something in me. I, together with everyone else, have been chasing it away. I wasn't worthy of myself, but I really changed then," I wrote and, at the next moment, crossed it out assiduously and even balled up the whole piece of paper that announced the remains of weakness or hidden artificiality which superfluous words always attest to.

"I wandered to a village in the south and was sick but then completely recovered," I declared instead on a fresh sheet, avoiding sentimentality. I reread it, was satisfied, and hurried on, again picking up speed. My pen screeched and scratched the paper, my neck and shoulders had become numb and sore, my chewed lips hurt, but I wrote, without noticing anything else, only following the colorful kaleidoscope flickering, alternating, with landscapes, human figures, interiors, and faces: the Parkers and Doctor Nemo, two Marias and the paintings of Archibald, Mia, Jeremy, round like a ball… It was funny, I played with them, like toys, and then Julian re-appeared, placed in the spotlight, and I only touched on him, as I should, hinting and not blurting out what, where, and how it ended.

"I don't know what happened to him," I admitted. "And I'll never know. Perhaps that's the beauty of it, perhaps that's the secret. And you, Gibbs…"

I thought about the last phrase, then grinned and left it as it was, breaking off with an ellipsis – the benevolent symbol of all possible endings. Those, of all kinds, are better to think up later – not once or twice, altering and imagining them differently. And he, if he wants, can search me out to reach an agreement on the most credible one.

I stretched and wiped my tired eyes, then carefully collected the sheets strewn across the table, stuffed them into an envelope, and licked it shut. It was already light outside – night was coming to an end. Something thundered on the street and predawn sounds could be heard in the building – occasional noises in the pipes, the quick steps of the chambermaids, some jingling and creaking. I sat, contemplating whether I should leave right now, before dawn, then decided to lie down for a minute, and instantly fell into a deep sleep, where nothing existed – neither faces nor thoughts.

The rays of the sun woke me. It was late, I had slept away the whole morning. The white envelope lay on the table; my raincoat and my unopened bag sat in the corner as they had yesterday evening.

"Go! Go!" I commanded, jumping up in a hurry and feeling full of energy. My stay here was over, I had nothing to do in that city. The road and my faithful car beckoned and longed to head out. I went downstairs, ate a quick breakfast, and soon stood by the registration desk with the keys and the envelope in my hands.

"This is for Piolin," I said coldly to the desk clerk, extending the envelope. "He still runs this place, right?"

"Yes, of course," he replied, glanced over the fat letters, and lifted his eyes to me. "Did you have a chance to hear the latest news?"

he inquired in a low voice after a second or two, and then blinked hesitantly.

"I heard it, heard it," I said even more dryly. "Pass on the envelope and don't worry about the rest."

"Will do," the clerk lowered his head. I paid and, a minute later, was riding down the half-empty avenue in the direction of the only asphalt road leading out of the City of M. into the heart of the country.

I felt good, although it was sad. The windows of the surrounding buildings looked down on me without interest but with reciprocal sorrow. We knew we would never see each other again but retained our indifference, as if obeying a rule or habit. I had attained everything I'd wanted here, and the city had kept everything it didn't want to give up, concealing it behind a strong lock. We were even, and still the sadness didn't let up – maybe because the days could never return. I had become older, although by only the tiniest bit, and every façade, in turn, had decayed a little, adding attrition and cracks. "Remain strong," I whispered occasionally to the silent houses – shifting gears a little more abruptly than necessary but otherwise not differing from the hundreds of other visitors who complete a short stay and hurry away.

I was in no rush however, and my direction remained unclear. I was just driving on randomly, heading toward no specific place and not wanting to name any new goals. Something glistened to my left – the gilded arc, the statue to we-know-who – meaning the city was already behind me. Then the incomplete Memorial appeared, from which iron rods stick out, and, right after it, the rickety sign with the traditional wish. Well, the same to you too, although you aren't going anywhere.

Out of the corner of my eye I noticed a figure on the shoulder to my right, just after the sign. A wizened man stood with his hand slightly raised, trying to hitch a ride from the cars rushing by. Following a sudden impulse, I braked swiftly, veered out of the driving lane, and backed up, jolting over the potholes on the side and cursing through my teeth at this unexplainable whim.

The hitchhiker was totally surprised. He approached me

indecisively, slowed before looking inside, then said in a high voice with a sort of challenge, "I'm traveling a long way – twenty miles from here if not more, although right on this road. And I can't pay you – my wallet was stolen!" When he finished the sentence, which he had trouble uttering, he shifted his gaze and didn't see me nod that he could come along. "Oh, excuse me, hello, I should have begun with that," he added, stuttering and again looking at me with strange round eyes that didn't have any eyelashes.

"Hop in," I said, trying to sound friendly and repressing a grin. "I'm headed the same way."

The stranger repeated, "I can't pay for it," but seeing I wasn't reacting, shrugged his shoulders and sat in the passenger's seat. I observed he didn't have any baggage and was dressed too lightly for the time of year.

"Don't think I'm like this," he said crossly after a few minutes, turning away from me and looking out the window. "I'd be happy to pay you or take the bus, but my wallet was really stolen and I don't have a cent."

"Don't worry, I wasn't thinking that at all," I replied indifferently.

"I'm not a swindler and I'm not in the habit of lying," he resumed. "It's just that some strange thing happened. I got involved, right in the middle of it, and now I'm going to another place, and I probably can't stay there long either, to tell you the truth... In fact, I'm an astrophysicist, I have a degree, though you won't believe me of course, and of course you're right not to."

"Why not?" I looked at him with interest. "I believe you, and am very glad to. Tell me, can I ask... It concerns... I've wanted to know for a long time: is it true that everything flies apart – and with incredible speed? I mean – the expanding universe and so on, or is that all nonsense? Excuse me for putting it so amateurishly, but it's fascinating, although I don't know much."

The stranger thought for a second, looking at the road in front of us, then said in the same piercing high pitch, "No, why, your question is quite on the mark," – and began to discuss the hypothesis of the Big Bang and the arguments raging around it. His eyes lit up, his face gathered in soft pleats, and his hands scurried this way and that in the air, tracing wild curves as if directing hundreds of simultaneous thoughts.

"There was an explosion, and everything blew apart – yes, that's probably right," he said, his pupils glittering. "But was there only one? That's the most important issue, and no one's provided an answer yet. So it's worth assuming, and beside – not only apart, it may also be toward, inward, and afterward a clash, a jolt, a new cataclysm! The theories look good when only the nearest is taken into account, but let's consider infinities – why just one of them may exist? Imagine: many – or no, let's just say two for simplicity: two big explosions, and at some point the particles will reach each other, meet, intermix – and what is that, an expansion? No, and no again. You shouldn't be lazy, you need to look from every perspective – only then will the whole picture emerge. Maybe there are clusters, fragments, scattered spots, and we're only inside one, taking it for the whole in our blindness. And they say all is clear…"

He turned to me as if searching for my support, gesticulating and agitated, repeated a few things a couple times, asked himself and agreed with himself. I, listening intensely and afraid of missing even one word, was full of sympathy for his uneasy passion. It was more remote and more hopeless than anything I knew, and I realized I'd never be able to have forms or sounds embody even a part of my compassion, even a tiny bit of my understanding, the mild hint at my own anxiety that couldn't be expressed or explained. Okay, the clusters, the clouds of matter, but even inside them everything was running off to immeasurable distances. How can you have the courage and capture all that with your eye, I thought, replying to my companion with interjections and nods and trying to remember at least something of what he was saying in order to contemplate it later, alone.

"All in all, I'll tell you," the stranger continued, grinning confidentially. "I'll tell you: everything is arranged in its own way, and there's no reason to be proud of a superfluous assumption – or, I should add, to be ashamed of it. The cosmos has no limit of variety

– every phenomenon contains its own essence, every object, every soul. Take neutrinos – the eternal breath of the universe that gives rhythm and dimension. But is it cyclical, this breath? That's a big question! And, by the way, does it have a beginning and an end? Or, for example, large stars – do you know that each has its own special fate? Oh, that's very interesting and even instructive in a way. Some gradually burn out – dragging along everything nearby, expanding, consuming planets, coldly dimming. Whereas others explode, unable to hold back their own power – and that's a completely different issue! Imagine how wild it is, how much dynamism and movement, energy and detritus, what diverse forms… This is where everything really flies away, even if we don't notice it from here. We just speak with academic boredom – oh yeah, one more new nebula, several tens parsecs in diameter, a trifle for universal measurements. But if you look back a couple of billion years – what a tremendously bright explosion… Unfortunately, quite often we just don't have enough passion," he added. "I thought about this all last year – at home and in the hospital. I was sick a lot last year… Stop!" he exclaimed suddenly. "We passed the turn. My fault, I was babbling away and missed it. Don't worry, I'll go by foot…"

We reversed, although the stranger tried to object, and I dropped him by an untraversable rut, almost a path, which disappeared into the roadside bushes. "Thank you," he said to me. "Thank you," I replied and, driving off, I saw in the side mirror he was still standing and looking after me.

I didn't ask him his name, but didn't reprove myself for it. He answered my question, and that was more than I could've expected. What's his name to me – it'll be forgotten, like any word, like a person you rub shoulders with for a short time. The trajectories intersect at a point, become close – or, maybe, just seem close. Even your thoughts may find momentary sympathy, but you can't avoid separation, just as you can't guess when your eyes will be unlocked – all the curved paths in the universe are too complicated for predictions.

In the meantime, my compassionate response still lived within me. I felt something shrink away and something else, imponderable, found the place it had once abandoned in bewilderment and confusion. Stars, stars, each has their own fate. They may not be immortal but what else should your soul stretch for?

I realized that life was long and I still hadn't lived half of it, although sadness remained in me, waiting in the corner of the vaulted hall like a crooked figure on the bench by a pillar. It had something to recall if the time came, but I now saw that the hall was enormous, and a myriad of sounds soared under the ceiling, reverberating off the walls and mosaic floor, switching with each other, contradicting, dispersing, joining together. The world suddenly grew larger – yes, I agreed dutifully, it isn't that small, maybe it doesn't even have borders. Vigilant signals-scouts, sent out in all directions, don't return, obviously not encountering any barriers. They fly, rush, don't slow, like star particles freed by a blast, echoing more and more quietly, then completely getting lost, each in its own space...

"Or in its own dimension," I tossed in immediately, as if twisting a polyhedral crystal before my eyes. "How many of these dimensions are there? Can all the theories be incorrect, limited by common numbers?" It seemed I was again reliving the forgotten expectations, and the question marks almost appeared here and there. Neither desires nor doubt or hopes were locked anymore in a constrained circle of things, doomed to a word, to a person or a place. Julian disappeared, moving into the past. Other people disappeared too – dissolving, fading, and liberating more in me than there was before. I understood that my freedom was absolute and real, even if well-wishers might want to feel my forehead, noting with concern: you aren't healthy. I'll only laugh – come on, it's you who's got a fever – and we'll remain with our own. But I'll know for sure where the riches lie, and to them, the others, it will never occur until the very end.

The asphalt rustled under the tires; the wipers whisked the misting rain off the windshield; everything was smooth and exact. A rare moment, I thought, I'll recall it and file it away as an approximation of perfection. It's a pity I can't share it with anyone – too many details, no hope of describing all of them. If simplified, it'll lose the essence, will get narrowed down to the banal, which is everywhere. Why do most books teem with banalities as well? What is it – weakness of spirit and eternal fear?

"I'm for myself!" I said aloud. There was a lot of meaning in that, as Gibbs affirmed before and I was confirming now. But no one could accuse me of repeating after him. Even if it sounded similar, one could never know for certain – and I was about to open my mouth to explain why but quickly checked my thoughts: no, you don't need to ramble on anymore. You've made your point and that's enough – hold your tongue: *silence still rules.*

There was a fork ahead of me, and I, without contemplating, glided into the right lane, to the exit for the capital. The hero is returning, even if no one is there to meet the hero. How refreshed you look, you're a different person. What's that on your cheek? – He doesn't say a word…

Because there's nothing to add, I admit with an innocent grin and immediately correct myself – you can't add anything that will make others listen. Words possess immense power, but indifference is also remarkably hard to break – an admirable fight, but I'm not fighting now. Even if I discard the blinkers or peel off the shells, it won't be interesting for many – and maybe just for me.

But sometimes even one participant is enough – so, let's throw the outer layers away:

The day is long, I'm saying, the day is long, and my car obedient, like a lively beast.

The stone steps lead down and sliding over them brings no joy, but not everyone is capable of that either.

Gibbs didn't die – he had a boat.

I know I don't have a secret anymore, but I am no longer ashamed of myself.

Also by Vadim Babenko:

SEMMANT
A SIMPLE SOUL

SEMMANT

An excerpt from the novel published in 2013

CHAPTER I

I'm writing this in dark-blue ink, sitting by the wall where my shadow moves. It crawls like the hand on a numberless sundial, keeping track of time that only I can follow. My days are scheduled right down to the hour, to the very minute, and yet I'm not in a hurry. The shadow changes ever so slowly, gradually blurring and fading toward the fringes.

The treatments have just been completed, and Sara has left my room. That's not her real name; she borrowed it from some porn star. All our nurses have such names by choice, taken from forgotten DVDs left behind in patients' chambers. This is their favorite game; there's also Esther, Laura, Veronica. None of them has had sex with me yet.

Sara is usually cheerful and giggly. Just today I told her a joke about a parrot, and she laughed so hard she almost cried. She has olive skin, full lips, and a pink tongue. And she has breast implants that she's really proud of. They are large and hard – at least that's how they seem. Her body probably promises more than it can give.

Nevertheless, I like Sara, though not as much as Veronica. Veronica was born in Rio; her narrow hips remind me of samba; her gaze pierces deep inside. She has knees that emanate immodesty. And she has long, thin, strong fingers… I imagine them to be very skillful. I like to fix my eyes on her with a squint, but her look is omniscient – it is impossible to confuse Veronica. I think she is overly cold toward me.

She doesn't use perfume, and sometimes I can detect her natural scent. It is very faint, almost imperceptible, but it penetrates as deeply as her gaze. Then it seems all the objects in the room smell of her – and the sheets, and even my clothing. And I regret I'm no longer that young – I could spend hours in dreamy masturbation, scanning the air with my sensitive nostrils. But to do that now would be somewhat awkward.

A SIMPLE SOUL

An excerpt from the novel published in 2013

CHAPTER I

One July morning during a hot, leap-year summer, Elizaveta Andreyevna Bestuzheva walked out of apartment building number one on Solyanka Street, the home of her latest lover. She lingered for a moment, squinting in the sun, then straightened her shoulders, raised her head proudly, and marched along the sidewalk. It was almost ten, but morning traffic was still going strong – Moscow was settling into a long day. Elizaveta Andreyevna walked fast, looking straight ahead and trying not to meet anyone's gaze. Still, at the corner of Solyansky Proyezd, an unrelenting stare invaded her space, but turned out to be a store window dressing in the form of a huge, green eye. Taken aback, she peered into it, but saw only that it was hopelessly dead.

She turned left, and the gloomy building disappeared from view. Brushing off the memories of last night and the need to make a decision, Elizaveta felt the relief of knowing she was alone. She was sick of her lover – maybe that was the reason their meetings were becoming increasingly lustful. In the mornings, she wanted to look away and make a quick retreat, not even kissing him good-bye. But he was persistent, his parting ritual enveloping her like a heavy fog. Afterward, she always ran down the stairs, distrusting the elevator, and scurried away from the dreary edifice as if it were a mousetrap that had miraculously fallen open.

Elizaveta glanced at her watch, shook her head, and picked up speed. The sidewalk was narrow, yet she stepped lightly, oblivious of the obstacles: oncoming passersby, bumps and potholes, puddles left by last night's rain. She wasn't bothered by the city's deplorable state, but a new sense of unease uncoiled deep inside her and slithered up her spine with a cold tickle. The giant eye still seemed to stare at her from under its heavy lid. She had a sense of another presence, a most delicate thread that connected her to someone else. Involuntarily, she jerked her shoulders, trying to shake off the feeling, and, after admonishing herself, returned to her contemplation.

Find out more about A Simple Soul at www.simplesoulbook.com

A SIMPLE SOUL

An excerpt from the novel published in 2013

CHAPTER I

One July morning during a hot, leap-year summer, Elizaveta Andreyevna Bestuzheva walked out of apartment building number one on Solyanka Street, the home of her latest lover. She lingered for a moment, squinting in the sun, then straightened her shoulders, raised her head proudly, and marched along the sidewalk. It was almost ten, but morning traffic was still going strong – Moscow was settling into a long day. Elizaveta Andreyevna walked fast, looking straight ahead and trying not to meet anyone's gaze. Still, at the corner of Solyansky Proyezd, an unrelenting stare invaded her space, but turned out to be a store window dressing in the form of a huge, green eye. Taken aback, she peered into it, but saw only that it was hopelessly dead.

She turned left, and the gloomy building disappeared from view. Brushing off the memories of last night and the need to make a decision, Elizaveta felt the relief of knowing she was alone. She was sick of her lover – maybe that was the reason their meetings were becoming increasingly lustful. In the mornings, she wanted to look away and make a quick retreat, not even kissing him good-bye. But he was persistent, his parting ritual enveloping her like a heavy fog. Afterward, she always ran down the stairs, distrusting the elevator, and scurried away from the dreary edifice as if it were a mousetrap that had miraculously fallen open.

Elizaveta glanced at her watch, shook her head, and picked up speed. The sidewalk was narrow, yet she stepped lightly, oblivious of the obstacles: oncoming passersby, bumps and potholes, puddles left by last night's rain. She wasn't bothered by the city's deplorable state, but a new sense of unease uncoiled deep inside her and slithered up her spine with a cold tickle. The giant eye still seemed to stare at her from under its heavy lid. She had a sense of another presence, a most delicate thread that connected her to someone else. Involuntarily, she jerked her shoulders, trying to shake off the feeling, and, after admonishing herself, returned to her contemplation.

Find out more about A Simple Soul at www.simplesoulbook.com

ABOUT THE AUTHOR

Vadim Babenko left two "dream" jobs – cutting-edge scientist and high-flying entrepreneur – in order to pursue his lifelong goal to write full-time. Born in the Soviet Union, he earned master's and doctoral degrees from the Moscow Institute of Physics & Technology, Russia's equivalent to MIT. As a scientist at the Soviet Academy of Sciences he became a recognized leader in the area of artificial intelligence. Then he moved to the U.S. and co-founded a high-tech company just outside of Washington, D.C. The business soon skyrocketed, and the next ambitious goal, an IPO on the stock exchange, was realized. But at this peak of success, Vadim dropped everything to set out on the path of a writer and has never looked back. He moved to Europe and, during the next eight years, published five books, including two novels, *The Black Pelican* and *A Simple Soul*, which were nominated for Russia's most prestigious literary awards. His third novel, *Semmant*, initially written in Russian and then translated with the author's active participation, is published exclusively in English.

Find out more at www.vadimbabenko.com

CPSIA information can be obtained
at www.ICGtesting.com
Printed in the USA
BVHW070224050920
587807BV00002B/10